CONQUEROR OF HER HEART

Everything was different for Cynthia. The color of the people's skin, their language, their ways. A wave of homesickness engulfed her, and she turned to her captor. "Why do you keep me here, Red Wolf? I just want to go home."

Red Wolf grasped her chin in his hand. "I believe the spirits brought you back to me. You think that you do not belong here, but I think that you do. You are a white woman who can understand, and I want to make you understand before you go away from me. I say there will be something special between us, even though you are white and I am Oglala Sioux."

Their eyes held, and to her own amazement, Cynthia did not resist when Red Wolf bent closer, moving his hand to her shoulder, and lightly rubbing her cheek with his own.

Her heart pounded wildly, and every part of her body tingled with excitement and apprehension. She felt her life changing before her very eyes, felt her soul being stolen from her.

The virile Indian crushed her to his chest, holding her soft form possessively against his hard frame. "Wakan Tanka has brought you here. Red Wolf wants you to stay. May it be so."

SIOUK SPLENDOR

F. ROSANNE BITTNER

ZEBRA BOOKS
KENSINGTON PUBLISHING CORP.

This book is dedicated to all my faithful readers who over the years have enjoyed my Indian-white romances. Here's another one, just for you!

F. Rosanne Bittner

This novel is based on true historical events, although all characters and major plots involving those characters are purely fictitious and a product of the author's imagination.

ZEBRA BOOKS

are published by

Kensington Publishing Corp.
475 Park Avenue South
New York, NY 10016

First printing: December, 1990

Printed in the United States of America

We did not think of the great open plains, the beautiful rolling hills, and the winding streams with tangled growth, as "wild." Only to the white man was nature a "wilderness" and only to him was the land "infested" with "wild" animals and "savage" people. To us it was tame. Earth was bountiful and we were surrounded with the blessings of the Great Mystery. Not until the hairy man from the east came and with brutal frenzy heaped injustices upon us and the families we loved was it "wild" for us. When the very animals of the forest began fleeing from his approach, then it was that for us the "Wild West" began.

Chief Luther Standing Bear
of the Oglala band of Sioux

I think of thee, when golden sunbeams shimmer
    Across the sea;
And when the waves reflect the moon's pale glimmer,
    I think of thee.

I see thy form, when down the distant highway
    The dust clouds rise;
In deepest night, above the mountain by-way,
    I see thine eyes.

I hear thee when the ocean-tides returning
    Loudly rejoice;
And on the lonely moor, in stillness yearning,
    I hear thy voice.

I dwell with thee: though thou are far removed,
    Yet art thou near.
The sun goes down, the stars shine out,
    Beloved,
Ah, wert thou here!

Henry Van Dyke
from Goethe's
Nahe des Geliebten

Part One

Chapter One

Cynthia Ann Wells had never seen the likes of Deadwood, South Dakota, in her sixteen years of life. For a young girl who had known nothing but a gentle, civilized life in Charleston, South Carolina, a frontier mining town was both frightening and fascinating. There could be no better sign of her preacher father's devotion to bringing sinners to Jesus Christ than for the man to give up the luxuries of the East for a crude and rugged town like Deadwood.

Cynthia clung to her father's hand, her mother and little brother Alex on the other side of her. They had brought their wagon from the small white frame house in which they lived beside the tiny, one-room church at the outskirts of town; both buildings had been hastily erected by the few civilized citizens of Deadwood in hopes of enticing a preacher to come there and help bring some kind of law and order and decency to the raw, wild residents of the little town that was exploding with new arrivals every day.

It was June 1875, and there had been an unusual amount of rainfall, leaving the streets such a quagmire that the family had been forced to tie the wagon at the end of town and walk to the supply store. Preacher Wells had not wanted to parade his lovely young daughter, whose budding beauty was obvious to anyone who looked

9

at her, through a town of wild, woman-hungry men; let alone bring his still-handsome wife along also. But there were certain things the women needed that he was not sure how to choose himself, and Mrs. Wells and both the children were getting very frustrated with their virtual imprisonment. Preacher Wells decided it was time to put their safety in God's hands.

The long skirt of Cynthia's plain gray dress brushed against clods of mud left on the boardwalk by the constant traffic of men. She wondered at the constant flow of people and wagons up and down the boardwalks and the muddy street, a grand mixture of miners, bankers, merchants, freighters, saloonkeepers, real-estate speculators, surveyors, lawyers, and even the bawdy, painted ladies and the gamblers her father preached about in Sunday services.

Cynthia decided it must be ladies of that very kind who approached them from the opposite direction this moment, although her father had said they could not really be called ladies. Cynthia stared at bright satin dresses and exposed cleavage, red lips, and feathered hats. Little Alex, nine, also stared, and both children got a jerk on the arm from their parents and strict orders to look away from those "wicked women," and Cynthia could not help wondering how they got that way, if they had families at one time like she did.

Two men suddenly came sprawling through saloon doors just ahead of the Wells family, forcing the four of them to jump back. The men began rolling around on the boardwalk and finally into the street, followed by a crowd of men from the saloon who cheered and cursed as they watched the fight. Preacher Wells quickly led his family past the scene, and Cynthia winced at the sound of well-aimed blows, fist against face, followed by grunts and growling.

"I have a feeling bringing law and order and Christianity to this town is going to be a monumental task," Preacher Wells told his wife.

Men sitting and standing along the boardwalk stared at Cynthia and her mother as they walked by, most of them eyeing Cynthia. She could feel their eyes on her, and her still-freckled cheeks turned crimson. She felt as though she were walking naked through the streets, and she was painfully aware of her breasts, which had developed to a prominently full, round shape in only the last six months. At first she had tried to hide them, keeping cloth tied tightly around them until it became too painful and constricting. Her mother had finally given her a cotton undergarment that fit her nicely, and she had told Cynthia that she must accept the fact that she was becoming a young woman and not be afraid or ashamed of it.

Having her first period five years ago had been traumatic enough for Cynthia, but at least that was something she could keep secret. Her changing shape was something she could not hide, and she had never been more aware of it than now, as she walked down the main street of Deadwood. She didn't know a lot about men, other than her parents warning her to be careful around them now that she was becoming a young lady. She knew about love, from her mother and father, and she vividly remembered a night when she was nine and heard strange noises from her parents' bedroom. She had gone to see what was wrong, and had seen her father on top of her mother. It had seemed almost as though he was hurting her, and yet as Cynthia peered through the crack in the door, the two had suddenly embraced and her mother had laughed lightly.

It was not until Cynthia had seen horses mate and had asked what was going on that she began to realize what her parents had been doing. Her mother had explained that that was how the mare became pregnant and gave birth to her colts. *"Is that how people get babies?"* she had asked her mother. She remembered how red her mother's face had become. *"Yes,"* the woman had replied. *"But first they must love each other very much and be married in*

11

the eyes of God. And they stay together for the rest of their lives. That is what is different between people and the animals."

Cynthia was old enough now to make the further observation that apparently some men and women thought nothing of mating without the legality of marriage. Her father and mother did not need to explain in detail the reasons for their warnings about "painted ladies" and staying away from the wild men of Deadwood.

Cynthia had never given such things much thought until only recently, in the deep of the night. Thoughts had come to her that she was sure were sinful, but sometimes she could not stop them. She knew that someday she would marry and have babies, yet at the same time she could not really imagine it actually happening to her.

Men watched Cynthia's lovely form; studied the long, straight, blond hair; noticed her big, sky-blue eyes. But most of them looked at her as a woman in the making, an innocent who still had a girlish look to her freckled face. She was tempting indeed, but most of the men, although hungry for something as pretty as Cynthia, kept their distance. After all, this must be the preacher's daughter; and the handsome woman walking with them, from whom the girl apparently got her blond beauty, must be the preacher's wife. Although the men were for the most part crude, rugged, and lonely, they held a good share of respect for the preacher and his family. There were plenty of whores in Deadwood with whom a man could vent his needs; women like Cynthia Wells were meant for better things, and most men who watched her hoped that maybe they would strike a rich vein of gold. Perhaps wealth would make them worthy enough to marry such a girl. Money could buy a lot of things, especially a woman's love. It was surely more important, even, than a good education or coming from a prominent family.

"Hell, it's only the rich businessmen or another

12

preacher who gets girls like that," one bearded onlooker muttered to another as the family walked by.

"You strike it rich and you've got just as much chance as any other man," his companion replied.

Both men laughed. "If the damned Indians would leave me alone, I might hit my fortune," the first man said then. "Damned Sioux are getting bolder and meaner. The damn soldiers better start doing their job or the hills out there will have to be deserted and all that gold will lay out there, just wasting away."

"Them soldiers are doing what they can. We aren't supposed to be here, you know, according to the treaty."

"To hell with the treaty! No damned savages who don't know the value of a gold nugget are going to keep me from getting rich. If they're too dumb to take advantage of the wealth that's laying under their precious Black Hills, that's their problem. I'm going back to my camp in a couple of days. Them scurvy heathens that attacked me the other day should be gone by then. If they think they scared me away for good, they'll find out different."

Cynthia and her family walked past more saloons, a liquor dealer, a dentist's office, a printing shop, and a lumber yard. They passed one of many banks, and Cynthia wondered if there was really as much money in the whole world as what passed through banker's hands in Deadwood. Her father had said upwards of $100,000 a day was handled in this town's banks. It seemed an incredible figure, and she was sure her father had heard wrong. The prices of supplies were tremendously high, but Preacher Wells had often come home praising the Christian outlook of suppliers who sold supplies to him at much lower prices because he was a preacher and the town sorely needed one.

"May God bless their souls," the man had said many times over. "It is warming to the heart to realize that even in a town like this one there are Christian people, good people who have not forgotten kindness and respect."

13

But the people Cynthia saw meandering the streets of Deadwood did not fit such a description, and she was sure that the percentage of kind and respectful people of Deadwood was very low indeed.

They finally entered the supply store Preacher Wells frequented most, and the owner, Arthur Bonneville, greeted them with a smile and a wave. "I see you brought the family along this time," the man called out.

Preacher Wells nodded, herding his wife and children to a counter stacked with rolls of material, while a few muddy, unkempt men inside turned and stared for a moment. Bonneville busily wrote up one order after another, and Cynthia watched him for a moment, wondering if a taller, more gangly man existed. Bonneville was rather homely, but his smile was warm; and Cynthia had to force herself to keep from staring at his hands, which were huge.

"I daresay the suppliers and bankers and saloon-keepers of this town will end up many times richer than most of the men who come here looking for gold," Cynthia's father muttered to his wife.

"I have no doubt," Mabel Wells answered, fingering some of the material.

Cynthia helped her mother search for just the right material for new Sunday dresses. Both mother and daughter looked forward to the project, which would help pass the lonely hours they spent confined to the parsonage. Little Alex, a stocky, blond-headed boy full of vigor and inquisitiveness, ran around exploring the supply store. His parents both wished there were more young boys the age of Alex with whom he could play, but most of the men who came to Deadwood did not bring families. Mabel Wells took care of her children's schooling herself, for there was still no school in Deadwood and little need of one. In spite of the sorry condition of the mining town and the lonely life it would mean for their children, the Wellses were sure they had done the right thing answering the call for a preacher. A

14

man of the cloth must go where God calls, to people in need of the Good Word. The children would simply have to adjust, but Mrs. Wells worried about their safety.

Preacher Wells waited in line at the counter with a list of needed supplies.

"You gonna survive the wild life of Deadwood, Preacher?" a man waiting asked him.

"God gives me the strength and patience I need," Wells replied.

"Well, I hope He protects you from the Sioux," the man answered. "I wouldn't be givin' any thought to goin' out and preachin' among the miners in the hills if I was you. The damn savages is givin' them men a hard time, I'll tell you. What do you think about the Indians, Preacher?"

Cynthia studied the material, but her ears were wide open to the conversation. She had not seen the elusive Indians on their trip West, nor had she seen any since coming to Deadwood. Her only knowledge of them was through news back East, and the gossip of the few citizens who came to church on Sundays. According to all of them, the Sioux were a sorry lot, wild and savage murderers, dirty and lice-ridden, a class of people no better than animals who would be better off wiped from the face of the earth.

"They are human beings, sir," Preacher Wells answered, "and they are God's children, the same as any man."

"God's children?" The man laughed. "The Devil's children is more like it. There's nothing about the Indians that can be connected to God. They're murderers and rapists, that's what they are."

"Please, sir, my wife and children are present," Wells told the man. "I would appreciate you being careful of your choice of words."

The man removed his hat. "Sorry, Preacher, but you ought to know what Indians are really like. You bein' fresh from the East and all, and never bein' out there in

15

the hills."

"Ain't you heard what the Sioux did to Henry Clymer's party a few days ago?" another man said to the preacher. "Left Clymer and the four men with him dead at his claim. Other than all of them bein' scalped, I can't even begin to describe what else was done to them. It ain't for the ears of your women. You call men who can do things like that the children of God?"

"They are simply ignorant of Christ and his love," Preacher Wells answered. "I understand your feelings, sir, but it is my duty as a servant of God to try to see the good in all men."

"Well, there ain't no good to see in an Indian," the first man answered. "Like they say, the only good Indian is a dead one."

Little Alex stared and listened with his mouth open. Cynthia wondered at the whole predicament. After all, these lands belonged to the Sioux under a treaty. They considered it their land. Maybe they didn't know any other way to try to keep the white out than to kill every one that they came across. She wondered how these white men would feel if some foreign power came to Deadwood and ordered them all out, as though that power had some unearned right to take everything over. She wondered if it was sinful to have at least a small ounce of sympathy for the Indians' side.

Still, in spite of her wonder over the fairness of it all, she was herself terrified of the Indians, for all she knew about them was what was printed in the Eastern papers, and what she had heard through gossip among those good citizens who managed to come to church. Everything she heard was bad, and her feelings toward this unknown species of mankind were a mixture of fear and curiosity.

"I am told many more soldiers have been brought into Fort Robinson," Wells was telling the two men. "Surely the soldiers will help stop all this violence."

"Preacher, there ain't enough soldiers anywhere to stop them redskins," the second man told him. "We've

16

got to do some of it ourselves. A bunch of miners are scouring the hills right now lookin' for the savage bunch that killed Clymer's party. They won't get away with it."

"Violence only breeds violence, sir," Wells answered. "Perhaps if we showed some kindness and patience on our part, held some respect for the Indians' point of view—"

"You're livin' in a dream world, Preacher," the first man told him with a chuckle. "If you saw with your own eyes what them savages can do, you'd forget all about the love of God. Indians don't know the meaning of the word love, I'll tell you that. That there Sitting Bull and Crazy Horse, they're the Devil's helpers, mind you. God meant for this land to belong to us white men, men who can appreciate the wealth God planted under this earth, men who know what to do with that wealth. The Indians just let it lay there like it was nothin'. It's up to us civilized people to make proper use of the land. I don't believe God minds if we rid this earth of all its heathens."

Wells shook his head. "You don't understand the true teachings of the Christ, sir. I do hope you will come to our Sunday services. At least come and let me pray for your own safety before you head back into the hills yourself."

"I'll think on it, Preacher," the first man answered.

Cynthia agreed with her mother on a lovely blue-flowered material with a white background. But her heart was strangely heavy in spite of buying the prettiest material on the counter. She knew she should be excited about making a new dress, but the talk about the Indians weighed heavily on her. She was old enough to know there had to be two sides to every dispute, and surely there was a side of this story in favor of the Indians, a rightness to their own point of view. Still, they seemed capable of such violence. Was it possible they were truly incapable of love, incapable of peace and reason? Of all the things she had heard about them, she had yet to hear something good.

17

"You should have worn your bonnet," her mother fussed as her father paid for their supplies. "I'll not let you go out of the house without it again."

"But there's no sun today, Mother. I hate wearing a hat."

"It isn't just the sun. You should keep your head covered. And the brim keeps your face partly covered. Too many men have stared at you today. It is very unladylike to go without your bonnet."

Cynthia reddened as she felt two men turn and look at her, overhearing her mother's words. She suddenly felt stark naked without the hat, and wanted nothing more than to get out of the store. She took the package of material and everyone else in the family gathered up an armful of supplies and headed outside, where the sounds of tinkling pianos, laughter and voices, and clattering wagons greeted their ears. They headed back toward where they had left their wagon, but as they neared it, they heard whistles and shouting, and a crowd was forming at that end of the street.

"Now what?" Preacher Wells spoke up. "Stay close to me, children."

"Hang the bastard!" someone shouted so loudly in the distance they could hear it.

"Look at him fight—just like a wildcat!" someone else yelled.

Cynthia's heart pounded with an unknown dread. She hated violence, and although she couldn't yet see what was happening up ahead, it surely involved violence. She followed quickly beside her father as they dodged and edged around the gathering crowd. Men came barging out of saloons, hardly noticing the preacher and his family, one man nearly knocking Cynthia over in his haste. He didn't bother to stop and apologize, but rather kept walking quickly toward the center of the oncoming crowd.

Finally the subject of the excitement came into view. "Dear God," Preacher Wells muttered. "How can

18

they do this?"

Cynthia strained on tiptoe to see, then caught sight of a young Indian man who could surely be hardly any older than she. His body was bruised and bleeding, and he struggled against the men who held him, ropes tied to his bleeding wrists, his arms outstretched between two strong men who pulled in both directions until Cynthia was sure his arms would come out of their sockets. The men were leading him down the street, jeering at him, spitting at him, throwing whiskey bottles and rocks at him.

Instantly Cynthia's heart went out to the young man. She hardly noticed that he was nearly naked, wearing nothing but a loincloth and ankle-high moccasins. His black hair hung long and straight, a red cloth tied around his forehead. A mixture of fury, terror, and humiliation was in his deep-set, dark eyes as he tugged wildly at the ropes, growling like an animal.

"What is this outrage!" Preacher Wells asked a man standing nearby.

"It's justice, that's what it is. That young savage was part of the bunch of renegades that killed the Clymer party. Them men there killed the rest of them—saved this one for some fun in town. Folks has to have their vengeance satisfied, Preacher, whether you like it or not."

Cynthia felt a lump forming in her throat, and tears stung her eyes, as a man riding a horse behind the young Indian man lashed him three times with a bullwhip, making him stumble. But the Indian made no sound.

"You're making yourselves into the very kind of animals you say the Indians are," the preacher protested.

The man to whom he spoke turned, smiling through teeth stained from tobacco juice. "Stay out of it, Preacher. This crowd is in an ugly mood. They might even turn on a preacher if they get pushed too far."

Cynthia felt sick to her stomach as she caught sight of the Indian's bleeding back as they passed by. "Stay right here," her father told them. "I'll be right back."

19

"Father!" Cynthia called out.

Preacher Wells charged into the crowd, holding up his arms, and Cynthia hurried after him, hardly hearing her mother's shouts to come back. She still clung to her package as she shoved her way through the men, no longer afraid of them, only angry at them. She came close to the edge of the circle of men that surrounded the Indian now. The young man held his head proudly as Preacher Wells held up his hands and demanded that the men stop their cruelty. Cynthia watched her father gratefully. Albert Wells was short and stocky, his hair already thinning. He was not a big, strong man physically, but he made up for it in strength and bravery when it came to standing up for what he thought was right.

"He's a dirty Indian! A murderer and a thief!" men shouted at the preacher.

"Get out of the way, Preacher! This isn't the Lord's business, it's the Devil's. The Indian is gonna' hang!"

"But first we'll have some fun with him!" one of the men holding a rope shouted. He gave the rope another tug, and the Indian man winced but still made no sound.

"We hold our own judgment here, Preacher," someone else shouted. "And Indians don't get no trial or jury. They'll soon learn they can't go around murdering innocent miners."

More shouts went up, and Preacher Wells continued to protest, insisting the Indian should be taken to Fort Robinson to answer to the proper authorities. Amid all the shouting and arguing, the young Indian man's dark eyes scanned the crowd, coming to rest on Cynthia. Suddenly for him all the voices dimmed, and he forgot his pain. Never had he seen a young white girl like this one, so perfectly formed, so very fair. Surely she was blessed by the spirits, her white-blond hair and blue eyes making her special. There was a kindness in those eyes that struck him, for out of the entire crowd, the pretty, freckled face of the young white girl was the only one that

20

looked back at him with a hint of sympathy and sorrow. He knew in that moment that she was not like the others.

For Cynthia it was the same. She no longer heard the shouting crowd. The young Indian man's dark eyes held her own like magnets, and for the first time she looked straight into the eyes of a Sioux Indian. It struck her that he was actually human! He had pride, he felt pain. For some reason she had almost expected that an Indian would not even be shaped like other men. But this one was not only shaped like one, he was terribly handsome, his dark skin glistening in sunshine that was finally breaking through the clouds; his black hair looking clean; his high cheekbones and full lips, the wide-set, dark eyes all contributing to a perfectly chiseled face. There was something in the wild look about him that almost hypnotized her, for behind that wild look she saw a human form, human emotions.

"There! You see?" a man near her shouted. "See how that heathen rapist is looking at your own daughter, Preacher? You know what he'd do to her if he caught her alone?"

Cynthia's face reddened deeply as men turned to look at her. She tore her eyes from the Indian, and her father stormed up to her. "I told you to stay with your mother!" he told her angrily. "Get yourself back there, girl!"

Cynthia blinked back tears and darted into the crowd, hardly able to see her way back to her mother, who immediately chastised her for following her father. "Just for that you will not start on your new dress for a full week, young lady!" the woman barked.

Cynthia didn't care any more about the dress. She could not forget the young Indian man, his torture. Was he afraid? Surely he was. Maybe he wasn't even guilty of what the men said. After all, how did they even know they had gotten the right Indians? These men had no right hurting him. He should be taken to the soldiers at Fort Robinson. Things like this could only make the Indians more angry. She struggled against tears as the

21

crowd got angrier, and finally her father was pushed aside, and the crowd continued down the street, jeering at the Indian, still tugging at the ropes and whipping him at irregular intervals.

"Father, what will they do to him?" Cynthia asked anxiously when her father came back to them, his eyes full of sorrow.

The man looked at his wife. "They are going to let him hang by his wrists all night from the big cottonwood tree at the other end of town," he told his wife sadly. "They want him to suffer. In the morning they're going to hang him."

Mabel Wells closed her eyes and shook her head.

"I heard once that hanging is the Indian's most dreaded way of dying—something about choking off the inner spirit so that it can never go to the great hunting ground in the sky," Wells said almost absently, a terrible sadness in his voice. "I should be able to stop things like this, Mabel."

Mabel met his eyes. "God doesn't expect you to be able to stop this kind of hatred, Albert. It will take some time. All you can do is pray for the soul of that poor young man."

Cynthia sniffed back tears. Her throat hurt terribly, and she wondered why she felt so terribly sorry for the Indian man. Perhaps it was because he looked hardly any older than she. But mostly it was the simple cruelty of the men who were leading him down the street. It would break her heart to see an animal treated even half that bad. To see it done to a human being overwhelmed and sickened her. How could men hurt someone that way? She had never seen this kind of violence and hatred.

"I should never have brought my family out here," Wells said sadly. "I'm sorry you had to see that, Mabel."

"You have answered God's calling, and I told you long ago that I would go wherever you go, Albert. Let's just get back to the house."

The man nodded. Their end of the street was actually

22

quiet, as nearly every man in town had followed the crowd toward the other end, where the Indian man would be hung by his wrists from the tree. The thought of it made Cynthia shudder. Surely they would continue beating him and insulting him all night long, stretching out the poor young man's agony and dread. And in the morning . . . She felt a chill move down her back. They were going to hang him! It just didn't seem right. If the white man expected the Indian to respect his ways, to trust him and have a desire to follow the white man's ways, then they should show the Indian true justice, show him that every man gets treated the same.

"From now on you do exactly as I say, young lady," her father was telling her. "You put yourself in great danger walking into that crowd of wild, angry men."

Cynthia hardly heard the words. She didn't care how much she got punished. It had been worth it to actually look upon a real wild Indian. And yet she almost wished she had not gotten such a close look, for she knew already that his dark eyes would haunt her. She felt strangely different, as though suddenly awakened to the real world, to the truth about men. Men could be cruel no matter what their skin color or customs. These white men were being just as cruel and bloodthirsty as the Indians could be. Where did it end? Where did God mean for it to end? She wished there were some way to help the Indian man escape, but he was surrounded by Indian-haters; and perhaps it would be terribly wrong to let him loose. Still, perhaps he had a reason for what he had done.

They walked back to their wagon, and Cynthia's father helped her climb into the back of it. All the way to the wagon he had patiently answered question after question from Alex, questions about hanging, about Indians, about what the Indian man had done. Cynthia's skin crawled when her father explained with as much care as possible what it meant to hang a man. The vision of the men putting a rope around the Indian man's neck, of the horror the Indian man would surely feel at dying that

23

way, made her feel sick to her stomach. She hastily wiped at tears that she could not stop, and her father patted her arm.

"I'm sorry about all of that, Cynthia. You'll not come into town again for a long time."

"It's all right," she answered, her voice thin. She looked at him pleadingly. "Isn't there something you can do for him, Father?"

"No one can help an Indian in this town, Cynthia. All I can do is pray for his soul, and for the souls of these men who know so much hatred. That is why we are here, to bring Christianity to the lost souls of Deadwood. Hanging that poor Indian boy is just something they will have to live with for the rest of their lives."

The man left and climbed into the seat of the wagon, kicking off the brake and heading back to the parsonage. Cynthia stared after the crowd of men, who had nearly reached the other end of town. The wagon moved around the end of some buildings, and the crowd disappeared. But she could still see the Indian man as vividly as if he sat across from her in the wagon.

Chapter Two

Cynthia turned restlessly in her bed, unable to go to sleep. The heavy rains had left a sultry humidity in the air, as the temperature actually rose through the night instead of falling. Everything felt wet. But it was not really the humidity that kept Cynthia from falling asleep. She could not get out of her mind the vision of the young Indian man being so helplessly tortured. She could still see his eyes, see the way he winced but refused to yell out when pain was inflicted upon him. And now Cynthia could still hear shouting and laughter and voices from town. Were they still hurting him?

She threw back a light blanket and sat up, rubbing her eyes and going to her window. It was closed against insects, but she reasoned it would be worth fighting insects to get a breath of fresher air. Still, when she opened it, the outside air was not refreshing at all. She made a face at the humidity and stuck her head out the window, leaning far enough out that she could see part way down the street in the distance.

Lanterns lit up the street and some of the buildings, mostly the saloons, which never seemed to close. She couldn't see all the way down the street, but she knew the Indian man was there, hanging by his wrists from the cottonwood tree. Were men hurting him while he hung there helplessly? It brought an unexpected pain to her

25

chest to think of it, and tears stung at her eyes. How would the fighting between Indians and settlers ever stop if people kept doing these things to the Indians? It seemed incredible to her that no one but her father had tried to stop the incident. They were actually going to hang that poor Indian man tomorrow, without giving him one chance to defend himself.

Now she could hear the tinkling piano music again. Apparently people were celebrating the capture and the coming hanging. It was as though everyone was having a good time. She reasoned that surely God did not look kindly on such behavior, that the men doing this to the Indian were just as sinful and barbaric as the Indian himself. What made their actions any less wrong than what the Indian might have done?

"*Judge not . . .*" She could hear her father's words—words read from the Bible. It was not man's place to judge one another. At least if judgment had to be taken, it was supposed to be after a trial, after a jury heard all the evidence. This was not how it was supposed to be done. This was not justice.

She pulled back inside, the nudging thought that had been plaguing her since earlier in the day beginning to crystallize. She had dared not even think it earlier, but deep in the night, with haunting pictures of what was happening to the Indian man, she allowed the forbidden thought to return. Someone had to help the Indian. Someone ought to go over there and cut him loose. Surely it was not wrong. Surely it was the Christian thing to do. If anyone else thought of it, they would not have the courage to actually do it; but Cynthia determined there could be no fear in doing God's work.

"*I was thirsty, and you gave me drink. I was naked and you clothed me.*" So many words of the Scripture raced through her mind. When a person helped another, it was like helping Christ. Perhaps God Himself had planted these thoughts in her mind, as though ordering her to

26

help the Indian. *"We are all God's children,"* her father preached often. He had said it that very day about Indians. Her young and compassionate heart could not bear the thought of the Indian man hanging at the tree, with no one to help him or care about him.

Her heart began to pound at the action she was contemplating. Perhaps this late at night she could sneak over to where the Indian was, and she could cut him loose herself! God would surely understand, if no one else did. But maybe she would never have to explain. Maybe no one would ever even need to know it was Cynthia Wells who let the Indian go.

She paced quietly on bare feet, breathing deeply, praying, trying to find the courage to do what was in her heart to do. She opened the door to her room, peering across the narrow hallway to her brother's small room. The door was open slightly. She peeked inside, and by the moonlight she could see he was fast asleep. There were only the two small bedrooms upstairs. Her parents slept downstairs, surely themselves lost in slumber.

Cynthia slipped off her nightgown and pulled on her cotton dress, which lay across the foot of her bed. Suddenly nothing felt real. It was as though she were reading all of this in a book, not doing it herself. Her body was clammy with perspiration from nervousness as she hastily buttoned her dress and tied a bow at the back. She felt for her brush on the dresser and quickly ran it through her long, straight hair. She picked up two quilts from a trunk in the corner, shoving them under the covers of her bed and patting the blankets around them to make it look as though someone was sleeping there.

Excitement and fear flooded through her as she picked up her shoes and went to the door and out into the hallway. She tried not to think about how dangerous it could be for her if some of the men in town spotted her. This time of night only drunk men would be up and about. She thought about her parents' warnings about men, but she was on a mission for God, and she told herself she must not be afraid. God would guide her and protect her.

She crept down the stairs, counting the steps and hanging on to the railing to step over the fourth step from the top, which always squeaked badly. She took a deep breath at the bottom of the steps and crept to the doorway to her parents' bedroom. She could hear her father snoring. She walked into the kitchen then, with only the dim moonlight that managed to filter through a couple of windows to guide her. But she knew the house well, knew where everything was kept. She felt gently along the porcelain shelf her mother used for kneading dough and cutting meat. She was sure she remembered seeing her mother's meat knife lying at the edge of it earlier in the day. Her fingers came in contact with the handle of the knife, and she gripped it in a sweaty hand.

She hurried to the back door then, afraid that if she hesitated a moment longer she would never go through with her good deed. She slowly slid back the bolt on the door and opened the door just enough to slither outside.

It was quiet and dark behind the house. Crickets sang loudly, and the air hung wet and warm. Cynthia quickly slipped bare feet into her shoes, then edged toward town, staying in the shadows, realizing she was more afraid of the white men in town than of getting close to the Indian. She headed for the rear of the buildings, clinging to the knife as she hurried along, keeping out of any light. She prayed there would not be any drunk men lurking in the shadows.

The piano music and laughter grew louder. She was approaching the heart of the raw, muddy town, and now she could hear the painted women, laughing and screaming. She wondered how any woman could lead such a life. Suddenly a back door to one of the buildings opened, and Cynthia darted back, cringing against the back wall of the building. A man came out and threw out a pan of water, then went back inside.

Cynthia breathed deeply to regain her composure, such as it was. She waited a moment longer. The man did not return. She hurried along then, past more saloons. As she broke into a near run she bumped into something, and several stacked buckets fell with a great clatter. Her heart pounded wildly as she ran even faster then, crouching behind a barrel. But after several minutes, no one came out to see about the noise, and she decided there must be so much noise inside that no one had even heard. She squeezed her eyes shut and thanked God that she had not been spotted so far.

She kept going, getting her foot caught once in thick mud that seemed to suck at her foot like quicksand when she stepped in it. She tugged with all her strength and got the foot out, then wondered how she would explain the mud to her mother. For now it didn't matter. Nothing mattered but to get to the Indian. She must be very close.

She reached the end of the main cluster of crude wooden buildings, then stopped, peeking around the corner. In the distance she could see several lanterns circled around a tree, so many that even from where she stood she could see the Indian man hanging by his wrists. Her eyes widened when she realized the miners had stripped him completely. Never in her life had she set eyes on a naked man, and she stared for a moment, realizing it was sinfully wrong, but unable to curb her curiosity. She hesitated, wondering if it was bad to step up close to a naked man, let alone an Indian. And yet the importance of her mission seemed to overshadow this unexpected setback. She told herself she must let nothing stop her. When someone is in dire need of help, one must overlook incidentals.

She moved closer, and she noticed the Indian look in her direction, as though, like a wild animal, he sensed she was there, even though he surely could not see her. Cynthia saw that only one man lay guarding the Indian, and he lay snoring away, a whiskey bottle still in his hand. She remembered her father once saying that drunk men sleep harder, and she was sure this was God's way of removing her last obstacle. She moved closer, then cautiously stepped into the light of the lanterns.

The Indian looked at her with a mixture of surprise and distrust in his dark eyes. Cynthia stared back at him, noticing there were bruises and red streaks of blood all over his body, at least from the waist up. She could not bring herself to look upon the rest of his nakedness from this close a range. The way he hung there, bloody and abused, reminded Cynthia of how Jesus had been treated before he was nailed to the cross. Surely this poor soul, heathen or not, was a child of God, and helping him was the only Christian thing to do. But she could sense the wildness about him. It was as though she had come to cut loose a wolf or a bobcat. She swallowed to find her voice.

"Do you . . . understand English?" she asked, her voice hardly more than a whisper.

The Indian nodded.

"Are you badly hurt?"

The pride and stubbornness returned to his eyes. He shook his head.

Cynthia stepped even closer. "I am called Cynthia. I've come to cut you loose."

The Indian frowned in disbelief. He studied the pretty face, remembering it from the crowd earlier in the day. Her father was the preacher. He knew about preachers and missionaries, but he preferred to worship Wakan Tanka.

"Why do you do this?" he asked her quietly.

"Because I am a Christian, and what these men are doing is wrong."

A hint of a grin moved across his full lips, and Cynthia was too innocent to realize he was grinning at her foolishness. If it was a white man who hung here, surrounded by Indians, no Indian would let him go. To the Indian, this girl was just another example of how soft some whites could be. But his grin faded when he saw real tears in the white girl's lovely blue eyes. She was not doing this just to ease her conscience, or for her God. She really cared. And surely she was a young woman of great courage to come here in the night and do something this town full of vicious men would be very angry for.

"I am called Red Wolf," he told her then. "I will not forget the kind white girl with the golden hair and the blue eyes."

Cynthia reddened, but she could not take her eyes from his for that moment. Even with its bruises and a cut lip, the young Indian man's handsomeness could not be hidden.

"If I let you go, are you strong enough to run away quickly?"

"I have suffered the Sun Dance sacrifice. What these men have done to me is nothing," he answered.

She wanted to ask what the Sun Dance was all about, but there was not enough time. "Promise me you won't hurt me, or make me go with you?" she asked him then.

"It is Red Wolf's promise."

Cynthia took the knife from where she had kept it hidden in the folds of her skirt. She raised it, and the Indian watched her cautiously, as though he thought she might use it to kill him rather than help him. She hesitated, watching his eyes again. "Please don't hurt me," she repeated.

He shook his head. "I do not break my promises."

Cynthia swallowed and raised the knife higher. The Indian was taller than she, and he hung with his toes barely touching the ground. The only way she could reach his ropes was to stand on her own toes and press against him, grasping one of his strong arms with her left hand while she began cutting with her right. The importance of hurrying, her fear of being caught, combined to make her hardly aware of the closeness,

31

other than to notice Red Wolf did not smell bad at all, nothing like whites claimed about Indians. He smelled sweet, like sage and leather.

As Cynthia sawed as rapidly as her thin arms could muster, Red Wolf breathed deeply of her own soapy scent. He felt manly desires at the feel of her breasts against his chest, the softness of her golden hair brushing against his face. Never in his entire life had Red Wolf been this close to any white woman, let alone one as beautiful and young as this one. He admired her courage, for surely if she was caught she would be severely punished. He thought how, if she were Indian, she would make a very good wife.

Cynthia wondered if she was really doing this, or just dreaming it. She prayed inwardly for God to hurry and make the knife go through the rope. Slowly the strands gave way, until finally the knife went through.

Red Wolf fell to the ground, his beaten body and aching arms giving way to the sudden freedom, his legs unable to support him at first. Cynthia was so close to him, her hand still clinging to his arm, that she fell with him. She quickly rolled away from him, getting to her feet and watching him with wide eyes, wondering if he truly would keep his promise now. Red Wolf rolled to his knees, hunching over in pain at first. He quickly pulled his wrists from the rest of the rope that bound them, rubbing at his arms to get the circulation moving in them again. He flexed his hands, then threw back his head and breathed deeply before slowly rising.

The Indian turned and faced Cynthia, and for a moment the air hung silent and dangerous. She clung tightly to the knife as he reached out and grasped her arm, leading her out of the lantern light.

"You are a good white woman," he told her. "I will not forget what you have done."

"Are you sure you're well enough to get away?"

"I have learned how to keep from feeling pain."

32

"Give me your hand," Cynthia told him.

Red Wolf reached out. Cynthia felt for his hand, then placed the knife in it. "You might need this."

Again there was a moment of silence, and Cynthia's heart pounded so wildly she wondered if Red Wolf could hear it. Would he turn around and use the knife on her? Or would he force her to go with him?

"Return quickly to where you came from," he told her then, "before you are caught. You are a good warrior."

"A warrior?"

"*Ai.* You are brave to go against your people, and brave to free a man who is your enemy."

Their eyes held in the moonlight, until raucous laughter from a saloon down the street interrupted the strange attraction they both felt.

"You must go, and so must I," Red Wolf told her. "Good-bye, white girl Cynthia. I will never see you again, but you will hold an honored place in my heart."

"Good-bye, Red Wolf. God be with you."

Reluctantly, Cynthia turned and hurried off into the darkness. Red Wolf watched until he was sure she was well on her way. He turned then to the man who lay sleeping on the ground. The man had stripped Red Wolf and had burned up Red Wolf's loincloth, his medicine bag and all its fetishes.

"You'll hang stark naked tomorrow in front of the whole town, you dirty redskin," the man had told him, before holding the end of a burning cigar to Red Wolf's groin and underarms while he hung helpless. For these things the hated white man must die.

Red Wolf wanted nothing more than to kill all of them, but this man would be a symbol to the others. He stepped closer to the snoring man, then rammed the knife into the white man's heart. The man made only a slight grunting sound before the life went out of him. Red Wolf wiped the bloody knife on the man's shirt, then removed his boots and cotton pants, carrying the clothing into the

33

darkness where he pulled on the pants and tightened them at the waist with the leather belt the man had worn in them.

He pulled on the white man's boots, then shoved the knife into the belt to hold it and hurried through the darkness to where he had seen a corral of horses earlier in the day before it grew dark. He took a bridle from a hook near the gate, then unhooked the gate and slipped inside the corral. Quietly he put the bridle on a horse, realizing it was probably not the proper bridle and bit for this particular horse, but it would have to do. He led the horse out of the corral gate, looking around for a moment before easing up onto the horse's bare back. His keen senses picked up no hint of having been discovered.

Red Wolf took another look in the direction into which the white girl called Cynthia had fled, and he felt a great surge of desire at the thought of her, wondering if he was foolish not to force her to go with him. But she had saved him from a most dreaded form of death. He must let her go free, but he knew she would always weigh heavily on his mind.

He turned the horse and rode out into the darkness.

Cynthia hurried back through the darkness, her excitement so great she was beginning to feel sick to her stomach. She had done it! She had let the Indian go! No one could hurt him anymore. God would be very pleased with what she had done. But at the same time, she suffered from a nagging, unidentifiable guilt, a gnawing fear that perhaps she had done something terribly wrong instead of very right. Surely it couldn't be wrong. She reminded herself that others would only *think* it wrong, because they didn't understand the Christian point of view. The men who had captured and tortured poor Red Wolf surely didn't know anything about Jesus or Christianity.

34

She hurried as quickly as she could, stumbling over the very buckets she had knocked over earlier, stepping on the still-wet ground where the man had thrown out the water. Several times she had forgot to lift her skirt, which meant the bottom of her dress would have mud on it; but she could attribute that to their trip to town earlier in the day. This was the same dress she had worn. She realized she could even blame the mud on her shoe on the earlier walk into town. If she could just get back home and back into bed, no one would ever know. They would probably suspect more Indians had come and had freed their friend.

The house finally came into view. Now it looked inviting. There was nothing she wanted more than to be back in her own bedroom, safe and sound. There she could take time to think about what she had done, could take time to think about Red Wolf, what it had been like to talk to an Indian. She had actually touched one! Cynthia Wells, daughter of a minister, had touched a wild Indian, had actually freed him from captivity! She couldn't believe it herself, and she knew no one else in town would ever suspect her.

She reached the back door, then removed her shoes and gathered up the hem of her dress, tucking it into the sash she wore around the middle enough that none of it would drag on the floor. She carefully opened the door. It was still unbolted. Apparently no one had awakened to discover it was not locked. She slipped inside, quietly closing the door and sliding the bolt shut. She stood still a moment. The house was silent.

Cynthia walked on bare feet to the bottom of the stairs, then counted again. The squeaky step was fourth from the top, eighth from the bottom. One, two, three, four, five, six, seven. She stretched her leg and avoided the eighth step, then ascended to the hallway and hurried to her room, quietly setting her shoes in a corner. She took off the dress and laid it back across the foot of her bed, then pulled on her nightgown. She took the quilts from her bed and re-folded them in the dark, laying them back on the trunk.

"Cindy?" someone said quietly.

Cynthia gasped and turned to see her brother standing in the doorway. "What are you doing up?" she whispered. "And I was dressing, you little devil! What are you doing in here?"

"I didn't see anything. It's dark in here."

Cynthia stepped closer. "Well, what are you doing in here?" she repeated.

"I had to go—you know. I had to use my pot. I saw a shadow and wondered if it was you. Where did you go? How come you're putting on your nightgown? You already put it on once."

Cynthia swallowed, trying to think fast. She pulled the boy into her room, closing the door and whispering.

"I just couldn't sleep, that's all. I went outside for a while."

Alex frowned. "Outside? In the dark? You ain't supposed to do that."

"Aren't. And I can do whatever I want."

"Not at night. Mother and Father say it's dangerous to go out at night."

"I know that. But I didn't go away from the house or anything."

"Why can't you sleep?"

Cynthia wanted to scream at him for all the questions, but she knew she must remain calm and make Alex believe her story. She led him to her bed and sat down.

"I couldn't stop thinking about that Indian man."

Alex rubbed at his eyes. "I know. Me either."

"Did you feel sorry for him too, Alex?"

"Mmm-hmm. Those men were being mean to him. I never saw anybody all beat up before, somebody that got whipped."

"Neither have I. I couldn't help wondering what God

would think of it. I don't think He would want anyone treated like that, not even an Indian. Father says Indians are the children of God, just like us."

"I know."

"It almost reminded me of how people treated Jesus when he was crucified."

"I wish he could get away," Alex told her. "I bet I could go over there and cut him loose."

"Alex!" Cynthia moved farther back onto the bed. "Would you really do that?"

"Sure I would, if I was bigger. But Mother and Father would probably catch me, and Father would take that willow whip of his to me."

"Well, I'm just glad to know you feel the same way I do. I'd do it too, but I'd probably get caught too."

"Do you think they'll really hang him in the morning?"

"Probably. Unless some Indians come in the night to cut him loose."

"Do you think they would come that close to town?"

"They might—to save one of their own kind. The Indians can be pretty cunning, you know. They can be around without anybody knowing it. That's what Father says."

"Father said too that if they hang him, he's going to go over there and pray for the Indian's soul. Do you think Indians have souls?"

Cynthia thought about the look in Red Wolf's eyes earlier in the day, the terror, the fierce pride. She thought about how surprised she was to see that he was only human.

"Of course they have souls," she answered. "They just think different than we do. I think maybe someday I'll be a missionary and I'll go to Indian reservations and make them Christians." She turned to her brother. "And you could be a doctor and come and help me."

Alex shrugged. "Mother says I'll never amount to

anything if I don't do better in my studies."

"You better get back into bed for now," Cynthia told him then. She was sure she had made him practically forget she had gone outside, and he certainly didn't suspect she had gone into town. "Goodnight, Alex."

The boy got up from the bed and went to the door. "Goodnight, Cindy. Don't go outside anymore, okay? Father says it's not safe outside after dark."

"I won't go. I'm going to sleep now."

Alex seemed satisfied. He left, closing the door after him, and Cynthia breathed a sigh of relief. She put a hand to her still-pounding heart and got up, going back to the window and opening it again. She leaned out. She could still hear the music and voices, and she wondered when someone would finally discover Red Wolf was gone. She was glad that apparently no one had yet, for everything seemed normal. She could hardly believe she had actually left the house, snuck down that very street, and cut loose the Indian man.

She took a deep breath of air and walked back to the bed, flopping down on her back. She had really done it. She felt proud, basking in her secret deed. She had dared the darkness, dared the danger of the rugged mining town, dared to walk right up to an Indian and cut him loose. Red Wolf could have killed her, or taken her away with him, but she had trusted in God, and had felt no fear.

She thought about Red Wolf, remembering the feel of his strong forearms in her hand, remembering how he smelled, and realizing as her face turned red in the darkness that she had been pressed close to him, that her breasts had actually touched against him. Surely her dress must have touched his nakedness, that forbidden part of man no woman should see unless the man was her husband. Was that bad? Surely it wasn't, for it was the only way she could cut him loose.

She wondered if her mother had seen her father that way. It was difficult to imagine her parents mating, but she had seen it once with her own eyes, although the memory was vague. Blankets were over them, and she had seen only her mother's bare leg, but she knew now what they had been doing. Yet whenever she looked at her parents, it seemed so unreal. Her mother was so proper and ladylike, so concerned over the correct way to dress and how a girl should conduct herself. But they had to have mated, or she and Alex would never have been born.

The thought of it brought mixed feelings to Cynthia's budding body. She remembered Red Wolf's naked body with a mixture of shame and admiration. He surely was the picture of man's splendor, yet to see a man that way was also frightening. The thought of mating gave her funny feelings inside. She could not truly imagine allowing a man to do such a thing to her, but at the same time, to her surprise, the thought also brought waves of curious desire she had never felt before.

Her whole body prickled at the memory of standing close to Red Wolf in the darkness, of watching his dark eyes. She remembered the feeling of pride and the odd desire she felt when he called her a brave warrior. She wished she could shout out to everyone what she had done—could tell Alex and her parents at least. She didn't even have any friends she could tell, and wouldn't dare even if she did. It must be her secret. She could only hope her funny feelings around Red Wolf had not been sinful, and that God would forgive her for accidentally setting eyes on a naked man. She would try very hard to forget what she had seen. She had done a very good deed this night. That was all that mattered.

She turned over in bed, and the security of being in her room and knowing Red Wolf was free finally brought on the sleep she had been unable to capture earlier in the night. She was not aware of the shouting that took place several minutes after she fell into a deep slumber.

"Ruben's dead!" a man told others inside a saloon.

"The Indian's gone!"

Commotion rumbled through the saloon and out into the street to other saloons. Before long most of the people who seemed to live by night, and even some who had been sleeping, were mingling around the tree, where Ruben Kinder still lay with a whiskey bottle in his stiff hand, a gaping, bloody wound in his chest.

"Must have fell asleep," people muttered.

"Poor soul never knew what hit him."

"Wonder how that heathen got loose."

"Somebody cut the rope!" another shouted, holding up the pieces that had been tied around Red Wolf's wrists. "Look here. A clean cut."

People mumbled, looking around at each other.

"Who the hell would have done that?" someone muttered.

"Maybe it was that damned preacher!" another fumed.

"Preacher Wells wouldn't do anything like that. He won't even leave his house after dark."

"He's the only one who spoke up in defense of the Indian," someone else put in. "It makes sense."

"That bastard Indian stole poor Rube's pants and boots—looted his body like it was nothin'."

"One of my horses is missin'," someone else yelled angrily. "Ten to one the Indian took it!"

"I say we go over to the parsonage and find out if the preacher did this," someone else put in, fist raised. "He ought to know that if he did, he's responsible for Ruben's death!"

Shouts of "Yeah! Yeah! went up from the angry crowd.

"Wait a minute!" The words came from the storekeeper Art Bonneville. "If the preacher did do it, it was only because of his Christian beliefs."

"He's got no right interferin' with the law of Deadwood, or what the majority of the people want. Let him keep his preachin' and practices to the church! Preachers ain't supposed to mix with the law!"

40

"I say it couldn't have been him," Bonneville answered. "The only way Preacher Wells would have freed the Indian would be if he could have taken him to Fort Robinson. He wouldn't free a savage just to turn him loose to kill again. He sure wouldn't have any part in letting the Indian kill Rube."

"Maybe he don't know the Indian killed Rube. Maybe he just cut him loose and then run off, afraid of being caught," someone else yelled out. "I say we at least go over there and question him."

Another uproar came from the crowd, several fists in the air. Men picked up Rube Kinder's body to carry it to the undertaker, while others picked up lanterns and headed for the parsonage.

Chapter Three

Cynthia jumped awake to the sound of someone pounding on the parsonage door. Her first thought was the memory of freeing Red Wolf, and she sat bolt upright, her heart pounding immediately at the sound of shouting men and more banging on the door. She hurriedly felt around for her housecoat, rising and pulling it on.

Had they found out so soon? Had men come to hang her? She told herself she must remain calm. She must look innocent. How could anyone possibly know it was she who freed the Indian? Had the drunk man not really been asleep at all? Perhaps he had slyly opened his eyes and had seen her! Perhaps he had let her free the Indian so that he could point a finger at the minister's daughter and tell the whole town what a bad girl she was. She breathed deeply to keep from crying as she went to her door.

"Cindy, what's the matter?" Alex asked. He stood across the hallway in his nightshirt.

"I don't know. Someone is at the door. I can hear shouting outside."

A shadow moved across the flowered wallpaper of the staircase wall as Preacher Wells moved through the downstairs hall toward the door carrying a lantern.

"Just a minute! Just a minute!" he was shouting.

Cynthia and Alex moved to the head of the stairs, sitting down on the top step to watch, while Mabel Wells, her hair still in a nightcap, moved to stand just beneath the banister, a heavy robe wrapped tightly around herself.

"Who's there?" Preacher Wells called out.

"It's Art Bonneville, Preacher," came a voice in reply. "There are some men with me. They want to talk to you."

Wells opened the door slightly. "What on earth do you men want this time of night?"

"Open the door wider," someone yelled. "Does he look like he just got out of bed?"

Bonneville held up a lantern of his own. "Hell, yes, he looks like he just got out of bed. What did you expect? I told you the preacher wouldn't do it."

"Wouldn't do what?" Wells asked again, opening the door wider. "What is this all about?"

Bonneville faced the preacher apologetically, while several other men shoved their way inside.

"You men will get mud all over my hallway!" Mabel Wells exclaimed, stepping back because she was in her housecoat. "All of you leave here at once."

"We want to know if your do-good husband here got the notion to cut that Indian loose tonight," one of the men shouted.

Mrs. Wells's eyes widened indignantly. "Mr. Wells would never do such a thing!" she barked. "He was sound asleep in bed when you so rudely barged into this house!"

"Hush, Mabel," the preacher answered. "I'll do the talking." He faced Bonneville squarely. "The Indian is loose?"

"Someone cut him down," Preacher Bonneville answered. "Nobody in this town would do that, Preacher, and you were the one to defend him earlier today."

"I certainly did, and I would do it again. But I wouldn't have gone out there tonight and cut him down. I'm sorry to admit I'm not that brave, for one thing; and I don't

44

believe in interfering with a town's law, no matter how much I might disagree with it. I will freely preach against the things I saw today, but I would never take a direct hand in interfering. Whatever you men would have done to that Indian, it would have been on your own consciences."

"There, you see?" Bonneville said to the others. "I told you he didn't do it."

"It's his word. That's all we've got to go on."

"The preacher wouldn't lie," Bonneville argued. "And look at him. Anyone can tell he just got up."

Cynthia watched, her whole body tingling with the excitement of it. She sat with her knees drawn up to her chest, her arms wrapped around them. Never had she known such excitement, let alone be the cause of it. She wanted to laugh and jump around at the trick she had played on these cruel men.

"I can't say I'm sorry someone cut that poor soul loose." Preacher Wells told the men. "But it wasn't I who did it."

"Well, whoever did it has some guilt of his own to suffer," Bonneville answered. "That redskin killed Rube Kinder—knifed him right in the heart, then stole his pants and boots and stole Hugh Black's horse."

A general mumble moved through the crowd, and Mrs. Wells gasped.

"Wow!" Alex muttered.

Cynthia felt as though someone were draining all the blood from her body. A man was dead! It must be the drunk man who was lying nearby! Red Wolf had killed him! And he must have done it with her mother's own knife! She couldn't find her voice, and tears stung her eyes. She felt as though she had killed the man herself. She might as well have, for it was she who cut Red Wolf loose, she who had handed him the knife, trusting him just to run away. She never dreamed he would kill the poor sleeping man who lay nearby!

"We'll find out who did it, and he'll pay," someone in

the crowd grumbled.

"It don't make any sense," another muttered.

"Gentlemen, have you considered the fact that other Indians could have come in the night and cut your prisoner loose?" Preacher Wells suggested. "No man in this town would have done it, and no woman or child would risk going out there in the night to do it. And certainly whoever did it would not have let the Indian kill Mr. Kinder. It couldn't have been anyone in Deadwood that did it. You know how sneaky Indians can be. I don't have any experience with them myself, mind you. But I've heard how good they are at hiding and being around when no one knows they're there."

Art Bonneville removed his hat and ran a hand through his hair. "Well, you've got a point there, Preacher. It could have been other Indians. But it would be the first time Indians have come close to town."

"We'd better be on our guard, stay close to the lights and stay inside as much as we can at night," another man put in.

"We're sorry to bother you in the middle of the night, Preacher," Bonneville told Wells. "But you were the only one we could think of who might think about letting the Indian go. You can see by what he did why we feel the way we do. They're thieves and murderers, the whole lot of them. If we could have hanged this one, we could have taught them a lesson. Maybe they would have thought twice about messing with the miners out in the hills."

"I still say it isn't right to take the law into your own hands," Wells answered. "Indians are the government's problem. Prisoners should be taken to Fort Robinson to the soldiers. Maybe if you had done that with this one, we wouldn't have this problem, and Mr. Kinder would still be alive."

Another rumble of mutters went through the crowd.

"I suppose you're right there, Preacher," Bonneville answered, twisting his hat in his big hands. He towered over Preacher Wells like a tree. "Maybe we'll do that next time."

"And you boys think about coming to church Sunday. By the way, I'll be glad to speak over Mr. Kinder's grave whenever you're ready to bury him."

"Probably first thing in the morning," Bonneville answered. "We'll get out of here for now. Sorry about the mud. My wife will be glad to come over and help the missus clean it up in the morning."

"It's quite all right. My daughter will help."

Men started leaving, a few more of them apologizing. Alex turned to his sister when he heard an odd whimper come from her mouth. She was rocking, still hugging her knees, and in the light of their father's lantern and a couple more still held by men in the room below, he could see tears on Cynthia's cheeks.

"What's the matter, Cindy?" he asked.

She made a choking sound. "I think . . . I'm going to be sick," she groaned. She suddenly jumped up and ran to her bedroom.

"Mother! Mother! Cindy's sick," Alex called out.

The remaining men left while Mabel Wells hurried up the stairs to Cynthia's room, where she was vomiting into her chamber pot. Alex stood staring while Cynthia's mother hurried to her side, pulling back the girl's long hair.

"Oh, dear! Cynthia, what is it? Is it something you ate?"

"No," the girl muttered through tears.

"Cynthia, you're crying!" She turned to her husband, who had reached the top of the stairs and Cynthia's room by then.

"What's wrong with her?" he asked.

"I think it's just the trauma of the day—seeing that poor Indian being beaten, hearing the foul mouths of those men—and now this sudden interruption tonight. Those men had no right storming in here like that and upsetting the children. They've never seen the kind of violence we saw today. Go downstairs and boil some

47

water for tea, will you, dear?"

Preacher Wells nodded and left. Cynthia straightened, covering the pot and shaking back her hair.

"Go and get your sister a piece of peppermint from the parlor table," Mabel Wells told Alex.

Alex hurried off, not wanting to miss anything. He flew down the stairs two at a time and hurried into the parlor to get the piece of candy from a bowl on the buffet. He couldn't imagine why Cynthia was so terribly upset. He thought the whole event was a wonderful adventure. He had never seen so many things in one day, nor known this much excitement. Why did girls get upset so easily? It wasn't like Cynthia at all, even though she was a girl herself. Usually she shared the same spirit of adventure that Alex did. And earlier when he talked with her, she had not seemed that upset over seeing the Indian's mistreatment. It was true the event had kept her awake, and she had had to go outside for a while, but . . .

"Outside!" he whispered to himself. Could it have been Cynthia? Was his sister that daring? Was she so upset over the Indian's treatment that she would have let him go? Surely not! Still, he had caught her coming back from somewhere. Maybe she had done more than just sit outside the door. Why go to all the bother of dressing if all you're going to do is sit outside on the step in the dark? She could have done that in her nightgown.

Not Cynthia! But it would explain why she was so suddenly upset enough to be sick. The dead man! If she had freed the Indian, she was responsible for Mr. Kinder's brutal killing!

He flew back up the stairs and into Cynthia's room, where her mother had lit and turned up a lamp. Cynthia was as white as her nightgown, and there were dark circles under her eyes. She was still crying, wiping at her eyes with a handkerchief.

"Oh, I'm so angry at those men for barging in here like that and scaring your sister half to death," Alex's mother said, taking the candy from him. "Here, darling, chew on

48

this peppermint."

Cynthia took the candy, glancing at Alex with a strangely pleading look. He knew she didn't want him to mention he had seen her sneaking into her room with all her clothes on. There could be only one reason why she didn't want her parents to know.

"I'm going back to bed," Alex told his mother then. He walked up to Cynthia and patted her head. "Night, Cindy."

"Goodnight, Alex," she said quietly, blowing her nose again.

Alex retreated to his own room, lying wide-eyed and thinking while his father brought up some tea for Cynthia and both parents talked to her about learning to cope with life's cruelties.

"I never should have brought you and the children out to this godforsaken place," the preacher told his wife and daughter.

"Albert Wells, there is no place that is godforsaken," his wife answered him. "You, of all people, know that. You're just speaking out of anger. God called you here, and Lord knows the Good Word is needed here. It won't hurt the children to learn about some of the evils in this world. It will help them know how to face such things, how to stand up to them and avoid them. But I do feel that today's events were a little too much too soon."

Cynthia sipped the hot tea, which soothed her aching stomach. But what was there to soothe her aching heart, and her painful guilt? She wondered if she would feel better if she told them, but she was too afraid. The townsmen might do something terrible to her, or to her father. He would lose the entire following he had struggled to get to come to church. The incident had been blamed on the Indians. All she had to do was let everyone believe that, and she was free.

But she knew she was not free at all. She would suffer just the same as if she was in prison, her guilt exposed to all the world. For she would have to suffer it alone, and

49

she wasn't sure how long she could keep her terrible secret. It had been a wonderful secret at first. Now it had turned ugly. Now she hated Red Wolf for making a mockery out of her good deed. She had never meant for anyone to be hurt.

Why? Why had he killed Rube Kinder? The man was just lying there sleeping. Surely it was true, then, what everyone said about Indians. Red Wolf had proved that they had nothing but murder and evil in their hearts. He had taken her good mother's meat knife and he killed Mr. Kinder with it, for no reason other than to take the man's clothes. She had given him the knife in kindness, to protect himself, and he had murdered a man with it. Perhaps she had been wrong about Red Wolf and other Indians having a human side. Perhaps she had been wrong and sinful to let him go. She had thought she was doing God's work, but now it seemed it was surely the Devil's work. Was it this easy for the Devil to get into someone's heart and mind? Was her faith so weak that Satan had tricked her so quickly?

"You lie down and try to sleep," her mother was telling her. "I'll look in on you in the morning, Cynthia. You sleep as long as you feel you need to."

"Yes, Mother," she answered quietly. She finished the tea and thanked her mother for thinking of it. "Tell Father goodnight for me. I'm sorry I made so much trouble. Tell him it's all right that he brought us here. I don't want him to feel badly about it."

"Everything will seem better in the morning when the sun rises. You'll see that life goes on, Cynthia," her mother answered, patting her back.

Cynthia moved under her blanket, feeling numb. Her mother covered her and kissed her forehead, then turned down the lamp and went out, taking the teacup with her. Cynthia lay staring into the darkness, and new tears came. What had she done! How would she live with this! Why had Red Wolf killed that man?

She wished she could talk to Red Wolf, tell him how

50

much she hated him now, how much trouble he had gotten her into when all she wanted to do was help him. She wished she could tie him back to the tree herself. He was nothing but a murdering wild Indian after all, and she shivered at the realization of how close she had been to him. He could just as well have stuck the knife into her own heart, and she wished now that he had. Death would be better than the ugly lie she had to live with now.

Still, she could not forget the look in his eyes. And he had not harmed her. Surely that had been a sign of appreciation for what she had done, and to show appreciation was to show human feelings. Why, then? Why had he killed Mr. Kinder? Didn't he understand that she would bear the guilt of it just as much as he? Did Indians think differently about such things? Never in her life had she been so disappointed in another human being. She felt betrayed, and more than that, she felt an utter fool.

Her bedroom door opened then, and Alex crept into her room.

"Cindy?"

Cynthia sniffed and sat up. "What do you want?"

Alex came closer, sitting down on the edge of her bed. "It was you, wasn't it?" he whispered. "That's where you had been when I saw you come back to your room."

Cynthia stared at him, her eyes adjusting enough to the darkness now to see him. "Don't tell," she whimpered after a moment of silence. "Please don't tell, Alex. They might put me in jail."

Alex touched her arm. "They wouldn't do that to a girl," he told her. "But I won't tell, Cindy, I promise."

Cynthia broke into new tears and reached out to hug her brother. "What should I do, Alex?"

Alex felt silly hugging his sister, but he felt sorry for her. He patted her back. "I don't know. Just don't do anything. They think Indians did it."

Cynthia sniffed, pulling away from him. "I know," she whispered through tears. "But I don't know if I can keep

51

it inside, Alex. I feel so guilty. It's like I killed Mr. Kinder myself."

"You didn't see the Indian do it, did you?"

"No. I just gave him the knife for protection, and then I ran away."

"Then it isn't your fault. You didn't know he'd kill Mr. Kinder." The boy frowned. "I wonder why he did it."

"I don't know. Mr. Kinder was just lying there sleeping. He was supposed to be guarding Red Wolf, but I think he was drunk."

"Red Wolf? You know his name?"

Cynthia nodded. "I told him mine. And I made him promise not to hurt me. He seemed . . . so grateful. And he was so badly beaten, Alex. I felt so sorry for him. I was sure . . . God wanted me to go over there and let him go. If only he hadn't killed Mr. Kinder."

New tears came. "Heck, Cindy, Mr. Kinder probably did something bad to him, hurt him bad. You know what they say about Indians getting revenge. Before the white man came along, they were always fighting each other. It's just the way they are."

Cynthia blew her nose again. "Maybe so. But it doesn't keep me from feeling partly responsible, Alex. Do you think God will forgive me?"

"He doesn't have to. You didn't do anything wrong. You were just being Christian. You felt sorry for Red Wolf and you let him go so nobody could hurt him anymore. You didn't know he'd kill Mr. Kinder. You don't have to feel guilty."

"But I do. Just going there was wrong. Mother and Father would never have approved. Not only did I free Red Wolf, but I went out alone after dark. Terrible things could have happened to me. I've never done something like this before, Alex. I'm so scared. If anybody finds out . . ."

"Nobody will. Just don't say anything and I won't either."

"Thank you, Alex. You're a good brother."

Alex shrugged. "It's just because what you did was so exciting, and brave. I wouldn't tell on something like that. If you broke a dish or something, I'd tell. But not something like this. You're my sister. I don't want those bad men in town to come for you. You better go to sleep now. Maybe you'll feel better in the morning."

Cynthia nodded, lying back in bed. Alex patted her arm and started to leave, then came back to the bed. "If I don't tell, will you tell me tomorrow what it was like? Will you tell me what Red Wolf was like?"

"I will," she whispered.

Alex ran out of the room and Cynthia blew her nose again. Why? Why? Why? She could not find a reason for what Red Wolf had done. She had actually had feelings for him, had actually looked upon him as a human being. She had touched him—an Indian! A murderer! She had freed a murderer! She had even looked upon his naked body. And worst of all, she had been attracted to the handsome, strong, dark Indian—a feeling absolutely forbidden for a white woman!

What a sinner she must be after all! It would take a lot of prayer to free her of this terrible guilt. But more than that, she knew it would probably take an open admission, but the thought of it terrified her. If Red Wolf had not killed Kinder, she could have considered telling her father. He might have even been proud of her good deed. Now she could tell no one.

She turned over on her side, weeping into her pillow, until exhaustion overwhelmed her and she finally fell back to sleep, her last thought being a fervent hope that the morning sun would lift her heart; that by some miracle she would wake up in the morning to discover this was all just a horrible nightmare.

Far out in the hills a handsome young Indian man rode through the darkness on a stolen horse, riding to freedom. But he knew he would not soon be free of the memory of the blue-eyed, blond-haired young white girl who had given him back to the land and his people.

Alex came running into Cynthia's bedroom at the same time his mother entered the room to tell Cynthia to get up and try to eat some breakfast. He wanted to see his sister in full morning light, to see if she had somehow changed. He wondered if the night before had even been real, and he knew when he saw Cynthia's face that it was. She looked haggard, circles under her eyes, her hair a tousled mess from tossing and turning through the night.

"Do you think you can eat, dear?" her mother asked. "Maybe I should see if there is a doctor in town. You don't look well at all. Surely there is more wrong with you than getting upset over that terrible Indian killing Mr. Kinder."

"No, Mother," Cynthia answered quickly. "I'll be all right. It might be something I ate, mixed with all the excitement. Those men did frighten me terribly."

Unknown to her mother, Cynthia had already been awake for over an hour. She had lain thinking, actually wondering herself if the night before had been real. But she knew the awful truth when her mother mentioned the killing. Red Wolf really had killed the man, and it was Cynthia Wells who had given him the knife, her own mother's knife.

"Well, I'm not so sure that's all it is," her mother told her, feeling her forehead. "You don't seem to have a fever. You get dressed and come downstairs and try to eat. At least drink some more hot tea."

The woman turned, then let out an exclamation of surprise. "Cynthia! Your dress!"

Cynthia's chest tightened with dread. It was time to start lying. That was the awful part about her secret. She would have to lie on top of all her other sins.

"Oh, it's just mud from yesterday," she told the woman, keeping her eyes averted from her mother's. "I got some on my shoes too."

"Not the mud, Cynthia. Why, this actually looks like blood!" The woman held up the dress, and Cynthia's eyes widened at the red stains on the front of it. Her face paled. Blood! Red Wolf's blood! It was like being branded. She swallowed, at a loss for words.

"How on earth did these stains get here?" Mabel Wells questioned.

Cynthia managed to look at the dress, then at Alex, pressing him with her eyes to come up with some kind of story. Alex rammed his hands into his pockets. "It's my fault," he pouted. "Cindy told me she'd wash the stains out before you saw them."

"*Your* fault! Please explain, young man."

Alex sighed as though feeling very guilty. "I killed a bird yesterday with my slingshot. Cindy held it and tried to save it, but it died. The bird got blood on her dress. She promised not to tell."

"And I didn't," Cynthia answered haughtily, as she would normally do if they were fighting.

"You didn't have to. All you had to do was let Mother find the bloodstains," Alex grumbled.

"That will be enough. Alex, you bring that slingshot down to breakfast and turn it over to your father. I've told you time and time again not to shoot at living things with it. You had better say an extra prayer in church Sunday for your sin. And you will not play with your slingshot for two weeks! Now both of you come down to breakfast."

"Yes, ma'am," Alex answered.

Their mother walked briskly out of the room, taking the dress with her. Alex turned scowling blue eyes to Cynthia.

"I'm sorry, Alex," she told him. "Thank you for giving me an excuse for the stains. I'll pay you back somehow, I promise."

The look of agony on his sister's face dispelled the momentary ill feelings Alex had for her. "It's okay," he told her. "Are you okay this morning?"

Cynthia swallowed. "I don't know. I hate telling lies, Alex. But those men . . . what would they do? And Father and Mother would be so angry."

"Maybe in a few days you'll feel better. They'll all forget about it. That Mr. Kinder was just a drunk anyway. I heard Mr. Bonneville talking about him once that other time Father took me into town with him."

"But he was a man, Alex, a human being. And now he's dead! It's so dreadful! I feel like I killed him."

"You didn't kill him. Quit saying that. Come on. Get dressed and come downstairs. When we go out to do our chores, you can tell me about the Indian. What was his name?"

"Red Wolf."

"Wow. You sure are brave, Cindy. I wish you would have taken me with you." He gave her a grin, his youthful excitement and curiosity overlooking the gravity of his sister's deed. "Hurry up and come downstairs."

The boy went out so Cynthia could dress. She felt like her arms and legs weighed fifty pounds each. Every movement was agony, and she wondered if it was from her lack of sleep the night before, or from guilt. She pulled on a plain, blue dress, then picked up a brush and ran it through her white-blond hair. She looked at herself in the dulled mirror, seeing before her a young woman guilty of murder. She imagined being marched to a platform, a noose being slipped around her neck. She put a hand to her throat, wondering how it felt to be hanged, wondering if the Indians' beliefs were true that anyone hanged could never make it to heaven.

She took several deep breaths for courage and calm, then went out and down the stairs. She felt her whole body going hot when her mother's words hit her ears as she entered the kitchen.

"I know it's around here somewhere," the woman was fussing. "I left it right here last night."

Cynthia walked slowly to the table, watching her

mother search for something, knowing what it was. Alex glanced at his sister knowingly, then looked back down at his plate.

"Cynthia," Mabel Wells said then, seeing the girl had come into the room. "Have you seen my meat knife? I'm sure I left it right here last night."

Cynthia wondered if her cheeks were as red as it felt like they were. It was time for another lie. "No, Mother. I don't remember seeing it. Are you sure that's where you left it?"

"Well, I could swear." The woman sighed in disgust. "How can a knife that big just disappear? I liked that one better than any of the others. It was so nice and sharp."

Cynthia put a hand to her stomach. Nice and sharp. Sharp enough to slice into Rube Kinder's heart. The smell of the breakfast food only made her feel ill. She stared at her bowl of oatmeal, unaware that her father's discerning eyes were fixed on her.

"Are you sure you haven't seen the knife, Cynthia?" the man asked, startling her with the question.

Cynthia raised her eyes to meet his dark ones. Most of the time her father's eyes showed nothing but kindness and gentleness, even when he was trying to discipline his children. But this morning she saw in them a silent accusation. Was it really there, or was it only her guilty conscience making it seem like it was there?"

"No, Father, I haven't seen it. I would say so if I had."

The man suddenly smiled. "Of course." He looked strangely relieved, then turned his eyes to his son. "Alex, you will be doing some extra chores around here for the next couple of weeks, for killing that bird. We have told you time and again—"

"Father, he didn't really try to kill it," Cynthia interrupted, feeling an obligation to stick up for her poor brother. "He was aiming at something else, and the bird flew by. It was just a strange coincidence that he killed the bird. We both tried to save it. That's how I got the blood on my dress."

57

The man eyed her again, as though he was not sure he should believe her. Then he grinned again. "So, you've matured enough to start sticking up for your brother instead of picking arguments with him, I see," he said. He sighed and stretched his arms. "Well, still in all, he has to learn to be more careful. We'll make it extra chores for one week, but he still goes two weeks without the slingshot."

Cynthia glanced at Alex, who only stared at his plate.

"We have to clean up the mess those men left in the hallway last night," Mabel told her daughter as she set a cup of tea in front of her. She sat down to the table then and began handing out biscuits.

"Wait until after the funeral, Mabel," Preacher Wells told his wife. "I saw Art Bonneville this morning when I took my morning walk. He said the town will bury Mr. Kinder at ten o'clock. The children will have to get their meal eaten and put on their good clothes."

Cynthia felt a lump rising in her throat. She looked at her father. "Why?"

"Why? For the funeral, of course."

She felt the awful hotness again. "You want me and Alex to go?"

"Of course," the man answered, buttering a biscuit. "You know the entire family always attends the funerals at which I speak. It's a matter of respect. Mr. Kinder has no family here, and he wasn't the most saintly person in Deadwood. If indeed there are any saintly people in this town at all. But he was a human being, with a soul, and I shall do my best to persuade God to take him under His wing."

Cynthia sipped the tea, keeping her eyes cast down again. The funeral! She would be expected to go to Rube Kinder's funeral—the very man she had helped murder!

"Perhaps Cynthia isn't up to it, Albert," Mabel told her husband. "She really looks peaked. I think she needs a doctor."

"Well, I'll see if there is one available."

"No, Father, please! I'm all right, truly. I'm just a little weak from being sick last night. I'm all right now." She wanted dearly to use sickness as an excuse not to go to the funeral. But she was afraid that if a doctor examined her, he would somehow get the truth out of her.

"Well, we will be the judge of that," her father told her. "You come to the funeral with us, and if you still feel all right after that, we won't get a doctor. But I insist you lie down for a while when we get back."

"Yes, sir."

"And eat some of that oatmeal," Cynthia's mother told her. "It will help revitalize your strength."

Cynthia set down her tea and dipped a spoon into the thick, hot oatmeal, forcing a spoonful into her mouth. Even though it was soft and creamy, she could barely swallow it. It seemed to hang painfully thick and heavy somewhere in the tube that led to her stomach, and she drank some more tea to wash it down. She wondered when she would ever again have an appetite. But more immediately important, how was she going to stand at the grave of Rube Kinder and listen to her father speak words over the man she had helped murder? She could already hear the people there singing a hymn, could hear her father's eloquent words and prayers. It was surely proper punishment for her sin, to have to stand at the man's grave. But the thought of it made her shiver.

She managed to down another spoonful of oatmeal, and her father again watched her, wondering at his daughter's strange behavior, the way she had actually seemed to be lying when she said she had not seen the knife. He knew Cynthia well, knew how difficult it was for her to tell a lie. But he told himself the girl truly was just sick; that she truly had not seen the knife; that the blood on her dress really was from a bird. He could not allow himself to believe the other conclusion he had drawn. It seemed too impossible, too incomprehensible. Not Cynthia. Not his own daughter. It was absurd.

59

Chapter Four

The Reverend Wells and his wife walked behind the coffin as it was carried into the crude, unorganized burial ground that had been quickly established near Deadwood. Most of the men who lay there were miners, some who'd died from Indian attacks, most who had died from disease or accidents. A few of the bodies buried there were men who had died from drunken fights, from accidents in town, and some simply from drinking too much.

Cynthia and Alex walked behind their parents, holding hands. Cynthia squeezed her brother's hand so hard he gave her a jerk. "Not so tight," he grumbled, frowning. But the look of devastation on her face made him squeeze her hand in return for support.

A line of men followed behind the minister and his family, and soon the coffin of Ruben Kinder was lowered into the newly dug grave. Several women were in the crowd that gathered around the grave, but only two of them were of the same caliber as the minister's wife—honorable wives of a couple of the businessmen in town. The rest of the women at the grave site were obviously whores. Their dark clothing could not hide their wild, frumpled look, nor the painted faces and dyed hair.

Cynthia stared at one of them, a young woman who could be pretty if she were not so painted. She was weeping openly. She wondered at the fact that such women apparently had feelings. Had she loved Ruben Kinder? Did he pick her out special, or was she just his favorite?

Preacher Wells began his oration, and Cynthia concentrated on watching the painted ladies. It was the only way she could keep from crying. Surely people would wonder at her crying over one of the town's worst drunks, and they would begin to think about it and perhaps figure out the real reason for her tears. She studied each prostitute intensely, trying to make up stories about how they might have come to be in Deadwood, doing what they did.

She shut out her father's words, refusing to think about God at all, for to think of Him made her think about her wretched sinfulness and guilt. Surely what she had done was worse then what these prostitutes did, and at the moment she wished she was one of them instead of a girl who had helped kill a man. Not only had she done the terrible deed that put Kinder in his grave, but she had become a liar on top of it.

Finally the sermon was over. Wells led those present in a hymn, and men began shoveling dirt into the grave. The sad, haunting hymn about death and the resurrection, combined with the awful sight of the coffin being buried forever, finally brought the tears to Cynthia's eyes. She covered her mouth, fighting with all her might to keep from sobbing openly, and two prostitutes standing across from her began whispering.

"Such a tenderhearted girl, to cry over an old drunk like Rube," one of them muttered.

"Some people cry over anything," the second answered. "Besides, she's young and inexperienced. Girls like the preacher's daughter think everyone is good. But there sure as hell isn't anything to cry about over ol' Rube."

They both forced back smiles, for the occasion was solemn, nonetheless, and even though Rube Kinder was not the most prominent citizen of Deadwood, the fact remained he had been brutally murdered by an Indian.

Cynthia was certain the women were talking about why she was quietly crying. Did they suspect the real reason? Would they start a rumor circulating through Deadwood? She was grateful for the wide-brimmed bonnet she wore this time, even though she hated hats. The brim hid her face enough that the women who watched her surely could not see the remorse and devastation in her eyes.

Cynthia breathed deeply to stop the tears, looking through an opening between two people across from her to watch the rolling hills beyond where they stood. Far out in those hills Red Wolf rode free. For all she knew he was raiding and killing more miners and settlers, laughing loudly at the foolish white girl who had let him go free. She wondered how he lived, if he ate raw meat and murdered for pleasure. Her vision of him was turning into that of the worst savage. She could see blood on his hands, blood in his mouth. She could see fire in his eyes, and his even, white teeth gleamed when he smiled his wicked smile. The picture of him in her mind was becoming totally distorted, and she wondered if he was using her mother's favorite knife to kill more people. She thought how brokenhearted her mother would be to know that.

The service finally ended, and the worst ordeal of Cynthia Wells's life was over. She hurried along, pulling on Alex, wanting to get far away from the grave, half expecting Rube Kinder to rise up out of it and point a finger at her. The preacher and his wife yelled at Cynthia and Alex to slow down and stay beside them, and once they were far enough from the grave Cynthia stopped and waited.

"You must be feeling better to run like that, Cynthia," her mother told her. "But you really shouldn't. Slow down now, and I want you to rest once we get back to the parsonage . . . after we first clean the floor, of course."

"Yes, Mother."

The prostitute who had wept over Kinder walked past them, still crying. Cynthia watched her, wanting to go up to the woman and tell her she was sorry. It seemed to Cynthia that it was surely her father's duty to try to comfort the woman, but she was equally certain her mother would never allow the good preacher to go and speak to such a woman. Apparently her father had already mentioned it, for her mother was patting his arm.

"You know you mustn't be seen in their company," she was saying. "Perhaps she will come to church. Then you could talk to her. And if any of these women come to church, we must let them inside, Albert. They are God's children too, and perhaps we can find a way to cure some of them of their wicked ways. But you mustn't go into their dens of iniquity."

Cynthia wondered if her mother was just afraid her father would be tempted by such women. Was it that easy for a man to fall into sin? Surely not her father. He was so good, so honorable, and so much in love with her mother. There was so much about men she didn't understand.

For Cynthia they couldn't get away from the graveyard and back home fast enough. When they finally reached their little white house, Cynthia began to feel somewhat more relieved. The worst was over—the terrible night, the awful first day, the sad funeral.

"Each of you get a bucket from the house and pump them full of water," Cynthia's mother told her and Alex.

"Yes, ma'am," Alex replied, running into the house and getting two buckets. He handed one to Cynthia, who waited outside. "Come on!" He looked excited, and Cynthia followed him to the hand pump, where Alex hung his bucket over the spout and began pumping deliberately slowly so that they could talk. "Tell me about it, Cindy. What was it like!" he asked her then.

Cynthia watched water trickle from the spout. "I don't know. I mean, when I was doing it I felt kind of numb. I wasn't really afraid. It was like . . . like something was making me do it." She looked into her brother's eyes. "I thought it was God. But maybe it was the Devil."

Alex's eyebrows arched. "I never thought of that." He pumped harder. "What was he like, Cindy? Did he understand English? What did he say?"

Cynthia thought again about the handsome Red Wolf. She had wanted so much for him to turn out to be kind and good. Why, oh, why did he have to kill Ruben Kinder? Why did he have to go and spoil her good deed, and spoil the romantic image she had of him.

"Yes, he spoke English," she answered. "He said he hardly felt the pain of his beating because he had suffered the Sun Dance. What do you think that is, Alex?"

Alex shrugged. "I don't know. Maybe Father would know. We could find a way, maybe, to ask him about it without him suspecting." He stopped pumping. "What else did Red Wolf say?"

Cynthia could not help the emotions she felt at the memory, in spite of what Red Wolf had done. If only she could be sure it wasn't the Devil who had sent her there.

"He told me he would never forget the kind white girl with the golden hair and the blue eyes who helped him. He said I was a good white woman, and a brave warrior."

"Wow!" The word came out in whispered awe from Alex's lips. "A brave warrior! He really said that?" Cynthia nodded. "That must mean a lot, for an Indian to say that to a white person," Alex continued. "I wish I was the one who had gone and let him go."

"No, you don't," Cynthia told him despondently then. She waited for Alex to take his bucket from the spout, then hung her own on it. "Then you would feel as terrible as I do about Rube Kinder's death. Did you see that painted lady who was crying? I bet she liked Mr. Kinder a whole lot. Do you think women like that really have feelings?"

Alex shrugged. "I don't know. I suppose. Father says the Indians are God's children, so I guess those bad ladies are too. And they look like anybody else, except for the way they dress and all. I guess they have the same

65

feelings. Do you think the Indians do too? I wonder if Red Wolf has a mother and a father, maybe sisters and brothers. Maybe he even has a wife! I've heard Father talk about how young some Indians are when they marry, only he says all Indian marriages are an abom—abom—"

"Abomination," Cynthia said, finishing for him.

"Yeah, that's it—abomination. He said Indians aren't married in the eyes of God—not legal, Christian marriages. He said they all live in sin, and that some Indian men have more than one wife. Do you think Red Wolf has a wife?"

Cynthia pumped harder, astounded that she had felt a tiny pang of jealousy at the remark. A wife! She didn't really know how old he was. She had only guessed he was perhaps eighteen. Maybe he did have a wife! Did Indians fall in love like white people? Did they consider husband-and-wife as sacred a relationship as white Christians did?

"I suppose he could have one," she answered, angry with herself for being upset at the thought of it. She realized then that saving Red Wolf's life had made her feel as though he somehow belonged to her. Yet it was a ridiculous thought, and she pumped even harder, for she realized that before she learned about Rube Kinder's death, she had even had romantic thoughts about Red Wolf—terrible sinful thoughts that no white girl should have for any man, let alone an Indian. She decided she would never tell her brother she had seen Red Wolf naked. He would tease her about it, perhaps go into such a fit over it that he would spill the story to their parents.

"Where is the water?" their mother shouted then from the back door. "What is taking the two of you so long?"

Alex grinned and picked up his bucket. "Come on, brave warrior," he told his sister with a giggle.

Cynthia took her own bucket from the pump spout and walked slowly toward the house. She realized she felt strangely different today, older, stronger, wiser, much more aware of life's realities—of sin and death, love and

66

hate, cruelty and betrayal. And for the first time she had
felt jealousy, the kind of jealousy a woman feels over a
man, the kind her mother felt, perhaps, over her father
going to call on a prostitute. The distrubing part was that
her jealousy was over a young Indian man who had
betrayed her, and who she was not likely to ever see
again.

She reached the back steps, where she heard her
mother fussing again over not being able to find her
favorite knife.

Sunday services came only two days after the day of
the funeral. Cynthia again gladly wore the bonnet. She
sat at the end of one pew, speaking to no one. Only a
handful of people attended, but that much was an
accomplishment for her father, who had managed to raise
church attendance from six to fifteen in only eight
weeks. Her mother played a piano that was badly in need
of tuning, one that was better fit for plunking out spunky
tunes to which prostitutes and miners could dance. After
all, the piano had been donated by a saloon. Cynthia's
mother had at first declared it should not be brought into
the church, but after much pleading from her husband,
the woman had relented.

"It is only an instrument, Mabel. It can be used for
good as well as bad. How it is used is up to the one who
plays it. If this is the only piano we can get, God Himself
has surely provided it. It is not our place to refuse it, if its
music is the Lord's music and will help bring more people
to church."

Now the good Mrs. Wells plunked out a hymn, while
the growing group of voices in Sunday church sang the
first hymn, a song about forgiveness for all past sins.
Guilt continued to plague Cynthia so that she could
hardly sing the words, and she kept her head bowed
through the sermon—one of repentance, of "seeing our
sinful ways and changing them," of "ridding souls of the

67

pain and agony of guilt so that we can be forever free, cleansed in God's eyes, able to face our Lord squarely when we stand before him on that day of judgment."

More hymns were sung, but Cynthia hardly heard the music. The last two days had been painfully long, her nights restless. She had had more time to think about what she had done, time to look across the softly blowing prairie grasses and wonder about an Indian called Red Wolf, to hate him for the misery he had created in her soul and yet to wonder about him.

She wasn't sure anymore how she felt about Red Wolf. She only knew she was so sick with guilt that she was hardly eating and was beginning to feel weaker and more miserable. The only man who could tell her whether what she had done was right or wrong was her own father, and she knew deep inside that she could not keep her secret forever, unless she wanted to be this miserable for the rest of her life.

The long service was finally over. Cynthia hung back while people left, stopping to talk to her father on the way out. Finally only the family was left. Cynthia walked up to her father, looking up into his soft, brown eyes, eyes that could sometimes show a stern anger, but that had always shown love, even in his most angry moments. Cynthia wondered sometimes how her father had looked when he was younger—probably slimmer and more handsome. She realized she knew little about her parents in their own youth, and all she knew about how they had come to be together was that her mother was the daughter of a minister back East, and that after Cynthia's grandfather died, Albert Wells had come to her mother's church as the new preacher, very young at the time, fresh out of the seminary. They had fallen in love and married. Cynthia had never known any of her grandparents, as her mother's parents had been dead before she was born, and her father's parents had lived much farther north and had died before Cynthia ever got to meet them.

"Father, I need to talk to you," she told the man aloud then.

"Wells's eyebrows arched in curiosity, and he looked at his wife. "Go ahead and see to dinner, dear. Take Alex with you."

Cynthia turned away, and Alex stared after his sister as his mother led him out. Was she going to tell? He wished he could be there to see it, wondered how his father would react. Cynthia waited until she heard the door to the little chapel close, then turned to face her father, taking a deep breath. She swallowed for courage, untied her bonnet, and removed it.

"It was me, Father. I cut the Indian loose," she told the man.

To her surprise the man showed no immediate shock at her words. He only stared at her, then slowly nodded. "So," he said calmly, "that is why you were suddenly sick that night."

Tears came to her eyes then and she hung her head. "I didn't know . . . he'd kill Mr. Kinder," she sobbed. "I feel like I killed him." Her body jerked in a sob. "I thought I was doing something good. I . . . felt sorry for the Indian. If I knew he was going to kill Mr. Kinder, I wouldn't have done it, Father. I'm so sorry! I don't know what to do—how to make up for it. Please don't let the men in town come and hang me!"

"Hang you! Is that what you thought they might do?"

She nodded, choking in another sob and taking a handkerchief from a pocket of her dress. In the next moment her father's arms were around her, and she wondered why she hadn't told him sooner. She wept aginst his chest.

"Oh, Cynthia, the people of Deadwood wouldn't hang a sweet, good-hearted young lady like you." He patted her shoulder. "I suspected all along, after the way you reacted that night, and then your mother finding blood on your dress and her knife coming up missing." He sighed deeply. "I didn't want to believe it, and I didn't want to accuse you. I knew that if you did it you would tell me eventually." He hugged her tighter. "But it was a terribly dangerous thing to do, Cynthia. You must never, never go into Deadwood alone like that, not even in the daytime."

"I stayed behind all the buildings. Nobody saw me," she answered. "When I got to the Indian, he was all bruised and bleeding. Mr. Kinder was lying next to him with a whiskey bottle in his hand, and nobody else was around." She jerked in another sob. "The Indian . . . spoke English. He told me his name was Red Wolf, and he could have killed me, Father, but he promised not to harm me and he kept his promise. He actually . . . spoke kindly to me . . . seemed grateful. I gave him the knife for protection, and then I left. But he turned around and used the knife to kill poor Mr. Kinder . . . Mother's knife! Mother's favorite knife! Oh, Father, I didn't know he'd do that! I didn't know!"

"Of course you didn't. You were doing what you thought was the Christian thing to do, Cynthia. Don't feel you have any guilt in the matter, because you don't. You are only responsible for cutting loose a man who was being brutalized, a child of God, no matter that he is a heathen. No one is responsible for Mr. Kinder's death but the Indian, and probably Kinder himself, for being such a slave to the bottle."

Cynthia drew back slightly, looking up at her father with tear-filled eyes. "What should I do, Father? I'm so sorry about all of it. And I'm sorry I lied to cover it up. Please give Alex's slingshot back to him. He only made up the story about the bird to explain the blood on my dress. He saw me coming back that night and he figured it out right away. But he promised not to tell because he was afraid too. He thought somebody might harm me."

"No one is going to harm you." Wells patted her arm. "I will see that the proper people are told, Cynthia. I will make them understand."

70

"Oh, I've made trouble for you, Father. You'll lose some of the people you've tried so hard to get to church."

The man frowned. "I don't think so. Those who are coming have learned about the love of God. They'll understand why you did it. Of course, there are some who think the love of God is for everyone but Indians, but I'll get over that barrier some day."

"Would God love somebody like Red Wolf?"

The man grinned and kissed her forehead. "God loves everyone, Cynthia. Always remember that. Even men like Red Wolf can be saved and can live for the glory of God. For now I am just glad that you finally rid your soul of your dark secret. Come now. We will tell your mother, and we will all pray together. Then we will have our dinner, and I will go and tell the others the truth about the Indian."

Cynthia blew her nose again, and walked out of the chapel with her father's arm around her. She felt silly for not having told him sooner, for her father was the most forgiving, understanding man in the whole world, as far as she was concerned. They headed for the house. She was not at all sure her mother would be as understanding, but she knew that if anyone could calm the woman, her father could.

They entered the back door and into the kitchen, where Mable Wells was peeling potatoes. Alex looked up from cutting bread at the table, his eyes wide with curiosity. His father looked at him sternly. "From now on, young man, you will not help your sister hide something so drastically important," the man told him. "You should have known it would be for Cynthia's own good that we know."

Alex hung his head, and Mabel Wells turned to her husband. "Know what?" She frowned. "Cynthia! You've been crying again. What is it?" The woman walked closer. "What have you two been talking about?"

Cynthia stared at the loaf of bread on the table while her father told her mother what she had done. She heard the gasps, heard the sudden tears of disappointment and shock, heard her mother say she didn't believe it. Her heart shattered at the realization of how the woman's heart was surely breaking.

"She thought she was doing the Christian thing, Mabel," her father was saying. "She's a softhearted girl who couldn't bear the thought of what those men were doing to the Indian."

"But the Indian killed Ruben Kinder!" the woman sobbed.

"Cynthia didn't know he would do that. When he killed Kinder, Cynthia had already left him. She thought he would just take the knife and run."

"The knife? *My* knife? That . . . that heathen is running around killing people with my knife?"

Cynthia broke into renewed tears.

"Mabel, who cares about the knife? It's just like the piano, remember? It is an instrument that can be used for bad or good, depending on who uses it. What's more important now is Cynthia. She feels like she's done something bad, and I have told her she most certainly has not. She acted out of Christian love for a fellow human being. What she did was dangerous and disobedient, but very brave and very Christian. You should be proud of her, not fretting over a knife."

The woman sniffed. "Yes. Yes, I suppose you're right, Albert. It's just such a shock. I . . . I have to get used to the idea of it."

"The blood on her dress was from the Indian, not a bird," Wells continued. "Now you know why Cynthia got sick the night they came and said the Indian had killed Kinder. Surely the way she reacted tells you she had no idea that would happen, how sorry she is about it. Our Cynthia has been living with a terrible guilt since it happened, and she needs to be free of it and to understand she only did the Lord's work—that God doesn't blame her for anything."

Mrs. Wells blew her nose. "What about the townspeople? What should we tell them?"

"The truth. They'll understand. Cynthia is soft-hearted and ignorant of the ways of the Indian. She doesn't understand the way they live and think."

"You certainly don't seem very upset about all of this," the woman told her husband.

"I suspected from the very first night. I was just waiting for Cynthia to come to me of her own accord."

"Well, you could have told me, Albert."

"If I had, you wouldn't have been able to wait. You would have questioned Cynthia."

The woman sniffed again, then spoke her daughter's name. Cynthia looked at the woman, seeing a mixture of stubborn indignation and hurt pride in her mother's eyes.

"I'm sorry, Mother. I just . . . I couldn't stand the thought of what those men were doing to the Indian, or the thought of them hanging him the next day."

A hint of forgiveness moved into the woman's eyes then. "It bothered all of us, Cynthia. But we have a strict rule that we keep religion to the church and let the town take care of itself. You must understand that out here feelings of hatred run high against the poor Indians. I know that is wrong, but that is the way it is. We cannot interfere with what happens to Indians, and it is dangerous to speak out for them. Your father will handle the matter in his own way, as he slowly brings more people into the church."

"Yes, ma'am."

"We are not living back East, Cynthia, where the laws are clear, the line between black and white very distinct," Cynthia's father put in. "Deadwood is a raw, uncivilized, lawless little mining town, full of men who have come here to be free of the constraints of Eastern laws; men who have come here with one thing in mind, and that is to get rich. It isn't right, mind you, but that is the way it is. This town and the mining claims are on Indian lands, or so the Indians believe. Perhaps they are right. But the smell of gold lures these men here to face whatever dangers they must face in order to find riches. We are here to serve them and to help them find the Lord, if that is possible in this haven of sin. We cannot win over men if we anger them by interfering with their idea of justice, especially where it involves the Indians. First we win them to the church, win their hearts to God—then we try to make them see that Indians are also the children of God."

Mabel Wells put a hand to her chest and gasped. "I just realized what could have happened to Cynthia! Oh, child, didn't you realize that heathen could have killed you too? Or worse?"

"I wasn't afraid, Mother. I felt God was with me, protecting me. I thought I was doing what He wanted me to do."

The woman closed her eyes, sighing deeply. "The next time you do something you feel is God's calling, you might discuss it first with your father." She put a hand to her face. "Oh, my! How will the people of Deadwood react to this?"

"I'll make them understand, Mabel," Wells answered his wife, giving Cynthia a squeeze. "You just go ahead with dinner. We will eat together and then pray together. Then I will go into Deadwood and tell them."

"Can I go with you, Father?" Alex asked excitedly. "I want to see what they say!"

"No, you cannot. I will go alone."

The man left Cynthia's side and Cynthia watched her mother's eyes. Mabel Wells was as loving as her husband, but she had a bigger pride, one that she often said she considered a sin. It was harder for her mother to forgive disobedience than it was for her husband. But for her children's sake she was usually able to rise above her pride and hurt. She managed a smile for her daughter, then reached out and hugged the girl. "Promise me you will talk to your father first before you decide to do something so foolish, child."

"I promise, Mother."

"Help me with dinner now. Then we must pray before your father goes into town."

Cynthia felt her stomach tighten. She was still not so sure the men of Deadwood wouldn't want to punish her some way. If only Red Wolf hadn't killed Kinder. There was a much greater chance the people of Deadwood would understand and forgive her deed if not for Kinder's death. How she wished Red Wolf would be caught and brought back. Sinful as the thought was, she would gladly go to his hanging. She thought how ironic it was that she had felt so sorry for him, and now wished she had never let him go.

But what bothered her most was that she still could not forget him, the dark eyes, the secret pride she had felt when he called her a brave warrior, the flutter in her stomach when he talked about her golden hair and her sky-blue eyes. It seemed as though that one night's adventure had changed everything about her, the way she felt inside, the way she looked at people. She wanted to understand Red Wolf and his kind. Why had he killed Rube Kinder? In spite of telling her father and mother what she had done, Cynthia still felt guilty. She wondered if she could just understand Red Wolf's reason, maybe she would feel better about the whole thing. She had seen such a human side of Red Wolf, had been so sure he had feelings like anyone else. Why, then, had he so easily killed Kinder? What was so terrible about a few whites coming into their land that made the Indians raid and kill? Why were they so angry?

She began cutting up potatoes, wondering what kind of food Red Wolf ate. But it mattered little. By now he had completely forgotten her, and she must forget him.

Chapter Five

Cynthia kept turning to look, hoping to see more people come into the church. But so far there were only Mr. Bonneville and six other regulars. It was time for her father to start his sermon, and still no more had come.

It had been a whole week since her father had gone to the citizens of Deadwood and told them it was his own daughter who had cut Red Wolf loose. She would never forget the look on her father's face when he returned.

"I guess I overestimated the ability of people to understand," he told his wife. "And people wasted no words in letting me know what a poor disciplinarian I am." He had looked at Cynthia then. "According to those I spoke with, I should give you a good thrashing. What do you think, Cynthia?"

Cynthia had reddened, looking down. "If you think it would make the townspeople happy."

"Oh, they think I should do it publicly." He had looked at Cynthia's mother again. "Can you imagine even suggesting such a thing?" He had taken Cynthia's chin in hand then and pulled her head up. "Don't hang your head, Cynthia. You did what was right. Most of the people in this town haven't the slightest understanding of compassion for a fellow human being. If I thought you needed a good thrashing, I would already have done it." He had sighed deeply then, as though carrying a great burden. "My duty here will be much more difficult than I supposed," he had told his wife, patting Cynthia's cheek while he spoke. He had put an arm around his wife then. "Fix me some tea, will you, Mabel?"

"Of course, dear. Was it that bad? Surely they understand—Cynthia is only sixteen, and she knows nothing about Indians."

"Apparently in Deadwood there are no excuses for helping an Indian, especially not one who has killed one of your own. But not to worry, Mabel. It will all blow over in time. What's done is done."

Cynthia had watched them, and she would never forget her father's words then.

"You know, Mabel," he had told his wife, "for the strangest reason I couldn't bring myself to tell them the Indian's name. It would make it much easier for the soldiers to find and identify him as Kinder's killer if I told them. But the way those people talked, I found myself wondering who was the worst sinner, the Indian or those men in town. I felt the strangest compulsion to deliberately keep the Indian's name from them so he would never be caught. I can't imagine why I did that. After all, he did kill a man."

"Perhaps it was just a matter of conscience. If you name him, he might be found easier—and then hanged. We don't know why he killed Mr. Kinder, or what we ourselves might do to someone who tortured us."

"I like to think I would never raise my hand to another human being," Wells had answered. "Christ tells us to turn the other cheek."

"I suppose we could never really harm another man. But we don't understand how Indians think, Albert. All I know is, from what I have seen in Deadwood, there are men here who are no kinder and no more civil than the Indians."

Cynthia watched her father now, saw the disappointment in his eyes as he rose to give his sermon. She loved him all the more for his understanding for what she had

78

done, his defense of her in town, and his refusal to tell the men Red Wolf's name. It was not that she cared one whit now for Red Wolf, for in her estimation he had still betrayed her. But it made her mad that the men in Deadwood wouldn't even try to understand why she had helped the Indian. Not telling them Red Wolf's name was a way of getting back at them for the meanness. She was even angrier now over the fact that so many had stayed away from church, no doubt to show their disgust over Cynthia's deed and to make sure the Reverend Wells knew how they felt.

Her father conducted his service with as much fire and sincerity as if the little chapel was full, and her mother pounded out the hymns on the "sinful" piano with more fervor than Cynthia felt necessary. The woman was obviously upset over the low attendance, and Cynthia felt sorry for them both. When the service was ended, Wells walked up to Cynthia and put out his hand.

"I think we should go into town today and get some more supplies," he told her, turning to his wife as she came up beside him.

Cynthia's eyes widened and her heart pounded. "To town? You mean . . . you want me to go too?"

"Certainly. Why not? It's time the citizens of Deadwood saw you walk proudly down the street, time they reminded themselves what a lovely, Christian young lady you are, and you are not ashamed of what you did. You were brave enough to go and cut that Indian loose at night, Cynthia. Surely you're brave enough to accompany the family into town today."

Cynthia smiled faintly, wanting to please her father. "I think I am."

"Of course you are. Let's go have our dinner now, and then we will pay a visit to Mr. Bonneville's supply store."

Cynthia moved mechanically through dinner, hardly able to eat with the thought of going into town, where everyone would stare at her. But her father had told her to be proud. He was sure she should go, and perhaps he was right. Maybe if she just started showing herself, spoke to people, let them see she was just a young girl trying to do a good deed, there would be less tension and animosity. Perhaps people considered her staying close to the house as a sign of shame and guilt.

They finished dinner and piled into the wagon, to which Cynthia's father had already hitched two mules. The Reverend and Mrs. Wells sat side by side in the wagon seat, and Alex and Cynthia sat in back. Cynthia breathed deeply as the wagon moved toward the now-dusty main street of Deadwood. Cynthia felt people staring, and she looked right back at them, holding her chin high.

Her father drove the wagon right through town and halted in front of the supply store. He climbed down and tied the mules, then helped his wife down while Cynthia and Alex jumped out of the back of the wagon. Cynthia was relieved to realize there were not nearly as many people milling about today as usual. This was Sunday, and she remembered her father talking about how many of the inhabitants of Deadwood slept half the day because of drinking all night the night before.

"The problem is especially bad on Sunday," he had told his wife. "Maybe I should change the time of my services so that more can come."

"If a man is wanting to find the Lord, he ought to be able to get himself up at a decent hour to do it," Cynthia's mother had answered. "It's certainly not much of a sacrifice."

A couple of wagons clattered by, and things seemed generally normal, but Cynthia stayed close to her father, still sensing the stares and an underlying current against her. What were people saying about her? Did they think she was bad? She hurriedly followed her parents into Bonneville's store, where Cynthia immediately walked again to the stack of material on one counter, pretending to be looking at it but really just wanting not to have to look at anyone.

"Well, the good Preacher Wells," a man standing inside said, a sarcastic ring to his voice. "You give your daughter that thrashin' yet? Maybe you'd, uh, like one of us to do it."

There was an ugly laugh, and Cynthia swallowed back a lump in her throat.

"I only punish my children when they have done something wrong," Wells answered the man. "Cynthia only did what she thought was her Christian duty. And I wouldn't touch or speak wrongly to my daughter if I were you, Mr. Drake. I am not a man of violence, but I have a father's protective instincts, and God is on my side."

"He might be on your side, but—"

"That's enough, Drake," came Bonneville's voice. "I don't want any trouble in this store, and Cynthia Wells is a proper young lady with a heart that happens to be too soft, that's all. She's hardly more than a child."

"Looks like a full-growed woman to me," Drake answered with the sneering laugh again.

"You save those eyes for the prostitutes," Bonneville answered him. "Now if there is nothing you need here, go on out until the reverend is through with his purchases. I'll remind you the reverend is a man of God, come here of his own free will from the comforts back East—not to get rich, but to bring guidance and God's word to worthless souls like you and me."

"Speak for yourself, Bonneville," the man called Drake answered. "I didn't come out here to hear about God. I came out here to find gold—and to kill Indians finding it if I have to."

Cynthia never looked up. She didn't want to see the face that belonged to the one called Drake. She remembered two buckskin-clad, dirty-looking men standing near the counter when she came in. Surely the one called Drake was one of them. She was proud of her father for speaking up to the man, and now more glad than ever that he had not told any of these men Red Wolf's name.

81

The door opened and closed, and Cynthia turned sad blue eyes to her father, who only gave her a smile. "Pick out some ribbon to trim that dress, Cynthia," he said with a wink. He turned to Bonneville with a list of needs, and Alex, who had stood rigidly beside his father, ready to fight the grown men who had confronted him if necessary, now went about snooping into everything in the store. Cynthia's mother, who had remained quiet out of sheer terror, let out a sigh of relief, sure her poor husband might have actually had to become physically violent if the awful men in the store had tried to lay a hand on Cynthia.

"They aren't all like those two," Bonneville was telling Cynthia's father. "Most folks do understand, Preacher. They'll all come around in time. Don't you worry about the church attendance this morning. It will come back up."

"I certainly hope you're right, Art."

"Sure I'm right. Now let's have a look at that list."

Cynthia and her mother picked out some satin ribbon for dress trim. This evening they would start on the ne dresses. Cynthia looked forward to the diversion. Maybe Mr. Bonneville was right. Maybe with a little more time things would be fine again. They made their purchases and picked up their packages, Cynthia's heart feeling lighter at Bonneville's words, and at the way her father had stood up to the man called Drake.

Preacher Wells opened the door for his family, but before they could go out, three women in bright dresses and rustling skirts barged through the doorway. Cynthia knew in an instant they were prostitutes, and she gawked at their shiny, red lips and the colors of blue and green over their thick-lashed eyes.

The moment hung awkward, as the three women stopped and stared before they came all the way inside, which prevented the preacher and his family from leaving. Cynthia began to redden under the hot glare of one of the women. She recognized her as the one who had cried the most at Ruben Kinder's funeral, the one Cynthia thought might have loved Kinder.

"Well, well," she said, sneering her painted lips. "If it isn't the little bitch that killed Ruben Kinder."

All three of them snickered and looked Cynthia over. Cynthia struggled against tears, her face feeling on fire.

"My daughter killed no one!" Cynthia's mother said. "She felt it her Christian duty to help the Indian man. She had no idea he would kill Mr. Kinder. And who are you to stand there and accuse another!"

"Mabel!" Preacher Wells said quickly. "Let it go. Let's just get home."

The three women sauntered aside just enough to let the family slip past them. "Pretty little thing, I'll say that," one of them observed with a snicker.

"Any time you need work, honey, we can give you a job," said the one who had favored Ruben Kinder.

They all laughed loudly then, their cackles making Cynthia think of witches. Surely that was what they were—sinful, wicked, cruel witches! She wouldn't tell her father, but she hated it here now—hated people like Drake and like the wanton women who roamed the streets. Sometimes she felt like she hated God, for leading her to do something that had brought so much pain to her parents and so much shame to her own soul. Most of all she hated Red Wolf.

They boarded the wagon. A few people said hello, no animosity in their voices. But Cynthia was devastated at the words of Drake and the prostitute. She didn't like people thinking bad things about her, not even people like that. She wondered at how they could stand in judgment, people who were themselves such sinners. How could they take her good deed and turn it into something so ugly.

Preacher Wells drove the wagon away, and Cynthia looked over at Alex. "I'm never coming back into town again," she told him with tears in her eyes.

"Sure you will. You shouldn't listen to those ugly,

smelly women," he answered, wrinkling his nose. "Did you smell that awful perfume?" He stuck out his tongue. "They're just jealous because you're pretty," he told her.

Cynthia could not help smiling. "You've never said anything like that to me, Alex."

The boy shrugged. "Well, it's true. Father said for you not to act ashamed, so don't. Let them talk. Father says God knows who's right and who's wrong. That's all that matters."

"Maybe you're right." Cynthia turned to look off to the west as the wagon headed back to the parsonage. The land stretched out like a swelling green sea, and in the distance thick pines made the hills that stretched toward the mountains look black: Black Hills. That was what the Indians called them. They were supposed to be sacred, so sacred, in fact, that the Indians had killed many white people for daring to invade them.

The hawk circled, its wings held out seemingly immobile while it floated gracefully on upper air currents. Cynthia watched, wishing with all her heart she had the freedom that hawk had. If it didn't like being in one place, it could just fly away to wherever it wanted to go. And animals knew who their friends and their enemies were.

It was not that way with people. Nearly two months had passed since she let Red Wolf go free. A couple of girls her age had come to town with their families, one of their fathers opening a barber shop, the other a restaurant. Although the girls were allowed to come and see Cynthia's mother for lessons, and their families came to church, the girls were cool to Cynthia, as though by having touched an Indian and let him go free she was somehow tainted. Cynthia was sure the towns-people had told the girls' families about the incident, and their parents had given them strict instructions to stay away from Cynthia. One of them had a little brother about a year older than Alex. The two boys had become fast friends. It was only Cynthia who was left out.

Now, with Alex always going off to play with his new friend, Cynthia was more lonely than ever. It was one thing to be lonely because there was no one near her age with whom she could associate. But to be deliberately shunned was much worse.

Every day she regretted more and more that she had let Red Wolf go. Every day she felt farther removed from God. And every day she hated Red Wolf even more. She continued to have visions of him laughing at her, and in the night she could hear the shrieking cackle of the three whores, see them pointing their fingers at her and calling her a murderer. Never did she realize there could be so much hatred in the souls of human beings. But now as hatred began to brew in her own heart, the feeling was becoming more clear to her. She didn't like feeling this way, but it hurt so badly to be accused of doing something wrong when she knew in her heart she had done the right thing.

Her father's words of comfort and of support did little to comfort her. It only made her feel more guilty, for she knew she was bringing pain to her family and making her father's job more difficult. Every day the man came home looking tired and upset, and every day there was a new rumor, and often a story backed by evidence, that the Indians were raiding and killing all over the Black Hills. The thought of it weighed heavily on Cynthia's heart. What if one of the raiders was Red Wolf? Was he still using her mother's knife? Had it become an instrument of evil in the hands of the man Cynthia Wells had freed?

Cynthia rose from the back steps, keeping an eye on the hawk, which flew farther away now. Watching it seemed to somehow lift her spirits. She felt a kinship with the hawk. It seemed to know how she longed for its freedom, longed to go far, far away from this place. She ran through the back field, past the water pump, past a pile of wood, past the crudely built fence that held her father's mules. She stretched out her arms and moved them like wings, continuing to follow the hawk.

She ran past the wagon and the stable. Her father was in town again, her mother busily sewing in the parlor. Alex was off playing with his new friend. No one saw Cynthia following the hawk, and in Cynthia's mind, probably no one cared. A stiff wind blew her white-blond hair back from her face, blew the skirt of her dress between her legs as she ran. The hawk circled again, riding the wind. Cynthia smiled at its beauty, its graceful movements, envied its ability to look down on everything from up high.

All the agony of the past days and weeks welled up inside her soul and suddenly brought forth a gush of tears. Lonely. She felt so terribly lonely and guilty. She had been to town only one other time since the day the whores laughed at her. It was like being in prison. Yes, she was in prison, being punished for helping a murderer. She cried and cried, falling to her knees and bending over. It felt good to cry this way, to let the tears come hard, to make loud noises.

She had tried to be brave for her father, putting on smiles and being proud like he had told her to do. But she couldn't keep it all inside forever, and she didn't want her father to know how badly she needed to weep. She covered her face and cried for several minutes, feeling suddenly weak and tired. She had eaten and slept too little over the past weeks, unable to get back all the good feeling about life and about herself she once had had.

She was scared now—scared she would never get over this—scared she would feel this way for the rest of her life, be shunned the rest of her life, never have any friends. She wanted so much to leave Deadwood and go back East, but her father's work was here, and he had been so kind and understanding, she hated to complain and upset him more. Somehow she had to bear this alone, but she wasn't sure how she would do it, for she couldn't even ask God for help now. Somehow she had lost Him, had been unable to pray. That was the worst loneliness of all.

Finally she was able to control the tears. She took her handkerchief from her dress pocket and blew her nose and wiped her eyes. She looked up into the sky with bloodshot eyes to see that the hawk was gone. She breathed deeply, getting to her feet and turning to go back home. A tiny alarm sounded in her heart when she realized she could not see her house. The rolling hills, with their hight crests and deep gulleys, did not leave an unending horizon as she had thought. She was in a gulley, unable to see above it.

How far had she come? It certainly didn't seem that far. She put a hand to her chest, realizing she was alone, much too far from the house. She had done another bad thing, wandering off like this. She had better get back quickly before her parents discovered what she had done. She looked around, trying to determine which way she had come. Suddenly she wasn't sure. She ran, picking up her skirts and heading for the crest of another hill.

Cynthia saw no sign of buildings, but she did see riders coming. She waved her arms, then dropped them, realizing they might be bad men, mean miners who might do bad things to her. Or, worse than that . . . Her heart began to pound wildly. They could be Indians! She had boldly displayed herself, but as she watched them ride even harder toward her, she began to see the dark skin, the long hair. Now she could hear their yips and war whoops.

They *were* Indians! She turned in the opposite direction and began running, praying her house would quickly come into sight. She tripped on her own skirt and fell face down, scratching her cheek on a rough plant. She quickly got back up and ran as fast as she could, wanting to scream but unable to find her voice. She reached the crest of another hill. There it was! Her house! Deadwood! But she was astonished at how far away it was. How could she have let herself do this?

She ran even harder, but already she could hear the pound of horses' hooves behind her, could feel the soft earth shaking, could hear clearly now the wild cries of the wild men bearing down on her. She prayed someone from town would see and would come riding out and scare off the Indians, but as she ran she reached another gulley. Now no one could see, and she winced and ducked as several horses thundered past her. She kept running, but one of the Indians rode his horse smack into her side, knocking her down.

She could hear their laughter now. She slowly got back up, straightening to see that they were circling her, talking among themselves in their own tongue.

"Go away!" she screamed. "You'd better go away or soldiers will get you!"

They laughed again. Her mind raced with confusion. They rode around and around her, so that she wasn't even sure how many there were. Four? Six? Eight? They all looked the same through her tears—all dark and wild—all showing the evil grin she had so often envisioned on Red Wolf.

Something poked her in the ribs and she screamed. Now a poke from the other side, a whack on the head. She put her arms over her head then as they continued to circle her, poking at her with the dull end of their lances. She tried to run again, but they left her no place to go. One kicked out at her, knocking her to the ground. Before she could get up one of them straddled her, and she felt a cold blade at the side of her face.

She stared into his dark eyes. He was not so different from Red Wolf, but he was not Red Wolf. He moved himself down slightly, taking her skirt and throwing it over her face, then ripping off all her slips and her bloomers. Cynthia screamed as loud as she could, flailing wildly at her abductor until she felt something sharp cut into her hand. Then came a hard blow to her face.

Someone jerked her up then. She felt sick and dizzy. Through blurred vision she thought she saw the Indians passing around her slips and underwear. They were laughing, holding them up. Then they stuffed them into painted leather bags that hung on their horses. Someone dragged her over to a horse and began tying something on her hand. She looked at her hand and saw blood running, dripping from it. She gasped at the sight, then began fighting the Indian who was tying a piece of cloth around the wound. She pounded and scratched at him while the rest of them laughed. Then she felt the sting of his quirt as he whipped at her several times with it about the face and neck until finally she stopped fighting him.

She stood there shivering and crying while the Indian returned to tying a cloth tightly around her wound.

"Red Wolf," Cynthia sobbed. "If you must take me with you . . . take me to Red Wolf. He . . . he'll tell you . . . I saved him once. You should let me go. I saved the life of one of your friends. Red Wolf. Do you know him?"

The man grasped both of her wrists with one strong hand and began looping a strip of rawhide around her wrists.

"Wait," she protested. "It's too tight. It hurts."

The words seemed to mean nothing to him. He kept hold of the other end of the rawhide and mounted his horse with the same ease in which a man would walk. He urged the horse into a fast walk, and Cynthia was obliged to run behind it or fall and be dragged.

"Wait! Wait!" she begged.

The other Indians rode behind them, poking at her again with the blunt end of their lances. Terror welled in her soul. How long would they keep this up? How much could she take? How far could she go without falling and being dragged? And surely it was only a matter of time, maybe just until they got a little farther from town, before they threw her down and each one of them did vile things to her. The thought of how it felt to have one of them ripping at her clothes made her gag with vomit. She could not imagine a fate worse than being raped by Indians. The thought of any man doing that to her had always been frightening, but this . . .

She tugged at her bindings. "Wait!" she screamed again. "Stop! Please stop! Let me go and I won't tell! If you take me with you, soldiers will come and kill you!" She jerked hard, terror and anger raging in her soul. The man who led her turned his horse and came back toward her. She looked boldly at him.

"Take me back, you dirty savage!" she screamed at him, surprised at her own anger and hatred, surprised that she could call anyone a name, feel this vicious. She screamed when his quirt came down across her face and neck again.

"Keep quiet, white bitch!" he told her. He dismounted again, coming close to her and painfully grasping her arms, jerking her close. "Keep quiet, or I, Many Bears, will tie each of your legs to a horse, and each horse will be ridden in the opposite direction until you are torn in half!"

Their eyes held challengingly, and Cynthia knew by the look in the eye of the wild man who had threatened her that he would make good on the threat if she didn't keep still. Horror rippled through her blood, while blood trickled from the tiny cuts on her face and neck where he had hit her with his quirt. Her hand was beginning to ache fiercely from the cut his knife had inflicted when she had tried to fight him, and it seemed everything hurt from the waist up, from so many blows from the lances and the quirt.

"Please," she said quietly. "Don't . . . don't hurt me until you have spoken to Red Wolf. You speak English. You know what I'm saying. Do you know him? Do you know Red Wolf?"

He grinned sarcastically. "I know him. So, you are the one who saved him from the white man's rope! Our people know the story. But it matters little to me. It is I, Many Bears, who has claimed the white woman with hair like the sun and eyes like the sky. You are mine! I care not that you saved Red Wolf. I have no rope around my neck. I do not need your help, white woman. It is *you* who needs help this time."

Cynthia shuddered when he reached around her and grasped some of her hair in his hand, a look of hunger she recognized even though she had never been with a man. Instinct told her what he was thinking, and she hoped she wouldn't throw up on him. If she did, he might tie her legs to the two horses like he said. This man was powerful, perhaps thirty years old, and vicious. There was none of the humanness in his eyes she had thought she had detected in Red Wolf's eyes. This man was different. This man was all that whites said Indians were, or so it seemed at this moment.

"If Red Wolf set eyes on you once and did not claim you for himself, then Red Wolf is a fool," he sneered at her. "He told us about the white men who captured him, and the white girl who let him go. Now I know he spoke the truth. And now I know how foolish he was." He yanked hard on her hair so that she winced, and then he laughed. "The spirits are with me today, white woman! Wait until Red Wolf finds I have captured the white girl who saved him! I will enjoy you, and then I will trade you back, for guns and food. White men will pay any price to get their women back from Indians, will they not?"

The man turned and re-mounted his horse, deliberately riding fast so that Cynthia could not keep up. He dragged her for many feet before stopping and getting down again, picking up her bruised and scratched body, and carrying her back to his horse. He plopped her on it and mounted up behind her, encircling her with an iron grip and riding off with her again. As they rode he said something to the others in their own tongue, and they all laughed again.

For the moment Cynthia was just grateful to be on the horse and not dragging behind it. Everything hurt, and she felt weak from loss of blood. The bandage on her hand was already soaked. She felt dizzy, and her head lolled back against the broad chest of Many Bears. She felt numb, confused. And she prayed inwardly that by some miracle Many Bears would not touch her before reaching the village or wherever it was he was taking her; that Red Wolf would be there and would help her. After all, he owed her that much.

But there were so many Indians, and they were so scattered. It was not likely Red Wolf would even be in the same village; and if he was, how could she put any faith in his helping her? He was surely no different from these men, and he had already betrayed her once. In her delirium she almost laughed, thinking what a fitting punishment she was getting for freeing Red Wolf. Now she would probably suffer untold humiliation and pain at the hands of Indians, and in the end, death. In a way, even this was Red Wolf's fault. If she had not freed him, she would not have suffered all the other problems. She would not have run away from the house today to follow the hawk and to cry.

Red Wolf. It all came back to Red Wolf. That one foolish night had cost her everything—her reputation, her friends, her family, her God, her pride. Now it would cost her her sanity, her purity, and probably her life.

Part Two

Chapter Six

"Albert, it's getting dark. What should we do?" Mabel Wells paced in the kitchen, wringing her hands, while her husband sat at the table, hands folded, head bowed.

"I don't know. I didn't say anything to anyone in town yet. I looked everyplace in town, Mabel—at least everyplace Cynthia would dare to go. She certainly wouldn't go into a tavern. In fact, the way things have been lately, I can't believe she would go into town at all."

"But if she did, so many people are angry at her. Maybe some of those miners . . . oh, Albert, you don't think some of those men would have taken her off with them!" Terror showed itself in her eyes.

Wells shook his head. "No. Angry as they all are, there are enough people in town who respect Cynthia as my daughter and who would not stand by and let ruffians drag her away. I just can't believe they would let that happen."

"Well, you're just going to have to go back to town and ask questions—tell them Cynthia is missing. Maybe someone will help us look for her. Some of the men could check the taverns and . . . and those horrible places where the prostitutes live. We have to be sure, Albert."

The man rose, going to look out the back door. "And if she is nowhere in town? What then? What is the alternative?"

His wife shivered. "I don't like to think about it."

He turned to look at his wife. "Indians?" Wells's eyes were bloodshot, his whole countenance weary.

Mabel's eyes teared. "But it couldn't be, Albert! I would have heard something—horses—Cynthia screaming."

"Maybe. You say the last you knew she was sitting on the back steps?"

The woman nodded. "Cynthia wouldn't be foolish enough to go wandering away from Deadwood!"

Wells rubbed at his eyes. "She was foolish enough to go and set an Indian free once. And she's been despondent and moody lately, ever since that incident in town with the prostitutes. Maybe she was daydreaming, wanted to be alone." He sighed deeply. "You know how it is out here. Sound gets muffled by all those gulleys and hills. You can't hear the town noises past the first hill."

Cynthia's mother grasped her stomach and turned away, noticing Alex standing in the doorway watching and listening, tears on his cheeks. "Did Indians take Cindy?" he asked.

The boy's father walked over to him, patting his shoulder. "Let's pray that isn't what happened to her, Alex. Come with me. We'll go back into town together and ask around. Maybe someone will help us look for her."

"Would the Indians kill her, Father?"

Mabel Wells stifled a sob at the remark, turning away to busy herself with washing dishes. *"I must keep busy,"* she told herself. *"I must not think the worst, not yet. Cynthia will show up. The Lord will protect her and bring her back to us."* She scrubbed at a pan, tears running down her face. Indians! No, no, not Cynthia! But if it *was* Indians, perhaps the one she had saved would discover her—help her. Surely he would be grateful enough to help Cynthia as she had helped him. But Indians didn't think like whites. Maybe he wouldn't be grateful at all. And maybe by the time he even discovered her, she would have already suffered unmentionable horrors at the hands of her abductors.

So young and innocent and pretty she was. The whole idea was sickening. Mabel cried harder, hardly able to see the dish she was scrubbing. And for the first time she resented her husband for bringing his family to the godforsaken place. Godforsaken it was after all. She had tried to defend it once, but she couldn't any longer. She felt suddenly distanced from God, unable to pray. If Cynthia had been taken by Indians, Mabel Wells's faith would be drastically shaken. Cynthia had suffered for doing what she thought was God's will, and now God had surely let something terrible happen to her.

Somewhere in the distance a coyote yipped, and night insects sang in rhythm. Cynthia shivered, a chill in the night air in spite of how hot the days were now. Her wrists were still tied, and the other end of the leather strap that bound her was tied to a small tree so that she could not run away. She lay curled next to the tree, with only the hard ground to lie on and no blanket to cover her. Without her bloomers and the extra slips she always wore, the thin cotton dress brought little warmth.

Everything hurt. Cuts and bruises from being dragged increased in their aches and stings as the hours wore on. Her face and neck felt on fire from the sharp little cuts from Many Bears' quirt. Her hair was tangled and had dirt in it.

The hours until Many Bears and the others finally stopped to make camp had been long and horrifying for Cynthia. It felt as though her insides had been shaken so that everything must be displaced, for Many Bears had ridden hard most of the way.

Part of the terrible ache Cynthia felt was from sheer terror and anxiety, wondering what Many Bears would do to her once they stopped. During the long ride he had often grabbed at her breasts, saying something to the

97

others in his own tongue and laughing. If Cynthia objected, he would pinch her cruelly, until finally she learned not to resist his hated touch.

When they finally stopped at this place, Many Bears knocked her from the horse like a sack of potatoes. Then he dragged her into some underbrush, and to her horror, pulled his privates from under his loincloth, laughing at the look on her face. He then proceeded to urinate, seemingly quite pleased at the good joke he had played on the terrified white girl. He covered himself again, then nodded toward her, pointing to where he had urinated. He jerked her over and lifted her skirt.

Cynthia realized he was telling her to relieve herself. Her terror made it easy to do just that, but she felt nauseous at the realization that Many Bears was watching her from behind. She could see his evil grin without turning around. He jerked her up before she was completely through, and she could still feel the burning sensation of urine dried on her legs, could smell it in her skirt. She had never experienced being this dirty, had never known this kind of pain and terror.

She waited, praying to a God she wasn't even sure heard her anymore, praying Many Bears would not do that one horrible thing he seemed to be threatening to do. She could not imagine a more hideous torture. She would rather he beat her to death than use her like the animals, take away her last bit of pride and self-esteem, submit her to hideous humiliation in front of the other men. If she lived through such a thing, she was sure she could never hold her head up in pride anymore, could never marry a nice man and be a normal wife and mother. She vowed that if Many Bears mated with her, she would find a way to kill him and then kill herself.

At a nearby campfire Many Bears and the other Indians sat eating and laughing, enjoying the warmth of the fire. Cynthia could smell the meat they were roasting, and in spite of her pain and terror, pangs of hunger gnawed at her insides. Her mouth felt as though someone had poured sand into it, and she wondered if she would die from hunger and thirst before Many Bears had a chance to kill her some other way.

She saw her abductor rise then, recognized his shadowy figure against the light of the campfire because he was much bigger than the other Indians. He was walking toward her now, and she whimpered with terror. Had he decided he had waited long enough? She scooted farther back as he came closer and knelt beside her. He jerked her head up, then shoved something into her mouth, forcing it between her clenched teeth. Cynthia realized to her surprise it was meat. She chewed on it eagerly while Many Bears held her up by a fistful of hair. She swallowed the meat and the man took something from around his shoulders and held it to her lips.

"Drink," he told her.

He tipped a canteen and Cynthia took a swallow.

"Soldier's canteen," Many Bears told her, taking the water away then. "I killed the soldier who used it." He leaned closer. "Maybe I'll kill you too, huh?"

"Why . . . are you doing this?" Cynthia answered in a shaking voice. "I haven't done anything . . . to you. I even . . . helped one of your own kind."

He set the canteen aside, grasping her chin in a strong hand while he still held her by her hair in his other hand. "You are white. It is not what you have done to me, white bitch! It is what your kind has done to my kind! For this the whites will suffer until they get out of the Black Hills!"

She could see his sneering grin by the moonlight. He moved his hand from her chin down over her throat to her breasts. "We do to white women what the miners do to *our* women! Then we get many guns and much food for returning the white women."

"Please don't touch me like that," Cynthia begged through tears.

"It will not be so bad," he told her with a smile. "It is no different from being with your husband, except that I,

99

Many Bears, am stealing what belongs to him, taking my pleasure with a white woman as white men took pleasure with my mother and my sister!" The words were hissed from anger and hatred.

Cynthia wanted to feel sorry for him. His mother and sister had been raped by white men? Did white men do that to Indian women? "I . . . don't have a husband," she whimpered.

Many Bears straightened. "No husband? How many summers are you?"

"I am sixteen," she sniffed, trembling.

"Sixteen summers—and no husband? Is he dead?"

"I have never had a husband."

He leaned closer. "You are untouched?"

"Yes."

He let go of her and rose. "Untouched you could be worth many horses to Many Bears, or much more in trade back to the whites."

Cynthia breathed a sigh of relief, but it didn't last long. He knelt close again, grasping her hair and touching his cheek to her own. "Or you could bring Many Bears much pleasure."

Cynthia struggled to think. Apparently her being a virgin had surprised him. "Wait and see, Many Bears," she told him, so engulfed with terror she wondered how she found the words. "I am worth more untouched. You said so yourself."

He straightened again. "It is true? You are the one who helped Red Wolf?"

"Yes. How else would I know his name? I took my mother's knife and I cut him down with it."

Many Bears rubbed his chin thoughtfully. "I will think on this." He picked up his canteen, and for a brief moment, as with Red Wolf, Cynthia caught a hint of human emotion within this wild man's countenance.

"Is it true, about white men doing bad things to your mother and sister?" she asked carefully.

Many Bears stood silently for several seconds. "It is

100

true," he told her.

Cynthia was astounded by the sudden sorrow in his voice. "I'm sorry," she told him.

Many Bears slung the canteen around his shoulder again. "If you were truly sorry, you would leave this land! How many of you must die first? How many of your women must be raped and tortured and killed before your men decide to take them back to where it is safe? Is the strange metal in the ground worth more to your men than their women and children?" He spat at her. "I have never known such fools as the white man!"

He stalked away without offering Cynthia a blanket or any more food or water. She didn't care, as long as he had decided not to rape her. She curled up closer to the tree, praying he would not come back that night.

The Reverend Wells stood in front of Art Bonneville's supply store, holding Alex's hand. Extra lanterns had been hung outside the door by Bonneville, after which the man had made his way through town asking men to come to his store for a meeting. Anything and everything was food for excitement and entertainment in a town like Deadwood. It was not difficult to get people to come. But this time of night, most of those who came were prostitutes and drunks, although a few of the businessmen, rousted out of bed by Bonneville, came grudgingly, some still in their robes.

Wells watched as men and women gathered around him. "Don't tell me you're gonna' preach to us in the middle of the night!" one man shouted.

The rest of the crowd laughed.

"This some kind of trick, Reverend?" another yelled out.

"I ain't about to give up my whiskey and women for no sermon!" said another.

Wells stood silently, squeezing Alex's hand, praying that by some miracle someone in the crowd would know

101

what had happened to Cynthia. Much as he detested the thought of it, if Cynthia had been taken by any of these men to be frightened and teased, it would be better than if she had been taken by Indians. But as he studied some of them, he realized there might not be much difference.

Bonneville finally returned, stepping up beside Wells and waving his hands for silence. "Quiet, all of you!" he shouted.

Alex watched the men, feeling suddenly very important, excited by the night meeting, even though his sister might be in danger. He was afraid for Cynthia, but at the same time he was proud of her. She had certainly been the cause of a wealth of excitement in Deadwood. He hoped that wherever she was right now, she would be as brave as she had been the night she rescued Red Wolf.

"The reverend asked me to call all of you over here because of something very serious," Bonneville was telling the quiet crowd. "His daughter Cynthia is missing."

A general mumble moved through the crowd.

"Maybe she run off with her Indian lover," the one called Drake said with a sneer.

Wells could no longer control his anger. He was too distraught over what might have happened to Cynthia. He let go of Alex's hand and charged off the boardwalk and into Drake. Bystanders pulled him away as he pummeled at Drake, who was much bigger and burlier than Wells, and who only laughed at the preacher's attack.

"Well, looky here! The reverend has a temper!" Several men laughed with Drake, as others yanked the reverend back onto the boardwalk. Wells breathed deeply for control, surprised at his outburst but feeling better for it.

"You better go ask God's forgiveness for that one, Reverend," someone told him. "I don't think preachers is supposed to be gettin' into fights."

There was another general round of laughter.

"I'll not stand here and hear my daughter being insulted. She could be in terrible danger!" Wells's voice broke on the last words, and he turned away for a moment. The crowd quieted a little and Bonneville stepped up to the edge of the boardwalk.

"This is no time for levity, and no time to be criticizing Reverend Wells. His daughter is missing, and he needs our help in finding her. I called all of you here to ask if any of you saw Cynthia Wells today."

People mumbled and looked around at each other, while Drake just stood grinning, thinking the whole matter humorous.

"Speak up if you've seen her," Bonneville told them. "If you know where she is, tell us. The reverend has no intention of punishing anyone. He just wants his daughter back. He knows how some of you feel about Cynthia for freeing the Indian. He knows some of you might have decided to tease the girl; get back at her somehow for what she did. He just wants her back and that will be the end of it."

Most shook their heads.

"Ain't seen hide nor hair of her for weeks," someone said.

"The girl hasn't even been to town for ages," one of the prostitutes added. "How would we know what happened to her?"

"She ain't in town," someone else said.

"Maybe she run off to the hills with some miner," another put in. "You never know what a girl that age will do. We already know that by her lettin' that Indian go. She's more than the reverend can handle, that's sure."

There was light laughter then, and Wells's heart felt like lead. No one in town had seen her. Cynthia would never run off with strangers. There was only one other possibility.

"I think Indians got her," he said then.

The crowd quieted again. Most of them, in spite of being drunk and in a joking mood, could see the agony in

103

the preacher's eyes.

"Please. I need the help of someone who knows Indians, knows how to read tracks and such. I want to search the hills behind the parsonage. Please have some mercy and understanding. Cynthia is my daughter, hardly more than a child, and totally innocent of how cruel men can be. If no one here in town has seen her, then it must have been Indians. All of you know what that means."

"Serves her right for lettin' that Indian go a couple of months ago," Drake sneered.

"Come on, Drake, don't rub it in on the preacher," another man said. He was of medium build with a heavy beard and hair so long that he wore it tied behind his neck, and dressed in buckskins. He stepped forward, looking up at Wells. "Name's Johnstone," he told the reverend. "Miles Johnstone. I've scouted these parts for a long time. I'll go check around for you."

Tears came into the reverend's eyes. "I appreciate it, Mr. Johnstone. God will bless you for being so understanding and for helping me."

Johnstone blushed a little and nodded. "Be ready first light," he told the reverend. "I'll come to the parsonage at dawn and we'll go have a look."

"Thank you. Thank you so much, Mr. Johnstone. My wife will be quite relieved too. It will be difficult to wait through the night, but I suppose we have no choice." He looked around the crowd. "Would any of you be kind enough to go along, just for protection?" he asked. "We can't be sure what is out there."

"I've got my business to think about," one man spoke up.

"I've got to get back to my claim," said another.

"Won't do any good any of us goin' with you," Drake told him. "If Indians did take her, she's long gone by now. And it's a sure bet she ain't no little girl anymore."

There were a few snickers, but several of the men pushed Drake away. "Go on with you," they told him.

"You got no call to talk like that in front of the reverend about his own daughter."

"She let the Indian go!" Drake grumbled.

"She didn't know what she was doing," someone argued. "No matter what she did, she's one of our own kind, and Indians might have her. We have to see what we can do."

"I tell you, she ran off with somebody," Drake insisted. "If she's wild enough to go right up to a naked Indian and cut him down, she's wild enough to run off with some miner. Maybe the girl is just lookin' for some excitement in her life. Lord knows it has to be pretty dull bein' the daughter of a minister." He shoved at all of them and stalked off.

"I'm sorry for those words, Reverend Wells," Bonneville said then, putting a hand on the man's shoulder. "I'll go with you and Johnstone in the morning."

"Thank you, Art," the reverend answered. "You're a good man."

"I don't know about that. I just know I don't like the idea of a sweet girl like Cynthia being in the hands of Indians."

Wells looked at the man with agony in his eyes. "Would they kill her, Art? Or would they torture her? Would they make a slave of her?"

"Now hold it, Reverend. Don't torture yourself with wondering what they would do," Johnstone said then. "First we have to determine if that is even what happened to her. As far as what they would do, it's hard to say. White women are often traded for food or guns, with no more harm done to them than the common ailments of having to live a harsh life to which they aren't accustomed. Some suffer worse fates. All we can do is pray that won't happen to Cynthia. Tomorrow morning we'll see what we can find out. If it looks like Indians took her, we'll go to Fort Robinson and tell the soldiers there. We're not going to find any men in this crowd willing to go into Indian country looking for her, that's sure. We'll have to leave that up to the soldiers.''

The reverend shook his head. "I never should have brought my family here," he said sadly, as the crowd broke up. "This is all my fault."

"You came here to bring God's word to a town full of sinners," Bonneville told the man. "There was nothing wrong in that, Reverend. You're the one who always says we have to accept all things as God moving in our lives, remember?"

Wells looked at Miles Johnstone. "Do you think, if it was Indians, do you think that if that one she saved sees her, he'd help her?"

Johnstone sighed deeply. "Hard to say. Those devils don't think like us, Reverend. They don't know the meaning of gratefulness and compassion. They aren't likely to give up a white girl as pretty as Cynthia just because she helped one of them. She is worth a lot to them—food, tobacco, horses, weapons, you name it."

"What about . . ." The reverend swallowed. "Would they rape her?"

Johnstone looked away. "The Sioux think that if they kill enough of us, rape enough of our women, we'll get out of the Black Hills. They're angry, Reverend, angry and even scared. They know the best way to torture and humiliate us is to steal our women and violate them. To them it's just an act of warfare."

Wells covered his eyes, and Alex could tell his father was crying quietly. It made a big lump come into his own throat. He wasn't totally certain what the word rape meant, but he knew it was something very bad and humiliating. His young heart was heavy for his pretty sister.

Hunger pains seemed to overshadow Cynthia's other physical pains as the second day of her captivity wore on.

106

She had not had anything to eat since breakfast at home the day before, other than the one piece of meat and the mouthful of water Many Bears had given her. Her lips were cracked and she had begged for water that morning, but Many Bears continued to deny her drink.

Cynthia felt numb now to the physical abuse. To her great relief, she began to reason that Many Bears only wanted to frighten her, see the terror in her eyes, watch her suffer. Somehow it made him happy. She didn't really care what he did to her as long as he didn't rape her, and that seemed more and more unlikely. Something about her being a virgin seemed to keep him from touching her, and she knew she could bear anything else he decided to do with her.

Life was fast becoming a matter of survival. She didn't care how she looked or how she smelled. She cared only that somehow she would live through this. She told herself over and over that God surely had a plan in all of this, a reason for making her feel sorry for Red Wolf in the first place, a reason for making her go and set him free, a reason for this ironic twist of fate that had landed her as a captive of a Sioux Indian called Many Bears, headed for the heart of Indian country. She had heard stories of how Indians respected captives who showed bravery. Red Wolf himself had called her a brave warrior. His reaction to her releasing him was proof to Cynthia that the rumors were true. She had seen honor in his eyes. But would he make good on that honor if he saw her now? Would he make Many Bears let her go?

Her head lolled against Many Bears' chest. She didn't care any more if she touched him. She was too weak to worry about what he would think. She closed her eyes and thought about home, about how worried her poor parents and little Alex would have been when they found her missing. Surely by now they were searching everywhere for her. If only she could tell them she was at least alive. She breathed deeply, telling herself that no matter what, she must survive, so that her parents' hearts would not be broken by finding her mutilated body.

But she wondered if survival would be worth it. She knew what most whites thought of other white women who had been Indian captives. They became outcasts among their own kind. She remembered her mother talking about it once. "A woman can't live with her own kind after something like that has happened to her," Mabel Wells had said. "Even if no Indian man has touched her, people don't believe it. It's a shame, that's what I say. A poor woman goes through all that and people at home treat her like it was her fault."

Cynthia wondered if that was how it would be for her. Maybe if she survived this, she would never be able to find a husband, never marry and have children, always be an outcast. Already the people of Deadwood looked down on her for freeing Red Wolf. Now it would be worse. Perhaps they were even saying she had gone off with Indians willingly.

Her eyes stung with tears at what this would do to her mother and father. Her father especially would be devastated, blaming himself for bringing his family to South Dakota. And what would little Alex think? She missed her brother, remembered how he had covered for her when she freed Red Wolf. She squeezed her eyes tighter against tears. She had quickly learned that Many Bears had no patience with tears, nor any sympathy for them.

"You white women weep too much," he had told her before knocking her to the ground with his quirt that morning. "Now you have something to cry about."

Cynthia struggled to understand this wild man with whom she was riding. There were moments when he seemed almost human, and other than hitting her with his quirt that morning, he had not abused her at all today. And sometime during the night he had come and put a blanket over her but had not touched her. She wondered if it was because she had shown some sympathy over his mother and sister being abused by white men.

She wished she knew more about this strange man, but she was afraid that questions would only rile him into hitting her again. He seemed to carry a great hatred in his soul. She had seen that same hatred in Red Wolf's eyes, and she began to wonder if it could simply be that these people were just plain mean and cruel and full of hate; or if there were things she didn't know about how whites had treated them. She wondered again about the Black Hills being sacred, and she thought about her father's teaching that these people were also the children of God. Cynthia saw nothing godly in Many Bears. But she wondered if perhaps God meant for her to bring His word to such men.

Silent tears trickled down her cheeks and dripped onto Many Bears' arm. He slowed his horse, taking his canteen from where it hung at the horse's side. He handed it to her.

"Here. Drink," he told her.

Cynthia took the canteen in total surprise. Did he know she was crying? She asked no questions. She took the canteen and guzzled as much as she could before he finally took it away again.

"Too much at once will make your belly ache," he told her. "Put cap back on."

Cynthia re-capped the canteen and Many Bears hung it where it belonged, never stopping the horse the whole time. "Couldn't you please untie my wrists?" she asked.

"No," he answered sternly.

They rode silently for several more minutes.

"Will Red Wolf be in the village where you're taking me?" she asked him then.

"Maybe. Red Wolf sometimes in our village, sometimes with Sitting Bull's people, the Hunkpapa."

"You mean there are different kinds of Sioux?"

Many Bears laughed. "You whites think we are all alike. We are different—the Sioux, the Cheyenne, the

Shoshone, the Comanche—all different. Even the Sioux are different. I am Oglala—same as Red Cloud and Crazy Horse. You have heard of these great leaders?"

Cynthia's heart pounded. Red Cloud! No Indian had caused more trouble for the settlers and soldiers than that one. Surely she would be skinned alive for the sheer pleasure of these wild men. "I've heard of them," she answered.

Surely, she thought, she was headed into hell. She would never see her mother and father and Alex again. Home seemed a hundred years and a million miles away. She looked down at her bandaged hand, wondering if it would get infected. Many Bears had not changed the bandage and had put nothing on it to help it heal. Over the last few hours the pain had suddenly grown worse, and it throbbed with every pulse of blood.

Her heart pounded with dread as Many Bears again moved his hand over her breasts. "Maybe Many Bears keep you after all—not trade you," he told her. "You would make a fine wife for Many Bears. You are built good—feed many babies, no?" He squeezed at her breasts, and she didn't know what to say to him, whether she should protest. She was never sure how he would react to objections. He slowed his horse then, saying something to the others in the Sioux tongue. They all slowed their mounts and headed for a grove of cottonwoods along a river, halting their horses in cool shade. Many Bears dismounted and yanked Cynthia to the ground, pulling her to a tree where he tied her as he always did when they stopped.

"Can I have more water?" she asked him.

"No. You have had enough until tonight." He turned and walked away, and Cynthia watched longingly as the horses fed to their content on the high grass at the water's edge and drank long, cool drinks from the river. One of the other Indian men with Many Bears lingered near her, looking her over, a grin on his dark, round face. His face was covered with pock marks, and she wondered

110

if he had had measles once. He knelt closer, and Cynthia cringed when he grasped the hem of her dress and threw it up over her head to see what was underneath.

"Get away from me!" she screamed.

Many Bears barked something at the man, who jerked her dress down and stood up, frowning at her. He stormed away, and the two men exchanged more angry words. Cynthia realized Many Bears was making sure the man knew she belonged to him personally. At least he was apparently not going to let these others do anything to her. She had that much to be thankful for. But she was not so sure Many Bears would wait until he arrived at his village to decide what to do with her.

Her only hope was Red Wolf. He would get her away from Many Bears and he would take her back home. Surely he would do that much for her. All she had to do was keep finding ways to keep Many Bears away from her at night until they reached his village. But maybe they would be found before they ever got there. Maybe her father had already determined what had happened to her, and he had gone to get soldiers to come looking for her. Yes. Soldiers would find her easily. They would take her away from this agony, this terror.

All day long Reverend Wells, Art Bonneville, and the scout Miles Johnstone searched the hills behind the parsonage. With every cry of a crow or a hawk, Wells was sure he could hear Cynthia calling for him, crying out with pain. What had happened to his daughter? He walked his horse back and forth, up and down hills and gulleys, through a soundless land, wondering if perhaps the Indians were right. This was a land that belonged to them. It fit them—big and wild and free. Maybe the white man didn't belong out here after all. After all, this land was promised to the Sioux years ago. But if the Indians were angry, why did they have to take it out on an innocent young girl who had done them no harm?

111

He prayed again that he was wrong—that Cynthia was not with Indians after all. But then he heard the pounding of a horse approaching. He turned to see that it was Johnstone. The man rode closer, a look of pain and sorrow on his face.

"Did you find something?" Wells asked the man.

Johnstone dismounted, reaching into a saddlebag and pulling out a ruffled slip. He held it out to Wells. "This belong to your daughter?"

Wells's eyes teared as he reached for the slip. "I . . . I am not familiar with my daughter's personals. But it's about the right size." He choked in a sob, curling the slip into his hands. "Who am I kidding? Who else would something like this belong to, clear out here? My God! What have they done to my Cynthia?"

Johnstone put a hand on the man's shoulder. "I'll ride you to Fort Robinson, Reverend. We'll tell the soldiers to be on the lookout. On the way we'll stop at Lead. There might be some soldiers there. That's all we can do, other than spread the word among the miners scattered in the hills. If you try to go riding into Indian country yourself, you'll only get killed. Your wife and son will suffer enough without losing you."

Wells nodded. "I suppose you're right," he said, his words choked. "We'll go back to the house. I'll pack some things for the ride to the fort." He walked to his horse, mounting up and looking out over the hills to the western mountains. Cynthia! His only hope was that soldiers would find her. But surely she had already suffered pain and humiliation. Surely it was already too late. Perhaps she was even dead.

Chapter Seven

Cynthia was sure she would die before ever reaching her unknown destination. She was equally sure no white man could have kept up the pace of Many Bears and the men with him. She was certain she was a hundred miles or more from Deadwood. By their third day of travel they were deep in the thick pines of the Black Hills, the sacred Black Hills. The beauty of the country could not be denied, but she was too weak to care.

Many Bears had become more belligerent again. She was not sure what had caused him to be more cruel, except that she must have unwittingly insulted him. He had brought her food and water the day before, a large piece of buffalo meat that tasted surprisingly good. Cynthia had eaten voraciously, and had even thanked him for the food. Then Many Bears had led her to a stream and told her to undress and wash. Cynthia had refused, mortified at Many Bears and the others seeing her naked.

"Do not disobey me in front of my friends," Many Bears had ordered her.

"I won't do it!" Cynthia had screamed.

"When you are my wife, you will change," Many Bears had told her. "You will like Many Bears. You will do what he tells you to do. Are you not grateful for the food I gave you?"

"I thanked you for the food. But I won't undress, and I will never be your wife!"

Cynthia shivered at the remembered look in Many Bears' eyes. He had stomped into the water and ripped off her dress, pushing her naked body, head and all, into the cold stream. Cynthia had screamed and struggled but had been much too weak to put up much of a fight. Her cut hand had ached fiercely as she grabbed at Many Bears, who'd scrubbed her with sand and then jerked her out of the water, dragging her onto the grass while the others watched and laughed. Many Bears had proceeded to take up his quirt and beat Cynthia several times over with its stinging strips of rawhide until she'd folded to the ground, begging him to stop. He had jerked her back up then, growling at her that white women didn't know how to obey and that they talked too much. He'd proceeded to put a deerskin shirt over her head, one that came to his own knees and on Cynthia hung past her knees. He'd then made her walk for the next several miles until they made camp for the night. He'd offered her a blanket, but no food or water until noon this third day.

Cynthia still shivered with the memory, wondering at the horror this man would put her through once he decided to make her his wife. She knew he would only make everything worse if she fought him, but she could not imagine lying still for a painted savage who knew of no way to make his women obedient other than to beat them. All of this pain and violence was new and shocking to her. This world she had been thrown into could not have been more foreign to her, and she wondered now if she would ever see her own world again. Surely no one would ever find her in these hills—so deep into Indian country that even the miners wouldn't come here, she was sure.

Pain plagued her every move. The insides of her legs were badly chafed from the constant riding. Her skin felt on fire from the sting of the quirt, and her hand was swelling, the pain growing more fierce. She was hardly aware that they were climbing now, the surefooted Indian ponies finding their way easily over rocks and around boulders that jutted out from the side of the hill they climbed. She thought how it was no wonder soldiers couldn't find the Indians when they were camped this deep in the hills, and her own hope of being found had dwindled. She wondered what kind of hell her mother and father must be going through by now, wondered what little Alex was doing, and tears stung her eyes.

"There," Many Bears told her then, pointing.

Cynthia blinked, and all her thoughts vanished, replaced only by a mixture of awe and terror as she followed Many Bears' outstretched arm and pointed finger. They were at the top of a very high hill. A small mountain would be a better name for it. Below them lay a huge Indian Village, a circle of tipis with several smaller circles of tipis within the greater one, all of them with openings that faced the east. Smoke drifted upward from several campfires. Hundreds of Indians milled about. Women were bent over fires. Children ran about, and dogs chased after them, barking and wagging their tails. Hundreds of horses grazed outside the village, which lay in a green valley between two pine-covered mountains.

"My village," Many Bears told her. "My wives will be happy to see me."

"Wives?"

"Many Bears has two wives—one of my choosing as a young man, the other her sister, whose husband was killed by white men. Many Bears has four sons, two from his first wife, one from his second wife. The other was my second wife's son when she came to me. Now you will be my third wife. You will help my wives with their work, help with the children."

Cynthia just stared, her heart pounding wildly at the realization that all of this was real. She was really the captive of a Sioux Indian man, who had brought her to a place where no one would ever find her, and who intended to make her his wife, or probably kill her if she objected. Her mind reeled with confusion as to what to do about her situation, while her body screamed with pain and weakness, reminding her there was really not much she could do but accept this horrible new fate, or die.

They began descending the hill toward the village. One of the other riders dragged behind him a travois loaded with the cleaned carcasses of two deer, and another carried a deer over the back of his horse. Cynthia remembered how easily Many Bears and the others had brought down the deer with silent arrows, how swiftly they had gutted the animals with their sharp hunting knives. She wondered again if Red Wolf still carried her mother's knife, and she shivered at the thought of it. If only she had never cut him loose, none of the horror that followed would have happened, and she probably would not be here now.

Excitement and noise within the village grew as Many Bears and the others came closer and were noticed. A great cry of reception came from the women, and men rode out to greet them, circling, yipping, and laughing. Cynthia wondered if they were glad for the meat, or glad for the captured white girl. Her thoughts swirled at the sight of Indians everywhere; painted tipis; colorful, beaded clothing; tinkling bells; black hair; beautiful, dark children who stared at her with wide, brown eyes; barking dogs; painted horses; the rich smell of meat being smoked; and staring women who pointed at her and carried on in a foreign tongue. Some were young and pretty, others old and wrinkled, some very fat and others looking too thin. Some of the children ran naked, and a few women sat outside their tipis breast-feeding babies, making no effort to cover their naked breasts.

A crowd gathered around Cynthia and Many Bears. Cynthia wondered how she must look by now, bruised, her hair tangled, cuts all over her, her eyes surely red and swollen from so much crying and lack of sleep. She had hardly any feeling left in her wrists, which were scabbed and calloused from being constantly tied.

Cynthia tried to pay no attention to the staring women, some of whom poked at her and all of whom were obviously talking about her. She scanned the crowd, looking for the face of the one man who just might help her out of this terrible situation. But Red Wolf was nowhere to be seen. She realized then that perhaps she wouldn't even recognize him. After all, there were hundreds of young men here, all with the same long, black hair. She had seen Red Wolf for only a moment, and in the dim light of a lantern. It was even possible he would not recognize her as the girl who freed him.

Panic began to overtake her as Many Bears rode up to a particular tipi. Bears were painted all over it, and a young woman stood just outside, holding a small baby. She frowned and watched as Many Bears dismounted, then lifted Cynthia down, plopping her in front of the young woman.

"This is Flowing Waters," Many Bears told Cynthia. "She is my second wife. The child she holds is my new son, Crying Owl."

Flowing Waters looked Cynthia over with disdain, disgust in her dark, jealous eyes. She moved those eyes to Many Bears. "Why you bring this white woman to our tipi? Why you not take her to the tipi where other women captives are kept?" She moved her eyes back to Cynthia, a wicked smile passing over her lips. "For the pleasure of all the men."

Cynthia shivered, realizing a fate much worse than being Many Bears' wife could await her.

"She will be my wife," Many Bears told Flowing Waters.

Flowing Waters spat at her and looked up at Many Bears. "White woman not make good wife. Better to trade her for guns! Food! White woman bring only trouble—soldiers."

"It is my decision." Many Bears shoved Cynthia inside the tipi, where two young boys sat eating, and a pretty

117

woman, slightly older than Flowing Waters, sat sewing a
moccasin. The woman looked up, her face lighting up
with happiness. To Cynthia's surprise, Many Bears
walked up to the woman and they embraced. Cynthia
found the gesture astounding, considering the cruelty
she had suffered at the hands of Many Bears. Was he
actually capable of caring? Did he actually love the
woman he embraced now? They seemed to have missed
each other.

Many Bears knelt in front of the two boys, saying
something to them in the Sioux tongue and tousling their
hair. He turned to Cynthia, his face showing the first
genuine smile she had ever seen on him, rather than the
evil, sneering smile he had offered her on their journey.

"My first sons. Little Arrow, who is seven summers,
and Gray Horse, who is four summers. Their mother is
my first wife, Basket Woman."

Basket Woman was pretty, and she looked at Cynthia
with a kind smile, surprising Cynthia even more. But the
smile faded when Many Bears said something to her in
their own tongue. Cynthia could see a hurt look in the
woman's eyes, but she did not make the objection that
Flowing Waters had made. Cynthia was sure Many Bears
was telling her he intended to make Cynthia his wife.
Basket Woman only nodded then, turning and sitting
back down to pick up the moccasin she was sewing.

Many Bears turned to Cynthia. "Stay," he told her. He
turned and left, and Cynthia looked around the tipi,
which was much larger inside than she had expected. She
thought of how much fun and how fascinating all of this
would be if she were just a visitor here, learning about the
Indians. The dwelling was amazingly clean, and beautiful
paintings decorated the inside. Piles of buffalo and deer
skins lay stacked in places, and Cynthia wondered if they
were beds. Terror rippled through her at the thought that
Many Bears could come back anytime now and decide to
make her his wife and get it over with. She turned her
eyes away from the piled robes, looking at various-sized

leather bags that hung from the tipi's support poles, each bag different, some fur-covered, some plain leather, some beaded and painted. She decided they must contain the various belongings of Many Bears and his family. Basket Woman sat on a chairlike device made of young branches woven together into a back support held up by bigger branches that formed a brace so that she could sit down and lean against it.

Cynthia guessed Basket Woman to be perhaps in her twenties, while Flowing Waters could only be in her teens. Yet Many Bears had said Flowing Waters had another son by her first husband. She seemed not much older than Cynthia, and Cynthia realized now why Many Bears had been so surprised to learn she did not yet have a husband. If she were an Indian, she would probably be married and have a couple of children by now.

"Do you . . . speak English?" she asked Basket Woman hesitantly.

The woman glanced at her and shook her head. Cynthia's heart fell. The only one who spoke English was Flowing Waters, and Flowing Waters apparently already hated her. Cynthia moved back, quietly sitting down, not sure what to do next. She looked down at her hand. The bandage on it was filthy, and her hand was red and swollen. Tears stung her eyes as she wondered if anyone cared, wondered if she was going to die from an infection.

Basket Woman looked at her again, then put down the moccasin and came closer, kneeling in front of Cynthia. She pointed to Cynthia's hand. Cynthia looked at her in surprise, holding out her hand. "I have a bad cut," she told the woman. "I think it's infected."

Basket Woman frowned, deftly untying the old piece of slip and unwrapping it. Cynthia winced with the pain as she peeled away the last layer of cloth, revealing dark red skin around a cut that was oozing with infection.

Basket Woman mumbled something in her own tongue, then moved to one of the many leather bags that hung about the tipi, reaching into one and taking out an

119

even smaller leather pouch; then moving to another parfleche where she retrieved still another pouch. She came back to Cynthia and took green moss from one of the pouches, taking hold of Cynthia's hand and placing the moss directly against the cut.

Cynthia winced with pain, wondering what on earth moss was going to do to help the cut but afraid to object. Then Basket Woman dipped her fingers into the second pouch. Whatever was inside, it smelled bad. The woman's fingers came out covered with a strange, thick, greasy substance. She lifted the moss and smeared the greasy ointment around the area of the cut, then replaced the moss. She began wrapping Cynthia's hand then with a clean piece of cloth.

Just having the bandages changed made her hand feel better. Cynthia smiled at Basket Woman, thanking her. Basket Woman did not smile back, but she did not sneer at her the way Flowing Waters had. She reached into the greasy substance then and began smearing some onto Cynthia's cuts. Almost instantly the sting in them went away, but Cynthia was not sure she could stand the smell.

Flowing Waters came inside then, leading a boy of perhaps three years by the hand, and supporting the new baby in her other arm. Cynthia guessed the older child to be the one Flowing Waters had by her first husband. Flowing Waters came closer, watching Basket Woman put the ointment on the cuts. She said something to the woman, her voice hard and biting. Basket Woman looked up at her and said something in return in a gentle voice. Flowing Waters tossed her head, looking down haughtily at Cynthia.

"You will not make good wife. You are too weak. Many Bears should trade you for food, tobacco, guns."

"I hope he does," Cynthia answered, feeling Flowing Waters' challenge. "I don't want to be his wife anyway. I don't want to be here at all."

Flowing Waters smiled. "You belong in the tipi for the stolen women, where the young men with no wives go to find their pleasure—where they teach the white women that they are not safe in this land. This land belongs to the Sioux! The white men killed my first husband, the father of my Little Beaver."

Cynthia felt her anger and her own pride building under the hot gaze of Flowing Waters. "I did not harm your husband. I would not bring harm to any of your people. I even helped an Indian once. He was captured by white men and brought to Deadwood to be hanged. But I cut him loose and let him escape! His name was Red Wolf. Do you know of him?"

Flowing Waters frowned, studying Cynthia's blue eyes. "You speak the truth?"

"How would I know all that? Ask Red Wolf. He would tell you. I'll bet you already know the story about how white men—miners—captured Red Wolf and killed many of his friends. A white girl set him free. I'm the white girl who let him go. I'm Cynthia Wells, and I want to talk to Red Wolf. He'll tell you to let me go back, to leave me untouched. I helped him. You know Red Wolf. I can tell by the look in your eyes. Go find him and he'll tell you I'm the one who helped him. Is this how you treat those who help you?"

Flowing Waters folded her arms, her dark eyes seeming to doubt Cynthia's word. "Red Wolf is on the hunt. He is not here."

"When will he be back?"

Flowing Waters shrugged. "Who can say? He went out, like Many Bears and those with him, only he went another way. Food is hard to find now. The miners take all of our game, scare many more animals away. There is never enough to eat. Our treaty says the white man does not belong here, but still he comes. And so we kill him, before he kills all the animals and we starve to death."

"Then tell Many Bears to wait. Tell him not to make me his wife or to send me to the tipi where the others are kept, until Red Wolf comes back. I helped him."

"You belong to Many Bears. He does not have to wait

for Red Wolf."

"But it isn't fair," Cynthia protested, unwanted tears coming into her eyes.

Flowing Waters smiled again. "Neither is it fair what the white man is doing to us. White men raped and tortured Many Bears' mother and sister, then cut them up like dead rabbits. You should be glad Many Bears has chosen only to make you his wife. It is an honor. But I do not want you to be his wife. I will make him take you to the tipi for the prisoners, where our men can do to you what white men do to our women. When they are through with you, then Many Bears can trade you back to your people!"

The young woman left, and Cynthia's heart pounded with dread. How much influence did Flowing Waters have over Many Bears? Could she really make him change his mind? How long would it be before Red Wolf came back? He was still her only hope. Without him she faced the humiliation of being forced to mate with Many Bears, or something even more horrible.

Basket Woman moved silently away, saying nothing. Rhythmic drumming began to beat somewhere in the distance, and Cynthia shivered at the added sound of jingling bells and chanting, singing voices. She felt more alone and abandoned than ever. Now even Many Bears was gone. Was he bargaining with someone for her? Were the men outside trying to talk him into taking her to the horrible place where women were kept for the pleasure of the young men? Her stomach churned, and she wondered if God even knew she was here.

She watched Basket Woman, remembering the greeting the woman had had for Many Bears. It seemed so strange that they had both actually shown affection for one another, that Many Bears had shown love and joy toward his sons. Did these violent people actually have regular families that they cared about? Flowing Waters hated her because whites had killed the woman's first husband. Had she loved the man? The look Many Bears

122

and Basket Woman had shared was not unlike the look Cynthia's own parents had often exchanged, one of love and respect. And yet there was a wild, cruel side to these people that did not match the tender moment she had seen Many Bears and Basket Woman share.

Utter weariness and pain overcame Cynthia's fears of what would happen to her next. The rhythm of the drumming outside lulled her, and her eyes began to droop. She could no longer bear sitting up, and she allowed herself the pleasure of lying back against a bed of robes. No one stopped her. No one shouted at her. The pain in her hand eased, apparently from the moss Basket Woman had put on it.

Cynthia allowed the badly needed sleep to come over her, hoping that by some miracle she would awaken to discover all of this horror was simply a nightmare. She would wake up and find she was in her own bed in her own room in the little parsonage. Her mother would come to wake her, and she would go down to have breakfast with her kind father and her little brother. She tried to say a prayer, but decided God surely could not be in this den of heathens.

She could see the hawk now. She watched it float freely on the wind. She wished she could tell Alex about it. She fell asleep thinking of Alex and of the games they used to play together.

Albert Wells walked out of the saloon-turned-meeting-room in Lead.

"Soldiers was through here just a few days ago." He could still hear the comment by one of Lead's citizens. "Hard to say which way they went."

Miles Johnstone walked up behind Wells, who stood leaning against a support post of the building's porch, his head hanging.

"I'm sorry, Preacher. I thought we could catch up with that detachment here. I don't know what else to do but go on to Fort Robinson for you and tell them what has happened."

Wells sighed deeply. "That will take you another five days. By then she'll have been missing eight days. By the time whoever is in command at Fort Robinson gets some men together and gets back up here, it will be another week or more. God only knows what will have happened to her by then."

"That's true, Preacher. But it will be better than doin' nothin' at all. I'm just sorry we can't round up enough men of our own to go look for the girl."

Wells snickered sarcastically, rapidly losing his faith in mankind. "One lonely, abused little girl can't win out over gold, Mr. Johnstone. These men have better things to do than risk their necks riding into the heart of Sioux country looking for someone they don't even know." He looked at Johnstone with red eyes. "I suppose it's the risk everyone takes coming out here, isn't it? It's part of the price we pay for expanding our frontiers, increasing our wealth."

Johnstone looked away. "I'm sorry, Preacher. I did what I could."

"I know that. And I appreciate it."

"I could go look for her on my own." The man turned back and faced Preacher Wells. Wells shook his head.

"No. I wouldn't ask you to do that. It's like committing suicide, the mood the Indians are in right now. We both know that. Cynthia could be anywhere. Within another week she could be clear over in Montana, or up in the northern Dakotas." He rubbed at his eyes. "You go on ahead to Fort Robinson and let them know. I'll go back to Deadwood and pray I run across some soldiers."

Johnstone pushed back his hat. "You could be in for a long wait, Preacher. The government has been tryin' to buy off more land from the Sioux for a long time now, and they won't sell. With the miners goin' into the Black Hills like they are, the Indians are just gettin' madder and madder. It's even dangerous for soldiers to be in that

124

area. I expect it won't be long before the government sends down orders for soldiers to ride in there and make sure all the Sioux get themselves onto what the government calls reservation land under the latest treaty. But the Sioux say that treaty isn't legal, and they won't be too anxious to come in. I expect they'll hold out most of the winter, and for now, the soldiers won't be too anxious to go riding deeper into Sioux country, and the government won't be too anxious to send them. Your best hope is that the Indians give up and come in on their own on account of hunger. When they do, if your daughter is still alive, she'll be with them."

Wells clung to the post. "Do you think she *is* still alive? What are her chances of survival, Mr. Johnstone?"

Johnstone removed a soiled, floppy leather hat, fiddling with it in his hands. "Hard to say, Preacher. If some Sioux warrior decides to take her for a wife, she'll be treated fairly decent, but life would still be awful hard for her compared to what she's used to."

"A wife," the preacher muttered. "My beautiful Cynthia . . ." His voice choked.

"It's better than most of the alternatives, Preacher. She could be sold off to some worthless whiskey trader, or used by all the young Indian men any way they want, or tortured and killed."

Wells seemed to wilt, and Johnstone could see the man's shoulders shaking.

"I'm sorry, Preacher. You asked me what her chances were. You might as well understand and be prepared. If she's taken as a wife and lives through it and is rescued, she'll need a lot of understandin' and love when she comes back. People can be pretty cruel to a white woman who's been with Indians."

"I know." The preacher's voice was gruff. "I should never have come out here. I was thinking of going back. Now I can't. I won't ever go back until I know what happened to my Cynthia."

Johnstone replaced his hat. "I reckon' I'll head on south to the fort. You better get back to the missus."

Wells nodded, unable to speak. There was nothing to do now but go back to Deadwood and wait . . . and pray, if, indeed, he had any faith left.

Cynthia felt herself being jerked to her feet. In her sleepy state she hardly realized what was happening at first.

"Come!" She recognized Many Bears' voice. "You will not be Many Bears' wife. Flowing Waters make too much trouble."

Cynthia was dragged outside the tipi, where frenzied drumming and dancing was taking place. Her heart raced with fear and dread as she roused from the first truly warm and relaxed sleep she had experienced in three days and nights. Now it was night again. Many Bears was pulling her through a crowd of trilling women, who poked at her and laughed at her. Some hit her with sticks.

"Where are you taking me!" she screamed to the powerful Many Bears.

"You will go to the tipi where enemy women are kept. Soon I will trade you—maybe to white soldiers—maybe to white traders. I will decide. You are worth much."

Cynthia's eyes widened with terror. "No!" she screamed, yanking on the painful rawhide Many Bears had again tied at her wrists. She pulled with all her might, but was no match for Many Bears, who simply dragged her when she refused to walk. "Don't take me there, Many Bears," she screamed. "I will be your wife. I won't make any trouble for you!"

"Better this way. I come visit you in tipi but you not be my wife. Then Flowing Waters make no fuss."

"You would let a woman . . . tell you what to do?" Cynthia struggled to get back on her feet, but Many Bears walked so fast she couldn't regain her balance. "Coward! You're a coward, Many Bears!"

126

The man paid no heed to her words. He dragged her past a fire around which Indian men danced and chanted. Beyond that was a line of grinning young men, who watched the young white girl with golden hair and blue eyes being dragged screaming past them. She would be a challenge. Each waited anxiously for his turn.

By the time Many Bears dragged Cynthia inside the intended tipi, she was screaming and weeping, still fighting with a strength she didn't know she had, a strength that came from sheer terror and fierce pride. She could not let this happen to her. But she had no chance against Many Bears, who pushed her down onto a mat and stretched her arms over her head, tying them to a stake. Much as she twisted and fought, he grabbed each of her thin ankles in his strong hands and tied her legs, spreading them to stakes set wide apart. Cynthia choked on deep sobs, her whole body numb with terror.

Many Bears rose. "It is done."

Cynthia did not question why the man did not take his own turn with her first. She screamed at him again to make her his wife instead, but the man walked out.

Cynthia lay weeping in the dimly lit tipi, hardly aware that only one other woman was inside, a Pawnee woman taken during a raid. She envisioned that the tipi was filled with horribly brutalized white women who by now were nothing but animals, who would be better off shot than returned to their own people. That was how she would end up—filthy and sinful and used, no good to anyone, white or Indian. She was not sure how long she lay there, how long it took for her tears to subside. She wished she could blow her nose, but she couldn't use her hands. She struggled against the rawhide strips that bound her to the stakes, horrified at the helplessness of her position.

Every nerve end came painfully alive then when a tall, dark figure entered the tipi. She felt vomit moving up toward her throat as he came closer. At first she could see only his buckskin pants, little bells tied into their fringes. He picked up a lantern, one Cynthia decided must have

127

been stolen off some poor settler. He held it close to her face, then said something quietly in his own tongue. She supposed he was studying her white skin and blond hair, getting himself more excited for the rape that was to come.

He set the lantern aside and knelt closer. She saw his dark skin, his bare chest, decorated only with several necklaces of silver and beads and bone. Long black hair dropped from around his back, and she smelled leather and sage. He brought his face closer into the light, and she decided she would face him boldly. If he was going to do bad things to her, she would not please him more by cringing and weeping and begging.

She met his dark eyes, and her heart felt a tiny prick of joy and hope.

"Red Wolf?" she asked, her voice a pitiful whimper.

Chapter Eight

"So, it truly is the one called Cynthia, the white girl with hair like the sun and eyes like the sky."

"Red Wolf?" Cynthia repeated, hoping against hope that here at last was help. Surely, after saving him from death, this young Indian man would not hurt her. "Help me, Red Wolf," she said in a near-whisper, unwanted tears coming. "I helped you once. Please . . . cut me loose. Please don't do something bad to me. Don't let your friends come in here."

An almost-teasing grin spread across Red Wolf's handsome face, and his dark eyes sparkled as though he had just heard a good joke. "Something bad?" He straddled her, touching the side of her neck with a strong hand, moving the hand down then, firmly but gently, over a breast, over her flat belly. "It is not so bad. Maybe you would like it." He leaned closer, resting his elbows on either side of her, watching her tears come harder. "Do you think it is different for our women when white men steal them away and do this to them?"

"No," Cynthia wept. "But I . . . would never say it was right. I didn't do anything to your people, Red Wolf. I even . . . let you go once."

A look of bitterness came into his eyes. "You are so ready to believe I would harm you—that all Indian men want nothing more dearly than to rape white women."

He straightened, his legs still straddling her. "How little you know about us! It is the *white* man who cannot keep his manpart small!"

Cynthia stared at him in surprise. He took a knife from its sheath attached to his weapons belt. It was a huge knife, nothing like her mother's kitchen knife. Fur and beads decorated the handle, which looked as though some kind of animal's teeth protruded from the end of the handle.

"Is it true?" he asked her. "Many Bears tells me you have no husband—that you have never been with a man. Does he speak the truth?"

"Yes." Cynthia sniffed, swallowing with apprehension as he moved back, running a hand down her slender leg to her ankle. He cut the rawhide strip that held her and she quickly pulled in her leg. Beneath her fear and dread, and hidden even from her realization at this tense moment, lay a tiny, secret pleasure at the touch of Red Wolf's strong hand against her breast, her belly, along her leg. It was not a sensation she could face or admit to at the moment, but it was there, a part of her budding womanhood that was not yet ready to be faced.

Red Wolf cut loose the other leg, and Cynthia instantly curled up defensively as he leaned over to cut loose the rawhide that held her hands tied to the stake above her head.

"I cannot cut loose your wrists yet," he told her, leaning close again. "I am taking you to my grandmother's dwelling. I can show no affection or mercy on the way there. You are the enemy, but you will belong to me now and the others will not harm you. But do not expect me to show kindness in front of them."

"But . . . what about Many Bears? He was going to trade me. He thinks I belong to him."

Red Wolf grasped her arm, helping her to her feet. "You belong to me now. You cost me much, my two finest horses and my best war shield."

"But Many Bears said he could get guns for me—food

130

and tobacco. He said it didn't matter that I had helped you."

"Many Bears could show no gratefulness in front of those with him. No enemy is to be treated kindly. He could not just give you to me."

"You mean . . . he brought me here deliberately, knowing you would come in here first?"

"Already I can tell you are like other white women. You speak too much." He took his knife and without warning he yanked at the buckskin shirt she still wore, pulling it out and ripping his knife through it, slashing it open.

"What are you doing!" Cynthia screamed. She pushed at him and he hit her across the side of the face, knocking her to the ground.

Red Wolf ripped the knife through the shirt again, pulling it off her in pieces as she hit and kicked at him, and her struggle caused several superficial cuts. "Stop it! Stop it! Cynthia screamed at him, but Red Wolf kept it up until Cynthia was entirely naked. He jerked her up. He shoved his knife into its sheath, then took hold of the end of the rawhide tied around her wrists.

"Now they will think I have claimed you," he told her. "They have heard your screams, and I will take you out of here naked. You are my woman now. They will not bother you."

She cringed, staring at him in utter shock. Survival instincts told her to calm down. He had apparently done this for her own good, although it seemed ridiculous that she should be grateful.

Red Wolf stared back at her for a tense, quiet moment, feeling a strange pull at the tears on her pretty face. His eyes dropped to her full, white breasts, the taut pink nipples that were peaked from her embarrassment at knowing he was looking at them. He watched her breasts rise and fall with her panting breathing, and he scanned her further, realizing with a sudden, intense desire that the hairs that hid her virginity were as sunny white as the hair on her head.

He met her eyes, and for a moment other things were forgotten. There was a strange pull between them, an unspoken attraction that neither of them would ever willingly admit at this moment, or even acknowledge to themselves. Cynthia watched Red Wolf's dark eyes take on a look of near-sympathy, but she dared not let herself believe that was what she really saw. In one moment he was being kind to her, in the next he was beating her. It had been the same way with Many Bears. He seemed to read her thoughts as he spoke then.

"It was necessary. I will not hurt you again. You gave my life back to me. Do as I say now. When we go out, pull at your ties. Pretend you do not want to go with me."

Cynthia frowned.

"Do as I say," he repeated. "Do you understand?"

Cynthia swallowed and nodded.

He turned and yanked on her, dragging her outside the tipi, where she cringed at her nakedness. Indian men watched, saying things that for Cynthia needed no interpretation. She could tell by their eyes, their chuckles. They laughed and made obscene gestures as Red Wolf dragged her past them, and Cynthia pulled at her ties as he had ordered her to do. That seemed to entertain them even more. Women also watched and laughed.

"You will like it," one who spoke English told her as Cynthia passed her. "Do not fight him, white girl. Red Wolf is handsome. He will make you feel good. I wish Red Wolf was my husband."

Women shrieked with laughter and spoke to each other in their own tongue. It seemed to Cynthia as though Red Wolf's tipi was ten miles away, and the few minutes it took to reach it seemed like hours. Finally Red Wolf was pushing her through an entrance flap and she ducked inside a large dwelling. A fire burned at the center of it. A small black kettle hung over the fire, and something cooked in the kettle that smelled good. Red

Wolf spoke up in his own tongue, and a voice answered, an aged, cracked voice coming from a tiny, shriveled woman who sat on the other side of the fire.

Cynthia had not even realized anyone else was inside the tipi until she heard the voice. She watched a figure rise and come around the fire toward her. It was an old woman, so shriveled with age that she was much shorter than Cynthia. Her long hair was pure white and tied into braids. Her tunic hung loosely on her spindly frame, and she looked up at Cynthia with a face that held seemingly thousands of wrinkles, then reached up with a bony hand to touch Cynthia's face and hair as Red Wolf said something more to the woman. She spoke up again, directing her words at Cynthia and patting Cynthia's cheek.

"This is Old Grandmother, my father's mother," Red Wolf told Cynthia. "I live with her and take care of her. I have told her you are the white girl who saved me from a hanging. She is grateful to you. She will take care of you. I go now."

Cynthia took her eyes from the old woman and looked at Red Wolf, realizing she actually didn't want him to leave. "Go? Where? You aren't going away?"

The teasing grin returned to his lips. "You want Red Wolf to stay?" His eyes moved over her nakedness, and Cynthia was angry with herself for acting as though she cared if he went away.

"No!" she answered quickly, her pride and stubbornness beginning to show. "And you owe me more than rescuing me from Many Bears," she added. "You had better take me back home, Red Wolf. You owe me a great deal after the way you betrayed me."

Red Wolf frowned. "Betrayed you? How did I betray you?"

She faced him squarely, sure she had the upper hand now because Red Wolf had saved her and seemed to feel obligated to her.

"You killed Ruben Kinder," she answered boldly. "I

didn't intend for you to do that. The whole town blamed me, and I feel like I had a part in it. You had no right to kill him after I was kind enough to let you go."

The teasing grin vanished from Red Wolf's face, and Cynthia's confidence waned as she saw hatred and bitterness return to his dark eyes.

"If Ruben Kinder is the man who slept nearby, then he deserved to die! Yes, I killed him! And I would do it to a hundred other white men who would do to me what *he* did to me! Now keep silent and let my grandmother help you, or I swear I will take you back to the prisoner's tipi and give you over to my friends!"

He turned and walked out of the tipi, and Cynthia stared after him, wishing she had said nothing. He had seemed suddenly human when he brought her inside to his grandmother, had looked at the old woman and spoken to her with affection. Old Grandmother, he called her. He took care of the old woman, just as her own people took care of their relatives. Again she was struck by the fact that perhaps these people really had feelings, actually loved their families. She had seen it in Many Bears' eyes when he spoke to Basket Woman.

Old Grandmother said something softly in her own tongue, patting Cynthia's arm. She led Cynthia to a bed of robes beside the fire, then walked to a parfleche nearby with a spryness that surprised Cynthia. To Cynthia the old woman looked as though she belonged in a grave, yet there had been a firmness in her hands that told Cynthia that what muscles were left in the old woman were still strong. Old Grandmother set several items down beside Cynthia, including a bowl of water. She set about then with what she apparently considered her task—to clean up the white girl and set her at ease.

Cynthia didn't know what to say to the old woman, who she knew wouldn't understand her anyway. She just watched in surprise as Old Grandmother cut loose her wrists at last, then began washing her gently. Cynthia was amazed at the woman's gentle touch, and the sparkling kindness in her eyes. Outside the frenzied drumming, chanting, and dancing continued, and Cynthia wondered what Red Wolf was doing. She couldn't remember if any other women besides the captured Indian woman were even in the tipi from which he had rescued her. Had he gone back there? She was shocked to realize the thought actually brought tiny feelings of jealousy, just as her thought of his perhaps having a wife had brought when she used to think of him when she lay awake in her bed at night.

Old Grandmother washed every part of her, then began rubbing a sweet-smelling oil on her scrapes and cuts. Cynthia wanted to ask a thousand questions about Red Wolf, and about Many Bears and why he had let Red Wolf take her. She wanted to know about Old Grandmother, about where the rest of Red Wolf's family was. But there was no way to communicate with the old woman, who went about her task as though she enjoyed helping Cynthia. She unwrapped Cynthia's bandaged hand and muttered a few words, then smeared the same bad-smelling ointment onto the cut that Basket Woman had used. She again packed it with fresh moss and wrapped it with yet another clean cloth.

Then the old woman took a brush made of quills and burrs from the parfleche and proceeded to brush the tangles and weeds from Cynthia's hair, muttering in her own tongue in a way that made Cynthia believe the old woman was admiring her hair. She sat still as Old Grandmother began braiding it then. She watched the old woman pick up a long strip of rawhide onto which seemingly thousands of colorful beads were sewn. She felt the old woman continue to braid her hair and realized she was braiding the pretty beaded strip of rawhide into it.

A strange, excited feeling came over Cynthia as she realized her hair would be braided and beaded like the hair of Indian women. All her fear of the moment was gone, as long as she was safe inside this tipi with Old

Grandmother, who was being so good to her. It gave her time to think, to realize that Red Wolf's cruelty had only been a show to protect her, and that apparently Many Bears had struck a bargain with Red Wolf. Had Many Bears meant to give her over to Red Wolf all the while, ever since hearing she was the one who had helped him? Had his own cruelty only been to help her—to show the others she belonged to him?

What strange rules these people had. Red Wolf had said Ruben Kinder had deserved to die. Apparently these people did not know the meaning of the word forgiveness. There was only right and wrong, and if a man was wronged, he took his revenge.

Old Grandmother finished braiding her hair, then got up and took a clean-looking tunic down from a hook. It was a light-colored doeskin, the breast beautifully beaded in the design of an eagle. She held it out to Cynthia, pointed to herself and then to Cynthia, indicating the tunic belonged to her but that Cynthia could wear it.

Cynthia took the dress gratefully, smiling and nodding to the woman, telling her "thank you" in English and hoping she understood. She gladly put on the dress to cover her nakedness. Old Grandmother gave her a braided rawhide belt and Cynthia tied it around her waist. Then the old woman took Cynthia's arm and indicated for her to sit closer to the fire. She dished something out of the pot that hung over the heat, putting the food on a tin plate and handing it to Cynthia. Cynthia wondered where the plate had come from, but for the moment didn't care.

Cynthia waited for the old woman to give her a spoon, but when she didn't do so, Cynthia realized they probably didn't even use spoons and forks. She was too hungry to care. She picked pieces of meat out of the stewlike concoction, and decided she was glad she didn't know what it was. It tasted too good to matter. She picked out pieces of turnip and onion and more meat until all the larger pieces were gone, then put the edge of the plate to her lips and tipped it, drinking out the rest of the mixture.

Old Grandmother looked pleased, dishing up some more for her. She looked so happy and eager that Cynthia didn't have the heart to tell her she was getting full. She managed to eat the entire second dish, but now her stomach was beginning to ache. The old woman used a gourd to dip some water from a wooden bucket. She handed it to Cynthia, and Cynthia drank the water eagerly.

Everything hurt, but at least she was clean and had a clean dress on. This was the most Cynthia had had in the way of comforts since Many Bears stole her away. She had no objections when Old Grandmother led her to a bed of robes, indicating that she should climb inside. Cynthia did so gratefully, so exhausted that she was soon asleep.

Cynthia had no idea how long she lay there. She only knew that somewhere deep in the night she woke with a start, taking a moment to remember where she was. She blinked, looking around the tipi, realizing the drumming had stopped and all was quiet. The fire was fading, but it was still light enough for Cynthia to see that Old Grandmother slept curled up into near-nothingness near the fire. On the other side of it lay Red Wolf, stretched out naked and lying on his back on a buffalo robe.

Cynthia stared, her thoughts and emotions totally confused. Should she hate him or be grateful to him? Was he a murderer, or had he been justified in killing Ruben Kinder? Was he a mere savage, or did he have human feelings? Was he bad, or good? And was she wrong to realize what a splendid specimen of man he was? Was she wrong to notice his fine build, the powerful muscles of his arms and shoulders, the handsome face and its firm jawline, the strong legs, the flat belly, the way his chest swelled quietly as he breathed . . . the size and mystery of that most manly part of him?

She chastised herself for looking at him at all, and she lay back down, wondering at how confused her feelings

137

were. She should still be terrified, but suddenly the terror had left her. Old Grandmother had cared for her as though she were Cynthia's own grandmother. Her own mother could not have done better. The tipi was big, and clean; the bed of robes on which she slept was soft and they smelled a little smoky but not at all dirty—nor did they have the bad smell of skins not properly cleaned.

This was a strange world into which she had been cast. How long would she be here? Would Red Wolf take her back right away? What were her poor parents thinking right now? And if Red Wolf did take her back, how would the people of Deadwood react? What would they think of her? Surely they would think the worst. No Indian man had done bad things to her, but she knew people back home would never believe her.

She lay back down, watching Red Wolf sleep, realizing gratefully that he had not tried to come into her bed and force himself on her. He had kept his promise not to hurt her again, and to her surprise she realized she believed him. Surely he was not all bad. He took care of Old Grandmother. Surely there was some goodness in the heart of the handsome young Indian who now "owned" her. But she realized her predicament was still precarious, and she vowed to be careful what she said to Red Wolf tomorrow so that she would not make him angry.

Red Wolf made a grunting sound then and stretched. Cynthia quickly turned over, keeping her back to him, not wanting him to know she had been staring at him. She did not see Red Wolf open his eyes and study the long, blond braid that stuck out from her blankets. She did not see the grin that passed his full lips again, nor did she know how badly he ached to take her and use her like any other enemy captive.

But there was something different about this white girl called Cynthia, something that went beyond the fact that she had saved his life. He knew he should take her back, but he wanted to keep her. Perhaps if he kept her long enough, she would not want to go back. For now he had no choice. He would be killed in an instant if he was seen with her. Soon they would head even farther north, for the summer celebrations. This white girl called Cynthia would simply have to go along, whether she liked it or not.

Cynthia awoke to see Red Wolf carrying a small armful of wood into the tipi. Old Grandmother looked up from a fire, over which sat a black skillet with what looked like the remains of the stewlike meal of the night before cooking inside, with more meat and turnips added. Cynthia sat up, rubbing at her eyes.

"What time is it?" she asked. "Have you been awake long?" She looked at Red Wolf, who looked at her with a look of disdain, shaking his head.

"Time? We keep no track of time like you whites. When the Sun Spirit rises, we rise with it. Come and eat. You will help Old Grandmother. From now on, you will get the wood and the buffalo chips for her. It is woman's work."

Cynthia frowned. "Buffalo chips?"

Red Wolf shook his head again. "You have much to learn." He picked up a piece of dried buffalo dung from a bucket. "The droppings from buffalo. After they are dried, they make good fire. Old Grandmother is too old to go out and gather them. And she needs help in scrubbing clothes, when she goes to the stream. She will show you how we wash our clothes, and how to make clothes and weapons from skins, so that you can do those things for her. She will teach you how to cook. Old Grandmother makes dog meat better than any of our old women."

"Dog meat!" Cynthia inched closer to the fire, looking at the skillet of food. "You eat . . . dogs?"

"It is good. You ate dog meat last night. It is better than the slimy eggs of the chicken that you whites eat."

Cynthia shivered, suddenly not hungry. She could not bring herself for the moment to realize that to others dogs might be considered as food, just like rabbits or deer or any other kind of meat.

"The dog spirit is a friendly spirit," Red Wolf told her. "They offer themselves to us willingly, and we thank their spirit after killing them, just as we thank the spirit of every animal that we kill for food." He set down the wood. "Soon the entire village will move farther north. We will hunt buffalo and you will learn how to use every part of the buffalo. Almost everything we wear and eat and use comes from the buffalo." He sat down on the other side of the fire. "But there are few left now. The white man has killed many buffalo. He thinks if he kills the buffalo, he kills the Indian. And I fear he is right."

His voice trailed off almost sadly, and Cynthia watched him a moment. He sat there wearing only a loincloth at the moment, his dark skin glowing from morning sun that peeked through the tipi entrance flap, which faced east. Cynthia moved a little closer, looking at him pleadingly. "Aren't you going to take me back, Red Wolf? You speak as though I'm going north with you."

He turned to look at her. It was the clearest view she had had yet of his face. She was astounded to see he was even more handsome in sunlight, with not a mark on the perfectly etched jawline, the high cheekbones, the straight nose. His black hair hung thick and long, brushed clean, with a round, beaded, leather ornament decorating one side of it. Their eyes held a moment, his dark ones making her feel somehow hypnotized.

"I cannot take you back—not until your family and all the soldiers have stopped searching for you. There has not been much time since Many Bears took you. All eyes watch for you. I would be shot the moment someone sees me with you. You will stay with Red Wolf for a while."

"How long!"

Red Wolf shrugged. "I do not know."

"But . . . my parents! They'll think I'm dead! Maybe they'll even go back East without me!"

"Then let them go. If all of you would go back, there

140

would not be this trouble."

"You're the ones who make the trouble," Cynthia answered, her voice rising with the terror that she would never see her family again.

Red Wolf faced her fully. "We?" He turned aside and spat, then looked at her again. "The white man comes. He makes the water dirty with his urine and garbage! The tree spirits cry with pain when the white man cuts them down to make his buildings that do not move. The earth spirit groans when white men pierce her with their sharp tools and dig into her heart to find the yellow metal that is so precious to them. Why is it so precious? It cannot be eaten. It cannot be worn on a man's back. The white man kills the animals, sometimes taking only the hide and letting the rest rot, while women like Old Grandmother starve to death because I and the other warriors cannot find enough food when we go on the hunt. White men take our land, so much of it that we feel choked to death! They kill us, men, women, and children, for nothing but the fact that we are Indian. And they steal our women and use them like pigs, then kill them and cut off their breasts to use for their tobacco bags!"

Cynthia gasped, turning away. "Stop it!"

"You say we make the trouble. Think again, white girl! We made no trouble at first, until we saw that the white man was not going to keep one promise he ever gave us!"

Cynthia swallowed back a lump in her throat. "But . . . I didn't do any of those things to you. Can't you . . . can't you just take me far enough that I could walk the rest of the way?"

"You speak like a fool."

Tears stung Cynthia's eyes. "But I . . . just want to go home. I miss my father and mother, and my little brother. I helped you, Red Wolf. I saved your life."

"And I saved yours." Red Wolf turned his eyes from her, staring at his grandmother. "Many Bears' second wife, Flowing Waters, would have killed you. She did not want Many Bears to keep you."

141

Cynthia blinked in surprise. "She would have killed me?"

"I returned from a hunt later in the day. Many Bears searched me out, told me he had a golden-haired white girl who claimed to have helped me escape from Deadwood. He could not just give you to me. It would have made him look like he had sympathy for you, and made it look like Flowing Waters rules him. So he traded you to me for my two best horses and my best war shield, one my mother made for me many years ago." He looked at her again, his eyes moving over her as though she sat there naked again. "I hope you will be worth the trade. I said I would take you out of danger only because you helped me once."

"But . . . why did Many Bears take me to the place where women prisoners are kept? Why didn't he just give me over to you?"

Red Wolf shook his head as though thinking her very stupid. "He did not want Flowing Waters to think he had sympathy for you. He only told her he would get rid of you—take you to the place where the young men can do what they want with you." His eyes moved over her again. "There I was to force myself on you and claim you. Today I will take the horses and the shield to Many Bears and ask if I can keep you for myself. Many Bears will keep his honor, and Flowing Waters will not harm you because you will belong to me then. She will think I have mated with you and wish to keep you."

Again Cynthia felt the startling pleasant sensation somewhere deep inside at the words, felt a sudden flush of warmth under his gaze. He had seen her naked. She wondered how safe she really was. Would he decide to act on what he was supposed to have done to her? These Indian men seemed so unpredictable. She would legally belong to him now, under Indian rules. Would he try to have his way with her and beat her if he didn't get it?

"Will I ever go home, Red Wolf?"

He studied the wide blue eyes, eyes that made him

142

want to fall into them. He wanted to feel his naked body rubbing against her smooth, white skin, wanted to see pleasure and desire in those blue eyes while he mated her. But she had not been touched by man, and he did not want to take her unless she wanted him in return. It was not likely that this girl with sunshine hair and such blue eyes would want him, a Sioux Indian man, that way. But maybe, after a time. . . .

"Someday," he answered, turning his eyes from her again. "Old Grandmother wants her hair re-braided. She likes to be clean and neat. Will you braid it for her?"

Cynthia watched him. "You love your grandmother very much, don't you?"

He watched the old woman. "She is good to me. My mother died of the smallpox when I was very young. My father was killed by white men only one year ago. He had been taking care of Old Grandmother. Now I will take care of her."

"I'm sorry about your father."

He snickered bitterly. "*Ai.* Before we are done many people will be sorry for many things." He turned hate-filled eyes to Cynthia. "It was men like Ruben Kinder who killed my father. That is why I and my friends raid mining camps and kill whoever we find. The kettle Old Grandmother cooks with, the plate you eat from, they are taken from miners. They killed my father, and I kill them."

"But how long can that go on, Red Wolf?"

He picked up a stick and poked at the fire with it. "Until the white man leaves the Black Hills—or until all of us are dead."

A silence hung in the air, and Cynthia shivered. "The white men will never leave, Red Wolf."

He looked at her, their eyes exchanging the realization of the alternative. "So be it," he said. "We did not start this war. The white men did. Hard Backsides did." He poked at the fire again.

"Hard Backsides?"

"Long-hair Custer. He can stay in the saddle a long time searching for Indians. So we call him Hard Backsides. It is his fault so many miners have come. It is against the treaty, but they come anyway. Miners raped and killed Many Bears' mother and sister. And we are hungry because the miners eat our game. All of us have been touched in some way by these white men. This is sacred land. They do not belong here. It is as I said. We will keep killing them until they go away—or until all of us are dead." He met her eyes again. "Will you braid Old Grandmother's hair for her?"

Cynthia nodded, seeing a side of him she never dreamed existed. He felt the way any man would feel if his land, his home, his family were being invaded and ravaged. There was a hurt deep inside. He grieved for his father. He was concerned over someone helping his old grandmother. He actually had human feelings!

"She was kind to me last night," she told him. "I like Old Grandmother already."

The old woman held out a plate of food for Cynthia. She took it but just stared at it. "I . . . I don't think I'm very hungry," she commented, staring at the meat.

"Eat it," Red Wolf told her. "It is considered an insult not to eat offered food. You will offend Old Grandmother if you do not eat it."

"But . . . it's dog meat."

"You ate it last night when you didn't know what it was. It will taste the same this morning. And you need the food. Eat."

Cynthia took a deep breath and picked out a piece of the meat, putting it into her mouth. It tasted as good as it had the night before. She chewed and swallowed while Red Wolf watched with a grin. She met his eyes then.

"Couldn't you at least send runners to tell someone I am all right?"

He laughed aloud. "And let soldiers follow the runners back?" He shook his head, taking a plate of food from Old Grandmother. "No. We will soon move on from

144

this place. No one in the village will speak of your presence until we feel it is safe to start bargaining for you. In the meantime you belong to me. Eat now. Then you will go with Old Grandmother and the other women to the stream to wash and you will braid Old Grandmother's hair. When the other women see you being kind to Old Grandmother, they will not bother you. If you show unkindness they will beat you. Soon some of them will be your friends and you will not feel so lonely."

Cynthia frowned. "How do you know I feel lonely?"

"Anyone is lonely when he is taken from his family and familiar places. It is the way I felt when the white men took me to Deadwood and I was surrounded by my enemy. Now you are surrounded by people you think are your enemy. It is lonely."

Cynthia was astonished at his perception of her feelings. "You're different, Red Wolf."

"Different?"

"You speak so well, as though you have schooling."

He shrugged. "Once, when my father rode with Red Cloud in the days when Red Cloud was strong and caused all the forts in the Powder River country to be abandoned, I stayed with Old Grandmother near Fort Laramie for safety. There white missionaries took a liking to me and taught me many things. But they never understood the Indian in me. They wanted me to understand their way, but they did not try to understand mine. Then they grabbed me one day and tried to cut off my hair. I fought them. I stabbed the man with his own scissors. I do not think that I killed him, but I will never know. I ran away. I waited a few days, then came back in the night for Old Grandmother. Together we found another Sioux village where we waited for my father to return." He looked at her questioningly. "Why is it you whites think your way is the only way? Why do you not try to understand us?"

Cynthia stared, amazed at his insight. "I don't know, Red Wolf. I never thought of it that way."

"There, you see? All of you see only your side."

"But I want to know, Red Wolf, truly. I want to understand your side."

He nodded slowly. "I will show you then. When you are through braiding Old Grandmother's hair, I will take you out into the hills and show you the land I love. You will learn to love it too, and someday when you go back to your people, you can tell them why we fight to keep the white man out of this land."

He started eating then, saying nothing more. Cynthia picked out the pieces of meat and turnip as she had done the night before, amazed that she was actually eating dog meat and finding it very good. Red Wolf and Old Grandmother conversed in the Sioux tongue, and the love between them was obvious. Cynthia drank down the broth from her plate then, wondering what her mother was making for breakfast this morning.

How far away her family seemed now. It was as though she had only dreamed that life. The awful ache of missing her parents and brother moved through her chest again so that it was hard to swallow. She watched Red Wolf rise then, standing before her in powerful and near-naked splendor. He was going to take her off with him into the hills today. She was not so sure she wanted to go, but she knew better than to argue about it. She still was not sure how far she could go against him without getting a beating. But she vowed that if he tried to have his way with her, she would fight him no matter what the cost.

Red Wolf walked over to a parfleche and reached inside it, taking something out. He came over to Cynthia and handed out her mother's knife. "This belongs to you."

Cynthia stared at the knife, the same knife surely used to kill Ruben Kinder. "I don't want it," she said quietly, tears stinging her eyes at the thought of it being her mother's favorite knife. "You killed a man with it."

He threw it at her feet. "That man beat me with a leather strap. And while I was tied with my arms

146

upstretched, he took his smoking stick of tobacco from his mouth and held its hot end to my flesh."

Cynthia looked up at him in horror.

"His death was easier than my torture," Red Wolf sneered. "He did not suffer!"

He turned and left, and Cynthia stared down at the knife. How she wished she could feel her mother's arms around her right now. But it was possible she would never see the woman again. She choked back tears and carefully picked up the knife, handing it over to Old Grandmother, gesturing that she was giving it to her as a gift.

The old woman's eyes lit up and she took the knife eagerly, nodding several times over. Cynthia thanked God for the old woman, who seemed to have a calming affect on Red Wolf. Old Grandmother might be her only hope of surviving the next few weeks or, God forbid, months. Old Grandmother began cutting through some of the bigger pieces of meat in her plate before eating them, and Cynthia thought about her father's words—about how an instrument could be used for good or for evil, depending on who was using it. It had been her mother's knife, then had been used to kill a man. Now it would be used by a grateful old woman for whatever menial tasks she would need a knife for.

Cynthia put her head in her hands and quietly wept for her mother.

Chapter Nine

Cynthia walked with Old Grandmother to a stream at the west end of the village, where women and children laughed and played in the water, some of them naked. Other women sat along the banks scrubbing clothes against rocks. Cynthia noticed their clothing was a grand mixture of skins and the same kind of cloth whites used to make clothes. Some women wore colorful cloth skirts and blouses, and she had noticed that many of the men wore cloth shirts. She wondered why they did not seem to be able to adapt fully to white man's ways. It seemed so simple. All they had to do was farm and build houses and live like whites lived.

Still, they seemed happy living as they were. Those who were naked in the stream didn't seem to be embarrassed or ashamed. There was a wonderful sense of freedom by the stream, so intense that it even affected Cynthia, who could not help smiling at the children. This morning, with the sunshine and the laughter, and being with Old Grandmother, Cynthia felt no fear. No one had bothered her, and after such a good night's rest and with a belly full of food, she was more at ease, able to look upon the strange people with whom she had been forced to live with a less-prejudiced view.

The children were beautiful, with creamy dark skin and huge, almost black eyes. Their round faces were framed with hair so black it almost had a blue cast to it. Cynthia realized they were like any other children, laughing and playing, their young spirits able to ignore whatever hardships and hunger they might be suffering. Was a child's spirit universal, no matter what the color of his skin?

She accompanied Old Grandmother to the stream, where they filled two buckets with water, then scrubbed a few clothes, mostly handmade shirts that belonged to Red Wolf. Scrubbing the shirts for Red Wolf gave Cynthia an odd sensation of belonging, a feeling of closeness to the young man who now "owned" her. She lay the clothing out on rocks and hung some on limbs and bushes to dry, noticing that here and there painted warriors stood silently watching, guarding their women and children. No man came to the stream to bother the naked women; there were no shouts from any of them that would indicate crude remarks were being made; and usually when she looked up, their backs were turned.

Cynthia thought about the men in Deadwood, the way they had looked at her when she walked down the street, the remarks and whistles they'd had for the prostitutes, the warnings her father had given her several times about going into town alone. It was different here. Now that she was considered the property of Red Wolf, there was an air of respect for her. There had been no threatening gestures or looks from the men in camp as they walked to the stream, and seeing the men standing guard made her feel safe, not watched. But safe from what? Her own people? She grinned at the silly thought and began unbraiding Old Grandmother's hair. She brushed it with the quill brush, and suddenly a young woman was standing beside her, holding out a little bowl made of bone.

"Here. Old Grandmother likes to have her hair greased a little so that it stays shiny and stays in place."

Cynthia turned to see Flowing Waters. She paled slightly, stepping back, a defensive look coming into her eyes. Flowing Waters frowned. "Do you not want the grease? I offer it in friendship."

Cynthia blinked in confusion. "Red Wolf said you wanted to hurt me."

Flowing Waters laughed. "When you belonged to Many Bears I wanted you to be dead. But you belong to Red Wolf now. And you are good to Old Grandmother. You do not act like other white women, who look at us like we are something ugly and dirty. Once at Fort Robinson, white women stepped back from Old Grandmother and made faces and talked among themselves. It made Old Grandmother sad."

Cynthia stepped closer and began brushing the old woman's hair again. "There's nothing so terrible about being old," she told Flowing Waters. "We all have to get old some day. My mother and father say old people are to be respected and listened to—that they're very wise."

Flowing Waters set down the bowl of grease. "*Ai*. It is also our belief." She sat down next to Old Grandmother and put her hand on the old woman's arm. "I love Old Grandmother. When I was twelve summers my mother and father died from white man's disease. Old Grandmother and Red Wolf took me in. Red Wolf was only fifteen summers, but he had suffered the Sun Dance and was a man. He is a good hunter and warrior. Old Grandmother helped me prepare then to marry Standing Eagle when I was thirteen summers." She looked off toward the village. "We were together only two summers before miners killed Standing Eagle." Her voice trailed off and Cynthia stopped brushing Old Grandmother's hair.

"I'm sorry about your husband, Flowing Waters."

The young woman looked up at her, the bitterness showing in her eyes as she looked Cynthia over and made her feel uncomfortable again. But the look quickly vanished, replaced by curiosity.

"You are different. Your eyes are true."

Their eyes held for a moment, two young women from two different worlds. Yet, Cynthia thought, not so different at all. "I was raised to care about people," she told Flowing Waters. "My father is a preacher—Christian."

A hint of bitterness came back into Flowing Waters' eyes. "I have known white people who called themselves that. But they were not kind at all."

"Then they weren't really Christians." Cynthia returned to brushing Old Grandmother's hair. "They said they were Christians, but they weren't Christians in their hearts. God's spirit wasn't inside them."

Flowing Waters frowned. "You have this spirit inside you?"

Cynthia thought for a moment, remembering how distant she had felt from God these past few days. But her father had taught her that if a person truly had God in their hearts, He never really left them. The thought brought a stabbing pain. How she wished she could tell her poor father she was all right.

"I guess I do," she answered aloud. She looked at Flowing Waters. "Will you help me braid Old Grandmother's hair. My hand is hurt bad and I can't use it very well. That's why I've been brushing her hair with my other hand."

Flowing Waters rose, taking up the bowl of grease and smearing it into the old woman's hair. "I will help you." She worked the grease through, then brushed the hair again and parted it through the middle. "Did Many Bears hurt your hand?"

"Yes," Cynthia answered, watching the Indian woman begin deftly braiding Old Grandmother's white locks. "The day he took me." She frowned. "Why did he do that, Flowing Waters? We were so close to town. Why didn't he just let me go?"

"To steal a white woman right from under her man's nose is considered not only brave, but a great joke on the

152

white man," Flowing Waters answered. "Many Bears and his friends still laugh about it. Many Bears belongs to the Strong Heart Society. He is a great warrior. Soon Red Wolf will belong to the same society. He has killed many buffalo, made war against the Pawnee and Crow, and he has raided and killed many miners. Soon he will be given the eagle-feathered war bonnet that was his father's before him. It has been saved for him by the old chiefs. Our great leader, Sitting Bull, also belongs to the Strong Heart Society."

"Society?"

"*Ai.* A good warrior always belongs to a society. My Standing Eagle was also a Strong Heart. There is also the Crow Owners Society, the Badger Society, the Omaha Society—and there is the Buffalo Cult, the Horse Cult, the Elk Cult—many groups to which a warrior can belong. Each has its own dance and way of dress and weapons and rules."

"You mean—like what we call clubs?"

"I do not know about white man's clubs."

Cynthia watched the braiding. "How old are you, Flowing Waters?"

"I am seventeen summers. What are you?"

"I'm sixteen." She hesitated. "How old is Red Wolf?"

"Red Wolf is twenty summers." The young woman looked at Cynthia with a teasing grin. "He is very handsome, is he not? Or do you white women think no Indian man is handsome."

Cynthia reddened. "I think he's very handsome."

"Now you know how good it feels to have a man inside of you," Flowing Waters said matter-of-factly, thinking Red Wolf had already claimed Cynthia.

Cynthia reddened more, wanting to declare that Red Wolf had done no such thing. But she remembered that he had told her the others must believe he had claimed her. "Yes," she said quietly.

"There," Flowing Waters said, stepping back a little.

"One braid is done. Now I will do the other. Is your hand getting better?"

"A little." She studied Flowing Waters' youthful beauty, finding it incredulous that one so young had already had two babies. "You speak good English, Flowing Waters, like Red Wolf."

"Some of us speak the white man's tongue better than others. Most of my people still speak only in our own tongue. I learned from missionaries around Fort Laramie, as did Red Wolf. He could have learned much more if they had not tried to cut off his hair."

"He told me."

Old Grandmother spoke up then, motioning to Cynthia.

"She wants to look at your hand," Flowing Waters told the girl. "She says you should not have got it wet."

"I had no choice," Cynthia answered, holding her hand out to the old woman.

"Red Wolf wanted to see if you would really help. He says you are brave and strong."

Old Grandmother studied Cynthia's hand.

"Will Red Wolf take me back home?" Cynthia asked Flowing Waters.

Flowing Waters smiled lightly. "Perhaps if you want to go. But now he has mated with you. Do you not wish to stay with him?"

Cynthia frowned. "You mean . . . like a wife?"

"*Ai*. You are special. Red Wolf took you after mating with you, instead of leaving you there for the others. Do you not know how kind that was? It means you are special to him." She looked at Cynthia. "Do you have a white man who is special to you? Many Bears said you had no husband."

Cynthia shook her head. "No, I have no husband. And there was no one special."

"I know white people. After a white woman has been with an Indian man, they treat her badly. Would they be

154

cruel to you if Red Wolf took you back now?"

Cynthia felt her heart sinking. "I don't know. Perhaps. But my parents wouldn't. They would still love me. It's only been five days, Flowing Waters. I miss my family. I . . . I haven't had time to know how I feel about Red Wolf."

"Soon it will be five weeks, then five months." She finished braiding Old Grandmother's hair. "It does not happen often, but I have heard of white women captives who chose to stay with the Indians rather than go back to the world from which they came. Perhaps you will feel this way too someday."

Cynthia fought an urge to cry. She didn't want to appear weak in front of Flowing Waters. "But I would never see my family again."

Flowing Waters frowned. "I suppose it is the same as when our people are forced to live in the white man's world. This is home to us—the Black Hills. Here we can breathe and we are alive. But you whites, you do not stay in one place. There seems to be no land that is special to you, so how can you miss it? You move from here to there in your white-topped houses on wheels. You come here and take things out of Mother Earth, hurt her with your picks and shovels, then you leave her wounded and bleeding and go to some other place. Do you have a land that is special to you? Do you understand that the earth is sacred?"

Cynthia swallowed back a lump in her throat. "I don't know what's right anymore. And I guess I don't have a place that is special. I'm happy wherever I am as long as I'm with my mother and father and my brother."

Old Grandmother spoke up.

"She says to come back to the tipi and she will put new moss on your hand," Flowing Waters told Cynthia. "Then you can go off with Red Wolf. She will come back for the clothes when they are dry. Old Grandmother says Red Wolf will take you into the hills today and show you

155

the land that we love."

"Won't there be miners out there someplace?"

"Not where Red Wolf will take you." Flowing Waters smiled slyly. "You will be alone."

Old Grandmother rose and began a brisk walk back to the village. Cynthia thanked Flowing Waters for the hair grease and followed the woman, still full of questions, and also full of apprehension over riding off with Red Wolf. But she was still afraid to object. Perhaps if she continued to cooperate Red Wolf would eventually take her back. If he took her back before he or some other Indian man touched her, she could still be accepted by her own people and would not be looked down on.

They walked back to the village, where fires burned, meat hung to dry, dogs ran and barked, and children played. A great herd of horses grazed to the south of the village, and sweet-smelling smoke hung lightly in the still air of morning. Cynthia noticed a few Indian men sitting around with whiskey bottles in their hands, and some lay flat on their backs sleeping. She wondered if they were still there from the night before. A small party of men was mounted on horses, and Cynthia watched them ride out. She wondered if it was to hunt for food, or to hunt for miners. She wondered where Sitting Bull and Crazy Horse were. Did such notorious leaders really exist? Were they right here in this village?

In some places men just sat around campfires smoking pipes. The women seemed busiest, either sewing or cooking or nursing babies or carrying wood. Most were still at the stream bathing and washing clothes. It struck Cynthia that the movements in this Indian village were not so different from when whites made camp while traveling by wagon train.

Women stared as she walked by. Some smiled, and Cynthia smiled back at them, still wondering how safe she was here. Apparently as long as she belonged to Red Wolf and did as he told her, she was in no danger. She wished she could understand what they were saying when one of them talked to each other and sometimes laughed after she went by.

She wondered if the miners and soldiers knew there was a village this big only a few days from the mining towns. Were these Indians planning to attack Deadwood? There seemed to be hundreds of warriors in this one village. She remembered her father mentioning that George Custer, the great soldier, was supposed to be rounding up these Indians and making all of them go to the Red Cloud Agency. Many more soldiers were supposed to be coming out soon. She wondered if she should tell Red Wolf. Her loyalty to her own people told her she should say nothing.

Yet she somehow felt like these people should be warned. There were so many women here, little babies, old ones like Old Grandmother. They all looked so happy here. Just as Flowing Waters had said, this was their home. Would she be considered a traitor if she told Red Wolf many more soldiers were coming?

Old Grandmother led her into the tipi, then washed and re-packed her hand, which was feeling much better. Then the old woman took a beaded leather headband from where it hung on a hook and she tied it around Cynthia's forehead. The old woman stood back and nodded, her eyes showing her appreciation for Cynthia's beauty. In spite of the remaining bruises and cuts, her provocative features shined—the perfect form and enticing curves beneath the tunic, the thick, braided blond hair, the wide blue eyes and full, pink lips. Old Grandmother knew this white girl would be a great temptation to Red Wolf, and she hoped her grandson would not get in trouble and that his heart would not suffer over the beauty who stood before her now, for surely the handsome Red Wolf had desires for this kind woman who had once saved his life.

Red Wolf entered then, and Cynthia turned. He was

still bare-chested, but he wore buckskin leggings. A bone hairpipe necklace graced his neck, and his long, black hair was tied to one side, the tail wrapped with beaded leather strips that hung down like ribbons over his right shoulder. His powerful upper arms were decorated with brass bands, and he wore a wide leather belt at his waist that sported the big hunting knife.

Red Wolf hesitated when he looked at her, and again Cynthia felt the strange pull deep inside as his eyes moved over her. He turned then and reached for a quiver of arrows and his bow, as well as a rifle. Cynthia wondered if he had stolen the rifle from some dead soldier or miner. It seemed incredible that this well-spoken, handsome young man had killed men, and she struggled to allow herself to understand why he had done it.

"Come," he told her. "Are you well enough to ride?"

"I think so." Cynthia swallowed, still not sure she wanted to go off alone with him. Did he have something more in mind than showing her the Black Hills?

Red Wolf looked over at Old Grandmother and smiled, saying something to her in the Sioux tongue. He looked back at Cynthia. "I have told her how nice her hair looks."

"Flowing Waters did most of it. I tried, but I couldn't because of my hand. Flowing Waters greased her hair for me."

Red Wolf nodded. "Is your hand getting better?"

"Some."

"There are chores that must be done. But you are still not well enough. Today I will show you the land that we love. Soon the whole village will move on and there will be much to do and little time for us to talk."

He walked out and Cynthia followed. Red Wolf shoved his rifle into a leather strap that held it at the side of his horse, a big Appaloosa gelding. He slung his bow around his shoulder, then turned and lifted Cynthia with ease, placing her at the front of his flat saddle made of leather stuffed with straw. A colorful blanket covered the saddle. Red Wolf leaped onto the horse's back from a standing position, with no help from a stirrup.

"*Ain't nobody can sit a horse like an Indian,*" she remembered a man saying on their trip to Deadwood. "*They can hang off the side and crook their arms through a rope and shoot a rifle or a bow right from the horse. They can race, dodge, turn on a dime. Tryin' to shoot an Indian off his horse is like tryin' to shoot the spots off a chipmunk's back. Them spots is a part of the chipmunk, and an Indian is a part of his horse.*"

Red Wolf reached around Cynthia. It was the first time she had been close to him without fighting him, other than the night she had cut him down. He moved one arm around her middle, and she was surprised at the gentle way he hugged her close, as though to reassure her not to be afraid. He took up the reins with his other hand and rode through the village. Men and women alike called out to him, and Cynthia could tell by the inflections in their voices and by their smiles that they were teasing Red Wolf about his white captive. Cynthia reddened as she realized they must think he was taking her away to mate with her again. The thought brought mixed feelings, for in spite of the fact that he was an Indian, Cynthia realized she felt attracted to Red Wolf. She knew it was wrong, terribly sinful; and she wondered if being around these people did something to a person. Perhaps they had a way of drugging their victims, or hypnotizing them. For she felt an odd freedom in her soul as she rode off with the wild Red Wolf into the land he called sacred.

Cynthia felt suddenly awkward and nervous. She was the one who came from a civilized world, who had the education and Christian teaching. And yet now she felt ignorant, for this was a world about which Red Wolf

159

knew everything and she knew nothing. As she rode with him into the thick pines, climbing away from the village, she could sense the delicious taste of freedom the Indian must feel. She could imagine better than she ever could before how difficult it must be for people like Red Wolf to be confined to one small section of land, to live in one solid house that could not be moved from one place to another.

"Once we roamed from Canada all the way south to the Arkansas River of Colorado," Red Wolf finally said. "And from the great river called the Missouri to the other side of the Rockies. Buffalo herds were so big that one could stand on a hill and see them for miles, thick and black. We used the buffalo for everything we wore, everything we ate, all of the tools we work with, to make our tipis, parfleches, cradleboards, everything. Now you see us using some white men's things—clothing and tools. It is because the buffalo are almost gone. If the white man does not stop killing them soon, there will be none left at all. We cannot survive without the buffalo. It is not just a thing to us. It is a spirit. The buffalo spirit lives in our very souls."

He headed up a rocky pathway that was steep at times, then would level off again. Cynthia quickly forgot her apprehension over the climb, for Red Wolf's Appaloosa seemed very surefooted, and she kept reminding herself of the words spoken about what good riders Indians were.

"We raid and steal because we are hungry, Cynthia, and there is not enough game to feed and clothe us any longer. The white man stole it from us, so now we steal from him. The white man shoots us down for no reason, so we kill him. He rapes our women, so we do the same to his."

Cynthia felt a shiver of fear sweep through her. Was that why he was bringing her out here, so that the others could not hear her screams? She felt frozen in place, unable to find a reply. They rode on in silence, and then she felt the gentle hug again.

"I do not bring you up here to hurt you," he told her, as though reading her thoughts. "But I will tell you that you are the most beautiful white girl, and the most caring, I have known, even though I have hardly known you long enough to be sure. I see the kindness in your eyes, the struggle to understand. I saw it the night you came to cut me loose. And no man needs to look upon you more than once to see your beauty. I have never before been attracted to a white woman in such a way that I did not want to hurt her."

They neared the top of a ridge, and he slowed his horse, then dismounted. "It is steep here. We will walk the horse." He lifted her down. Cynthia grasped his bare shoulders for support, and she caught the sweet scent of sage and leather. Their eyes met as he lowered her, and she was angry with herself for being so terribly attracted to an Indian. She was sure she had somehow been swayed by her surroundings, swept up suddenly in this feeling of freedom. She had been so quickly transported into another world, and here, so far from reality, so far from all she had ever known, she felt entirely different, as though she were floating in some kind of dream world and none of this was really happening to her.

Red Wolf took her hand and led her to the top of the ridge. There were no trees here, and Cynthia gasped at the sight. Mountains and ridges cascaded all around, covered with dark pine. She could see the Sioux village far below on her left, and in the distance to her right lay another village. Red Wolf pointed to it.

"Sitting Bull and Crazy Horse are there," he told her. "Soon that village will join ours and we will go farther north. There we will stay for a while, where the game is better, and there we will talk about what to do about Hard Backsides and about the miners."

"The government is sending even more soldiers," Cynthia told him, wondering why she had said it. "They

161

want all of you to go to the reservation."

"I know. Scouts have told us." He grinned a little. "But you did not know that I already knew. Why did you tell me?"

She reddened and looked away. "I don't know." She folded her arms and shivered at the sight below her. "This is beautiful, Red Wolf. It's like God lives here."

He was silent for a moment. "Now you understand, God *does* live here, your God and mine. Who is to say He is not the same? The Sioux believe God created this place as a gathering place for all the animals. Now the white man has invaded it. He has chased away the animals, dug his pick into Mother Earth. He cuts down her trees to make houses. We pick up only dead wood. A tree is life, and it takes many years to be tall and strong. God created the tree to protect the land from flooding, to give a home to the birds of the air, to bring cool shade to man and to produce foods for him. Enough trees die by the choosing of the Great Spirit to provide the firewood we need. But the white man will not wait for a tree to die. He kills it."

He walked away from her, looking out over his village far in the distance. "And the white man also has no respect for the animal spirits," he continued. "He kills them just for a little food, leaving the rest to waste. Sometimes they kill a buffalo and take only the hide. The first time I saw this the food came up from my stomach, the sight made me sick. Surely the Great Spirit will destroy the white man someday for what he does to Mother Earth and to the animals and the trees. It is the same with the water. So many white men come now, washing and urinating and dumping their filth into the streams, that they are no longer clean."

It struck Cynthia as she watched him that he looked almost beautiful standing there framed against the Black Hills that stretched out behind him, a wild man in a wild land. He fit it so well, and she realized it was as though God had made the Indian for this land, this land for the

162

Indian. Never before had she seen with such clarity why the Indian fought so hard to keep what he considered his share of the earth.

"This land is sacred," he told her, making a sweeping motion with his arm. "Do you not feel it?"

He met her eyes, and standing there in a tunic, a beaded band around her head and moccasins on her feet that Old Grandmother had given her that morning, Cynthia felt like an Indian herself.

"Yes," she answered.

Their eyes held for a long, tense moment. Even though she had never been with a man, she understood the look in his eyes at that moment, and she turned away quickly.

"We belong here," Red Wolf continued. "Not on the reservation. We have lived one way for hundreds of years, and now the white man wants us to change in a day. It cannot be done, not even in a year, perhaps not in a hundred years. If we have our way, we will never change, and we will live in this land of our choosing, free of the white man."

"They'll never give up, Red Wolf. You can't keep up the fight forever. Surely you know that. You're smarter than the others."

"Not smarter. I just had the chance to learn more. I know you are probably right. But no matter how educated she is, if a woman is protecting her child, she would fight a hundred men even though she knew she could not win. She would strike out at them and let them stab back at her until she would fall to the ground. Even then she would keep fighting, struggling to keep the enemy from getting her baby. That is how we feel about Paha Sapa."

Cynthia turned and looked at him again. "You're different, Red Wolf. You aren't like the others. You could be a spokesman for your people."

"And who would listen? You saw how I was treated at Deadwood. To those people I am no different. And

163

inside . . ." He put a fist to his heart. "Inside here I am no different. I am Sioux, soon to join the Strong Heart Society. I thought once that I could be like the white man. But when they started to cut my hair, I knew I could not be. And I knew they looked upon me still as unequal."

"There could be more than one way to help your people. If things get worse, if the whites take over all of this and you are forced onto a reservation, you know enough to help your people, Red Wolf. You could represent them to our government, make sure they get treated fairly. You could show the whites how civilized and educated an Indian can be."

"Civilized? Is the white man civilized when he tears up the land and when he murders us on sight and rapes our women? Is he civilized when he makes the water dirty? Is he civilized when he rides into our villages when we are harming no one, and burns everything in sight, murders our women and children, cuts the insides out of our women and the privates off our men?"

Cynthia reddened and turned away. "I can't believe they do those things."

"They do. Ask any of our people. All of them can tell you things that would make a weak white woman faint. I was with Many Bears when he found his sister and mother. Their breasts were gone and their bellies cut open!"

"Stop it!"

"Now you understand our bitterness! Now you understand better why our own hearts are bad! What right do the whites have coming here onto land promised us under his own treaties with us? You tell me. What gives him this right?"

She felt tears stinging her eyes as she struggled to find an answer, but there was none, other than greed and selfishness and prejudice. She gasped when she suddenly felt a hand on her shoulder. Red Wolf was standing behind her.

"I am glad Many Bears captured you," he told her. "Many times I thought about the white girl who saved me that night. I wanted to talk to her again, to make her understand how it was I ended up being dragged through the streets of Deadwood for a hanging. I did not want her to think of me as just an animal. I saw something in her eyes—a desire to understand. That is what I am doing now. I am trying to help you understand. Some day, if you must go back, you will know. You will not look upon us in the same way. And perhaps you can make others see."

"Please take me home, Red Wolf. I don't belong here."

"Don't you? It is not the color of skin that matters, Cynthia. It is the heart—the spirit. Do you not feel what I feel when I stand up here?"

An eagle cried out and they both looked up at it. Cynthia felt an excited chill, the thrill of freedom she had felt the day she watched the hawk. "The day Many Bears captured me, I was too far from my house because I had been watching a hawk," she told Red Wolf. "I wanted so badly to be as free as he was, to be able to fly like that." She turned to Red Wolf. "Is that what you mean?"

"That is part of it. And up here I feel close to Wankan Tanka, the Great Spirit who rules all the earth and the animals."

Cynthia watched his eyes, hoping that in this soft moment perhaps she could convince him to take her back.

"Why do you keep me here, Red Wolf? Why is it so important to you that I understand? Why don't you torture me and kill me like you would any other prisoner? You act as though I belong here, but I don't. I just want to go home."

He grasped her chin in one hand, studying the faint marks left from Many Bears' quirt and wishing he could

165

wipe them away. "I keep you here without harming you because I believe the spirits brought you here. You were led to me that night, and somehow I knew it was not the last time I would see you. When Many Bears told me he had a white woman who said she had once saved me, I knew then that there was something special about you. You think you do not belong here, but I think that you do. You are a white woman who can understand, and I want to make you understand before you go away from me. But I must tell you that I do not want you to go away . . . ever. I do not know why. I only know that the spirits brought you to me, and there will be something special between us, even though you are white and I am Oglala Sioux."

Their eyes held, and to her own amazement Cynthia did not resist when he bent closer, moving his hand to her shoulder and lightly rubbing his cheek against her own. His gentleness surprised her, as did his sweet smell and the affectionate words.

Her heart pounded wildly. She had never had such feelings before, had never felt so alive, every part of her body tingling with excitement and apprehension. She felt her life changing before her very eyes, felt her soul being stolen from her. Yes, surely these people could hypnotize, for this young man she should hate for totally disrupting her life was pulling her close and she was letting him. His strong arms encircled her, pressing her soft breasts against his hard chest.

"Wakan Tanka has brought you here. Red Wolf wants you to stay. *Hetchetu welo*. May it be so."

"Red Wolf!" They heard someone calling then.

Red Wolf let go of Cynthia, and she stood feeling numb and confused as Red Wolf ran part way down the ridge. He called out in the Sioux tongue and Cynthia heard a female voice call back. It sounded like Flowing Waters. Red Wolf came running back to her then, his eyes full of grief and fear. "It is Old Grandmother! Flowing Waters

166

has come looking for us! Old Grandmother has collapsed! She cannot move!" He grabbed Cynthia's hand and took his horse by the bridle in the other hand, leading both of them back down.

Cynthia felt strangely sad that something was wrong with the old woman she had known only hours. She thought about the white women stepping back from her and whispering, wondering how Old Grandmother's heart must have hurt when that happened. She wondered if Old Grandmother was pretty when she was a young girl, and what life was like for the Sioux then. Surely it was a time when there were no white men at all in this part of the world.

She hurried along with Red Wolf, forgetting to wonder at the moment what might have happened between herself and Red Wolf if Flowing Waters had not come along and broken the strange spell Red Wolf had put on her.

Chapter Ten

They rode hard, Cynthia sure this time that Red Wolf's horse would stumble and fall. But the surefooted animal and its skilled rider scampered to the bottom of the high ridge without a mishap. Cynthia clung for dear life to the animal's mane as she rode slightly bent over in front of Red Wolf, squeezing her legs together to hang on. While her heart was full of sympathy for Old Grandmother, she felt a momentary excitement at the hard ride.

Cynthia had never ridden a horse this fast, never felt the wind rushing past her this way. It seemed odd to have no schedule for chores, no time set aside for lessons, no thought to time for anything. She realized that she could not recall any of the women at the stream scolding the children for anything, and many of the children ran naked. She remembered wishing when she was smaller that she could run naked too. The tunic she wore, and the moccasins, were so much more comfortable than the stiff, hard clothes she had always worn before, and if she was not still somewhat afraid for her life, and worried over her parents' emotional suffering over her disappearance, she could almost enjoy this new, free existence.

They thundered through the village, and Red Wolf dismounted before the horse even came to a halt. He did not stop to help Cynthia down, and she slid off the horse by herself, feeling women and children staring at her. She started inside the tipi, but a big-boned, stern-faced Sioux woman stepped up to her, putting out her arm and shaking her head.

Cynthia stepped back, feeling a certain grief of her own when she heard Red Wolf cry out from inside the tipi. Moments later he appeared at the entrance, holding his frail old grandmother in his arms. Cynthia stared as women began keening, letting out their shrill cries of grief. Red Wolf's face was hard-set, and there were tears on his cheeks. A leather sack was in one of his hands as he turned and started walking away from the village with Old Grandmother still in his arms, and Cynthia wondered what could be inside the sack.

Cynthia began walking behind Red Wolf, and they were followed by most of the people in the village, the eerie wails of the Indian women making Cynthia shiver and bringing a heavy grief to her own heart. She had known Old Grandmother for only one night and this morning, yet she felt someone dear to her had just died. Her feelings startled her, and mixed with her confusion over her predicament, her lingering fears, and her own worry over her parents to make her burst into tears as she continued to follow Red Wolf. Would she ever see her parents again?

A long procession followed Red Wolf for close to a mile, to a distant hill, where several scaffolds were erected. It was the first time Cynthia had set eyes on an Indian burial ground, but she knew by instinct what it was. She had heard about how the Indians often put their dead loved ones up high, rather than bury them in the ground. "They believe the spirits of their dead can more easily reach heaven that way," her father had told her once. "I am told that to the Indian, heaven is a place where there are many buffalo, more game than a man could ever need. It's always green and warm. And I expect to the Indian, heaven is a place where there are

170

no white men."

Cynthia continued behind Red Wolf as they neared the sunny hillside, where she could see the wrapped bodies of others lying on raised platforms where the animals could not get to them. Cynthia shivered at the sight, and suddenly someone grabbed her arm.

"You cannot go there." The words came from Flowing Waters, who had had trouble keeping up with Red Wolf when they were riding, and who had just now caught up with the procession. "It is forbidden for white men to set foot on our burial grounds."

Cynthia stayed back and watched as Red Wolf laid Old Grandmother on the ground for a moment, bending over her and rocking as though in great grief. She gasped then when he took out his hunting knife and slashed at his chest.

'My God, what is he doing!" she exclaimed.

"It is our way of grieving. We inflict physical pain to help ease the pain in our hearts. And at the same time we sacrifice our blood to Wakan Tanka to plead on behalf of the loved one that they be taken to the great hunting ground in the sky."

Cynthia closed her eyes and cried.

"You grieve for Old Grandmother, yet you hardly know her."

"She was good," Cynthia sobbed. "It's easy to cry for her." She sniffed and looked at Flowing Waters. "And I feel so sorry for Red Wolf. She was all he had left."

Flowing Waters nodded. "Now he has you. Perhaps Wakan Tanka brought you here for a reason. You come, and now the Great Spirit takes Old Grandmother. Is it not a sign?"

Cynthia just stared at the woman, shivering at the strange thought, again feeling that she had lost total control of her own destiny. "I don't know," she finally answered. She tore her eyes from Flowing Waters, unable to accept or comprehend the meaning of the woman's words.

She watched as Red Wolf walked to a small grove of trees and began cutting branches to build a scaffold. Blood poured from gashes on his chest. Some of the other women began helping, while more stood around Old Grandmother crying and chanting. Some made a circle, clasping hands and beginning to sing with an eerie rhythm, swaying to the words Cynthia could not understand.

Soon the scaffold was completed. Red Wolf laid Old Grandmother on a mat made from branches and blankets, the blankets brought by some of the other women and tied to the branches with rawhide. Red Wolf wrapped Old Grandmother in another blanket so that she was completely covered. Then he and some of the men who had also come raised the mat, setting it into notches on poles that were set in the ground.

Then Red Wolf picked up the leather sack he had brought along. From it he took some things Cynthia realized must have belonged to his grandmother—a mirror, some moccasins, and some other things she could not see from where she stood. He placed the items on the mat around his grandmother's body. Then a new grief gripped Cynthia's heart as she saw him take out the knife she had given Old Grandmother just the night before, her own mother's knife. Old Grandmother had been so happy with the gift. It made Cynthia even sadder over the old woman's death, and she wept not only for Old Grandmother, but for her own mother, for the knife brought back all the memories. She shivered at the irony that the knife she had used to free an Indian man weeks ago would now lie resting on a burial scaffold. How shocked her mother would be to know where her knife was right now.

Red Wolf went to his knees beside the scaffold then, bowing his head. The entire procession and ceremony had taken over two hours, but Cynthia had hardly noticed time passing. Soon some of those present began leaving. After another two hours all but Flowing Waters,

Red Wolf, and Cynthia had left.

"We must go now and leave Red Wolf to his grief," Flowing Waters told Cynthia.

"No. Let me stay," Cynthia answered.

Flowing Waters' eyebrows arched in surprise, and she looked from Cynthia to Red Wolf, then smiled wryly in spite of her grief. Yes, this white girl was different from the haughty bitches she had had occasion to know in the past. There was surely a purpose for her coming here.

"You may stay," she told Cynthia. "But do not go near him or set foot onto sacred ground."

"I won't."

Flowing Waters turned and left, and Cynthia sat down in the grass to wait for Red Wolf. She looked down at the injured hand Old Grandmother had so recently bandaged for her. She thought how thin was the line between life and death. She felt suddenly awakened to thoughts and realities she had never considered before being captured, and she felt older, somehow wiser. Agonizing grief swept through her soft heart then when Red Wolf stretched up his arms and threw back his head, letting out a long wail of grief, sounding like a wounded animal. Cynthia no longer wondered if these people were capable of loving.

The day warmed, and Cynthia had had too little time to heal from the physical and emotional trauma of the last several days. Hard as she tried, she could not stay awake as the sun rose higher and cast its heat on her, while the air hung silent except for the occasional song of a bird.

Hours had passed, and everyone had gone back to the village. Only Red Wolf and Cynthia remained, but Red Wolf stayed by his grandmother's scaffold and seemed hardly aware of Cynthia's presence. The village lay beyond a rolling hill, and the lay of the land kept any of its noises from reaching the burial ground. Cynthia wondered, as she grew tired and lay back in the grass, if the silence here was one of the reasons it had been chosen for a burial ground.

She stared up at puffy, white clouds, seeing different shapes in them, a dog here, a woman there. She wondered if the Indians found any spiritual significance in the clouds, for they seemed to find spiritual connections with practically everything. Her eyes began to droop then in her exhaustion, and soon she drifted off to sleep, a soft breeze caressing her face.

The sun moved across the sky, across the captured white girl and a young Indian man who sat beside his grandmother's burial scaffold. Cynthia had no idea how long she lay there before she realized the wind was blowing harder. It stirred her awake, and she opened her eyes to see someone standing over her. He was just a dark figure, the setting sun behind him. She gasped and sat up, just as a cloud moved over the sun. She could see then it was Red Wolf.

Cynthia stared at the scabbed blood on his chest. She backed away slightly, meeting his eyes and seeing the agony there. They were red and swollen, and there were streaks left on his cheeks where tears had been. She realized then that when he was captured by the men at Deadwood and dragged to the tree to be hanged, there had been no tears. This young man would never cry out of fear. This man could kill his enemy with no remorse. Yet now he had wept over his grandmother.

She saw him raise his chin slightly, his dark eyes searching her own. His jaw flexed in an effort to speak, even though he was consumed with grief.

"You stayed," he said quietly.

Cynthia nodded. "I felt bad—about Old Grandmother—felt bad for you."

He looked away for a moment, the stronger wind blowing his dark hair away from his face. He had loosened it, and it floated free with the breeze, somehow making him seem wilder. "Do white men weep when loved ones die?" he asked.

She watched him with a lump in her throat. "Yes. There is nothing wrong with crying over something like that."

He met her eyes again, and Cynthia felt as though some unnamed, unseen power was enveloping her. Their eyes held for a long time, both of them feeling the same force, feeling the same sudden lack of control over their own lives. He reached out his hand, touching her face.

"Old Grandmother told me this morning that she had a dream last night. In the dream she saw you and me together, but we were much older. Old Grandmother's visions have always come true." He studied her intently. "What do you think of that dream?"

Cynthia swallowed. "I . . . I don't know what to think."

"I think it is very strange how we have come to be together. I think it was meant to be."

Her eyes teared. "You aren't going to take me back, are you?" There was disappointment in her voice.

"I told you I cannot take you back right now."

"I mean—not ever?"

Their eyes held again. "That is up to you, in time." His hand was still at the side of her face, and she was surprised at the shiver of desire that swept through her as he rubbed his thumb across her cheek. "You have a good heart, Cynthia. I am glad that you waited. My heart was happy when I walked by and saw you lying here. And I felt strong desires as I stood and watched you sleep. I am tempted to do what I have told the others I have already done." He felt her tense, and he smiled sadly. "Do not worry. You are fast becoming special to me. When I take you, it will be because you are willing. And for now my heart is full of grief over Old Grandmother." He moved his hand down her neck, over her shoulder and arm, grasping her uninjured hand. "Stay with me, Cynthia. Do not be afraid of me. I can take care of you. I am a good hunter and provider. I feel something very strong when I

175

am near you, and I knew when I stood over you that you were special, for you understand my grief, though you hardly know me."

She turned away, pulling her hand away, her mind a tangle of confused feelings. "It isn't right that we should stay alone together, with Old Grandmother gone."

"What is not right about being friends? I will not touch you unless you are willing. Do you think I will not keep this promise?"

"I don't know what to think."

"There is no one to know but my people, and in their eyes it is not wrong that we dwell together. Flowing Waters will teach you how we make our clothes and weapons, how we cook and how we clean our things. I will have no one to do these things for me. I must be away, hunting and making war on the enemy. I do not wish to come back to nothing. My heart is too empty now. It hurts too much."

Cynthia saw smoke rising beyond the hill then. "What is that? Something is on fire."

"It is my tipi."

"What!" Cynthia turned to face him.

"It is the custom. Necessary items are removed from a tipi where someone has died and the tipi is burned. It is bad luck to dwell in a tipi where someone has died. I will need a new tipi. I will hunt the buffalo and bring you skins to clean and cure for a new tipi. Flowing Waters can help you learn how to do this. You can paint pictures on it that will show it belongs just to us. You will live like the other Indian women, learn to do things our way. Would you not like to do that?"

She saw the strange pleading in his eyes, was touched by his loneliness. "I guess I have no choice. But . . . where will we live until a new tipi is made?"

"We can live with Flowing Waters and Many Bears."

Her eyes widened. "But there is also Basket Woman, and four little ones! Won't it be too crowded?"

Red Wolf smiled sadly. "They will make room. And

many nights I will be gone. In the day I am seldom inside the tipi, and neither shall you be. If we are successful in the hunt, you will be very busy cleaning skins. By the time it is cold enough that we all must be inside the same time, we will have our own tipi."

Cynthia thought about her poor parents again. Already Red Wolf talked of still being together when the weather turned cold. That was four or five months away. She decided she must stop thinking of her old life. Apparently she was destined to live this new one, at least for a while. If she was to survive, she had to learn the ways of the Sioux. And for now she must not think about what Red Wolf surely expected of her eventually. He said he would not touch her unless she was willing, which as far as she was concerned meant he would never touch her at all. And as long as he did not, there couldn't be anything so wrong in staying together. She would simply refuse him until the day came that she could go home, and that would be that. Nothing would be held against her once she got back to her own people if no Indian man had touched her.

She felt a strong but gentle hand at her waist then, and she wondered who she was fooling. This young Indian man had some kind of powerful effect on her that made her lose her senses. She actually felt attracted to him at times! And she realized with sudden clarity and embarrassment that it was not Red Wolf she did not trust. It was her own feelings.

"Come," he told her. "We will go back now. Old Grandmother goes to the place in the sky where there is only peace."

Cynthia looked up at him. "Why did you put my knife on the scaffold?"

His eyes saddened. "She was happy with your gift. When we bury our loved ones, we place all the things they loved most beside them. And we give them weapons to fight any evil spirits that might try to keep them from getting to heaven, and to use to kill and prepare their food

177

once they reach that happy place. We give them their moccasins because it is a long walk."

Cynthia's eyes teared. "I'm glad you put the knife there. I hardly knew her, but I grieve for her. Now something of mine will always be with her. Somehow that makes me feel better."

"*Ai*. It helps the grief to know a part of yourself has gone with them. I placed my bone necklace across her breast. She made it for me many, many years ago."

Cynthia walked beside him. They crested the hill, and walked toward the village below. Cynthia felt as though she were walking through a doorway, leaving her old life behind and entering a strange new one. She felt a heaviness in her chest at having to leave Old Grandmother behind, alone on the scaffold. But she said nothing to Red Wolf. He was suffering enough grief already. Her heart went out to him, and she hardly realized that she had slipped her own arm around his waist as they walked.

Cynthia saw new looks on the faces of many of the Indian women who greeted her and Red Wolf when they returned. They smiled at her, and a few came up to her and stroked her hair, saying words she could not understand. But their gestures and eyes told her they suddenly looked at her as a friend and not an enemy.

"They respect you for staying out there with me," Red Wolf told her as they walked toward Many Bears' tipi. "They think you are good inside, not bad like most whites. They have accepted you now, for you grieved over Old Grandmother."

Cynthia smiled back at them, feeling awkward, but at the same time feeling a rush of relief. She was making friends among these strange people. One woman hurried up to them carrying a heavy buffalo robe, which she handed to Red Wolf. She said something to him, sorrow in her eyes. Red Wolf turned to Cynthia.

"We have our first robe. That was Little Deer. She has given us this robe as a gift. She knows we must have a new tipi."

As they approached Many Bears' tipi, Cynthia was astounded at the sight of even more women, and some of the men who were still in camp, all standing ready to greet Red Wolf and all bearing gifts of either skins, utensils, or food. Each took a turn laying his or her gift near the tipi entrance and each had a word of consolation for Red Wolf, who turned and smiled at the look of surprise on Cynthia's face.

"Did you think we do not understand kindness? They all grieve for me and have brought me gifts to start a new life . . . with you. They think since you stayed out there with me and grieved over Old Grandmother that you intend to stay with me forever."

Cynthia reddened and turned away, looking at the many gifts. "There is so much, Red Wolf. Shouldn't we do something in return?"

"They do not expect something back. We all take care of each other, Cynthia. If one of them has trouble, or is hungry, I will help them. All food from a hunt is shared so that no one gets fat while another starves. It is the way. We will invite some of them to come and eat with us when we cook the food they have given us. And we will have a celebration when our tipi is finished."

Cynthia could not help the wave of desire that moved over her at the way he spoke of "we" and "us" as though he took it for granted they would be together now. The words had the tone of husband and wife, and it gave her shivers. Even if she could have such feelings for Red Wolf, she thought it surely would be terribly sinful and wrong. She could never have such a relationship with this wild Indian.

"Come. We will put some of these things inside. Some we will pack into the buffalo robe, and tie it together and leave it outside. Soon we will pick everything up and move on north."

Cynthia wondered at what a strange day it had been. She moved almost as if in a daze, helping Flowing Waters and Basket Woman, her lessons in how to make clothing starting that very day as Flowing Waters gave her a pair of moccasins she had started to make for Many Bears.

"I want them to be for Red Wolf now," the young woman told Cynthia. "They will be my gift to him, for I cleaned and beaded the skins myself. You can sew them together, for you must learn."

Cynthia studied the hundreds of tiny beads sewn into the outer skin of the moccasins, marveling at the intricate work and the beautiful design. "The blue beads here represent water, the gift of life," Flowing Waters told her, pointing to blue beads on the toes. "Water is my sign. The yellow stands for the sun, who rules over the universe and is a friend to water. We must have both to live. The sun is very important. Our tipi entrances must always face the place where the sun rises. And the sun is round, like the circle of life. Life is one great circle, never ending. Old Grandmother is dead, but she lives on in her children and grandchildren. The circle of life never ends."

Cynthia began sewing the moccasins as Flowing Waters directed, using a bone needle and thin strips of rawhide. She prayed she would do a good enough job that Red Wolf would not laugh at her work. Again she felt the ignorant one. She knew how to mend the white woman's way, but this was an entirely different way of sewing, and she marveled at how sturdy Indian clothing seemed to be.

Many Bears finally returned from a hunt, bringing two rabbits with him. When he learned of Old Grandmother's death, he looked stricken with grief, and he went off to be alone. Cynthia watched Flowing Waters clean one rabbit, and she helped clean the second one herself. But she couldn't do as much as she would have liked because of her wounded hand. Flowing Waters insisted she must be careful using her hand too much for now. Cynthia was disappointed, for she wanted to show them she could be just as strong and do just as good a job as the Indian women. Or was it only Red Wolf to whom she wanted to prove herself?

In no time at all Basket Woman was making a good-smelling stew out of the rabbit meat, and when the sun fell behind the western mountains, all of them sat around a fire inside the tipi eating the stew. Cynthia sat slightly behind Red Wolf, feeling like a foreigner as the rest of them spoke in the Sioux tongue. She watched as Flowing Waters and Basket Woman put their children down for the night, and she saw the tender love the women felt toward their children. She marveled at the realization that she had seen no Indian children misbehaving that day. They were obedient and happy. She wondered if she would ever cease to be surprised by these people.

Then Flowing Waters began making up an extra bed of robes. "This will be for you and Red Wolf," she said matter-of-factly.

Cynthia's heart leaped with embarrassment and apprehension. They all thought she had already mated with Red Wolf! They expected them to sleep together! She turned wide, frightened eyes to Red Wolf, who only grinned, and suddenly all her good feelings toward him left her. She wanted to hit him for the look on his face, and she made up an excuse to go outside, wondering if she should try to run away. She moved into the darkness, wanting to cry, wondering which way to go, knowing how angry and probably embarrassed Red Wolf would be if she did try to run away. Maybe he would catch her, and then he truly would rape her out of anger.

In the next moment she heard his voice behind her. "We must sleep together, Cynthia. If we do not, they will know, and they will laugh at me and think me less a man for being too soft. I will not touch you wrongly."

She shivered, folding her arms protectively. "How can I believe you won't, when you'll be lying that close to me?"

"Because I have promised I will not. And I have told

181

you I would not touch you unless you were willing. Please come inside. It will be bad for me if you do not. And my heart is too full of grief over Old Grandmother for me to want any woman this night."

She found herself wondering just how many women he had been with, and it brought a surprising jealousy to her heart. But at the same time she could feel only fear at the thought of him taking her virginity. She wished she knew more about what it was like, wished she could understand how a woman could actually enjoy such a thing.

"Please don't be lying to me," she said, her voice shaky.

He came closer, putting a hand on her shoulders. "I do not lie."

He led her back to the tipi, and she felt herself literally shaking as they re-entered it. She felt clammy from nervousness. Already Flowing Waters and Basket Woman lay under blankets. Flowing Waters' arms were outside the blankets, and Cynthia saw that they were bare. Her eyes widened then as Many Bears removed all his clothing. Cynthia quickly turned away, and then Red Wolf was untying her tunic at the shoulders. She folded her arms tightly so that it fell only past her shoulders, and she quietly shook her head. Red Wolf turned her, and he saw the terror in her eyes. He leaned close to her ear.

"Trust me," he whispered.

She met his eyes and he smiled, not a victorious, lecherous smile, but one that was kind and loving. She wondered at the incredible fact that she was actually supposed to trust this savage who had killed men and had probably raped and killed women. She looked over at Many Bears, who had climbed under Flowing Waters' blankets, his back to Cynthia. She quickly dropped her tunic then jumped under her own blankets as fast as she could, but not quickly enough to keep Red Wolf from catching sight of her creamy breasts, and her round, white bottom. He almost groaned with the pain of wanting her. But he had made her a promise.

He undressed, while Cynthia lay curled up defensively, her back to him. Red Wolf smiled at her innocence and climbed in beside her, thinking how foolish he had been to promise he would not touch her wrongly. He turned his back to her and their bottoms touched. Cynthia felt as though fire was ripping through her veins. But she refused to acknowledge her feelings, for her fear of the unknown and of committing an atrocious sin was much stronger at the moment than the rippling desires Red Wolf stirred in her. How she managed to fall asleep at last she was not sure, but late in the night she was aroused by strange sounds from where Flowing Waters and Many Bears lay, almost as though someone were gasping with pain. She raised her head, and almost gasped at the sight of their naked bodies, Many Bears moving between Flowing Waters' legs.

She quickly turned away, scrunching down under the blankets and trying to cover her ears. Were Flowing Waters' groans and heavy breathing from pain or pleasure? She remembered the night she had caught her parents doing the same thing.

Red Wolf stirred and she curled up into an even tighter ball, sure that if he awakened and saw what Many Bears was doing, he would decide to do the same thing to her. She lay frozen for several minutes, and finally the sounds stopped. She heard soft laughter from Flowing Waters. She had apparently enjoyed it! There were a few murmured words, and then all was quiet again. Cynthia breathed a sigh of relief that Red Wolf seemed to have slept through it all. She fell asleep, unaware of the smile on Red Wolf's lips, for he had opened his eyes and had seen her lying with her hands over her ears.

Chapter Eleven

"We searched for two weeks, Reverend Wells, but there was no sign of the girl among any of the Indian villages we searched." A Lieutenant Wilson sat in a cushioned chair in the parlor of the preacher's home. "We were lucky to even be able to search those we did. The Indians are techinically at war right now, as you well know, over this mess of miners in the Black Hills. It's all we can do to keep up with the problems that has created without riding all over the Dakotas to find one girl."

"You mean—you're just going to give up?" Preacher Wells asked, his voice heavy with grief.

The man sighed deeply at the terrible sadness in the eyes of the preacher and his wife. "I'm terribly sorry to put it so bluntly, but I think you should face the fact that Cynthia is most likely dead somewhere. We checked a lot of mining camps, and none of them have been approached by any Sioux who wanted to trade the girl for something. That is usually what they do once they get their hands on a white woman or white children. They use them for ransom, to get guns or tobacco or whiskey—whatever. If they haven't approached someone by now, they apparently have nothing to trade, which means the girl is probably dead."

Preacher Wells held the man's eyes. "Tell me the other possibility. Could she be being held a prisoner?

Some kind of slave to some . . . some cruel Indian man?"

The lieutenant dropped his eyes. "I suppose that's a possibility."

Mabel Wells let out a pitiful groan and covered her face with her hands, while Alex stood aside listening, his lips puckering in anger and sorrow. Preacher Wells rose and walked to stand near a window.

"I don't know what to do," he said, his agony apparent in his voice. "She's been gone nearly six weeks now, what with the time it took to get help and the time it took you and your men to get into Indian country and back." He stared out across the open plains. "Six weeks." He swallowed back a lump in his throat. "The worst part is, we don't know whether to mourn her death or rejoice that she might still be alive. If she *is* alive, she might be better off dead." He shook his head. "I almost wish you would have found her body, Lieutenant."

Cynthia's mother burst into tears and left the room.

The lieutenant rose. "We'll keep doing what we can, Reverend. Between the miners coming and going, and our own Indian scouts, perhaps we will hear something more conclusive."

Wells turned to face the man. "If she is alive . . . what would it be like for her? Would it be constant torture?"

Wilson fingered his hat, wanting to give the reverend some kind of hope. "Not necessarily. If Cynthia is a smart girl, and brave, and you say she is both, she will quickly understand that cooperation is the key to staying alive. There is really no predicting an Indian, Reverend. She could be repeatedly raped by any number of bucks, or she could be claimed by just one who will keep her for a wife. The latter would be the most merciful. If it's just one man, and she cooperates, life would be bearable until she could find a way to escape." The man watched the preacher seem to wither. "I'm sorry to put it that way, but I know you want the truth. As long as your wife has left the room—"

Wells put up his hand. "I know. I know." He met the

186

man's eyes squarely. "Is that all?"

The lieutenant frowned. "Reverend, you don't want to put yourself through this."

"It's all right. I have to know what to pray for, what to be prepared for."

The lieutenant nodded. "Well, sir, sometimes captives are turned over to the Indian women to do with what they please. Sometimes they make her a slave to help with their chores. Sometimes they kill her, perhaps even out of jealousy, if one of their own husbands wants to keep the captive for a wife. Sometimes a captive will be tortured to death during some kind of celebration dance, but usually that is reserved for male captives. And sometimes . . ." The lieutenant hesitated.

"Yes, Lieutenant?"

"Well, sometimes a captive will stay with the Indians willingly."

"Willingly!"

"It's not unusual, especially if the captive is young enough. Some that have been captured as children become totally Indian in their ways and beliefs, and they are as impossible to tame as a real Indian. They refuse to come back to their own people and will fight them just as mightily as any full-blood. In a few instances young women captives have been known to willingly become a young buck's wife."

"You mean . . . *love* them? Have children by them?"

"Yes, sir. The most famous case is the Parker girl, down in Texas—captured by Comanche Indians, her whole family murdered. She was only nine. By the time she was found again, she was a full-grown woman, totally Indian at heart, with several children by her Indian husband. She tried several times to escape from her own people and go back to the Comanche. The famous Comanche leader, Quanah Parker, is her half-breed son. Of course, that was many, many years ago, but the fact is, those things can happen. But then she was only nine. Cynthia is what? Sixteen?"

187

Wells rubbed at his eyes. "Yes. And she was very pretty. And she was so spirited and brave. I just can't believe she's dead. But I don't want to believe the alternative." He met the lieutenant's eyes. "So what do we do now? Just wait?"

"I wish I could give you a better answer. But that's what it amounts to. We aren't giving up, Reverend. We will keep a constant lookout, keep asking questions, keep drilling the Indian scouts. And we are always out in the hills scouring for trouble. The Sioux refuse to accept the government's offer to buy up more Indian lands, and President Grant has ordered that all Sioux be rounded up and brought inside reservations lands. The trouble is, the Sioux won't recognize the last treaty and they refuse to come in. Rumor is General Crook himself will be coming out here to head an even stronger campaign to round up the Indians. Lieutenant-Colonel Custer is doing what he can in the meantime, and we have Shoshone and Crow scouts helping us. Finding one little girl isn't as easy as you might think, Reverend. It's a big country out there, and no one knows it better than the Sioux—every crook and cranny of it. And with more and more Cheyenne joining them, their numbers are getting bigger every day."

Wells put his hand on the lieutenant's arm. "I know you're doing your best. It's just . . . so hard . . . thinking about my sweet, innocent daughter in the hands of those fiends. I try so hard to tell myself I must love them, forgive them—tell myself they are God's children also. It was easy to say when I was removed from it. But now my daughter is at their mercy, and I wonder if the Indian even understands that word."

Wilson put a hand over the reverend's. "Many of them are more human than you might think, Reverend. They're a frightened, threatened people, and they would rather die than give this land over to the white man. They're angry, and when an Indian is angry, he knows of only one way to react, and that is through violence and

188

revenge. It's their way of life. But they can also be kind and loving, and very, very wise and prophetic. And there is hope for your daughter if she can find the young Indian man she rescued from a hanging. It's possible Red Wolf would help her. The Indian has a strong sense of justice. I am told Red Wolf has had some Christian teaching and that he speaks English. He is supposedly quite intelligent, albeit still as wild as the rest of them, but more intelligent, nonetheless."

"If she could find him, would he bring her back?" the reverend asked, new hope in his eyes.

"It's awfully hard to say. He might, after a time. He might be too afraid of reprisals right now. The memory of nearly getting hanged is still fresh in his mind. He might wait for things to cool down."

"And in the meantime?"

The lieutenant shook his head. "I can't say, Reverend. I just can't say. It's awfully hard to predict how an Indian will behave. But I'm sure he'll feel he owes her, so to speak. The problem is, we can't be sure she would even find him. There are a lot of Indians out there, moving about in different tribes. The only time most of them are all in one spot is during the summer celebrations farther north. But the mood they're in right now, no soldier detachment is going to go near a gathering like that. I'm afraid we just have to wait things out. But if Cynthia remains missing much longer, I wouldn't hold out too much hope that she's alive. I truly am sorry I can't give you better news."

"I know." Wells walked toward the exit and the lieutenant followed. "Thank you, Lieutenant, for your efforts. We'll stay right here in Deadwood, in case you come up with something. We aren't leaving until we know for certain what has happened to our Cynthia."

The two men shook hands. "I'll be sure to inform you of any news," Wilson promised. The man left, and Wells went back to stand near a window, while Alex went through the kitchen and back door, sitting down on the

189

back steps. He stared out over the endless horizon to the north, wondering if he would ever see his sister again.

They rode through wild, beautiful country, a land of rolling green hills with darker, forested hills to the west. The Sioux were headed for the summer celebrations, but were also hunting for buffalo as they journeyed. The first hunt had brought nothing, and Red Wolf had sulked angrily for days over the scarcity of game because of the white man.

Cynthia had lost all track of time, except that she was sure two full moons had come and gone since she was captured, or was it three? She wondered what her parents would think if they knew she was dressed and living as an Indian; if they knew that the notorious Crazy Horse rode with the very tribe she rode with.

It seemed to Cynthia that the Indians' numbers were swelling daily as other tribes joined them along the way, many of them Cheyenne. She sometimes walked with Flowing Waters beside the various travois that carried their belongings and the littlest children; and sometimes she rode a horse beside Red Wolf, who owned several horses, and very proudly, for several of them had been stolen from Crow or Pawnee, some from whites.

Cynthia had lost all fear of Red Wolf and the others. She had slept beside Red Wolf many nights, and had worked right alongside Flowing Waters and Basket Woman, learning the ways of an Indian woman. Her hands were becoming calloused, and her fair skin was turning from red to a softer brown. She wore her hair in a thick braid down her back most of the time to keep it out of her face, especially when helping skin and cut up an animal. She became adept with a knife, and learned the many uses of an animal, and she marveled at how the Indians wasted nothing.

Memories of home and family were fading, for the world she had once known now seemed like only a dream.

She was beginning to enjoy this life of freedom. Red Wolf and Flowing Waters had taught her many things, and Red Wolf had become a patient, devoted friend. There were no more teasing words about mating, and Cynthia wondered at times if he had lost all interest in that. She told herself it was best, and yet strangely, it upset her. On several occasions she had awakened to lovemaking between Many Bears and Flowing Waters or Basket Woman, and she had seen no ill effects on the women. In fact, they seemed quite happy and contented the next day. Her own curiosity was nudging her.

But it was more than curiosity. She was seeing Red Wolf in a different light. He was not a savage warrior who might rape or kill her. He was simply a young man like any other young man, and one who had become a friend with whom she could talk. Together they had talked of the differences between white man and red, talked about what life was like back East where Cynthia had once lived, talked about the history of the Sioux. Through Red Wolf Cynthia had learned a great deal of Sioux beliefs, and could even speak and understand some of their words. She had developed a great sympathy for their viewpoint, and most important, she saw them as human beings, angry, frightened, confused, threatened.

Most of all she saw Red Wolf as a young man who was capable of loving, a young man who, in spite of his warrior ways, understood compassion and had shown it to Cynthia. Every day it was becoming more difficult to ignore the feelings he stirred deep inside her young body; more difficult to ignore Red Wolf's undeniable hand-someness, his hard, muscular build, the softness that sometimes showed in his deep-set, dark eyes. There was an earthy scent about him, a certain power that emanated from him, a masculine strength about him that ran deeper than just the physical. He was a young man who was also strong on the inside. And no matter how Cynthia tried to keep from admitting to herself that she was attracted to Red Wolf sexually, the lovely ripples of desire would not stop teasing her whenever he came close, his long hair hanging loose, his lips full and sensuous, the little bells tied into the fringes of his clothing seeming to beckon her.

Red Wolf seemed to fit his homeland perfectly, as wild and beautiful as the land, his skin matching the red earth.

"We are getting stronger," he said then as he rode beside her. "More and more Cheyenne join us." He pointed to a contingent of Indians approaching them from the west. "One day we will be so strong, all white men will have to leave. Already we have chased many of them out. Some day we will also send the Pahuska away, no?"

Red Wolf grinned, and Cynthia smiled back at him. She knew by now that Pahuska meant Long-hair Custer and his soldiers.

"Maybe you will, Red Wolf," she answered. "But you had better take me back to my parents when you chase out all the whites, or I might never find them again."

His dark eyes moved over her, drinking in the soft, pale skin of her slender leg, which showed from her tunic, pulled up while she rode. He met her eyes then, his own showing disappointment. "So, you still wish to return to them?"

Cynthia sobered, looking straight ahead then. "It wouldn't be right to just stay with you forever, Red Wolf. I have learned many things, and I've grown to like your people. I even like this life, this freedom. It's exciting and different, and I've learned so much—things I could use to help the Indians when I return to my own people." She faced him again. "But I am still white, Red Wolf. I don't really belong here. You know that."

"And you still have no feelings for Red Wolf?"

Cynthia reddened, turning away again. How could she tell him? She must not! It wasn't right. It just wasn't right. Her mind must be playing tricks on her. It was all a part of the hypnotic effect these people and this life had had on her. She had lost all her senses. Suddenly a strong

192

arm was whisking her off her horse, and she gave out a little scream as Red Wolf set her in front of him on his own horse, holding her sideways and keeping a powerful arm about her middle.

"Red Wolf has strong feelings for Cynthia," he told her in a voice gruff with desire.

"Red Wolf, don't," she told him, keeping her head turned away. "You've left me alone all this time."

"Yes, and it has not been without great suffering!" he answered. "How many more nights must I lie naked beside the woman I desire, the woman I wish to have for a wife?"

Cynthia looked at him in surprise. They had been simply good friends all this time. He had not spoken of these things since those first couple of teasing days after he took her from the tipi where she had been held captive.

"Surely you have known how I feel, Cynthia," he told her. His horse slowly moved with the rest of the procession, but neither of them seemed aware of their surroundings at the moment.

"Red Wolf, you promised you would leave me alone." She looked down. "You said that after a while, if I still wanted to go back, you would take me."

"Yes, I promised. And I will still keep it. But that does not mean I cannot try to make you stay." She shook her head, but he pressed his arm tighter. "The spirits mean for us to be together, Cynthia. That is why you came and cut me loose that night, and why you ended up in my village. We are meant to be together. I have seen your goodness, your strength, your bravery. I have never wanted a white woman this way, and I do not know how right or wrong it is for an Indian man to love a white woman. But such are the feelings I have for you. I do not want to take you back—not ever! Please say you will stay with me!"

Cynthia looked at the difference in skin color where her hand rested against his powerful forearm. Surely it

193

was wrong! But his words cut deep into her heart. This wild Indian man was baring his soul to her. He had done it in many other ways, in telling her about his people, his fears, his beliefs—but never so clearly had he spoken of his feelings for her.

"I . . . I need to think, Red Wolf. I'm all confused."

"Tell me you do not have strong feelings for Red Wolf. Tell me you have not thought of turning to me in the night and letting Red Wolf come inside of you."

"Don't!" she whispered, shaking her head.

"Look at me, Cynthia." His grip tightened, and she reluctantly met his eyes. "I told you I would wait until you were willing. Now we are close, one in spirit, for we have spoken many days and nights about what is in our hearts. We have shared our God, our sorrows, our beliefs. The only thing we have not shared is our bodies. Tell me you never think about sharing your body with Red Wolf. Tell me, if you are able to so boldly lie."

Their eyes held, and her body felt on fire. He moved a hand over her belly and upward, pushing up on one breast, desire ripping through him at its full softness through the tunic. Cynthia grasped his wrists and jumped down from the horse, running back to join Flowing Waters.

Scouts rode up then, before Red Wolf could turn and ride back to Cynthia. They spoke excitedly, and then Red Wolf rode off with them. Cynthia felt suddenly disappointed, but also afraid—afraid of her own feelings, for she was not at all sure she could have resisted Red Wolf if they had been alone.

"What is happening?" she asked Flowing Waters.

"The scouts say they have found a herd of buffalo. We will make camp soon and the men will go on the hunt. Now you will see what the buffalo hunt is like— learn to skin a whole buffalo and what we do with all the parts." She smiled. "Red Wolf will kill as many as he can. He is anxious to have enough skins so that we can make a dwelling where he can be alone with you. He

194

tells us the reason he does not mate with you in our tipi is that white women think it is wrong to mate unless no one else is around. Is this so?"

Cynthia knew it would cause Red Wolf much embarrassment if she told Flowing Waters the truth. "Yes," she answered, her cheeks reddening.

"Then we must quickly sew together enough hides for your own dwelling, so Red Wolf can be happy with his woman."

Cynthia watched Red Wolf join several Sioux and Cheyenne men, yipping and celebrating the finding of a herd. Again she felt she had somehow lost total control of herself. Red Wolf was right. She had thought about sharing her body with him, but only in dreams and fantasies. She never looked at it realistically, but she could not deny the glorious feeling she had experienced when his hand touched her breast. Her eyes teared at the thought of her parents. If she gave herself to Red Wolf, she could never go back. Never. It had come down to making a choice, and she was not at all sure anymore that she could continue to choose her parents and her old life.

This time the hunt was successful. The work involved for the women was to Cynthia unbelievably hard, and she scowled at Red Wolf, who sat near a fire with a circle of men smoking a pipe, while the women worked rigorously with the skins and meat that had been brought back to camp, also by women, after first gutting and skinning the great beasts where they lay slaughtered far from the village.

For the Indians it was a time of great celebrating, even for the women, in spite of the work. Anytime a good supply of meat was found, it was a time for rejoicing. Cynthia had to admit deep inside that she'd been relieved when Red Wolf came back unharmed, for just before his arrival two warriors had returned badly wounded—one from being thrown from his horse by a charging buffalo, another with several broken bones from being thrown when his horse stumbled into a buffalo wallow.

"Often a hunter is killed," Flowing Waters had told Cynthia. "I always pray for Many Bears when he goes on the hunt."

Upon seeing one of the great beasts up close, Cynthia could well understand the danger of hunting them. She had been in this land for several months, but this was her first close view of a buffalo. Now came the task of learning its many uses: the meat, smoked, dried, made into jerky and pemmican; the hide, tanned and used for all forms of shelter, containers, and wearing apparel; the horns, made into cups, ladles, spoons, rattles; the bones, used for knives, arrowheads, shovels, sled runners, war clubs, awls, tool handles, and some for ceremonial objects; the hair for padding, ropes, and headdresses; the hooves for glue; the tail for fly brushes and whips; the bladder and stomach for pouches, water vessels, cooking vessels; the sinew for thread and bowstrings; the brains for tanning hides; and dried buffalo chips for fuel and ceremonial smoking.

The uses of the buffalo seemed endless, and the Indians' ability to turn all parts into useful objects was astounding and something to be admired. Never before had Cynthia been so struck by the importance of this animal to the survival of Red Wolf's people.

The sun set behind the western mountains, and there was still much work to be done. But first came the celebrating. Cynthia felt as though it were all a strange dream, being in the midst of the rhythmic drumming and the wild chanting and singing. Warriors danced around a huge central campfire, including Red Wolf, who was now a full member of the Strong Heart Society and wore eagle feathers in his hair. He had proven his manhood by snatching the eagle feathers himself from a high mountaintop two years earlier when his people visited the "land of the bubbling waters" far to the west.

"Yellowstone," Cynthia told him. "My people also consider it a special place."

Soon Red Wolf's people would celebrate another Sun Dance. Cynthia hoped she would not have to witness the bloody ritual. Still, when she thought about Red Wolf suffering that way, it brought forth again the wicked desires he stirred in her, for he was surely strong and brave.

Cynthia retired to Many Bears' tipi, while outside the frenzied dancing and wild singing continued, rising in crescendo, building in its excitement, the drums growing louder. Some of the Indian men were drinking whiskey, and Cynthia suddenly did not want to be seen. Would some of them suddenly change their minds and decide to add to their celebrations by burning a white girl at the stake? Their wild, seemingly heathen celebrating frightened her, for in all this time she had never been among so many of them at once, nor in the midst of such seemingly uncontrolled celebrating. Cynthia wanted to remain as unnoticed as possible. She had already washed her hands and arms of buffalo blood, and she moved under the robes of her bed, a terrible weariness coming over her after the hardest day's work she had ever experienced.

Her aching body was fast approaching sleep when she was suddenly aware of the presence of another inside the tipi. She opened her eyes to see Red Wolf standing over her.

"Red Wolf! I thought you would be celebrating half the night. The drumming frightens me. I'm just going to go to sleep."

Red Wolf knelt closer, and she could smell whiskey on his breath. Her heart beat in alarm and she curled up. "I will continue my celebrating in here, with my woman," he told her.

"Go away," Cynthia told him. "Not this way, Red Wolf."

He leaned over her, a silly grin on his handsome face. "There is only one way, white woman. And you have kept me from you long enough. You want Red Wolf, and Red Wolf wants Cynthia."

He yanked away her covers and grabbed her close, rolling on top of her.

"No!" Cynthia screamed. "Please, not like this!"

She pushed at him, but he buried his face in her neck, licking at her skin, while one hand moved under her, over her bottom. He pushed up her tunic, grasping at untouched places, while Cynthia screamed and fought him. She pulled hard on his hair, then butted him in the chin with her head. Red Wolf cried out and rolled off her, just drunk enough to be too slow to catch Cynthia as she quickly jumped up. She grabbed up a lance lying nearby, and she held it defensively.

"Touch me again and I'll kill you with this!" she screamed at him. "I mean it!"

Red Wolf stared at her angrily. "You want Red Wolf. I can see it in your eyes!"

"I don't want you this way—all whiskied up and forcing me," she yelled back, her eyes tearing. "You've taught me not to be afraid of you, and now I know I have to be!"

Red Wolf rose, blinking, looking confused, his anger seeming to leave him. "No, Cynthia." He rubbed at his eyes. "You do not have to be afraid of me. I thought . . . when Indian women celebrate such a great hunt, it is common to mate . . . out of joy and happiness."

"I'm *not* an Indian woman!" Cynthia ran outside, hurrying around the tipi into the darkness, her heart pounding with a mixture of fear and desire, for she could still remember the feel of Red Wolf's hands at her bottom, the fiery desires at the feel of his tongue licking at her neck. But it was too sudden, too forceful. And she didn't want him touching her because of whiskey. Now she was afraid she had angered him too deeply. Perhaps he would come after her, hand her over to the other men, and say he was done with her, tired of her objections. He might send her back to the place where all the men come and use captives! She ran through the darkness, hardly aware of where she was going, until suddenly she tripped and fell. She felt something hard slam into her forehead as she pitched to the ground. Then all was darkness.

Chapter Twelve

Cynthia's mind swirled with visions of the paintings inside a tipi, her parents and brother and home, a gutted buffalo, dancing, chanting Indians, horses and dogs, joy and terror, and the face of a young Indian man close to hers. At times she heard voices, but could not seem to open her eyes.

"Why did she run away?" a woman was asking.

"The drumming frightened her," said a man's voice. "She thought we were going to hurt her."

She recognized the voice, and something about the answer didn't sound right, but she couldn't reason why at the moment. She did remember running, but from what?

Something cool was placed on her forehead.

"If she does not come awake soon, it could be very bad," said the woman's voice again. "Two Dogs will come back soon and sing over her again and make the magic smoke. Her spirit has run away, Red Wolf. Only her body lies here. We must pray for her spirit to return."

"*Ai*," came the soft reply. "My heart will be sad if it does not come back."

"You are her friend. I do not understand why she would run from you. Surely she knows you would not hurt her."

There was no answer.

*　　*　　*

Cynthia blinked open her eyes to see an old Indian man shaking something over her and chanting. She let out what she thought was a scream, but it was a mere moan. She tried to rise, but the pain in her head forced her back down. The Indian man said something to her she did not understand, and then quickly left. Moments later Red Wolf came inside alone. Cynthia's first memory on seeing him was of his attack on her, and she made a little whimpering sound, trying to scoot away from him.

"Do not be afraid of me," he said softly, kneeling down beside her and taking her hand against her will. "I will not hurt you, Cynthia."

"You're a liar," she answered weakly, her eyes tearing.

"No. I drank the firewater. It put a wicked spirit in me. I will not drink it again. This is my promise."

She turned her face away. "I don't believe you anymore. I just want to go home."

Red Wolf sighed deeply. "All right then. I will take you."

She faced him again, her eyes wide with surprise. "You will?"

He put a big hand to the side of her face. "When I found you hurt, and thought you would die, my heart was sad, for it was my fault. And now you will never be able to have the feelings for me that I have for you. And I cannot go on wanting you as I do and not touching you. You are unhappy here, and now you have bad feelings for Red Wolf. I broke my promise to you. I will take you back as soon as you are well enough to travel."

Cynthia swallowed, her mind racing with indecision. She had not really expected him to say he would take her back. "What if you get caught?"

He shrugged. "I will have done the right thing. My feelings for you are too deep for me to trade you to cruel whiskey traders or to another warrior. I have no choice left but to take you back to your family and hope I do not get caught. If I do, then so be it. I will die knowing you are safe and happy."

Cynthia put a hand to her forehead, wincing with pain and feeling a lump there.

"You were badly hurt," Red Wolf told her. "You have been lying with no spirit for almost three days. I did not think your spirit would return to you. My heart is happy to see you awake and speaking. Wakan Tanka has smiled upon me and has granted me my prayer." He smoothed the hair back from her face, and Cynthia noticed cuts on his arms.

"What happened to you?" she asked.

"It was my sacrifice to the spirits to make you well."

Cynthia frowned. "You did that for me?"

His only reply was a soft smile. Cynthia wondered at his rugged strength, all the scars that were signs of his suffering in the ritual of manhood and in his grief over Old Grandmother, and now over *her;* as well as a scar on his left arm and one just above his right knee from battles with the Crow and with miners. It felt strange to know he had actually sacrificed his blood for her.

"Soon we will move farther north for the celebrations," he was telling her. "When the village moves on, I will ride south with you and you will be done with your unhappiness." He moved back from her. "Are you hungry? Thirsty?"

Cynthia watched him move toward a pouch of water. He was again the Red Wolf she had come to know well over the past two months, not the Red Wolf who had attacked her. He wore only leggings—no shirt. He retrieved a ladle of water and came back to her. She noticed his lean, muscular stomach, the strong arms decorated with copper bands. He shook his hair back from his handsome face as he bent closer. "Here. You should have some water."

Their eyes held as he gently grasped her behind the neck and raised her head just slightly. He put the ladle to her lips and she drank a little. He set the ladle aside then, moving his other arm under her shoulders to support her as he leaned over her.

"I am sorry, Cynthia. I did not mean for it to be that way. But perhaps you are right after all. Our worlds are too different. I must take you back." He leaned even closer and pressed his cheek to hers. "I will miss you," he whispered.

Cynthia remembered with mixed feelings how it felt when his hand touched her bottom. What would it be like if he had done so gently, if she were willing? He seemed so genuinely sorry now. Again his soft, human side surfaced, so that he was hardly any different from the way a young white man would surely be in the same situation. In fact, there were white men she was much more afraid of than this Indian.

Red Wolf rose and left her then, and she lay quietly looking around at all the items hanging from their places inside the tipi—quivers and bows, parfleches filled with supplies, a cradleboard, Indian clothing. There were paintings of bears and streams and the sun on the tipi skins, and outside she could hear the noises that had become familiar to her now—barking dogs and laughing children, horses thundering past, men and women speaking in a tongue foreign to her. She had come to understand a few words, such as *wasicus* for white man, *sotaju* for smoke, Pahuska for Long-hair Custer. She had seen the Sioux as simply human beings, with feelings no different from her white relations; and with beliefs and customs deeply ingrained, beliefs and customs the whites thought could be changed in a matter of days with the right religious teaching and if the Indians would simply live like the white man. But she knew now that the Indian spirit was mighty, and determined, and their ways had been practiced for hundreds, perhaps thousands of years. They could no more adapt to the white man's ways in a short time than white men could suddenly learn to live like Indians.

Her eyes teared, for she realized she had grown to love them all. She was not really sure she wanted to go home now, and that brought on feelings of guilt, for surely her family was sick with worry and grief. But life with the Sioux and Cheyenne was not so terrible, and she had experienced a wonderful freedom. She saw the land through different eyes, recognized its beauty and sacredness with much more clarity than she ever had before. Everything was so changed now. She knew she could never go back and be the same Cynthia who left, and the thought of rejoining her old life sounded suddenly dull and burdensome, with so many rules and schedules. Back home it seemed almost a sin to laugh, but these Sioux laughed readily. It seemed they were always teasing one another, telling stories, laughing in spite of their sorry state, for they were a hunted harassed people who never knew if they would find enough food to stay alive.

Now she realized why there had been such a celebration after having such a successful hunt. Now she understood why Red Wolf had drunk the whiskey. Finding a good supply of food was like realizing a victory over the white man. It meant the Indian could keep going, keep fighting. She had watched the pipe ceremony, had seen with her own eyes an eagle come to circle right over the heads of praying warriors. Surely these people had a connection with nature that white men could never grasp. And surely this beautiful land through which she had traveled with Red Wolf belonged to the Sioux. It was no wonder they were so angry over the intrusion of the white miners, who tore up the land with their picks and explosives.

It all came to her so clearly now, as though the blow to her head had made her think better, understand better. The Sioux belonged in this land and the white man had no right trying to steal it away. She thought about the grin on Red Wolf's face the night he attacked her. He was simply happy, celebrating the generosity of the buffalo spirit, which had provided much food and other needed items for them by allowing its herd to be found. He was celebrating life, for that was what the buffalo represented to these people.

A tear slipped down the side of her face, for what she realized most of all was that she was falling in love with Red Wolf. She was committing one of the greatest sins a white Christian girl could commit. But was it wrong to love? Weren't these people God's children, just like the Bible said, like her father had preached? Was there some purpose for her being here, and could she really leave Red Wolf now? Surely he loved her. He was going to risk his life to take her back, and he had cut himself when he prayed for her life. Of course! It was not a joke. Red Wolf really did love her, and more and more she had been unable to look at him as an Indian. He was simply a young man who loved her and would probably die for her if he had to. And she loved him.

But it was surely wrong! She had already told him she wanted to go back, and now he was agreeing to take her. Yes, this was the time to let it be, the time to do things the right way. She must take advantage of his willingness to take her back, and then she would end all of this. She would be back where she belonged, and she would still be untouched. In time she would surely forget these feelings she had for Red Wolf, and she would be left with the memory of her exciting life among the Sioux Indians. She would have grand stories to tell her children and grandchildren, and she would have a new understanding of these people that she could share with those who had to deal with them, and with missionaries who wanted to Christianize them.

Why, of course! That must be what God wanted of her—to understand these people enough that she could come back one day as a missionary and teach them. Surely that was her reason for being here, for going through all the terror and then the learning, and the loving. Now Red Wolf would take her back and she would be much wiser and more experienced. People would come to her to learn about the Indians. Back East she would be envied and questioned, a center of attention. For she,

Cynthia Wells, had lived among the Sioux Indians, during a period when they were literally at war with the whites!

Red Wolf came back inside, carrying a bowl of stew. He sat down beside her. "You must eat something."

He set the bowl down and reached around her, stacking robes and blankets under her shoulders so that she could sit up slightly. Her head hurt again, but not as much, and she breathed deeply of his sweet scent as he leaned close to her. Yes, she loved him, in spite of his attack, for that had not been the Red Wolf she knew. She loved him, but she must never tell him so. He'd said he would take her home. She would leave it at that. It was the only right thing to do.

He picked up the bowl then and started feeding her. She swallowed some from a spoon made of buffalo bone, and her heart pained at the sorrow and disappointment in Red Wolf's eyes. Surely he was hoping she would change her mind. Why would an Indian man love a white girl? Was it the same for him? Did he just look at her as a young woman he loved and wanted, forgetting that she was white? Didn't he realize it was just as wrong for him as it was for her?

"When will we leave?" she asked.

He hesitated, just staring at her for a moment with dark eyes that made her insides melt. "Two or three days, if you can travel by then."

"Fine," she answered. She swallowed back a strange lump in her throat. "It's best, you know."

His eyes looked watery. "I know."

"I think I understand," Flowing Waters told Cynthia, as she packed some food into a leather bag for Cynthia and Red Wolf. "If whites stole me away, I would want to come back to my people, even if I should learn to love a white man."

Cynthia did not reply. Flowing Waters thought she

207

loved and had mated with Red Wolf. Now the first part of that belief was true, but Cynthia didn't want to think about it. She was leaving, and that was that. She felt as though she were in some kind of trance, her movements directed by some outside being, her body moving mechanically. She didn't really want to go! But how could she tell them otherwise? And it was the right thing to do. She missed her parents and brother terribly, but now she realized how much she would miss these people—little Gray Horse and Little Arrow, Little Beaver and Crying Owl—such beautiful children, their faces animated with joy and innocence, little knowing what must surely lie ahead for them. She would miss Basket Woman and Flowing Waters, who had taught her so much. The tipi they had been making for Cynthia and Red Wolf was nearly completed, but Red Wolf would share it with someone else eventually.

Cynthia tried to ignore the terrible jealous feelings that created deep inside. It was only right that Red Wolf take an Indian wife and that she go home and someday marry a white man. She kept telling herself she must not acknowledge her feelings for the handsome young Indian man who had managed to wedge his way into her heart.

They walked outside, and Basket Woman began taking down the tipi. The village was preparing to move on. This was the last Cynthia would see of these people she had come to call friend. Flowing Waters held out the beautifully beaded parfleche full of food.

"You must keep the parfleche when it is empty," she told Cynthia. "It is my gift to you. I made it from the hide of one of the buffalo Red Wolf killed. Do you like the beadwork?"

Cynthia's eyes teared. "It's beautiful. How did you sew on so many beads so quickly?"

"I sacrificed much sleep," Flowing Waters answered. "I wanted very much for you to have something from me when you go back, so that you do not forget me."

Cynthia met the young woman's eyes. How incredible

that they were so much alike in so many ways. Cynthia had come to look at the young Indian woman as just a friend, like any girlfriend she might have in her own world.

"Thank you, Flowing Waters. I don't have anything to give you in return."

"I know. It is enough that you gave your knife to Old Grandmother."

Basket Woman walked up to them, handing out a beaded belt. "Please accept my gift," she told Cynthia through Flowing Waters. "Your good spirit will always be with us, even though you are gone in body."

Before Cynthia could answer, other women approached her, handing out gifts of beaded necklaces, a tunic, hair ornaments, more food, a knife, a deerskin blanket. Cynthia could make no reply, for the lump in her throat was too big. But her tears and her smiles told the Indian women of her gratefulness. Flowing Waters helped Red Wolf pack the gifts onto the extra horse he would take along as a pack horse. All too quickly Red Wolf was lifting Cynthia onto the lead horse. He eased up behind her then, and women and children ran along beside them for a ways, smiling and waving, shouting things in the Sioux tongue. Cynthia bent down and hugged Flowing Waters once more as the young woman ran alongside Red Wolf's horse.

"I'll tell all my friends about you—my best friend among the Sioux," she told Flowing Waters. "I'll tell my father to tell the soldiers to leave you alone. I'll have him write the President." She was yelling now as Flowing Waters fell behind. "I'll tell them to make people stay out of the Black Hills!"

They crested a hill. Cynthia kept looking back around Red Wolf's shoulder until she could no longer see the village. Never had her loyalties been so torn. She turned back then, staring straight ahead, while Red Wolf's arm tightened around her, and again she forced back an urge to admit to the truth. She must hang on. She must get home and end this craziness, get her mind and heart back to normal. Her head ached with a need to turn to Red Wolf and tell him she loved him, that she didn't want to go home after all. But she told herself to be strong, very strong. She must do what was right for the Christian daughter of a man of God. She must be wise, for surely, after all she had been through, she was a woman now, and not the innocent girl who had been stolen away.

They traveled for a week, and Red Wolf was strangely quiet and remote. When he talked, it was only about the land. He would point out distant mountains and ridges that the Sioux used for landmarks, and he told her stories of his boyhood. He told her more about his encounters with the missionaries at Fort Laramie, and some humorous stories of run-ins with white settlers. Cynthia talked more about her way of life, and how she wondered what people would think of her when she returned.

Red Wolf made no attempt to change her mind, and he spoke no more of wanting her. At night he made up separate sleeping mats for them. Cynthia thought how frightened she would be if she were lying out on the open plains in the darkness this way alone. But she was not afraid with Red Wolf along. He knew this land, every inch of it, even in the night. He knew every sound, and he seemed to be able to smell the presence of an animal before it even showed itself.

Cynthia knew he was doing the same thing she was doing—trying to harden himself against his feelings. He had promised to take her back, and that was exactly what he would do. She felt sorry for the lonely look on his face, for the loss of his grandmother was still fresh in his heart. She felt almost as though she should stay and take care of him, for even though he was brave and skilled in the hunt and in making war, he should have a woman to come back to, a woman to mend his clothes and moccasins, to cook for him, and to . . .

She shook away the thought as they moved now through thickly forested hills. The sun was setting. It was time to make camp again. An hour later he drew the horses to a halt and dismounted. "Get a fire together," he told her. "I am going to see if I can find some fresh meat before it is completely dark. I want to save the dried meat in our supplies if I can."

He took a quiver of arrows from his gear and slung it around his shoulder, then took up his bow. His dark eyes met her own then. "Do not be afraid. I will not be far away."

Their eyes held. "I'm not afraid."

His eyes moved over her strangely, and then he nodded and left. Cynthia wondered at how she heard no sound at all as he took off through the trees. She turned and began gathering some sticks for a fire. She soon had one going, then began unloading needed supplies from the horses. She tied the animals and made up two beds, then built a stand over the fire with notched branches, from which she would be able to hang a kettle.

She sat down and watched the fire then, thinking how pleasant and peaceful this journey had been compared to her rough and frightening journey north with Many Bears. It was all different now. She was going home. But she wondered if it would still feel like home, if she could ever look at her own people in the same way again. She wished there were not these cold, hardened feelings between herself and Red Wolf. She did not want to leave him this way, the old feeling of warm friendship gone. It had changed. It was as though if they couldn't be lovers, then they couldn't be friends either. She was proud of how strong she had been about the whole matter, but her heart was sad over losing some of the special joy she had found in being friends with him.

She rested her head on her knees, staring at the fire, then looked up when she heard the sound of horses approaching. She rose, alarmed. More Indians? What if they were enemy Indians? They would kill Red Wolf and

211

steal her away, and her fate could be a hundred times worse than it had been with the Sioux! She backed toward the horses, intending to inch her way to the pack horse, where the rifle was kept, even though she was not at all sure how to use it. But all too quickly four riders came over a ridge just ahead of her—white men!

They seemed to have been riding hard, apparently unaware anything was up ahead of them. The leader drew up his horse, staring at Cynthia in surprise.

"What the —"

The other three men rode up beside him, all four of them staring at Cynthia.

"You see what I see, Rex?" one of them asked.

"A white girl—wearin' Indian dress!"

"It's her, I bet! She's the one them soldiers was askin' about down south of here!"

The lead rider grinned, his eyes moving over her. "Could be." He rode a little closer. "What's your name, girl? You the one got stole from Deadwood?"

Cynthia remained speechless. She knew men like this. They were the kind who had dragged Red Wolf down the street in Deadwood. If they knew he was close by . . .

She shook her head.

"Damned Indians probably got her all mixed up," one of them spoke up.

The one called Rex grinned. "Yeah. Probably from rapin' her till she was crazy."

They looked at each other and snickered.

"Hey, Rex, you best look out. She ain't alone. No little white girl would be travelin' alone like this, two fine horses—plenty of gear. They's two beds made up here."

Rex turned his eyes to search their surroundings. "Most likely just one Indian—and most likely a buck. If he comes back and finds us here, he won't hang around. He'll take off like a scared rabbit." The man dismounted walking closer to Cynthia, who stared at him wide-eyed. He needed a shave, and he wore knee-high boots and a red flannel shirt. A floppy hat dangled over his unkempt hair, and he grinned at her through yellow teeth.

"How about it, missy? You travelin' with some big buck that's been layin' on you? You can tell us. We'll get rid of him for you."

"You get out of here!" Cynthia managed to squeak out.

The man chuckled and turned to the others. "Looks to me like we found us somethin' better than gold for the time being," he told them. He looked back at Cynthia as the others laughed and dismounted. "Here's how it goes, missy. We have us a fine time with you, then we kill you and tell the white folks back at Deadwood that we found you raped and murdered by the Indians. Ain't nobody gonna' think any different, and we've had ourselves a dandy time." He licked at his lips. "Fact is, we can keep you long as we want. Don't matter much when we claim we found you." He leaned closer. "Now all you got to do is tell us who you're with and where he went."

Cynthia prayed Red Wolf was close by. But even if he was, how could he fight all four of these men? They would kill him! Not Red Wolf! "I'm alone," she sneered, trying to appear brave.

In a flash the man's arm flew forward, and he grasped her around her tiny neck with a big, strong hand, squeezing. "Don't lie, little girl, else we'll make it all the worse for you, you hear? Now who are you with and where did he go?"

Cynthia grasped at his wrists with both hands but could do nothing. She kicked at him, but he only laughed and squeezed harder. Suddenly there came a whirring sound and a thud, and the man grasping at her neck went still, his eyes bulging. He staggered slightly, then fell forward, an arrow in the middle of his back. His fall knocked Cynthia down with him, and she scrambled away gasping for breath.

"Sonuvabitch!" someone cursed.

There came another whir and a thud, and a second man went down. Cynthia looked up to see Red Wolf then. He

213

came crashing through the trees, giving out a piercing war cry. He headed for a third man, wielding his knife. The man scrambled to get a hand gun from his belt, and Cynthia grabbed up a thick branch from the ground. The fourth man let off a shot at Red Wolf just as Red Wolf landed into the third man. The shot nicked Red Wolf in the left arm, and Cynthia saw the blood spatter as the force of the shot knocked Red Wolf slightly away from the third man, who then pulled his pistol from his belt while the fourth man scrambled to re-load his own pistol.

Everything was happening in only seconds. Cynthia was by then close to the fourth man, and she whacked his arm hard with the tree branch, while Red Wolf threw his knife. It landed with a thud in the third man's heart. Blood spurted in every direction as the man went down. Cynthia's blow to the last man had caused him to drop his pistol. He let out a string of curses as Cynthia kept swinging the tree branch at him, whacking at him about the head. He finally grabbed the branch away from her and started to hit her with it. But at the same time a shot rang out, and a hole opened up in the man's forehead.

Cynthia shuddered and stared as he stumbled backward and fell dead. For a few seconds everything was suddenly silent. In a matter of seconds all four men lay dead, and Cynthia realized they would have brought her more harm than any Indian men had brought to her.

She turned, seeing Red Wolf standing a few feet away, a smoking pistol still in his hand. He had picked up the third man's gun and used it to kill the remaining attacker. He stood there panting, blood pouring down his left arm, and it hit Cynthia with full reality how she would have felt if Red Wolf had been killed.

She ran to him then, and he swept her up in his good arm while she hugged him around the neck. "Red Wolf!" she whimpered.

"I am all right. What about you?"

"I am all right, I think. They were going to rape me and

kill me and blame it on you!" She pulled back a little. "When I saw them shoot you . . ." She touched his arm above the wound. "Oh, Red Wolf, you're bleeding."

"It is just the flesh."

She met his eyes, and she knew he saw the love there. "I cannot take you back now," he told her. "Not after this. When these men are found, their friends will be very angry. If we were found, they would kill me, and they might do to you what these men were going to do. Now it is too dangerous not just for me, but for you too. I am sorry, Cynthia."

She lay her head against his chest. "It's all right. I don't want to go back now anyway. I didn't even want to leave before, but I thought I was doing the right thing. Now I'm afraid too. Take me back to your people, Red Wolf. We'd be safe if we stay with the whole village."

"This is truly your wish?"

She looked up at him, studying his handsome face, the way his hair fell across it in wisps when the wind blew it. She reached up and pushed a piece of it back. "You fought for me today. When I thought that man was going to kill you, I knew how much I love you, Red Wolf." Her eyes teared. "Wrong as it might be, I can't leave you. I think it's like you said. I think we're supposed to be together."

His eyes lit up with joy. "*Ai.* Your words make my heart sing." He pulled away from her. "Come. We will speak of these things later. We must leave this place quickly. There might be more of them. If we are lucky, it will be a long time before these men are found."

Cynthia moved as if in a daze. She had admitted her love for Red Wolf. There was no going back now. She could no longer bury her feelings. She felt like an Indian herself now, as she moved among the dead bodies of white men. She had actually had a part in this! She might even be as wanted as Red Wolf. She had actually defended an Indian man against white men!

She was certain no one in Deadwood would believe her

215

story—that the white men would have brought her more harm than Red Wolf. Most of the people of Deadwood were already against her for freeing Red Wolf in the first place. She would be considered just as guilty as Red Wolf. People were so ready to believe that all Indians were bad.

They quickly picked up all their gear. Cynthia tied a piece of cloth around Red Wolf's wound. Red Wolf took food and tobacco from the white men's gear, as well as their guns and ammunition. Cynthia was surprised to find herself helping him pilfer the dead men's supplies.

"I should take the horses, but they might be recognized, and they would leave too much of a trail," Red Wolf told her. "We will leave them." He lifted her onto his horse and picked up the reins of the pack horse and they rode out, heading back north.

It was done. Cynthia knew her whole life would be changed forever now. But she didn't care. She was with Red Wolf. She loved him. He kept a tight arm around her, and she knew that soon, perhaps even this very night, once they got far enough away, Red Wolf would make her his woman. Her body felt on fire, but her heart pounded with apprehension. What would it be like?

"Soon we will find shelter," he told her then. "This is as far north as most white men come. I do not think we will be followed or that those men will be found for a long time."

She leaned her head back against his shoulder. Suddenly it seemed the only thing about her that was white was her skin. She had given her heart to an Indian, and now her own was Indian too.

Chapter Thirteen

Red Wolf kept moving for several hours after dark, and Cynthia found herself wondering if he had the eyes of a wolf and was able to see in the dark. After all, his guiding spirit was the wolf, and Red Wolf spoke of the animals almost as though they were his kin. It was easy now for Cynthia to understand why soldiers had such a hard time finding the Indians, for they were as cunning as their wilder relations that roamed on four feet.

She no longer held any doubt in her heart as to the rightness of what she was doing. It felt good to admit to her love, to lean against Red Wolf's powerful chest and relax in the wonderful peace of saying what was truly in her heart. She had complete trust in her skilled warrior, who had this night saved her from rape and murder at the hands of her own people. They had saved each other's lives, and had been drawn together unexpectedly. They came from two different worlds, but the feelings they held for each other were the same. Cynthia knew her love for Red Wolf ran too deep for her to ever go home now and be the same person, or to be happy in her old life.

"I will tell my people how bravely you fought," Red Wolf told her. "They will be glad to see you coming back with me."

"What about all our gifts? Shouldn't we give them back?"

"No. They would not expect it. They will just be happy to see you return. We will keep their gifts. We will need them when we start living together. Perhaps when we get back the tipi will be finished."

His arm tightened around her, and she felt the lovely desire ripple through her insides.

"You will be my wife now, and we will have sons," he told her, rubbing his lips against her hair. "We will keep the white man out of these hills, for our numbers are growing and we are stronger."

Her head lolled against his chest and her eyelids became heavy. They had already traveled all day and now half the night, and the strain of her attack and the horror of the ugly fight had left her exhausted.

"When are we going to stop, Red Wolf? I'm so tired."

"We will stop now then. I think we are far enough away for the night." He drew the horse to a halt and lifted her down. "We can make no fire. For tonight it is not safe. Can you see well enough by the moonlight to take down some of the gear?"

"I think so."

"I will tie the horse and leave everything on them in case we must quickly flee. Make up the bed and I will keep my rifle close by. Are you hungry? I have pemmican."

"Not really—just tired." She began removing blankets, realizing he had said bed, not beds. She felt suddenly clammy and nervous as she began spreading out the blankets. "What about your arm?" she asked.

"The bleeding has stopped. Tomorrow, in the daylight, you can wash it and tie it again. It does not hurt much." He finished tying the horses and came back over to her, laying the rifle near the blankets. He rose and faced her, putting his hands to her waist. In the moonlight he looked to Cynthia like some wild, beautiful creature come out of the forest to steal her away. "Come and lie with me, Cynthia," he said, his voice a gruff whisper from desire. "It will not be like that night I drank the firewater. I will make you my wife, the Indian way. We

218

will be one, and your God and mine will smile upon us."

She felt herself going rigid, and her arms hung at her side. "I'm afraid."

He leaned closer, touching his cheek to her own. Shivers of passion rushed through her, passion awakened by her own admission of love and the great freedom and relief that seemed to bring. She did love him so, but she felt awkward and inexperienced. She kissed his cheek, and he drew back.

"What was that you did?"

"What?"

"With your mouth on my cheek."

Cynthia smiled, feeling a little less stupid, for she knew about something he did not. "It was a kiss. It's what white people do as a sign of affection, except they usually do it on the lips."

Red Wolf frowned. "You mean, your lips . . . on mine?"

Cynthia felt the fires burning, and her breathing quickened. "Yes," she answered in a near-whisper.

Red Wolf leaned closer. "Show me," he told her.

She felt frightening yet thrilling sensations as he pressed his hardness against her belly and pushed himself close to her, his strong hands at her lower back. Cynthia studied his hypnotic dark eyes in the moonlight, then closed her eyes as she placed her mouth against Red Wolf's.

Instantly she knew she was lost forever. Instantly a woman's passions ripped through her girl's body, as their mouths pressed tight and their youthful desires surfaced full force. Red Wolf groaned, parting his lips and licking at her sweet lips, his hands pressing against her bottom. Cynthia wrapped her arms around his neck, and the kiss lingered, while Red Wolf grasped at her tunic, pulling up on it until his hands were caressing her bare bottom.

Cynthia's heart pounded wildly, and her breath came in gasps when Red Wolf left her mouth then, moving his lips over her cheek.

"I like this thing called a kiss," he told her, his voice strained with passion. "I want to mate with you, Cynthia. I want you to be my woman."

She whimpered as his fingers moved over secret places while she stood there pressed against him. Red Wolf licked at her cheek with wild passion while his fingers felt the sweet moistness that told him she wanted him.

There was no stopping now that both of them had given in to their love and desire. Red Wolf hooked a leg behind Cynthia's and kept a supportive hold behind her back as he lay her down on the blanket, both of them kissing wildly. Never had Cynthia been so afraid but also so excited. She didn't know what to do, but she knew she did not have to know. Her tunic was pushed to her waist, then up over her breasts.

She gasped in pleasure as Red Wolf's fingers found their mark, bringing out a wanton abandon Cynthia had never before experienced. She grasped at Red Wolf's hair as his mouth covered a breast, gently drawing forth almost painful pleasure from somewhere deep in her soul as she experienced for the first time the feel of a man tasting of the pink fruits of her untouched breasts. She arched up to him, wanting . . . wanting to feed him, to please him . . . wanting the glorious ecstasy he drew forth from her as his fingers probed and massaged places she had never offered to a man before. She had saved those things for the man she would love, and the man she loved was Red Wolf, no matter what anyone else might think of her decision. They would be married. Who was to say the Indian way was anymore wrong or right than the white man's way? There was really no difference, other than a piece of paper. A man and a woman still vowed their love before God, promised to love each other to the death, and mated.

Suddenly a wonderful explosion deep inside her made her cry out with the pleasure of it. Red Wolf was moving on top of her. Somehow he was naked from the waist down. She had not even realized he had removed his clothing. She felt his hardness against her bare belly, and she whimpered with a sudden apprehension, but there was no time to protest, for he was quickly between her legs, and in the next moment she felt the quick, painful thrust.

She cried out at the shock of it, yet somehow the pain was strangely satisfying. Red Wolf came down close to her, licking at her neck, groaning words of love in the Sioux tongue while he grasped her bottom from underneath and pushed deep. He moved with a teasing rhythm, and it seemed only moments before he suddenly pushed extra hard, then relaxed.

He remained on top of her, moving his arms under her back and shoulders to embrace her. He laughed lightly, kissing at her face wildly. "My woman, my wife," he said softly. "It is done. You are mine forever now, no matter what happens, Cynthia. You are mine! Red Wolf's!"

The trauma of the moment overwhelmed her, and she wrapped her arms around his neck, breaking into tears. How long could they really stay together? Had she done a terribly foolish thing? Would their two different worlds tear them apart?

"Oh, Red Wolf, I love you! I love you! Don't ever take me back! And don't let them come for me!"

"I will never let you go! Never! You are mine!"

He kissed her over and over, raising up slightly on his elbows. "Did I hurt you?"

Cynthia wiped at tears. "It hurt bad. But that's probably how it's supposed to be. It will get better, won't it, Red Wolf?"

He grinned the teasing grin. "Why do you think a man and woman keep doing this? You heard for yourself Flowing Waters' sounds of pleasure in the night when Many Bears mated with her."

Cynthia put a hand to his face. "You won't take another wife, will you, Red Wolf? I couldn't bear it. Promise me I will be your only wife."

He kissed her mouth again. "You are the only wife I

221

will ever want. Our men do not take wives just for pleasure. It is to help those who have lost their husbands. It is not like the white man thinks. Sometimes when a Sioux man takes a second wife, it is only to make sure she is protected and fed. Sometimes he never mates with her. But I will take no second wife, not even for those reasons." He tangled his fingers in her straight, blond hair, which now was wildly tangled. "I am happy, Cynthia. Tell me you are also happy."

"You know I am. I was just afraid to tell you before, Red Wolf. Afraid of how wrong it might be. Mostly I was afraid . . . afraid of letting myself learn to love you, and then losing you. How long can we really be together Red Wolf?"

"Forever." He kissed her again. "Forever and forever. They will never find us, and soon we will be rid of all the whites in the Black Hills."

She hugged him again, wanting desperately to believe him. But she knew Red Wolf looked at the picture through the eyes of a man totally innocent of just how many whites there really were back East, and how determined the white man could be when it came to gold. She knew enough to realize his future, and their love, could be doomed, but she didn't want to think about it now. She didn't want to face reality any longer, for she loved Red Wolf, and she could not hold back that love any longer.

"Yes, forever and forever," she answered.

Their lips met again, and then Red Wolf's moved down over her neck, lightly sucking at her breasts again, while Cynthia felt fire move through her blood.

"I want to do it again," Red Wolf told her. "I was too quick the first time, for I have longed for you such a long time." He kissed at her chest. "When it feels better for you, I will make it last much longer, and you will be a happy woman." He moved his lips back up to her mouth, licking and kissing at it. 'The more we mate, the sooner it will feel better to you, Cynthia," he told her. "I want you again. Tell me you want Red Wolf too."

"Yes," she whispered, kissing him back. "I want the hurt to go away so that I feel the same pleasure Flowing Waters felt. When they mated, sometimes I wanted to turn to you in the night, Red Wolf. I was just so afraid of my feelings."

"*Ai.* Then you have loved Red Wolf for a long time."

"Almost from the beginning."

"And you have been in Red Wolf's heart since the night you cut him down from the tree."

She felt the ecstasy returning as he swelled inside of her. She had seen him naked already, knew what that part of him looked like, but she never knew it could change this way. She had never been quite sure what happened to a man when he mated, but now as he became firmer and began moving inside of her again, she understood. It was glorious, beautiful.

She ignored all the warnings of such a forbidden love. She loved an Indian, but he was at the same time just a man—a man who had first become her good friend, a man who had saved her life, a man who loved her just as devotedly as she loved him. She would have to change her whole way of life to be with him, but that didn't matter. For to live any other way now, without Red Wolf, would be impossible.

In moments they were moving again in the sweet rhythm. The pain was not as great. Red Wolf caressed her lips with his own, quickly catching on to this new way of showing love, and quickly discovering that when he moved his tongue over Cynthia's lips she seemed to take even more pleasure in the kiss.

Cynthia in turn felt wildly bold, strangely void now of all inhibitions and modesty. She wanted to please her husband; and that was how she thought of him. Red Wolf was her husband—the Indian way. His gentle kisses and caresses made her respond automatically, and even though she still felt pain, she found herself moving rhythmically with him, almost enjoying the pain. For a few minutes they were both lost in their own ecstasy, relishing in the wonderful releases of finally sharing bodies.

The sweet explosion came again, and Cynthia arched up to him, supported by his own big hands. Never had she felt such utter ecstasy as this strange new feeling he created deep inside her, making her insides pull at him.

They relaxed together then, and Red Wolf pulled a blanket over them. The night hid them. Tomorrow they would continue their journey back north, back to a whole new life for Cynthia Wells.

For Cynthia the world became a wonderland of green prairie and fresh air and wild freedom. The pine of the Black Hills suddenly smelled sweeter, the bird's song was more melodic, and she felt melted into nature, a she-wolf to the male wolf who had claimed her. The ugly encounter with the white men seemed like nothing more than a bad dream, more unreal the farther they got away from the site.

Love had shrouded all reality, all ability to distinguish right from wrong. Love had painted for her a rosy picture of the future. Perhaps her name would become famous as the white girl who had mysteriously disappeared from Deadwood. Perhaps people would think God had snatched her up into heaven, and indeed He had. He had given her Red Wolf, and her heart felt freer and lighter than it had in a very long time. She wasn't lonely anymore, and she was afraid of nothing. She was Red Wolf's wife, and she would be brave and strong and learn to live like an Indian.

They split up the supplies between the two horses, and Cynthia rode the pack horse so that they could make better time the next day. They covered so many miles Cynthia could not begin to decide just how far they must have gone. But she kept up with Red Wolf, determined not to slow him down and risk the danger of someone who might have found the dead men catching up with them. Her insides hurt from the night before, but it was a delicious hurt, and she wanted to prove to Red Wolf she was just as strong as any of the Indian women. She suffered lingering headaches from her head injury of several days earlier, but that too she ignored. The important thing was to keep riding, to put as many miles between themselves and the dead white men as possible.

Red Wolf kept looking over at her and smiling, asking if she was able to keep going.

"I'm fine," she answered. "We have to get as far as we can, Red Wolf."

He smiled the handsome grin that made her insides stir anew. And Cynthia Wells knew she had been branded, just as surely as if a hot iron had been held against her skin. Nothing could change that now. Even if she was found, she would tell them she didn't want to go back. She would perhaps go home and say a last good-bye to her family. She would make them understand, somehow, and she would come back to Red Wolf. He was her life now, not her mother and father and brother, although it pained her heart to think of possibly never seeing any of them again. She prayed they were well, and she would miss Alex terribly, but once a woman took a man, she should cleave only unto him. That was what the Bible said. And Red Wolf was her man now.

The sun rose and moved across the sky and began to set, shining down on the young couple so much in love. Cynthia wondered at what a big land these Dakotas were. And so beautiful. It was no wonder the Sioux didn't like the white man coming here and destroying everything. She could see the contrast now between the way the Indians lived and the slovenly, wasteful way the white men of Deadwood lived, with their whiskey and their harlots and a hunger for gold that made them fight and cheat and kill to stake the best claim.

The Indians had lived on top of that gold all these years and had never needed it. It was nothing to them, for their way of life was simple and clean. Everything they needed came from the land and the animals. There was no need for gold.

"I know a good place to make camp," Red Wolf told her then. They had been riding in open land, but he headed his horse up a ridge then and Cynthia followed. Soon they were into the rich-smelling pine trees, fallen needles padding the sound of their horses' hooves. Cynthia could hear the sound of rushing water, and as they rode deeper into the trees and crested the ridge, she saw below them a rushing stream.

"It is a good place," Red Wolf told her. "Hidden, and the water is good. Come. We will swim."

He laughed, riding down the slope to the green grass and sparkling water below. The stream was banked on both sides by high ridges, with just enough flat ground on either side to make camp. Trees reached their needle-covered branches up toward the blue sky above, and it was obvious that anyone on either side of the ridges that hid them would never know they were there. Cynthia followed, then reddened as Red Wolf quickly dismounted and began removing his clothes.

"Come on!" he shouted. "It has been a hot day, and a tiring one. The water will give you new energy and cool you." He ran and jumped into the stream, paying no attention to the dried blood on the flesh wound of his arm. He fell back into the water laughing, rising up again in naked splendor, his dark wet hair slicked back from his face. Cynthia dismounted and walked closer, wondering as she stared at him if there could be a more beautiful specimen of man anywhere. His muscular arms and shoulders narrowed down to a slim waist and flat stomach. His buttocks and thighs were hard with muscle, and he was a good runner. Cynthia had watched him in racing games against other warriors. She wondered how many white men could withstand the rigorous tests of manhood that Indian men put themselves through. He sat back down in the water.

"Are you not coming? You will feel much better, I promise."

"I feel funny undressing when it's still daylight."

He threw back his head and laughed. "Cynthia, you are my woman now. We have mated, and I have slept next to your naked body every night since we went to Many Bears' tipi. Do you think I did not look at you many times when you were sleeping?"

Her eyes widened and she got redder. "Red Wolf!"

He jumped out of the water then, running after her. She screamed and started running away, but he caught her and held her arms while he untied her tunic at the shoulders. "You must obey your husband," he told her, smiling.

Cynthia screamed and laughed as he yanked the tunic down. He grabbed her wrist then and ran with her toward the stream, stopping at the edge. "Take off your moccasins," he told her. She hurriedly removed them and he pulled her into the water. They fell into it together, laughing and splashing each other.

"You were right," she told him. "It feels wonderful!"

They got into a wild water fight until Cynthia fell weak and laughing backward into the water. In the next moment Red Wolf reached under her and grabbed her up, standing with his arms around her waist then, looking down at her full, white breasts, the pink nipples peaked from the cold water.

"You are so beautiful," he told her, his dark eyes dancing. "I have the most beautiful woman in all this land, with her golden hair and blue eyes and pale skin and her nipples pink like berries."

Cynthia felt the beautiful desire he stirred in her come alive again. She closed her eyes, panting from their water play, and felt on fire at the feel of his eyes drinking in her nakedness. There was a time when she never dreamed she could let any man look at her naked, but this Indian man took away all her inhibitions. He seemed to control her with those dark eyes and that melting smile.

In the next moment his mouth was covering hers in a heated kiss, his tongue pushing into her mouth as though to mimic what he would soon do to her. He made her breath come in gasps as he left her mouth then, moving down to lick at the water on her neck, her shoulders, her chest, her breasts. He picked her up and carried her to the bank, setting her on her feet.

"Wait," he told her. He went to the horses and took down a blanket. The horses grazed quietly, occasionally going to the stream to drink, while their owner returned to his woman. He spread a blanket out on the grass and sat down, pulling Cynthia down with him. He grasped her shoulders and laid her back.

"I will dry you off," he told her, his eyes smoldering with desire. He bent down, licking at her again, moving over her arms, her breasts again, her belly, down her thighs, his soft tongue setting her on fire. She whimpered his name as he lightly licked the crevices of her lovenest, and she lost all modesty as he sat up then and drank in the sight of her as he gently moved his fingers to her secret place and made her open herself to him. This new abandonment of herself to her man quickly brought the sweet, pulling climax again, and he knew by her rhythmic gasps that she was ready for him.

He moved on top of her, their wet bodies sliding easily together, and she pressed up toward him as he entered her, for she wanted to feel her breasts against his chest. It all seemed so natural to her already. Womanly instincts brought forth by his invasion of her made her arch up to him, meet him with the same sweet rhythm with which he surged into her. She moved her hands over his muscular arms, his shoulders, down across his chest as she lay back then. He groaned when she touched his nipples, and she opened her eyes then, meeting his dark ones, seeing there a fiery passion, wondering if that same passion shone in her own eyes. She thought how strange that if he had forced her to do this, she would have hated him. But now she wanted him as much as he wanted her,

228

and she never dreamed doing this could be so beautiful and bring such splendid ecstasy.

It was all so natural and necessary. When a woman loved a man this much, surely there could be nothing wrong in giving him his pleasure and taking so much pleasure in return. Surely this lovemaking was only an extension of their love and friendship, just another part of the whole circle of love. If this was wrong, God surely wouldn't have made this the only way to get babies. And surely He wanted it to be pleasurable, so that mankind would continue to reproduce itself, and so that babies would be born out of love.

Red Wolf groaned and stiffened, and Cynthia could feel his life spilling into her. She hoped that soon that life would take hold, and she could give Red Wolf a son. He relaxed beside her then, pulling her close. Cynthia wondered if she ever in her life would know another moment this peaceful. They lay together quietly, their naked bodies wrapped around each other. The horses grazed nearby, while the water flowed behind them with melodic splashing and rippling. Above them the pines swayed in a light wind, and the rich smell of pine filled Cynthia's nostrils. She felt as though she had dropped out of the world outside this place, and she wished in that moment they could always stay right here, sheltered from all the things that lay waiting in that outer world to tear them apart.

She hugged Red Wolf's head to her breasts. She would not let it happen. It would always be like this for them. There would be no more Indian wars, no soldiers to come after the Sioux. They would stop looking for her, and all the whites in the Black Hills would give up and go home. She would remain behind to live forever in the Dakotas, with an Indian man called Red Wolf. Her throat tightened with the beauty of the moment. If only it never had to end.

Chapter Fourteen

It was several days before they came upon the fresh trail of the migrating Sioux and Cheyenne.

"Even more have joined them," Red Wolf said, studying the wide trail of hundreds of horses and travois tracks. In another two days they came upon the huge camp. From a distance Cynthia could hear drumming and chanting.

"The celebrations have begun," Red Wolf told her. "There will be even more to celebrate when we arrive. Follow me, my wife."

He rode faster then, and Cynthia pressed her legs tight against her horse, whipping at it lightly with a quirt Red Wolf had given her to make it go faster. She only vaguely remembered Many Bears using a quirt painfully on her nearly three months earlier. Now she used one herself, but not painfully for she loved horses as much as Red Wolf, and she was proud of how well she was learning to ride.

They reached the edge of the huge village, hundreds of tipis set in circles, all of them facing east. Newcomers who did not know about Red Wolf and Cynthia stared at the white girl dressed like an Indian. Red Wolf shouted words of greetings to men and women alike as he rode by.

"*Hohahe,*" many of them replied. "Welcome!"

The camp was alive with activity, and a very large tipi

231

had been erected at the center of the village. Cynthia stared at it as they rode by, sure it was for some kind of special ceremony. The Sun Dance? Red Wolf had told her about the ritual, and she hoped a white woman would not be allowed to enter, for she was not sure she was "Indian" enough to bear watching the grizzly ordeal, although she respected the religious significance it had for Red Wolf's people.

Cries of joy and greetings went up then when Red Wolf found his own people. A smiling Flowing Waters came running from a campfire, Little Crying Owl strapped to her back.

"What is this! My friend Cynthia has come back!"

Several people gathered around, with Red Wolf and Cynthia suddenly the center of attention. Red Wolf told Many Bears and others present what had happened. Faces turned somber, and Cynthia knew they were worried about the trouble their encounter with the white men would cause. Red Wolf said something that seemed to ease their minds, then he turned to her, waving his hand toward her and making the sign for "wife." Faces turned to smiles again, except for one wrinkled old man who stepped up to Red Wolf while Flowing Waters and other women hugged Cynthia.

"She will bring you much trouble, Red Wolf. She can never truly be Indian, and her people will keep looking for her. You should have left her there and come back without her."

"I could not do that, Two Owls. She is in my heart. She is my wife."

They spoke in the Sioux tongue, and Cynthia did not hear them, nor would she have understood.

"We are strong now, Two Owls," Red Wolf went on. "The soldiers cannot defeat such a large village as this."

"There has already been trouble. Scouts tell us Three Stars Crook is coming to our land. He is a bluecoat who stops at nothing, and so is Hard Backsides. I see black days ahead, Red Wolf. It will not be good for you to have

232

this white woman among us. If she is seen even one time, the bluecoats will hound us until we are forced into the land to the north, where the Queen Mother rules instead of the Great White Father who directs the soldiers."

"They will never make us leave this land, Two Owls! We are many now. We are strong! And I will not make my wife go away. She has a good heart, an Indian heart. She is mine, and I will not give her up!"

Two Owls, one of the old and wise warriors who was a man of many visions, scowled. "Heed my warning. I see bad days ahead. They will be bad for her too. She will have to be very strong."

"She *is* very strong."

Two Owls smiled then, but sadly. "You are young. Your manpart is eager for the beautiful white girl, and it is hard for you to think wisely. It was like that once for Two Owls. I see by your happy eyes that you will not listen, and so I will pray for you, Red Wolf."

The old man walked off, and Red Wolf stared after him. In the distance drums beat and warriors danced, and Red Wolf breathed deeply with pride and the firm belief that there was strength in numbers. Old Two Owls had let old age make him think in a self-defeating way. He turned to Cynthia, but already she was being dragged off by the women.

"We must finish the tipi!" Flowing Waters was telling her.

Red Wolf smiled. Yes. They must finish the tipi, for he wanted to be alone with his new wife.

Cynthia sat with her hair brushed out long, a beaded band wrapped around her forehead. She wore a bleached tunic given her by Flowing Waters, and she sat in a circle of women watching her husband dance around a night fire. It was the dance of the Strong Heart Society, warriors whose purpose it was to meet any emergency, to defend the tribe and to take care of the poor and needy.

Red Wolf's father had passed his grand eagle-feather headdress on to Red Wolf, and now he wore it proudly, as he danced with the other Society members to the rhythmic drumming. He carried a banner, made of feathers fastened horizontally to a long strip of red flannel and tied to a staff.

Another piece of dog meat was passed to Cynthia. She had gotten over her initial revulsion toward eating the tender meat of young dogs, for she had known them only as pets when she lived among her own kind. But to the Indian dogs were pets, work animals, and food. Their meat was very important in several religious aspects, and when a dog was killed for food, it was with the same reverence and a thanking of the spirit as when any other animal was killed. Its meat was considered a treat, and Cynthia had learned early on never to refuse offered food. It meant great insult to the one who offered it.

She took a piece of the meat and passed it on, taking a bite of it while she watched Red Dog dance and sing, shaking his rattle made of buffalo bone and filled with small stones. His shirt was fringed with hair-locks from the buffalo, and his shirt and leggings were beautifully beaded, and eagle feathers decorated both his rattle and his lance. Cynthia studied her husband intently, struggling inside to understand everything about him. When he was like this, all Indian, she felt more removed from him, and the reality of their differences hit her harder. When they were alone in their tipi, and he spoke to her in English, he seemed hardly any different from some white boy she might know, and she wondered what Red Wolf would be like, and how much he could accomplish, if he had a white man's education.

She shook away the thought, telling herself she was allowing herself to think too "white" again. Those thoughts were something her father would have. But she must be Indian now, and she must stop looking at her husband as something far removed from what she was. For he truly was her husband. Flowing Waters and

Basket Woman and several other women had worked all that first night finishing the tipi for them, and by the second night she and Red Wolf had a dwelling all their own, where they had enjoyed a night of heated lovemaking. It was like a honeymoon, and all night long that second night they had been teased mercilessly by Flowing Waters and others, who walked around outside the tipi joking about the young lovers and what they were probably doing inside.

This was their third night after returning. Many other celebrations had been going on all around them, and in two more days the sacred Sun Dance would be held.

"We will paint each other," Flowing Waters had told Cynthia. "You will be so beautiful! I will cover you with painted flowers, and Red Wolf will feel great desires when he sees how beautiful I make you. It is part of the celebration, that we paint ourselves however we wish. And we will paint our children too."

Cynthia finished her meat and continued to watch the dancing until she felt drawn into the fire. The wild singing and drumming had a hypnotizing effect, and somewhere late into the night she lay down on her side and fell asleep. She stirred awake when she felt someone lifting her, and she looked into the face of Red Wolf. It was painted with red streaks, and he still wore the headdress.

"I want my woman," he told her. "This time you will not run away from me."

She put her arms around his neck. "I won't," she answered sleepily resting her head on his shoulder. He carried her into their tipi and lay her on their bed of robes. He untied her tunic at the shoulders and pulled it off of her, then slipped off her moccasins. She had taken on the custom of wearing nothing under her tunic, learning to enjoy the wonderful freedom and comfort of the way Indian women dressed.

Red Wolf rose, looking like the grand warrior that he was, and Cynthia put aside the sudden vision of him riding into battle against soldiers. She did not want to think about it. Surely it would never happen. He pulled off his headdress, then rid himself of the rest of his clothing. His eyes held hers fast as he knelt over her. His face was sober, a look of power about him that told her he too was thinking about soldiers and white men."

"I am not your enemy, Red Wolf. Don't look at me that way."

His eyes softened and he leaned closer, touching her hair, her face. "*Ai*, you are not my enemy. But sometimes I wonder how it is I have given my heart to a woman with blue eyes and light skin, when out there everyone else with light skin *is* my enemy."

"Not all of them are, Red Wolf. It isn't the color of the skin. It's what is in the heart. Don't let your thoughts of the white men you hate make you hate me." Her eyes teared and he smiled sadly then.

"I could never hate you," he told her softly then. "No matter what ever happens, I could never hate you. I will love you to the death, Cynthia Wells."

"And I will love you," she whispered.

Both of them were thinking of the dangers that lay waiting for them, and both of them felt the sudden desperate fear of being torn apart. He met her lips, kissing her wildly then, possessively, savagely. He grasped her legs under her knees and drew them up, then guided himself into her, taking no time for preliminaries. Neither of them needed them. It was enough to be one, to flow into each other and give and take and please and claim. In this one act they were not different. When they were as one, they lost all fear, all worry. This was something they shared equally, and surely their love could overcome any obstacles that lay ahead of them.

They mated wildly, each hardly able to get enough of the other, pushing, grasping, their skin quickly damp with perspiration, their groans of pleasure easily heard outside the tipi. But no one thought anything of it. It was the natural thing to do, something many other husbands and wives were doing, for these were good times, times of celebration, times of strength and full bellies.

Cynthia wondered at the thin line between love and hate. Red Wolf's face was still painted in red streaks, and he could easily be a hated warrior, forcing himself on her. Yet he was simply the man she had chosen to love, and she gave herself to him willingly, just as he had once predicted she would. If he had done this to her that first night in the prisoners' tipi, she would have hated him. But he had kept his word. He had waited until she was ready, and now she wondered why she had waited so long.

They moved with the rhythm of the drums, and in that moment Cynthia Wells was not a white girl at all. She was wild and free, as Indian as the man who was mating with her. There were few traces left of the old, shy, innocent Cynthia. She knew now—so many things. It wasn't just that Red Wolf had taught her about being man and wife; he had taught her so much more—about life and love, about the inner spirit, joy and freedom. His was a way of life totally foreign to whites; and Cynthia wished there was a way to make whites understand the Indian spirit, appreciate the land and the animals as the Indians did, and give up their silly but determined search for gold. They didn't belong here. This was Indian country—Red Wolf's country—and now it was her country too. She felt the same pressing need to protect it as did Red Wolf.

She took his life into her belly, hoping each time he did this to her that that life would take hold and grow into a baby for Red Wolf.

Cynthia surprised herself at how well she adapted to the migrating life of her Sioux husband. Life consisted of settling, then moving on again, following the game. For the rest of that summer of 1875 they stayed to the north, and it truly did seem as though the soldiers and white men had forgotten all about them. But deep inside she knew it was foolish to think that could last forever, for occasionally Red Wolf and other warriors would leave for several days at a time, sometimes a week or two. When they returned, they brought with them new food supplies, stolen horses, blankets, and clothing.

Cynthia would ignore the vague feelings of guilt she felt when Red Wolf returned from what she knew was raiding. After all, the white men did not belong in this land. They had done terrible things to the Indians, especially to women and children. And game was not always easy to find. If the Indian were left to his old ways, he would not need to raid. But now the whites were taking all that was vital to Indian survival, so the Indian took back from the white man. Cynthia's heart, her thinking and reasoning, had become like the Sioux, for the most important person in her life was Sioux.

They moved through the rugged country of the northern Dakotas, across the Yellowstone River into Montana, through country more spectacular than Cynthia had ever seen in her life. This truly was God's country! It seemed filled with a strange spirit that made a person feel at one with the land. They moved south into Bighorn country, and never had Cynthia Wells felt more alive and happy than when moving through the spectacular mountains. No wonder the Indians didn't want to lose this! The scenery was magnificent. The land was untouched, clean and wild and still full of game.

"We come here to be cool in summer," Red Wolf told her. "And to be closer to Wakan Tanka. Here we are high, close to the heavens."

Nights were filled with drumming and joyous chanting, as Red Wolf's people reached out for guiding spirits, offering gifts of song and prayer to Wakan Tanka. To Cynthia their singing was a beautiful form of worship, and her own heart soared when she sat in campfire circles. Sometimes she half expected God Himself to come down from the sky and stand among them.

Life was good! It was spent in traveling, celebrating, hunting, storytelling, and making love. There was a lot of hard work, yet Cynthia hardly noticed. Each day passed swiftly, and there were delicious moments alone with Red Wolf, making love beside a stream or alone in their tipi at night.

Red Wolf was her whole world now, her reason for existing. The world of bustling, rude miners and the muddy streets of Deadwood were gone now. There were no dirty-talking men here, no painted, whoring women. There was no loud piano music and evil laughter. There were no rigid rules and stiff, uncomfortable clothing. Day-to-day living was not quite as comfortable, but Cynthia was willing to make the sacrifice. She was proud of how she was learning to sew skins into clothing, to stretch and dry a hide to make a sturdy war shield. She worked painstakingly on beading Red Wolf's clothing and moccasins, and she learned to cook the Indian way.

Her own God became mixed in her heart and mind with Wakan Tanka, and she was not so sure there was any difference. Many of Red Wolf's beliefs were no different from general Christian beliefs, and in many ways, these Sioux and Cheyenne were more Christian than many whites she had known who professed to be Christians.

Cynthia's only disappointment and worry was that after several weeks of making love, she still had not gotten pregnant. She wanted more than anything to give Red Wolf a child, but every month the dreaded curse came that sent her to the menstruation lodge. And every time it happened she sat in almost constant prayer that she would get pregnant, giving no thought to the danger of having a baby in the wilds with no white doctor to help her. After all, the Indian women did it. They knew as much about having babies as anyone. When it happened, she would be strong and brave, and show Red Wolf she could give him a healthy son or daughter with no complications.

Summer moved into autumn and autumn into winter. They moved south across the Bighorn River into Wyoming, then east. Now things were becoming more dangerous. The Sioux had to come down out of the mountains for the winter. That meant coming closer to white settlements again.

It was December when they moved past a small ranch, making no aggressive moves. But Cynthia could hear hollering from down below, and suddenly shots were being fired from several ranch hands. Cynthia gasped when two Sioux men and a woman fell from their horses, and quickly Red Wolf and several other young warriors went galloping off, yipping and shouting. Cynthia watched in terror as many shots were exchanged then. Other Indians picked up the bodies of those who had been shot from their horses, and Cynthia watched Red Wolf and the men below begin slaughtering the ranch hands.

She turned away, her feelings torn. The people below were her own kind of people. But if they had not shot at the Indians, there would have been no attack. Why did they have to fire for no reason? Why didn't they try talking first? Such encounters frightened her, for they reminded her of her own race, reminded her she and Red Wolf must surely be living on borrowed time.

She looked again at the scene below, and the cabin and several outbuildings were already going up in smoke. The Indian men were heading back with stolen cattle and horses, and Cynthia shuddered at a fresh scalp hanging from a leather strap around Red Wolf's horse's neck. She turned away, and they moved on without speaking until it was time to bed down for the night. Cynthia had become adept at quickly erecting and tearing down their tipi. Now it was up again, and she cooked fresh beef in a black kettle over a fire.

"You are quiet," Red Wolf told her.

She raised her eyes to meet his. "All the time I've been with you, that's the first time I've witnessed a raid on a white settlement. It makes me feel strange—traitorous."

Red Wolf lay against a backrest made of willow branches. "You are sorry you are with Red Wolf? You

240

want to go back to your people?"

Cynthia shook her head. "It just gives me a funny feeling, that's all. I know they shot at you first."

"Red Moon Woman was badly hurt. So were two warriors."

"I know. And so were a lot of white men at that ranch—probably all of them killed."

"It is the only way to get the message to them that they must leave."

Cynthia's eyes teared. "I just wish there was some way you could all get along—some way to settle all of it."

"Do you think *we* do not wish this?"

Cynthia swallowed back a lump in her throat. "I know that you do."

Red Wolf sat up straighter. "Cynthia, we have tried. We have listened to the white men, to the important ones who are sent here by the Great White Father in Washington. We listened to their promises, and we signed their treaties. We kept our part of the bargain, but they did not. They make up treaties to suit themselves. If something happens that they cannot keep their promises in one treaty, they decide to change it and make us sign a new one. We do this over and over, and always the treaty is broken again. We are angry and do not know what else to do now but fight them. Don't you understand how we feel about the white man's broken promises? Don't you see we have tried the peaceful way? It was the white man who chose this fighting, not us."

She nodded. "And what about . . . when the soldiers come?" she asked, her voice shaky. "They won't be as easy as the settlers."

"We are ready for soldiers. I hope Hard Backsides himself comes after us. It will be his last mission."

She looked at him, feeling a sick fear. "Red Wolf, it scares me when you talk like that. What would I do if you got killed? Would I stay here among the Sioux? Would I have to go to some other warrior and be his wife? I don't want to. But I don't think I can ever go home now either."

"Come here," he told her.

She moved away from the fire and settled down beside him. He turned her, laying her back against the backrest and leaning over her. "The spirits are with me. Nothing is going to happen to me. But if it does, you can go to Many Bears. He would not make you be his wife in the way you are saying. And now that Flowing Waters and you are such good friends, she would bring you no harm. If you wanted to go back to your people, Many Bears would take you."

She reached up, touching his handsome face. "I don't think I can ever go back, Red Wolf. But I'm so scared I'll have to someday. I just wish . . . I wish I could have a baby. That way no matter what happens to us, I would always have something of you with me. I'd love our baby to the death, no matter what anyone else might think of what I've done."

He smiled softly, leaning forward and kissing her lightly. "You will have a baby, wife of Red Wolf. You must relax and not think about it so much. The spirits will make my seed grow inside of you when it is right."

He met her lips again, their talk of having a baby drawing forth still-passionate desires in the young couple. He eased her tunic up over her hips, and she raised up slightly so he could push it to her waist. His kisses grew deeper, and his strong hands grasped at her knees and pulled them apart.

"We will just have to keep tempting the spirits to give us our wish," he told her as he removed his loincloth, the only piece of clothing he was wearing inside the warm tipi.

"Red Wolf . . . the supper," she protested.

"It will wait." He moved his bent legs up under her thighs, using them to raise her slightly. He guided himself into her, supporting her under the hips with his strong hands, both of them in a sitting position, their eyes holding challengingly as he began rhythmic thrusts.

Cynthia placed her hands on the dirt floor on either side of the backrest, helping push herself to him. She smiled and gasped at how quickly and easily they did this. It was like breathing. In seconds he made her want him, through delicious kisses and his sure, dominant attitude, with strong hands that pulled her to him, telling her he wanted his woman.

His breathing became more labored as his powerful hips moved back and forth. "Untie your tunic," he told her, his voice gruff with keen satisfaction. She did as he asked, letting the tunic fall to her waist so that her breasts were bared. His eyes glistened with desire at the sight of their beauty, the pink tips that made his mouth water. "You are so beautiful, Cynthia."

She grasped his forearms, closing her eyes then, resting her head against the backrest and breathing deeply, a thrilling climax rippling through her then, pulling at him so perfectly that he groaned with the thrill of it. He moved deeper then, in quicker thrusts, whispering words in the Sioux tongue, and Cynthia felt as free and wild as any Indian. His life spilled into her then, and he held himself fast inside of her for several seconds, praying himself that this time the seed would take hold.

He relaxed then, pulling himself away from her and leaning forward to kiss her again. "We will defeat the soldiers," he told her. "We will defeat all of them. Do not be afraid for Red Wolf."

She hugged him around the neck and he pulled her up away from the backrest, embracing her tightly. "My beautiful Cynthia," he whispered.

Chapter Fifteen

Cynthia huddled under a heavy buffalo robe she shared with Red Wolf. They sat close to the fire at the center of the tipi, turning a piece of venison, the product of pure luck on Red Wolf's part. Game had been much too scarce this winter, and it seemed to Cynthia that her belly was never quite full. It had been a bitterly cold winter, and for the first part of it snow had fallen so deep it was impossible to go far to hunt. Rations had been quickly used up, and the hundreds of Sioux and Cheyenne in their particular village and other villages camped deep in the Black Hills were sharing what little they had with others, especially the little children.

Now Red Wolf and Cynthia shared what they had with Many Bears and his two wives and four children. The two older ones sat bundled near Many Bears, their big, brown eyes peeking out from under blankets hooded around their heads. They sat quiet and listening, obedient and, as far as Cynthia was concerned, much too somber for little children. Hunger seemed to have a way of taking the smiles from their faces and the joy from their voices. The two babies slept in cradleboards near their mothers, both Flowing Waters and Basket Woman watching Cynthia turn the venison with almost longing looks on their faces.

"Things will not get better when the snow is gone," Many Bears told Red Wolf. "The runners came today,

245

while you were out hunting."

Cynthia felt her heart tighten. There had been some bad news.

"What did they tell you?" Red Wolf asked.

"Soldiers are coming, many of them. That soldier leader Three Stars Crook sent them. As soon as the snow melts, they will come for us to make us go to the reservation and stay there. Hard Backsides will lead some of them—and one called Terry and another called Reno. Many soldier leaders—many soldiers—many big guns. We will have to stay hidden deep in these hills. We will not be able to go far from here to hunt. Soldiers will be everywhere."

Red Wolf let out a kind of sneering snicker. "Let them come," he answered, his voice quiet but gruff with contempt. "Do they not know how many numbers there are of us now? In the spring we will gather together again. There will be thousands of us! They cannot round up that many Indians at once. We will fight as we have never fought, and neither Long-hair Custer nor any of the others will be able to make us give up all this land that is ours by treaty. The Great White Father in Washington will see that we are not so easily frightened."

The air hung silent for several long seconds as Cynthia turned the meat again. Her chest felt tight, and an awful, unnamed dread made her want to cry. Soldiers were coming, just when she had gotten used to this life, and just when she was more and more sure she must be pregnant, for she had gone two full months without a period. She had not even told Red Wolf yet. She had been hoping the terrible cold would break, and there would be a great mid-winter hunt that would bring in a good supply of meat. Then there would be something to celebrate, and she would tell him. Now perhaps she should tell him anyway. Perhaps it would brighten the current depressing situation, take Red Wolf's mind off of his hunger and the threat of soldiers.

But she could not help wondering what kind of danger more soldiers could mean to her existence with Red Wolf. All it would take was one raid, one man spotting a white woman among the Indians, and Red Wolf's people would be pursued relentlessly until Cynthia was rescued. She smiled sadly at the thought, for she did not need rescuing. Her own people would be sure she had suffered some kind of terrible fate at the hands of Red Wolf. They would probably even think she had gone mad if she told them she wanted to stay with her Sioux husband. She could already picture the shocked looks on their faces.

"Perhaps we should just go peacefully," Many Bears said then. "I fear for my wives, my children."

"No!" Red Wolf stood up. "There are many of us, Many Bears! We can defeat them!"

Many Bears looked up at him, his face looking strangely drawn and tired from losing weight over the winter. "These numbers of our people are all we have! When our people are killed, there is no one to come and take their place! But when soldiers and settlers are killed, there are always more to come and replace them! Their numbers are as many as the blades of grass on the prairie! No more will be coming to take our places, Red Wolf! This is all we have!"

Cynthia swallowed back a lump in her throat. She had hated Many Bears when she first arrived with him after he had abducted her. But she had grown to like and respect him, for he was a good provider, and was kind and gentle to his wives and children. He was a good hunter and a good friend to Red Wolf, and she had always felt obligated to him for allowing Red Wolf to claim her. She had never seen him look so defeated. The winter's ravages had aged him.

"The white men frighten easily," Red Wolf argued.

"Only the farmers and miners. But not Hard Backsides, and not the one called Crook."

Red Wolf fell to his knees, leaning closer to the fire,

his dark eyes drilling into Many Bears. "Do not speak like a man already defeated, Many Bears. It is not like you. You are an honored warrior. This land is ours, and it will remain ours as long as we show the *wasicus* we will not be easily defeated. First comes our pride, Many Bears. If we must sacrifice our women and children, they will give their lives gladly. It is the way."

Many Bears looked from Red Wolf to Cynthia. "And will Red Wolf's woman also give her life if she must? Will she fight the white man as a Sioux, or will she run to them if they come here?"

Cynthia met his eyes squarely. "I will fight them like a Sioux," she answered, her voice steady. "Don't you know by now where my heart belongs, Many Bears?"

"I know where it *should* belong, but I am seeing blue eyes and pale skin and hair like corn silk."

"You also see a woman who is carrying Red Wolf's baby in her belly. My first loyalty goes to the father of my child."

Many Bears' eyes widened in surprise.

"Cynthia!" Red Wolf exclaimed.

The faces of Flowing Waters and Basket Woman lit up with joy. "It has finally happened?" Flowing Waters asked her. "You are with child?"

Cynthia smiled and nodded, turning to face Red Wolf. "I was going to tell you when we were alone again. But I want everybody to know where my loyalty lies, Red Wolf. You know I would never go back to my people willingly."

Red Wolf smiled, but Cynthia detected the sadness and the worry behind the smile. Flowing Waters and Basket Woman laughed lightly. News about the baby seemed to change the atmosphere of doom that had filled the tipi only moments before.

"We will celebrate this meat we have to eat, thanks to the deer spirit," Red Wolf said then, moving to sit beside Cynthia. "And we will celebrate the life that grows in my woman's belly." He met Many Bears' eyes. "Now you know where she belongs, and to whom she will give her loyalty when the time comes."

Many Bears nodded. "*Ai.* This is good news, Red Wolf. More children means the survival of our race, no matter what happens to us. We must have many, many children, and we must teach them the old ways, no matter how hard the whites try to change us."

Red Wolf nodded, and Cynthia took the meat from the spit and began carving it, giving a juicy piece to each of the adults and the two older children. They all chewed slowly, wanting to savor the rare treat.

"Why did you not tell me sooner?" Red Wolf asked Cynthia, snuggling under the several robes and blankets that covered their naked bodies.

"I wanted to be sure. I actually meant to wait even longer, but Many Bears challenged me, and I couldn't resist."

Red Wolf grinned, his dark eyes sparkling with love. He moved on top of her and kissed her eyes. "It is good. I am a happy man this night." He moved a hand down over her belly. "You are still the same. When do you think our child will come out?"

"About seven months, I think. Sometime next fall."

Their eyes held, each realizing the unpredictability of their future. Cynthia could no longer imagine a life without Red Wolf, nor could she imagine having his child without raising that child among the Sioux. She knew already how a half-breed child by a white woman and an Indian man would be treated in her own society. He would be shunned and humiliated. She would never go back to that world, for now besides loving Red Wolf, she would have his child to protect. That child's only chance for happiness was to grow up among the Sioux.

"We'll make it, Red Wolf. God meant for us to be together."

He kissed her lips, loving her in a special way now,

loving her more than he thought possible. His lingering kiss turned to a harder, hotter kiss, for always there was this driving need to make sure she was still here in his arms, that no outside forces had stolen her away. Now it was more important than ever to protect her and keep her with him.

Cynthia reached around his neck, returning his kiss with fervor. This man had fathered her child. Her own people would never consider them married, but in Cynthia's heart, and she was sure in the eyes of the God who had brought them together, they were as married as any couple with a marriage license, and happier than a lot of them. Among Red Wolf's people she had learned more about God and sharing and love and friendship than she had learned among any whites outside of her own family. And she had learned more than that—things even her family had not taught her—about struggle and hardships, about how it felt to have a foreign people come and try to steal everything that belonged to you, about spirits and nature and how to live off the land, surviving without a dime of white man's money. She had learned to understand the fear of a people who simply were incapable of thinking like a white man, incapable of breaking promises, incapable of greed and lust and material desires.

"Make love to me," she whispered as Red Wolf's lips moved over her cheek to her neck.

He nuzzled her, licking and biting at her neck in a way that made her shiver with desire, and she opened herself to him readily, wanting him quickly inside of her, as though to prove to herself this was all still real. He was quickly ready for her, and he eased himself into her with a soft groan. She whimpered with the sweet union, arching up to him eagerly. Their bodies quickly heated up beneath the blankets, making them forget there was a chill inside the tipi in spite of the fire.

Cynthia closed her eyes and simply enjoyed the

moment, digging her fingers into his arms as he raised up, bracing himself with his hands and moving in a circular motion that always made her gasp for more, and which quickly brought the lovely climax, pulling her into his web of fiery pleasures that made her forget everything around her but this moment, this man, this bed of robes.

She breathed deeply, opening glazed eyes to see a dark, handsome man moving over her, to see the inside of the tipi swirling around her, the Indian clothing and weapons, the Indian paintings, the sweet smoke drifting upward through the smoke hole at the top of the tipi. This was her world now, a world of skins and animals and spirits and sun and beauty; a world of sweet freedom and dark people and campfires. The center of that world was a man called Red Wolf, whose life spilled into her belly then. But this time they did not have to wonder if the seed would take hold, for already it had sprouted.

The month was March 1876. "When the Geese Return from the South Moon," some Sioux called it. Others called it the "Moon of Falling Rains." It was Cynthia's third month of pregnancy, and still nothing showed, but she was relieved she had gone another month without a period. She was more sure than ever now, for she had even felt odd little flutterings in her belly.

The rains did fall, just as the Sioux said usually happened this time of year. They mixed with melting snow, and the ground became a quagmire in many places, making travel difficult if not impossible. Red Wolf's village remained in the hidden valley where they had camped most of the winter, waiting for the weather to warm more and for things to dry out before they ventured out in search of food. All of them knew this time how dangerous it would be, but in this particular area there was simply not enough game. They would have to risk the dangers of running into Hard Backsides or

251

some other regiment of soldiers, for if they did not, they would die anyway—of hunger. There was no choice, and it made Cynthia's heart beat harder with apprehension every time she thought about leaving this lovely valley where she had spent the winter huddled under blankets with Red Wolf, or sitting with Many Bears and his family sharing stories of ghosts and spirits and past war and hunting experiences.

She had gained some lovely memories here, memories that would be hers to keep forever. This place had become special, and she didn't want to leave it, ever. But leave it they must, and what bothered her the most was Red Wolf's comment that they must wait until the ground is dry. "We can ride harder and faster then if we have to run from the soldiers—or if we are the ones doing the chasing."

Red Wolf and the rest of them expected a confrontation before the summer of 1876 was over, and Cynthia was becoming desperately afraid for her husband's life, and for the baby that grew in her belly.

By the end of March, some warm, dry days came—soft, sweet-smelling days during which a return of thousands of birds brought their lovely chirping; days of greening grass and budding wildflowers. Children came out of their tipis and ran and played again, but some of them were much too thin. Horses began fattening up on new grass, and the smell of pine sap was rich in the air.

Cynthia hauled clothes and blankets outside to air them out, hoping the smell of smoke would eventually come out of them. She cooked outside, glad for the warm, open air again. Many long weeks spent mostly inside the tipi made her long for the wonderful sunshine and the spring breezes. Red Wolf and other warriors were restless, eager to get back to riding free and hunting, ready for any white men who might try to come against them.

Cynthia prayed they would be able to hunt with no

problems. Red Wolf was thinner, for he had shared his already meager rations with Cynthia, insisting she eat not only her share but part of his own.

"You are carrying my child," he would tell her. "You must eat. I want a healthy son. You are my woman. You must do what I tell you."

Cynthia had been tempted to argue the point, but when it came to the baby, she knew he was right. But it made her feel guilty to still be almost at the same weight she had been before winter set in while others looked so thin. At least now that spring was here, there was hope of finding a fresh supply of meat. In the meantime, they would have to subsist on dried meat, which she intended to boil with a little fat to make it softer and more edible. She walked to a stream to get a bucket of water, and it was then she heard the shouts of the village people.

Cynthia turned to see them pointing toward the crest of a hill to the south. She stared at what looked like approaching Indians, and she quickly filled her bucket and headed back toward her tipi. Already warriors from their own village were riding out to meet the oncoming Indians. Cynthia knew enough about Sioux trappings now to know that the Indians approaching were not Sioux. They looked like they were Cheyenne, but she did not remember seeing them before. In moments the women from her own village began wailing, and the women who straggled in with the oncoming Cheyenne men were crying and trilling in that eerie way Indian women had of mourning.

The Cheyenne men looked very upset, anger was the proper word. They began talking loudly to Red Wolf and the other men present, gesturing in sign language, using a mixture of Sioux and Cheyenne, sometimes pointing to the south. Cynthia felt her heart quickening, felt the fear and apprehension she had so tried to conquer building in her soul again.

There had been some kind of trouble. Cynthia set

down her bucket and walked toward the new arrivals, noticing that some of them had bloodstains on their clothes. She approached one of the Cheyenne women who was carrying a baby, and it was not until she got close that she noticed that the baby was dead, its head horrifyingly smashed.

Cynthia gasped and stepped back, staring as more women passed by, some with faces that only stared blankly. She spotted Flowing Waters then and ran to her side. "What is it, Flowing Waters!"

The woman turned eyes to her that almost frightened Cynthia, they were so full of hatred. "Soldiers!" she sneered. "The one called Crook! He attacked their camp, thinking they were Sioux. They killed many women and children, burned their tipis and supplies."

Before Cynthia could reply Red Wolf was shouting her name, running up to her. "Hurry!" he told her. "Gather up the tipi. We must leave quickly!" He half dragged her to their tipi, while other women immediately began dismantling their own dwellings.

"Red Wolf, what's happening?" Cynthia asked, her heart pounding.

"Crook! They will follow these Cheyenne who have come to us for help. We must leave this place or they will attack all of us!" In seemingly seconds the tipi was down and being folded for travel. "We will split into smaller groups for now," Red Wolf was explaining.

"Red Wolf, we can't!" Cynthia argued. "You said we have to all stay together to be strong."

"We do." He began loading his horses, which he had already brought out of the huge, grazing herd just that morning to check over and exercise. "But for now we must confuse the soldiers. Better they find only a few of us than the whole tribe. We will gather together again in another place. Soon we will be together in greater numbers than ever before. You will see."

Everything was happening quickly, and in an amazingly orderly fashion, for these were a people who had learned how to pick up and move on a moment's notice. Tipis were rolled up, their poles and skins attached to horses and travois. Fires were doused, horses readied, even little children helping with the preparations. All Cynthia could think about was whether it would be her own little group the soldiers would follow. In a smaller group they wouldn't have a chance, and if she was spotted . . .

She struggled against tears of panic as the entire village was gathered up in minutes and began heading north, accompanied by the straggling, beaten Cheyenne.

"The stupid soldiers thought they were Sioux," Red Wolf said bitterly. "Their camp was peaceful. They had done nothing wrong, and there were many women and children among them. The soldiers attacked without warning, killing many, burning everything. The Cheyenne men are very angry, as well they should be! There will be blood to pay!"

Cynthia said nothing, and she was filled with a terrible dread. All she could think about was the words both Flowing Waters and Red Wolf had spoken: *The soldiers thought they were Sioux.* If that was so, then apparently a large contingent of soldiers was scouring the area, looking for Sioux. They were being hunted like animals!

They rode for miles northward before finally breaking into smaller groups. Many Bears and his family stayed with Red Wolf, to Cynthia's relief. She did not want to be parted from them. Approximately fifty other men, women, and children stayed with their group, and led by Many Bears, they headed west, while other groups broke off and scattered in several directions.

"Let the one called Crook decide which tracks to follow," Red Wolf said haughtily. "Already runners are going to all the other villages, telling them to wait another month, then begin gathering at the Rosebud and the Valley of the Greasy Grass—the place where the river

255

the whites call the Little Bighorn flows. Then you will see how many Sioux and Cheyenne there are in this land, Cynthia—and so will the soldiers discover they cannot fight us!"

He spoke so confidently that Cynthia breathed easier. Surely he was right. He had been through these things before. The warriors were experts at fooling the white men. Indians were seldom found easily, and she knew that if their numbers grew more than the great gathering she had seen the summer before, there would be thousands of them. Surely they truly could fight anything the soldiers sent against them. She had to believe it. She had to have something to hope for.

They made camp deep in the Black Hills. The night was quiet, and they shared what food they had with some of the displaced Cheyenne who had stayed with their group.

"It is bad," one of the Cheyenne men told Red Wolf in English. "You must keep your white woman hidden. If they spot her, they will take her away. You must not try to stop them or they will gladly kill you. Get away, so that you will live to take her back. Remember my words."

Red Wolf threw down a bone. "They will not take her. They will follow the trail of another."

"There are many soldiers. It is possible they will break up their own numbers and come after our many small groups."

"Then they will die! If they split up, they will be weaker!"

The Cheyenne man nodded. "Perhaps. But I tell you, there were many of them—hundreds. It is good we will gather together ourselves. It is a time to be very strong, Red Wolf, to stay together and fight together."

"And we will! Soon we will all meet again at the Valley of the Greasy Grass."

"Mmmm, it will be good. I will not die before I sink my

lance into the soft bellies of those white soldiers."

"Or bend it on Hard Backsides' rear," Red Wolf answered with a confident grin.

The Cheyenne man laughed then. "*Ai*, that would be a sight to see! Perhaps his backside is hard, but his front side is as soft as any other white man. Someday I would like to wear that man's sun-colored scalp in my belt!"

Both men laughed, and Cynthia retired to her tipi, lying down on the bed of robes. She felt drained from the excitement and tension of the day, felt physically beaten from the hurried and unexpected trip. She stared at a dwindling fire, too tired even to add wood to it. She shivered at the thought of soldiers out there somewhere searching for them, and she snuggled deeper into the blankets, her eyes feeling heavy.

She drifted off, unsure just how late it was when Red Wolf finally came to lie beside her. She was vaguely aware that he kept his clothes on, and she knew in the deep recesses of her sleepy mind it was because he wanted to be ready to jump up and ride and fight if necessary. She felt him taking her into his arms, felt his unspoken fear as he tangled his fingers in her hair.

"I love you, Cynthia Wells, and I love the baby in your belly. Always remember that."

The words had a strange finality to them, and she hugged him close, refusing to let the tears come. She had to be strong now, show him how brave she was. "And I love you so, Red Wolf. I will always, always love you. You were first to take me, and will always be first in my heart."

Both wanted to believe the best; but both knew the worst possibilities. Things had to be said . . . just in case.

"The first time I set eyes on you, that night you came to cut me down, I felt a fire for you," he told her softly, kissing at her hair. "The fire grew hotter, and will never be extinguished. Always there will be a burning ember in my soul for my Cynthia. You have made me so happy, my beautiful white woman."

"And you have made me happier than I knew possible, my Indian man." She turned her face up to his and their lips met in a soft, beautiful kiss of honor and deep affection. The moment was intense, special, sweet. They did not make love, for this went beyond lovemaking. This feeling ran much deeper than the physical bond. She fell asleep in his arms. It seemed she had lain there only minutes, but suddenly it was morning. She awoke to the sound of thundering hooves—and a new sound—the clink of sabers, and a soldier's trumpet blaring out an "attack" signal.

Chapter Sixteen

"Soldiers!" Red Wolf leaped to his feet and pulled a sleepy Cynthia up with him. "Do not take anything! Put a blanket over your head and run to the creek bed with the other women and the children!"

Cynthia grabbed up a blanket, her heart pounding furiously. Red Wolf picked up his rifle and bow and arrows, while all around them the trumpeting grew louder, and soldiers yipped and shouted the same as attacking Indians would do.

Red Wolf pushed Cynthia through the tipi entrance. Outside, everything was chaos, women and children and old people hurrying to the north end of the camp.

"Run with them!" Red Wolf told her. "Hide yourself. I will come for you later." He pushed her toward some women who ran by. There was no time for "I love you" or "good-bye," no time to wonder what would happen to their tipi and all their gear.

Cynthia ran blindly, keeping the blanket hooded over her head so no one would see her blond hair. It seemed incredible that she was running from her own people, but she was just as frightened now as she had been that first day Many Bears stole her away. Women screamed and children began crying as shots seemed to be firing everywhere. Cynthia gasped when she saw a woman fall ahead of her, a gaping bullet wound in the side of her face. A small baby the woman had been carrying landed a couple of feet from its mother; and Cynthia grabbed it up, hardly aware the blanket fell away from her hair when she did so.

She held the baby close to her bosom as she kept running while shots and shouting filled the air. She looked back once to see two soldiers ripping the clothes from the dead woman and cutting at her breasts.

"My God, no!" she groaned. The things Red Wolf had told her were true. She had not wanted to believe his tales of rape and mutilation of women and children by soldiers. Surely men who wore a uniform and represented the United States would not commit such atrocities against the enemy! But she was seeing it now. Her stomach churned and she found her feet again, quickly pulling the blanket back over her head while she held the baby in one arm. She was sure the two men mauling the Indian woman were too involved in their heinous crime to notice her.

She half slid down an embankment that led to a creek, and she saw several women there. "Flowing Waters!" she called out, wanting to be with someone she knew. Flowing Waters moved from behind some brush on the other side of the creek.

"Here! Hurry, Cynthia!"

Cynthia splashed through the creek, just then realizing she did not have on her moccasins. She held the baby tightly and went to her knees beside Flowing Waters, breaking into tears.

"They killed a woman . . . right in front of me," she sobbed. She looked into Flowing Waters' terror-stricken face. "This is her baby."

Flowing Waters hugged her own baby tightly. "We must pray our men defeat the soldiers, or it will be bad for us."

Little Beaver and Gray Horse stared at Cynthia, eyes wide with terror, and Basket Woman sat behind them, holding Little Arrow, her head bowed. All along the creek women and children huddled, their whimpers of fear and quiet tears combining to create a sorrowful moaning sound in the air. Cynthia cried with them, hugging the Indian baby tightly and rocking back and forth as shots continued to be fired.

"If it is possible, the warriors will try to lead the soldiers in the opposite direction," Flowing Waters told Cynthia, her voice thin with fear.

Cynthia could not reply. All she could imagine was Red Wolf dying. How could she live if anything happened to him? The smell of smoke filled her nostrils then, and she looked up through the trees to see smoke wafting into the air above them.

"They are burning the village," Flowing Waters said.

"But . . . all our things . . . our tipi," Cynthia sobbed.

"*Ai*. Now you know how it is for us. We will have to start over. Now you know why we fight, why we hate."

Cynthia just shivered, rocking with grief. The tipi had become so special. She had helped make it herself, out of precious buffalo skins Red Wolf had so faithfully hunted. Their home would be destroyed! And what about Red Wolf? Would she ever see him again?

They heard horses coming then and she cringed. "Down there!" someone shouted. "I saw a white woman, I tell you!"

"Come on, men! The rest of the women and children are down here!"

To Cynthia's horror soldiers began firing into the huddled mass of women and children. The air was suddenly filled with screams and women began running. Flowing Waters yanked Cynthia to her feet and tore the blanket from her head.

"No!" Cynthia screamed.

"I am saving your life!" the woman shouted. "If you run with the blanket on your head they will shoot you down!"

"Let them!" Cynthia tried to pull the blanket back over her head, but Flowing Waters threw it aside. "Save

261

yourself, Cynthia! It is what Red Wolf would want! You are no good to him dead!" The woman picked up her other son and ran. Basket Woman was already fleeing with her two children.

"Flowing Waters, wait for me!" Cynthia shouted. She ran after them, her mind racing with confusion and sick fear. She stumbled over dead bodies, and then to her horror, a soldier rode in from their left, charging directly into Flowing Waters and trampling Little Beaver before knocking Flowing Waters to the ground. Crying Owl was ripped from Flowing Waters' arms and tossed to another soldier, who dangled the baby by a foot and ran his sword through the infant. By then Flowing Waters was fighting viciously with the first soldier, who punched her hard with his fist and then began tearing off her clothes. Two more soldiers joined the scene, fumbling at their pants while Flowing Waters was pinned to the ground.

Cynthia turned away. Flowing Waters' screams pierced her heart like a sword.

"She's a beaut!" someone shouted. "These tits will hold a lot of tobacco!"

"Cut them off now while she's still alive," someone growled. "That will teach her!"

Cynthia stumbled away, still clinging to the baby. Dead women and children lay everywhere, but a few were still running. Cynthia headed up the opposite bank, praying somehow she would escape, find Red Wolf, be safe in his arms again. But then she heard a rebel yell behind her, and she turned to see two men charging down on her. She tried to run faster, but someone grabbed her by the hair then, jerking her back so violently that she dropped the baby.

"Look at this!" someone shouted. "I told you I seen a white woman!"

Cynthia heard a gunshot nearby.

"Whooee!" another shouted, circling Cynthia, who struggled to get her hair free. "Ain't she a looker? Wonder how many of them bucks got a turn with her?"

262

"Maybe we should find out for ourselves what she's like," the man holding her said with a grin. "Any white woman who's been with them bucks ain't worth nothin' to her own folks anyway. Maybe she's grown kind of wild. Maybe she'd like it."

"Let me go!" Cynthia screamed. "I'm Cynthia Wells! I'm a preacher's daughter, from Deadwood! Let me go with the Indian women! They've done nothing to you!"

The men laughed. "A preacher's daughter, huh?"

"Let her go, Stewart!" came another man's voice.

The one holding Cynthia's hair turned his horse, not letting go of Cynthia. She stumbled sideways, her head screaming with pain.

"Sir, look how she's dressed! She's as Indian as the rest of them!"

"I don't care how she's dressed!" Cynthia looked up at a middle-aged man who looked like a soldier with rank. "You touch that girl wrongly and I'll have you court-martialed. Enough atrocities have been committed here today. This woman is white! She might be the one I've been looking for all these months." The man rode closer.

"Sir, she's wild as hell. If I let go of her, she'll run off after them other Indian women."

"Are you Cynthia Wells?" the officer asked.

Cynthia stared up at him. Something about his eyes made her trust him.

"Yes," she answered, her face stained with tears.

The man reached down and grasped her arm. "I am Lieutenant Wilson, Miss Wells. Your father will be overjoyed to find you're still alive. Come with me."

The first man let go of her hair and cursed as he rode off. Cynthia stared up at Wilson, who held her wrist firmly. "I don't want to go with you," she whimpered. "I want to stay with my husband's people."

The man frowned. "Your *husband!*"

"Please," she sobbed. "I am Red Wolf's wife now. I love him. I don't want to go back!"

"You don't know what you're saying. The Indians

263

have probably beaten and raped you so often you've lost your mind."

"No! No one ever hurt me! They just . . . they didn't bring me back at first because they were afraid. And then I didn't *want* to go back. I married Red Wolf—willingly."

The man shook his head. "Married? The Indian way? That's no marriage for the daughter of a minister. You come with me now, Miss Wells. After a while you'll get your mind straightened out and realize where you belong. I understand you've been through a lot. I don't blame you for your confusion. It happens." He pulled on her arm. "Get up now on this horse with me. I've been searching for you for months. I'm taking you back to Deadwood."

"Please, no! I have to know if Red Wolf is all right!"

"He's most likely among the warriors we left dead back there. A few got away. Right now, girl, you've got to face reality. I'm not about to let you go back to those Indians, so just get up on this horse. Don't make me have to tie you."

The tears came again. Cynthia looked around at dead bodies, then looked down to see the baby she had been carrying lay nearby, its tiny face shattered by a bullet.

"No!" she screamed. "No! No! No!" She yanked violently at Wilson's grip, wanting to get to the baby, to pick it up and at least give it a proper Indian burial.

"Now stop that!" Wilson told her. He dismounted, keeping hold of Cynthia's wrist and bending it behind her. He pushed her to the ground, bringing her other wrist behind her and putting handcuffs on them. "My name is Lieutenant Wilson. I'm damned sorry, Miss Wells, but I'm just doing my duty."

"Is it your duty to murder women and little babies?" she screamed. "Is it your duty to rape? To slice off a woman's breasts while she's still alive?"

"The men sometimes get carried away, Miss Wells. There is a lot of hatred that has built up over the years." He jerked her up. "Those are isolated instances, and I try

264

to keep them from happening. I have never killed an Indian woman or child."

"You're in charge of them!" Cynthia screamed. She turned her head and tried to spit at him, but Wilson was much too strong for her. He picked her up and threw her over his saddle, then wrapped rope around her and under the horse's belly so that she could not wiggle off.

"I told you I try not to let these things happen. Now please cooperate, Miss Wells. I really don't want to be rough with you. You're making this very difficult for me." He came around to stand near her head. "Don't you understand how distraught and devastated your parents have been? Don't you understand you don't belong out here? Don't you want to see your mother and father again?"

"I just want to be with Red Wolf," she sobbed. "Please! Please at least search through the bodies back at the village. Please! I promise to cooperate if you'll cut me down and just let me see if Red Wolf is among them!"

Wilson sighed. "All right. But I'm leaving the cuffs on, and I'll keep a rope tied to your wrists with the other end tied to the pommel of my saddle so you can't run off." He took hold of his horse's reins and walked the horse along the creek, then headed up the embankment. They walked right past Flowing Waters' naked, mutilated body. Her throat had been cut, and her two babies lay nearby. Cynthia felt vomit rise in her throat. Flowing Waters! She had been her best friend, had helped Cynthia learn all the Indian ways. She had helped sew Cynthia's tipi. Cynthia thought of Old Grandmother, and she was glad the old woman had not lived to see this.

"Oh, God, why? Why?" she sobbed, crying so hard then that it felt as though she would not be able to get her breath. Wilson led his horse away from the scene at the creek and back to the village, where soldiers were pilfering burned tipis, picking up souvenirs that they could tell their grandchildren they had taken after a "brave battle" against the "mighty Sioux." The horse finally came to a halt and Wilson untied Cynthia and pulled her off the horse.

"What you got there, sir? Your own personal prize?" someone shouted. Laughter followed.

"That will be enough!" Wilson answered. "This girl is the captive from Deadwood. I will be taking her back to her parents. If any one of you touches her wrongly or insults her, you will answer to me!" He took hold of Cynthia's arm and led her around the camp.

Cynthia struggled to stop crying so that she could see better. Her stomach ached fiercely at the horrible sight—dead warriors, men she had known, friends of Red Wolf. They lay bloody and strewn about. It was obvious that any who had not been killed with a first shot had been finished off, for many had bullet holes in the middle of their foreheads.

"Please wipe my eyes so I can see better," she asked Lieutenant Wilson.

The man pulled a handkerchief from his pocket, feeling sorry for the girl, sure she had somehow been cruelly manipulated by the Indians. Here was another white girl who did not want to go back to her own people. It seemed incredible that it could happen, but he was seeing it with his own eyes. He wiped at her face and nose, then led her through the bodies. Some were already being gathered up for a mass burial.

It was a nightmare for Cynthia, but she was determined to look at every dead body at the site. When she finished, she broke into tears of relief. Red Wolf was not among them, and neither was Many Bears. She sank to her knees and bowed her head.

"Thank you, God. Thank you," she sobbed. She looked up at Wilson. "He isn't here." She rose then, tossing her hair back behind her shoulders. "You didn't get him, Lieutenant Wilson," she said proudly then. "And you never will! And someday I'll be with Red Wolf again!"

The man shook his head. "Things will never again be

266

the same for the Indians, Miss Wells. Don't you realize that? This is just the beginning of the end for the Sioux."

"There are more of them—many more! You were lucky this time, but soldiers will pay for this!"

Wilson looked alarmed. "How many more?"

Cynthia only smiled bitterly. "I'll let you wonder about it, Lieutenant. You just remember Red Wolf will be among them, and he will be very angry over losing his wife! You haven't won a victory here today—*sir!* You just fed the fires of hatred that burn in the belly of the Sioux! They will fight harder than ever now, and someday Red Wolf will come for me!"

"Not once we get you to Deadwood, and you will have full soldier escort all the way. Now let's go." The man lifted her to his horse and mounted up behind her.

"Do what you want," Cynthia told him, hating him just because he was a soldier. "Red Wolf and I will always be together, even if I never see him again. I'm carrying his baby, and that's something no one can take away from me!"

Wilson seemed to hesitate for a moment. "My God," he muttered before kicking his horse into motion.

Cynthia only smiled. Red Wolf was still alive, and his baby was still in her belly. The entire company mounted up and moved out then, headed for Fort Robinson. But there would be another stop first—at Deadwood—to deliver a white girl who had been missing for nearly a year.

Red Wolf searched the faces of the straggling women and children that he and the others had fought so hard to save. Blood still dripped from a deep wound in his leg, suffered when a soldier had shot at him while on the chase. Once Red Wolf and others realized there were far too many soldiers to fight them all, they had quickly mounted their horses and tried to bait the soldiers by leading them away from the women and children. But not all of the soldiers had chased after the remaining warriors. Some had stayed behind.

Runners had been sent to alert the rest of the Sioux and Cheyenne who had split into other small groups. They must gather together again. This atrocity must be avenged! The soldiers would pay for the years of broken treaties and for what they had repeatedly done to Indian women and children; for their attacks on innocent villages of Indians who were not making war against them. They would pay for allowing white miners and settlers onto this sacred land, and for coming here to protect the trespassers!

Red Wolf desperately screened the surviving women, hoping against hope that Cynthia would be among them. There was much wailing and crying, and many of the women were wounded. Red Wolf spotted Many Bears then, his arm around a weeping Basket Woman. To Red Wolf's relief the woman held Little Arrow in her arms, and Gray Horse stood beside her, his round, brown face stained with salt streaks left by tears. He clung to his mother's tunic, sucking on his thumb, and Red Wolf was shocked by the look in Many Bears' bloodshot eyes.

"They raped and killed Flowing Waters," the man told Red Wolf, his voice heavy with hatred. "Little Beaver and Crying Owl are also dead." Fire seemed to glow in the man's eyes. "I will kill many soldiers for this! Many soldiers!"

The man stumbled away, then went to his knees and raised his arms, throwing back his head and letting out a long, piercing cry of anguish. Basket Woman stood crying quietly. Red Wolf put a hand on her shoulder.

"Basket Woman," he asked in the Sioux tongue. "What about Cynthia?"

The woman shook her head. "I . . . do not know. I saw her . . . for just a moment, when they were . . . raping Flowing Waters. Cynthia saw. She was . . . holding a little baby she took from an Indian woman who was killed. The blanket had fallen away from her hair. She ran

268

one way . . . I ran another. I do not know what happened to her after that, Red Wolf. I am sorry."

Red Wolf squeezed her shoulder. "I know."

"If the white men see her hair, they will not hurt her. She is one of theirs."

Red Wolf swallowed back a lump in his throat. They might not hurt her, but they would most certainly take his Cynthia back to her people. He had wanted to charge all of the soldiers the day of the battle, fight to the death for Cynthia; but he remembered old Two Owls' advice that he was no good to her dead.

"Cynthia," he groaned. How could he rescue her now? The soldiers who had found her would join up with the rest of the troops. Until the Sioux and Cheyenne could gather together in stronger numbers, they could not fight the bluecoats. There was no time now for anything but sending runners out to the far corners of the Dakotas and into Powder River country. They must get themselves organized after the long, cold winter—gather at the Valley of the Greasy Grass—build their numbers to so many that the soldiers could never defeat them. Red Wolf knew he would find no help in going to recapture one white girl, no matter how much his people might have loved her. For the moment it was far too dangerous. All that mattered now was to avenge what had been done to their people, to show the soldiers and settlers for once and for all they did not belong in this land.

Red Wolf walked several yards away from the others, not wanting them to see his tears, for they were for a white girl. He felt he had somehow failed her, for he had promised they would not be apart. Now she was gone. He might never see his child, the baby they had so badly wanted, the baby that had brought them so much joy. He folded his arms and bent over in agony at the thought of possibly never holding his Cynthia close again, never being inside of her, never being able to enjoy her sweet love and companionship, never seeing his own child. It seemed incredible that just two nights ago he had held her close, whispering words of love.

If he could not get to her, would she one day forget about her Red Wolf? Surely not! She would have his baby. And he knew she would love the child with great passion. But he knew white men well enough to know they would be cruel to the child, and he felt the bitter pain of being helpless to protect the baby and its mother. How cruel and ironic that it was his paticular tribe that had been followed by the soldiers. But then perhaps if not then, it would have happened another time. Surely he had been foolish to think he could keep a white girl forever. It was foolish, youthful passion on his part, but that passion still burned hot in his soul.

Cynthia Wells belonged to Red Wolf! He would try to find her. But if not, nothing that happened to either of them from now on would change the fact that she belonged to him, body, heart, and soul. For now, he must help his people. It was what Cynthia would want. He smiled sadly at the thought of her trying to rescue an Indian baby, and he prayed the white men had not been cruel to her.

He threw back his head, tears streaming down his face. "Cynthia!" he groaned. "Cynthia!" How could he go on without her? He would pray to find a way to get her back, and he would not rest until he did.

Cynthia picked at her food, aware that the eyes of nearly every soldier in the camp were on her. She wondered how she looked to them, her hair stringy from never being combed after being rousted out of bed so cruelly the morning of the attack. Her tunic had spattered blood on it, and her face and arms were covered with dirt from being pushed against the ground by Lieutenant Wilson.

They had joined a huge camp of soldiers, and she knew it would be impossible for Red Wolf to rescue her. She prayed that he would not even try, for surely he would be killed; if he succeeded, the soldiers would only track him and attack another Sioux village. Cynthia did not want to be responsible for another atrocity such as had happened the first time. Her stomach still churned at the memory of what she had seen, and again tears filled her eyes at the thought of her last vision of Flowing Waters.

Her good friend was dead. Red Wolf was out there somewhere in a wild land she would probably never get to see again. There would be no more storytelling around campfires; no more snuggling under blankets in their own tipi. There would be no more riding free, chasing the buffalo, celebrating a good hunt, no more traveling through a beautiful land she had come to love. Worst of all, Red Wolf would not hold her in his arms tonight, would not make love to her tonight, perhaps not ever again. She would go back to a place that would seem foreign to her now, to a people she no longer knew. She would be changed, and her family would not love her anymore. She would be an outcast among her own people, yet would never be allowed to return to the people she loved and to whom she had given her heart.

One soldier strolled by as Cynthia tried to force down a piece of meat. She had no appetite, but she wanted to stay healthy for the baby's sake. She thought about all the times Red Wolf had given up food so she could eat more.

"What's it like, missy? Did they rape you? Torture you?"

Cynthia looked at the man with as much hate in her blue eyes as any Indian woman would hold for a soldier.

"Leave her alone, Sergeant," Lieutenant Wilson spoke up. "It's none of your business."

The sergeant snickered and walked off, and Wilson, who sat to Cynthia's right, apologized for the man. Cynthia stared at her plate of food.

"It doesn't matter. I know what to expect." She looked at the lieutenant. "It's true they didn't hurt me, Lieutenant Wilson. I swear it. Red Wolf himself never touched me until I decided I wanted him to." She held his

271

eyes squarely, proudly, not caring what he thought. She was Red Wolf's wife.

"Don't you realize what you've done, Miss Wells? What you're saying?"

"I know exactly what I'm saying. I saw more cruel violence and hideous crimes committed back there by soldiers at that Indian camp than I ever saw committed by any Indians while I was with them." The lump came back to her throat. "And they call themselves men. They don't know the meaning of the word! You want to find good men—brave, strong, honest? You'll find them among the Sioux and Cheyenne, not here."

"I realize you witnessed some very terrible things, Cynthia. But that's war. Things like that have been going on for hundreds of years. I try to keep it from happening, but I can't be watching every man every moment. Most of them handled themselves very well. We're here to dig all the Indians out of those hills, Miss Wells, and we will do it, one way or another. They must learn to stay on the reservation."

"This land *belongs* to them! They have a signed treaty."

"When that treaty was signed no one knew gold would be discovered on this land."

"Gold!" She spat. "Let the white men go find it someplace else!"

"Cynthia, this country is growing and changing. The Indians will just have to grow and change with it. It can't be stopped. You're white. You must know that. You didn't really think you could stay forever with Red Wolf, did you?"

Her eyes teared so that she could not see her food. "I love him," she said quietly. "Don't you understand that? He is my husband. I'm carrying his child." She turned tear-filled eyes to the man. "Can't you just let me escape? I'd never tell. It would be so easy for you."

The man sighed and ran a hand through his hair. "No. You don't really belong with them, Cynthia. They have just got your thinking all turned around, and all I can

272

think about is the look on your father's face when I told him all the possibilities of what could have happened to you. The man has been praying for months to find out something about his daughter. Now I have you right here, and you're going back, Cynthia. Don't you want to see your parents?"

She sniffed, thinking of her mother. It had all started so innocently. She was going to free a young Indian man so he wouldn't be hanged. Now the knife she had used, her mother's favorite, lay on a burial scaffold with Old Grandmother. An Indian baby was growing inside of her, and the man she loved had red skin and wore feathers in his hair.

"Yes, I would like to see them. But only to tell them I'm all right. Then I want to go back."

"That will be entirely up to them. It's not in my hands to decide your future, Miss Wells. My job is to take you back. After that your parents can do whatever they want."

Cynthia picked at her food again. Maybe by some miracle her parents would let her go back to Red Wolf. It was the last tiny bit of hope she had left. Maybe once they knew she was carrying his baby . . . She managed to swallow a piece of meat, realizing how shocked and distraught her parents would be when they found out she had loved an Indian man and was pregnant by him. The Cynthia Wells who would be returned to Deadwood would not be the Cynthia Wells who had left.

"You're welcome to bathe and wash your hair in a tub inside my tent later if you like," Wilson was telling her. "I imagine you would like to clean up. It might help keep these bastards from staring at you. I even have one of your dresses with me. Your father gave it to me—wanted me to have it just in case by some miracle I found you and you needed it. Now the miracle has come. Would you like to wash and change into it?"

Cynthia stared at her plate. "Yes. I guess so."

Wilson studied her a moment, wondering at the kind

273

of man Red Wolf must be to have practically turned this girl against her own people. Was it possible he really had been kind to her and had not forced her? It was hard to imagine so much human emotion could be wrapped around an Indian man. And the girl had wept over the death of an Indian woman who she had said was her best friend. It was actually as though Cynthia Wells thought of the Sioux as her family!

"I'll get the dress," he told her, rising from the campfire.

Cynthia set down her plate and rested her arms on her knees, putting her head down. Perhaps the lieutenant was right. Perhaps thinking she could live forever with Red Wolf really had been a silly dream. She was white. She would put on a calico dress again, and be suddenly transformed outwardly. But inside she knew she would never be white again. It didn't seem fair that the color of her skin should keep her from what made her happiest. Who had invented all these strange rules about life? Who made the law that a white woman could not love an Indian? She was sure there was nothing in the Bible about it. Why was it treated as though it was a sin? Surely it wasn't a sin to love a man as much as she had loved Red Wolf.

"Here you are," the lieutenant said then.

Cynthia raised her head and the man laid a blue flowered dress across her arms. Seeing the dress brought forth all the reality. She remembered the day she had picked out the material for the dress, shopping in Deadwood with her mother and father. She was Cynthia Wells, a preacher's daughter from Charleston, South Carolina. And yet she wasn't that Cynthia Wells at all. The Cynthia Wells who had worn dresses like this one had died the day Many Bears took her away. That Cynthia Wells would never come back. There was only this Cynthia, the one whose heart belonged to an Indian man. She rested her head against the dress and wept.

Chapter Seventeen

People stared as Cynthia rode through town. "It's her! It's the preacher's daughter!" she heard some of them whisper.

"My God, what she must have been through!"

"Oh, I wouldn't mind being captured by some big, handsome Indian buck," one of the prostitutes quipped. Cynthia heard laughter then.

"Serves her right," someone else said. "Her freein' that damned renegade last year."

"I wonder how they found her."

"Cynthia! Cynthia Wells!" someone shouted, running toward her. "My God! Your father will be beside himself with joy!"

It was the storekeeper, Art Bonneville. Cynthia looked down at him as she rode by, this time sitting her own horse and riding beside Lieutenant Wilson. "Hello, Mr. Bonneville," she said quietly.

Bonneville frowned, detecting the sadness in her voice and wondering why she wasn't happier to be home. Perhaps she had suffered so greatly all her spirit was gone.

"God bless you, child," he told her. He dropped back and watched as she rode on, staring straight ahead and giving no acknowledgment to any of the others. "Poor girl," he murmured.

"Look at her skin, so brown from the sun," another said as they passed by more townspeople. The streets buzzed with gossiping people, some of whom followed Cynthia and the lieutenant to the parsonage. As Cynthia and the lieutenant approached the familiar little church and the white frame parsonage Cynthia could already see her father running toward them. Someone had run ahead to tell him his daughter had been found.

"Cynthia! Cynthia!" he was shouting. "Dear God, I don't believe it! Cynthia!" The man reached up and grabbed her off her horse, hugging her tightly and breaking out in tears. "Praise be to God!" He wept. "Praise be! Praise be!"

In the next moment her mother was there, crying and carrying on, while Alex stood back a little, scrutinizing his sister carefully. It was Alex who sensed immediately she had changed.

Cynthia let her parents have their due. Surely they had suffered a great deal. It felt good to see them, but different. Her joy would be so much greater if she knew she could go back to Red Wolf. She noticed how different her father smelled, realizing she had long been away from the smell of hair lotions and lilac water. Fake smells. That was what whites used. Fake smells. Red Wolf had always smelled good, so manly. But he didn't need all the strange greasy creams in jars that whites seemed to need.

Her parents wept openly, both of them hugging her so hard she could barely breathe. Finally they let go of her, both of them reluctantly, standing back and looking her over, trying not to look shocked at her tanned skin, and the white line around her forehead where she had obviously worn a headband.

Cynthia blinked back tears. She didn't want to hurt them, but she also did not want to hide the truth any longer than necessary. They had to know.

"Father, Mother," she said then. "I wish I could have let you know I was all right. But Red Wolf was afraid to

276

bring me back, afraid people would misunderstand and arrest him."

"What's this?" Her father frowned. "You speak as though you're defending the very heathens who stole you away! Surely you have suffered, Cynthia. Surely they . . ." His eyes moved over her thin frame.

"I wasn't hurt, Father. In fact . . ." She looked at her mother. "I want to go back, after we've had a chance to visit. I have so many things to tell you—things I learned about the Sioux, how I grew to love them." She looked at her father then. "Please let me go back, Father. Red Wolf . . . he's my husband now. I'm carrying his child."

Mabel Wells gasped, stepping back from her daughter. "No!" she cried.

Cynthia stood straight and proud. "Mother, it isn't so terrible. I love him. I married him willingly and I'm having his baby."

Her father made an odd choking sound, then coughed and turned away for a moment, looking out over the plains. What had happened to the innocent girl who had been abducted a year ago? What had the Indians done to her to make her speak this way? Had she been raped so many times that she didn't know her own mind anymore? But she looked fine. She didn't look abused.

Alex stared at the new sister who had come home. He was full of a thousand questions about the Indians, and despite his parents' reaction, he was proud of Cynthia. She had survived a terrible ordeal and had made the best of it.

"Why don't we go inside, Reverend Wells, and we'll talk about all of this," Lieutenant Wilson was saying, his hand around a shocked Wells's shoulders.

"What is she saying! What is my daughter saying!" Wells groaned.

Cynthia watched him seem to shrivel before her eyes. Her eyes teared at the effect her news had had on him. Surely her father and mother would hate the baby in her belly. She had hoped their Christian love would apply to their grandchild in spite of his being half Indian, but already she could see the battle that lay ahead of her. And already she knew they would never let her go back.

"Red Wolf," she whispered. If her parents didn't let her go back, she truly might not ever see him again! How could she go back alone? She wouldn't know the first place to look, and if soldiers didn't find her, wild animals might, or she might just die from the elements or be abused by miners. She had to think of the baby now. It was her only link to Red Wolf. She put a hand to her chest, telling herself she must stay calm, but her own tears came then, for she realized with staggering reality that she hated this place now. She hated Deadwood and she hated its people. She hated this small frame house that was now so confining, and she hated the uncomfortable stays and long sleeves of the dress she wore.

"You all right, sis?" Alex was asking her then.

She turned to her brother and hugged him, bursting into tears. "Tell me you understand, Alex. I loved Red Wolf. I loved living with the Sioux. I want to go back."

"Didn't you miss us?" he asked.

She pulled away, surprised at how much he had grown and how long she really had been gone. This life seemed so strange to her now. "Oh, Alex, it's all so different." She wept. "If you lived among them, you'd know what I'm saying. You would learn to love it too, and to love the Indians."

Wells had got control of himself, and he turned to his daughter, putting an arm around her. "We have much to talk about," he told her. "Come into the house, Cynthia. Tell us all that happened, how you came to be stolen away." He hugged her tightly. "I don't care how things stand right now. I just thank God that my daughter is back and safe. Surely you're terribly confused right now. God only knows what you've been through."

He led her toward the house; and she realized that for

her parents to even begin to comprehend how she felt now, she would have to tell them the entire story. She had spoken too soon in her anxiety to be allowed to go back. She had to handle them carefully, for this whole thing was a terrible shock.

People stared as she followed her family into the house. She thought how innocent and naive she had been when she lived here a year ago, and how totally ignorant about Indians. Her parents were just as ignorant about them. She had to make them understand. It was her only hope of ever seeing Red Wolf again.

"What should we do, Albert?" Mabel Wells asked her husband. "She isn't our Cynthia any more."

The two of them sat at the table in the kitchen. It was two o'clock in the morning, and neither of them had been able to sleep. The house was quiet, and they spoke in low voices so their daughter would not hear them.

"I don't know." Wells rubbed at tired eyes. "She's so confident about what she wants. My God, Mabel, she's carrying Red Wolf's baby, and she doesn't even act like she thinks there is anything wrong with it! She really thinks she's married to him! Our own daughter! Our sweet, innocent Cynthia—pregnant by an Indian, and *proud* of it!"

Mabel closed her eyes and put her head in her hands. "They must have done something to her. I have heard the Indians use certain herbs and such like drugs. Maybe they did something that affected her mind."

Wells shook his head. "She seems very clearheaded to me. And after some of the things she told us, about what the soldiers did to those poor women and children, a man can understand how they feel." He looked at his wife. "I'm a Christian, Mabel—a preacher, no less. I can't help understanding how the Indians feel—seeing clearly that it isn't right for all these miners to be coming into land promised them by our own government. I have preached that the Sioux are God's children, to be loved like any man. But when it comes to my own daughter . . ." He sighed. "I feel so guilty saying they're God's children, but feeling at the same time that they aren't good enough for my Cynthia."

Mabel put a hand over her husband's. "It isn't that they aren't good enough, Albert. It's that the two cultures are much too different. Cynthia is young. She thinks she can survive anything. She thinks she's in love, but only because Red Wolf saved her and became her only friend. I think because she had no choice but to stay with them, she looked too much to this Red Wolf to protect her. Perhaps just being around him so much led her to *believe* she loved him. But by then her life had been so changed, so removed from all she had ever known. She has to realize that no matter how much she thinks she could have survived with them, she couldn't. She's *different*, Albert! She's *white!* She isn't meant to live that way. The Indians are born to it. Cynthia wasn't. If our daughter goes back to those people, it means an early death. And we both can see what lies ahead for the Sioux. There is going to be more fighting, and eventually, whether it's right or wrong, they are going to be compelled to live on reservations. We can't have Cynthia living that kind of life."

Wells ran a hand through his hair. "Are you saying we have to tell her she must stay with us?"

"Of course we have to tell her that! It's the only right thing. After a time she'll gradually slip back into her old life, remember who she is, what she is. She'll begin to see it's the only right thing to do."

"And the baby?"

Mabel Wells's cheeks colored. She looked at her lap. "I find it so hard to accept that she actually willingly got pregnant by an Indian." She fingered with the lace on her skirt. "There is nothing we can do about the baby. It's

280

done now. She'll have it, and she'll love it as any mother loves what comes from her womb. But we both know how such a child would be treated around here. We'll have to go back East, Albert. She can have the child there. It's . . . it's possible you won't be able to preach anymore. I'm not sure how people at home will accept it all."

"There's more reason than the baby to go back, and we both know it," Wells added.

His wife met his eyes, and they both knew.

"If we don't take her back East," Wells said aloud, "she'll try to run away and get back to Red Wolf."

"I know," Mabel answered sadly. "That is why we must leave quickly. Part of the reason I couldn't sleep was because I half expected her to try to sneak out tonight. We can't trust our own daughter, Albert. And right now she doesn't know what's good for her. In time she'll realize how much we love her, that we only want to do what's best for her." She squeezed her husband's hand. "We can't let her go back, Albert. We must be strong about it. She'll fight us at first."

The man nodded, his heart heavy with grief over how his daughter had returned a stranger. "I know."

"It's harder for you to be firm with her. But if you love her, Albert, you can't let her go back. If she goes back we'll never see her again, and she'll die some obscure, early death and be buried on an Indian reservation. This Red Wolf is a Sioux Indian, Albert. Our two cultures couldn't be more different. How do we know he wouldn't tire of her in time and sell her off like a can of tobacco? How do we know he won't take another wife, or two or three? Cynthia can't live under those conditions. She seems to love him so much, to be so sure of his love and protection. But we can't take the risk that she might be wrong. Even if she *is* right about the man himself, life would still be very dangerous for her, very hard. And we would never see our daughter again. God has brought her

281

back to us. Surely He means for us to keep her now. Somehow we will have to accept and love the baby. He or she will be our grandchild, carry *our* blood too."

The man kept nodding. He leaned back in his chair. "So, when do we do it?"

"As quickly as possible. This house and most of the furnishings belong to the church. They will send out someone else. We can have our personal things packed in a day, if need be. That Lietuenant Wilson is still in town. We can ask him to escort us to Julesburg, where we can catch the Union Pacific."

"Julesburg is a good two weeks' traveling from here. That Red Wolf might come after her."

"No. The lieutenant said he probably wouldn't right away. Things would be much too dangerous right now for him to come alone, and the lieutenant thinks that right now he would get no help from the Sioux. They will be gathering together to concentrate on revenge for the soldiers' attack and the broken treaty. He said Crazy Horse and Sitting Bull are on the warpath again and they won't rest until they drive all the miners out of the Black Hills. No Indian is going to risk coming this close to a settlement the size of Deadwood. The lieutenant said they're scared and angry now. They'll regroup and try to decide what to do next. That gives us a little time to get Cynthia away from here. I think we should spend the rest of the day packing and leave early tomorrow morning."

Wells rubbed at the back of his neck. "It's all so different now. I feel like our family has been destroyed."

"She'll come around and be our daughter again eventually, I'm sure of it. In the meantime we can't hate her or accuse her of wrongdoing, Albert. She really believes in her mind that she has done nothing wrong. And if she wants and loves her baby, we have to love and want it too. We will have to bear the insults and heartache such a child is going to bring."

He studied his wife quietly for a few seconds. "What

282

do we do if Cynthia violently objects to leaving? She's liable to run off, you know. She won't like this."

"We'll tie her if we have to."

"Our own daughter!"

"Albert, we have to do whatever is necessary to get her away from here. We know what's best for her. If we must restrain her, I know it will tear at our hearts, but we have to remember it's for her own good."

He closed his eyes and hung his head. "Why has God done this to us?"

A lump rose in Mabel Wells's throat. "I don't know, Albert. Perhaps to test our faith, to test our ability to love and accept. I only know we must not blame God; and we must not waver in what we know is right for Cynthia."

She reached out and he clasped her hand. "It's decided then," Mabel added, squeezing his hand. "We'll go back to Charleston, right away."

Cynthia sat in the parlor, watched by a young soldier who stared at her as though she were a harlot but said nothing. She could not believe her parents were actually taking her back East, and so quickly.

"They're afraid," she thought. *"They're afraid of Red Wolf coming for me."* And surely he would have come eventually. She knew how difficult it would be for him to come now, and her heart ached that perhaps he had been wounded. What if he lay bleeding and in pain somewhere, calling out for his Cynthia?

Apparently her father knew she might try to run away, to get back to Red Wolf on her own. He had placed this soldier in their house to watch her like some kind of prisoner while the rest of them packed. If she had known her parents would do this to her, she would have snuck out the night before. Tears came to her eyes again at the realization that they had not understood at all. All her stories, her pleadings, her sincerity had been for nothing.

They simply could not believe she could actually be in love with an Indian man.

How suddenly all her happiness had ended. Red Wolf! Where was he? Was he all right? What would he be thinking now? She prayed he would be smart enough *not* to come for her right away. He would surely be caught and shot. But that left only one alternative. She would be dragged back East. Perhaps she would never see her husband again.

She wanted to love her parents—not to blame them. But it was difficult not to hate them for not respecting her feelings. Why couldn't they just understand? She had been so sure that they would.

Alex walked by carrying a box. He looked at her through the parlor entrance as he passed, stopping for a moment to stare at her. He smiled then. "You'll be okay, Cindy. You'll be happy again when we get home."

His eyes had been sympathetic, and she felt relieved that at least her brother seemed to understand a little. He didn't hate her and call her stupid. Alex had always liked adventure, and he'd seemed to admire her the night she cut Red Wolf loose; and even more now that she had lived with Indians. Perhaps his young mind didn't comprehend her pregnancy or how she got that way. But she knew what others in this mining town would think. They would think like the soldier who stared at her now, thinking his dirty thoughts. She looked at him suddenly then, her blue eyes fiery and challenging.

"Stop looking at me, soldier."

He smiled slyly. "Can't blame a man for looking at a pretty girl."

Cynthia glared at him. "Stop looking at me, or I'll tell Lieutenant Wilson you tried to bother me. He'd have you punished."

The man's eyes turned sullen and he moved to lean against the entrance to the parlor, his back to her. Cynthia's father came into the room then, the sorrow in

284

his eyes evident, making Cynthia feel guilty. He came close to her, kneeling in front of her.

"I do hope you realize we're doing this for your own good, Cynthia. I'm sorry about the soldier guard for my own daughter. But while you're so mixed up, I'm afraid you'll try to slip away on us."

Cynthia looked at her lap. "I would." She met the man's eyes. "Please, please, Father, let me go back! I love Red Wolf. He's the father of my child. He's my husband! Please let me go back!" Her eyes teared and her throat ached.

Wells took her hands. "I can't. You are my *daughter*. I can't have my daughter living under those conditions. I can't risk never seeing you again, or risk my daughter dying young. I want back the daughter who left here."

Cynthia pulled her hands away. "That daughter can never come back." She looked at her lap again. "That daughter had never loved a man before, had never known nature, had never known the freedom of being one with the land, the joy of living off the land." She met his eyes. "That daughter never knew what prejudice really meant, or how wrong her government was in the way it treated some of its people. And that daughter wasn't carrying a man's baby."

Wells frowned, shaking his head. "Don't you love us anymore, Cynthia?"

"Of course I love you. You're my parents. But I also love Red Wolf. Doesn't the Bible say that when a woman takes a husband she must turn only to him and give up all other things?"

"But he *isn't* your husband, Cynthia, not in the Christian way."

"He *is!* What's the difference if I never signed a piece of paper, Father? God knows how much we love each other. He brought us together. We are as united in heart and mind as we were in body, and I know God—"

"Stop it!" The man rose. "Don't talk to me about be-

285

ing united in body, Cynthia! Not my daughter, not my innocent child!"

"But I've done nothing wrong, Father. Please, please let me go back!"

Tears trickled down her face, but Wells shook his head. "Someday you will understand, Cynthia. You will realize that you could never have survived that life. Surely you know how much we love you, child. We're doing this to help, you, not hurt you."

"But you *are* hurting me! I just want to be with Red Wolf. I want him to see his baby! It isn't fair to him!"

"For all you know the man is dead. And even if he isn't, it will happen sooner or later. You told us yourself what a good warrior he is. There will be a lot of trouble over the soldiers going into those hills to roust out the Indians. Your Red Wolf will be right in the middle of it. There will be more fighting, Cynthia, and I will not have my daughter in the middle of it! I'm sorry, child. God knows how sorry I am! If I could see any better way to do this, I would take it. But that's no life for you, and the sooner you realize it the better. I see no alternative but to get you out of this country as soon as possible." His voice broke and he ran a hand through his hair, turning away from her. "We were so close once, Cynthia. Remember? Remember when you came to me and confessed to letting Red Wolf go that night? Do you remember how understanding I was about it?"

More tears slipped down Cynthia's cheek. "I remember."

"Then surely you know how very much I want to understand, how much I want you to be happy, how much I support your beliefs. But I can't let my daughter go and do something that will bring her an early death." The man seemed to be struggling not to break down. He turned back to Cynthia, tears on his cheeks. "Please tell me you understand that much, Cynthia—that everything I do is because I love you. I'm not blaming you for

286

anything, child. I'm not accusing you of doing anything wrong. I think you're just a very mixed-up young woman right now, and carrying Red Wolf's child makes you feel even closer to him. But we're determined to get you out of this country, Cynthia, and we will not change our minds about that."

Cynthia's heart ached at the look in her father's eyes, his own tears. She realized she had hurt him deeply, but her own hurt that he didn't understand her feelings ran even deeper. She stared at him, remembering how kind and generous and forgiving he had always been. Never had she felt so torn.

"Don't you realize how much I blame myself for all of this, Cynthia?" he was saying. "If I hadn't brought you out here, none of it would have happened. I'm so sorry, Cynthia. Please tell me you forgive me."

Her tender heart would not let her speak cruelly to him, for she knew he truly did believe he was doing the right thing. "Father, I don't need to forgive you. You did what you thought was right. Everything that has happened has been because of my own decisions, like when I cut Red Wolf down, and when I strayed too far from the house. You didn't have anything to do with that. And I don't regret for one minute what happened after Many Bears captured me. I'm telling the truth when I say none of those Indian men touched me. And Red Wolf never did either, until I let him. I love him, Father, the same as Mother loves you. There is no difference at all."

Their eyes held for a long time. The man nodded then. "I suppose you do. But you have to face the fact that Red Wolf lives in a harsh world full of danger. Even your baby would be in great danger. You told us what the soldiers did to some of those Indian babies. Do you want that to happen to yours?"

"Red Wolf would never let it happen."

"Cynthia, you know he can't always stop it. He might

be brave and skilled and all the things you say he is, but he's only human, Cynthia. The fact that soldiers attacked that camp where they found you—what they did there—that should show you that Red Wolf cannot stop such things; and it's going to get worse. At least for the time being you and your baby will be safe. Isn't that worth something to you?"

"But I don't want to live without Red Wolf," she squeaked, the tears coming then.

"Cynthia, you'll have his baby to keep forever. We promise to love the child as we would love any grandchild. Maybe someday, when you've had time to get back to the kind of life that you are meant for, and if, after a time, you still feel the same way you do now, and things are settled down with the Indians; maybe then we can talk about it again. You'll be older and able to make your own decisions. I suppose then, if you want to come back, there won't be much we can do about it. But for now, you know we're right, Cynthia. And if you have ever loved me, I beg of you, child, don't make me have to restrain you some way when we leave. Promise me we can trust you not to try to run away. Don't tear my heart to pieces by making me have to tie you."

Their eyes held for long, silent seconds. "You really would tie me?"

Another tear ran down his cheek. "Yes, Cynthia, I would."

She jerked in a sob and looked at her lap. "I won't make you do that, Father."

He leaned forward and hugged her, and Cynthia cried on his shoulder.

"Thank you, child," he told her in a near-whisper.

After several more minutes of crying he let go of her, petting her hair. "You want something to eat? You have to take care of yourself, you know, so you have a nice, healthy baby."

She wiped at her eyes. "Not right now, Father."

The man patted her shoulder, then rose and left. Cynthia looked up at the soldier, and she could tell through her tears that he was staring at her again.

"Best you go back East, little lady," he told her, humor in his voice. "Half-breeds in these parts get treated worse than full-bloods."

Cynthia looked at her lap, putting a hand to her belly. Yes, this would be a very bad place for her child to grow up. If she couldn't go back to Red Wolf, it was better to go home to Charleston. She wasn't sure what they were going to tell people there. They would worry about that when the time came.

She rose and went to a window, staring out over the open plains. Red Wolf was out there—somewhere. How she longed to get on a horse and be Indian again, to ride free over those plains and go and find her husband! But she was carrying a baby. She would be found, and even if she wasn't, she had no idea where to go to find Red Wolf. There were all kinds of dangers to consider, not the least of which was the cruelty of some of the white men camped in those hills.

She could only pray that Red Wolf would understand that what she did now was only because it was best for the baby. She felt as trapped as a prisoner, but she was left with no choice. It was senseless to make her poor father tie her to restrain her. To try to go back to Red Wolf now was suicide anyway. Her only hope now was that in time she might be able to go back, after things were settled with the Sioux. Then she could take her child and go and find Red Wolf. He would be so happy and surprised . . . if he was still alive.

She covered her face and wept. Who was she fooling but herself? It was over. That was the reality of it. It was over, and she would not see Red Wolf again.

"We're just about all packed, Father," she heard Alex shouting as he ran through the hallway. "Lieutenant Wilson says maybe we can start yet today. He says there's

289

plenty of daylight left."

Cynthia ignored the rest of the conversation. Of course. Why wait another night, another hour, another minute? Why not get it over with? She looked down at her pink dress, touching it. She rubbed at her arms, wondering if all of this was even real. Which part had she dreamed? This part, or the time she'd spent with Red Wolf?

She put a hand to her belly. Both were real. She had truly been Indian, for a while. Now she was white again. She was Cynthia Wells, the preacher's daughter. If not for the baby in her belly, it would almost seem as though she had never been stolen away, had never been the wife of a warrior called Red Wolf. But in her heart she would always be his woman, a warrior's woman, willingly, lovingly, with all the passion her soul possessed. Nothing would ever change that.

Chapter Eighteen

Cynthia walked to the pond behind the house located a half mile from the city of Columbia. A member of the Methodist church where her father had preached before going West had sympathized with the returning Wells family and had let them use this country home, which he had vacated but had not sold yet. Her father was waiting for a new preaching position, and in the meantime he was trying to get a teaching job.

The house they had been given to use was a pleasant one, a one-story brick structure that was neat and well kept. But it felt strange to be living inside any kind of house. Cynthia got out of it every chance she found, longing for the open air and the sunshine. Now she sat by the pond, staring at how the cypress trees and magnolias were almost perfectly reflected in the still waters.

How different this place was from the wild, open country of the Dakotas. South Carolina was beautiful too, more beautiful than she had remembered. Perhaps it was because Red Wolf had taught her to appreciate the land. She looked at such things through different eyes now, and she wondered what Red Wolf would think of South Carolina, with its wooded hills and green mountains, the thick colors created by a host of flowers, the never-ending green of things. There were no horizons here like in South Dakota, no endless rolling plains, no magic Black Hills. But surely this beautiful place was also sacred. Now that she thought like Red Wolf, she could see the sacredness of all nature. Surely there were once Indians here who loved this place the way Red Wolf loved the Dakotas. But the Eastern Indians were gone, most of them extinct, most of those left living in Indian Territory.

Her throat tightened. Was that what would happen to Red Wolf? How would he ever be able to bear living in captivity? It would kill him. She could only pray that he would use his remarkable intelligence to his own good, use it to better himself and to help his people once the day came that they could no longer live the old way. Now that she was back home, she could more clearly see what surely lay ahead for the Sioux. It tore at her heart, but she knew she was better off to be out of the entire situation for the time being.

But there was no Red Wolf to love, to hold her, protect her. No Red Wolf. The thought made her whimper, and she sucked in her breath, then broke into pitiful sobbing. How could she bear this? How she longed to feel Red Wolf's arms around her, to hear his voice speaking quietly into her ear. How she ached to see his handsome smile, to feel his strong hands moving over her naked body, relaxing her, loving her. She could almost taste his kiss, feel the wonder of having him inside her. How was she to go perhaps forever without feeling that again?

She knelt by the pond, touching a lily and peering into the water to study her own reflection. A young woman looked back at her, a young woman with long, straight hair that she now wore in a prim bun; a young woman who had once ridden free on the Dakota plains wearing an Indian tunic, but who now wore the stiff clothing of a white woman; a young woman who was once painted from head to toe with flowers for the summer celebrations, but whose face was now plain, void of color other than the natural hint of pink in her cheeks.

Anyone looking at her now would never know the

difference, except for one thing. She sat down in the grass, touching her swelling stomach. She was almost six months along already. It had been nearly three months since she was taken from Red Wolf that terrible morning. She could still remember the feel of the buffalo robes, the smell of Red Wolf, the texture of his straight, black hair. She could see his smile, hear his voice, smell the smoky interior of the tipi. Now all that was gone. The tipi had been burned. There was no Red Wolf.

But there was this lingering remembrance, this life inside her belly. It moved. It lived. It was a part of Red Wolf. She still wasn't very big, but big enough to show, and big enough to stir up the gossip. She couldn't help feeling sorry for her parents, who were constantly having to explain their daughter's condition.

"She was captured by Sioux Indians," they would say. They never mentioned that she had loved Red Wolf, and Cynthia did not bother trying to explain. Here people sympathized with her, and that was what her parents wanted. Somehow it made her pregnancy more acceptable for people to think she had been raped. How ironic that they would be more shocked and appalled at the simple truth that she had loved an Indian man and had married him and gotten pregnant by him. They actually respected her more for having been raped, and for now being willing to keep the half-breed child she would have.

"What a Christian heart she has," they would say, "being able to bear this child and wanting to keep it."

"We must love the baby as one of God's children," her mother would reply. "He is, after all, our grandchild. We cannot give him away. We feel there is some purpose in all of this. If it is God's will that Cynthia have this child, then we must accept it."

"How strong you are," some would comment.

"What a terrible ordeal!" others would say, staring at Cynthia as though she were some kind of circus creature. She knew what some of them were thinking, wondering— their supposed Christian minds wallowing in the mud of lustful curiosity.

"What is it like to lie with an Indian?" some of them seemed to want to ask. *"Are Indian men made differently? Do they beat you first? Were you ever tortured? Was there more than one?"*

Cynthia was not about to answer any of their unasked questions. She knew by instinct that no amount of explaining would satisfy them. They didn't want to hear about how beautiful the spirit of the Indian was. They didn't want to believe Indians could love and be kind. They didn't want to know she had been in love and had given herself willingly.

She rested her head against a rock and looked up at the sky. The clouds that floated past her now had first floated over the Dakotas. How may days ago? How long did it take the sun to get from her to Red Wolf? She wished she could travel that fast. She could be with Red Wolf again in half a day. Where was he now? What was he doing? She had had an anxious feeling all day, a sick feeling of apprehension that she attributed to her condition. She closed her eyes, feeling the sun on her face, pretending she was lying beside a creek with Red Wolf and they were letting the sun dry them after swimming naked together.

Now she could see him bending over her, feel his lips kissing her. She could taste his mouth, feel his hands moving over her, remember the power she felt in his arms when she grasped at them. Her clothes were gone, and Red Wolf was moving on top of her, his lips gently tasting her breasts, his hands moving under her hips. Then he was inside of her, filling her with his magnificent manhood, bringing out all her passion and joy, whispering her name.

"Red Wolf! Red Wolf!" she whispered. She rolled to her side, the tears coming again. There would never be another man in her life, she was sure. How could any white man live up to Red Wolf? And what white man would even want her now that she had been with an Indian? Her parents only loved and accepted her because

294

she was their daughter. But an outsider would never accept her enough to want to take her for a wife. It didn't really matter, because she had no desire for any man but Red Wolf and couldn't imagine that she ever would. And yet again it was painful to think that she would never know the joy of mating again, the glorious ecstasy of sharing her body with a man. Yet it couldn't be ecstasy unless it was with Red Wolf.

She lay there daydreaming about Red Wolf, hardly aware that her father had come home shouting to her mother.

"Mabel! Mabel, come quick! Look at this!"

There was a pause. "Oh, my God!" the woman said then. Moments later Mabel Wells was calling to her daughter. "Cynthia! Cynthia, come inside! Hurry!"

Cynthia stirred from her sweet dreams and sat up, looking toward the house. Her mother stood in the doorway waving a newspaper. "Come and see this, Cynthia!" The girl got up and walked back toward the house, wondering what could be so exciting. She went into the kitchen, where Alex stood staring at the paper.

"Wow!" the boy murmured.

Mabel took the paper from her son and handed it out to Cynthia. "Look at this. Now see what your loving, kind, abused Sioux Indians have done and tell me they are not savages!"

Cynthia took the paper, opening it to the headlines. CUSTER MASSACRED AT LITTLE BIGHORN. Cynthia felt a tingle in her blood. "General George Armstrong Custer and five companies of the 7th U.S. Cavalry, an estimated three hundred men, have been slaughtered to the last man by Sioux Indians at the Little Bighorn River in Montana," she read.

"Hard Backsides!" she said in a near-whisper. She could not help a hint of a smile. "They really did it. Red Wolf said they would get him someday, and they did!"

She sat down in a chair while her parents and brother stared at her. Cynthia read eagerly. The article posed several possible reasons for the massacre, which was still under investigation. It told of a range of reports on the number of Indians involved, from several hundred to several thousand. Cynthia's eyes teared, her heart swelling with love and pride, for she would never forget the awful things done to the Indians the day she was stolen away; never forget her last sight of her dear friend Flowing Waters, and the two precious children; never forget the shattered head of the little baby she had tried to rescue. Surely Red Wolf had been a part of this massacre of Hard Backsides. How eagerly he would have ridden down on those soldiers! He would have taken out all his frustrations over losing his white woman on those men.

She could see him riding with the other warriors, circling Long-hair Custer and his men, yipping and calling, his face and horse painted, his heart hungry for revenge. Many Bears would have been there too, seeking revenge for losing Flowing Waters and the two babies.

"What a wonderful victory for them!" she commented, looking up at her parents then with tear-filled eyes.

"Cynthia, how can you talk that way?" her mother asked. "Don't you understand how terrible this is? Those were innocent young boys who were killed."

"And so were the women and little children innocent that the soldier killed the day I was taken." She stared at the article again. "I hope Red Wolf was there. I hope he's the one who killed Hard Backsides Custer!"

"Cynthia, you're talking foolish," her father told her gently.

"Am I?" She set the paper down and looked up at him. "I wish you could understand. You think I was drugged or tortured or something. But I am the same Cynthia, and I was never abused. I loved Red Wolf, and I learned to love his people. I understand why they did this, Father."

The man sighed. "Right or wrong, this is just an example of why it's a good thing you're away from there. Things will be worse than ever for them now, Cynthia.

More soldiers than they have seen yet will be sent out there. All the Sioux have done here is cut their own throats. Do you understand that much at least?"

She put a hand to her chest, it ached so. "Yes. I understand that much."

"Red Wolf and the others will be hounded and hunted and killed until all the Sioux are finally on reservation land. Their old way of life will be over, and you wouldn't want any part of the way they will have to live from now on. You're better off here, and so is Red Wolf's son or daughter."

Cynthia looked down at her swelling stomach. "Yes, I suppose so." "*Red Wolf!*" she thought. "*Were you there? Oh, I hope your bullets and arrows found their mark! I hope you celebrated that night! I hope you wished we could celebrate together, the way we used to celebrate a good hunt.*"

Jealousy stabbed at her heart at the thought that maybe after a time Red Wolf might take an Indian wife. Would he forget about her someday? Would the memory fade until she was but a whisper in his mind? He was a man with needs. Surely he would take another woman, even though he might not love her as he had loved Cynthia. Perhaps that was what would happen to her too. She would take a husband simply to be secure and have a home of her own. But she would never love him in the way she had loved Red Wolf.

She rose from her chair. "May I keep this paper?"

Her father looked at her as though she were a stranger. "I suppose. I can get another. I am surprised at your attitude, Cynthia."

"You shouldn't be."

"Just don't go around telling others you're glad about it. They wouldn't understand either, and we have all already agreed it's useless to try to explain."

Cynthia walked past him and down the hall to her room, going inside and sitting down to read the article more closely. George Armstrong Custer was dead. It seemed impossible. She couldn't help being glad. If it weren't for Custer spreading the word that there was gold in the Black Hills, Sioux land wouldn't have been so filled with whites in the first place. It served him right.

Someone knocked on her door then, and she looked up to see Alex coming in. "Cindy?"

"What do you want, Alex?"

"Will you tell me what it was probably like—Red Wolf and those Indians riding against Custer? I like to hear you tell about how they dressed and all that. Do you think there really were thousands of them?"

Cynthia smiled. "Yes, Alex, I'm sure of it. There were more Indians in one place than General Crook or Longhair Custer could have known."

Alex sat down beside her. Her brother seemed to be the only one who came close to understanding how she really felt, who never looked at her accusingly. Alex understood, for his young boy's heart was as spirited as an Indian's. Cynthia gladly told him again what life had been like among the Sioux, for every time she was able to talk freely about it, her heart felt lighter, happier. In the telling, she could be close to Red Wolf again.

"He would have been painted," she began, "nearly naked because of the hot weather. He would ride his painted pony bareback, and I can just see him charging down on the soldiers, screaming a war cry, his long hair flying in the wind. . . ."

He walked into Lieutenant Wilson's quarters, standing proud and silent. Wilson looked up at him, an extremely handsome Indian but at the moment looking ragged and dirty, for earlier in the day he had been herded into the fort with the few remaining warriors of the small band that had been captured just that morning. Since the Little Bighorn, there had been a heated campaign to bring in all Indians and end this thing for once and for all. The Sioux and Cheyenne had split up into many bands, most of

298

them caught and killed or arrested over several months. The Indians' ability to hide and fight soldiers in numbers far greater than their own had earned them considerable respect from many soldiers, and Wilson did not doubt that they could learn a lot about fighting from these rugged red men of the Plains.

"So, you are Red Wolf," Wilson said then.

The man before him glared at him with dark, vengeful eyes, his long black hair full of dust, a soiled headband tied around a deep gash near his temple. Blood still trickled from a wound on his right forearm, and he wore only a loincloth and buckskin leggings. His shoulders were powerful, his stomach flat and muscled. His broad chest was decorated with a bear-claw necklace and another necklace made of porcupine quills. A copper band decorated one firm bicep.

Wilson struggled with the thought of this man actually loving a white girl gently, and yet he surely had, for no one could mistake the love Cynthia Wells had in her eyes when she spoke of him.

"I am Red Wolf," he answered proudly. "What is it you want with me? Am I to be hanged? Shot?"

Wilson smiled and shook his head, rising from his chair. "No. Actually, I just wanted to meet you. I wanted to see the young warrior who made such an impression on a white girl named Cynthia Wells."

Red Wolf's countenance immediately changed from hate and contempt to a sudden softness. His breathing quickened, and Wilson was struck by the love that shown in his dark eyes. "You have seen her? You know where she is? Can I see her?"

Wilson smiled sadly. "No. She has been taken back to the land of the rising sun, Red Wolf, a journey of many weeks from here, white man's land."

Red Wolf's face fell. "You knew her? Is she well? Does she still carry my child?"

"She did when she left here. That's all I know. That was nearly three months ago. I am the one who took her back to her parents."

"Where? Where is she? I could find her someday!"

Wilson folded his arms. "No, Red Wolf. I would never tell you where she went. Don't you understand it was best? Look at you. You've been through hell, and if she had been with you, she would have gone through it too. She probably would have lost her baby, maybe been killed herself. Now you'll be living on a reservation. Is that the kind of life you would have wanted for a girl of Cynthia Wells's breeding? She could never have stood it, Red Wolf."

"We will be strong and free again!" the young man answered, holding his chin high.

Wilson sat down on the edge of his desk. "Face the truth, Red Wolf. It's over. Crazy Horse is dead at the hands of his own people. Sitting Bull is in Canada. The moment he returns, he'll be arrested and brought to the reservation. Personally, I don't think any of it is right. But unfortunately, I have no say in it, and my own heart is bitter over what your people did to Custer and all those innocent young men at the Little Bighorn. But I can actually understand it to some extent. At any rate, it's over, Red Wolf, and you have to face that fact and learn that your people have to change, or die."

Red Wolf swallowed, feeling the reawakened agony of losing Cynthia. To hear someone talk about her brought back all the pain, all the passion. "Please," he begged. "Tell me where she is."

Wilson shook his head. "I can't do that. She'll learn to adjust and so will you. In fact, her father will probably get transferred to yet another place, and I won't know myself where he is. I just thought you would want to know that she was all right the last time I saw her."

His eyes teared. "Did she speak of me?"

Wilson actually felt sorry for the bloodied warrior who stood before him. "Yes. She spoke of you. She didn't want to leave at all. She wanted to come back to you. But after a time she'll understand, as you will, that it was all for the best."

"But what about my child? I have the right!"

"No. You don't have that right. He'll be raised in her world, Red Wolf, and I'm sure he'll have a good life. He'll be loved, that is certain. But he'll be living in a world so foreign to you that if you went there right now, you would soon die. It would be like taking a fish out of water for you to leave this land. By the time you could go into the world of the white man, much time will have passed, too much for you to try to step back into Cynthia's life."

Red Wolf turned away, afraid for the soldier to see his tears. "Why did you call me here?" he asked, his voice strained. "To torture me with talk of Cynthia?"

"No. I only told you what I know so that you would be at ease as far as what might have happened to her after she was taken from you. I called you over here for another reason."

Red Wolf stared at a picture of Abraham Lincoln that hung on the wall. "What do you want, *wasicus?*"

Wilson rose and walked back behind his desk. "Cynthia told me something about you that got me to thinking. She said you spoke English very well, and that you seemed very intelligent. She said you were special, different, and that she thought you could do a good job of representing your people to the white man."

"So?"

"So, things are going to change, Red Wolf. There is a lot of legislation going on in Washington, where our Great White Father resides and rules over his people like your chiefs do. Believe it or not, there is a lot of sympathy on the part of white citizens back East to look out for the best interests of the Indians."

"They kill us and herd us onto reservations, then feel sorry for us, is that it? They want to soothe their guilty consciences." He turned fiery eyes to Wilson. "You whites have a strange set of codes!"

Wilson sighed. "Yes, I suppose it seems that way." He stepped closer to Red Wolf. "This country is changing,

Red Wolf, and nothing can stop it from happening—nothing. Some things are going to happen no matter how anyone feels about it. I'm asking you to think about that—to think about how effective a handsome, intelligent young man like yourself could be in helping represent his people, in making sure they get fair treatment. It won't help having reservation agents and other whites speaking on their behalf. They don't really understand, and half of them are crooked to begin with. What they will need is someone from their own blood speaking for them—someone who truly understands their needs, their fears, their beliefs. Someone like you."

Red Wolf frowned, shaking his head. "What do you expect me to do?"

"I want you to think about Cynthia's words. I want you to honor her by living up to what she believed you were capable of doing. I can tell in this short conversation that she was right. I think you are a very intelligent man, Red Wolf, and that with some education, you could be very successful in winning certain rights for your people by representing them before Congress and the white leaders who make these decisions. It would be a long road. You would have to learn many things, travel East and go to special schools, learn the white man's ways, how he thinks and feels. It would not be easy, but you would be doing it for your people, and for Cynthia Wells."

Red Wolf breathed deeply, again touched just hearing Cynthia's name. How many nights had he ached to hold her again, longed to taste her lips, to be one with her? He would never love another, never forget his white woman. He stared again at the picture. "Who is that?"

"That's Abraham Lincoln. He was our President during the Civil War—the white man's war back East."

Red Wolf nodded. "I know about him. Cynthia told me. He freed men you call Negroes, men with very black skin and hair who were kept as slaves. I have seen such men. We call them Buffalo People." He felt the painful

302

awareness of how deceitful the white man could be. "This Lincoln freed the Buffalo People, but the Sioux, who were in this land first, are *not* free. Why is that, *wasicus?*"

"That is one of many injustices I can't defend, Red Wolf. But even the Negroes have to live among the whites, learn to live as white men do. They don't have a land of their own either. They don't live on reservations. So freedom for them will not be so easy as you think. And perhaps someday the Indians will learn the white man's ways enough to be able to move away from the reservations and live among them."

Red Wolf shook his head, his back still to Wilson. "No, *wasicus*. It is different for the Indian. He will never truly be like a white man. Away from his homeland, he will get sick and die. I see it now." He faced Wilson again. "I will think about what you have told me. Perhaps I will get this learning you speak of. I will harden my heart against the longing to be in the land of the Great Spirit and be strong so that I can bear living among the whites long enough to get this education. But then I will come back. I would never be able to stay away from the sacred hills for long. To be away from them is to drain the blood from my body. I take nourishment in them, draw life and strength from them and from my people." He stepped closer, his dark eyes drilling challengingly into Wilson's. "I will consider this education. But for one reason only. We can no longer hope to defeat the white man in battle. There are too many of you, and your guns are too big. But perhaps there is another way to beat you—to learn to *think* like you, and then use it against you!"

The words were spat out in a sneer, and Wilson could see this young man would surely be a challenge to fight physically. Perhaps he would one day be a mental challenge for the best in Washington.

He smiled slyly. "Make Cynthia Wells proud, Red Wolf. She said you were different, and I believe you are. Accept what is and go on from here. Use your energy and your intelligence for your people, and learn to forget Cynthia Wells."

Red Wolf's eyes teared again. "I will use my intelligence and learning for my people. But I will never—*never* forget Cynthia Wells! A fire for her will burn inside me forever!"

Never had Cynthia known such gripping cruel pain. "She's too young," she vaguely remembered the doctor saying. "This is not going to be an easy birth."

She had lain in labor for hours, and she kept calling for Red Wolf. If only he could be here. Had it really been six months since that awful day the soldiers came? Would she wake up and find it had been six years? If only he could know his child was being born.

She screamed, she cried, she passed out, then awoke to screams again. Never had she been more terrified than of this awful pain. Was something wrong? Would her baby die? No! She must have this child! It must live! It was all she had left of Red Wolf, her only link to the sweet love they had shared. Again came the cold, cruel fingers of pain that ripped at her insides and made her body do things against her will. She clung tightly to her mother's hand as the woman coached her, soothed her damp face with a cool cloth, told her to relax and just let the baby come.

Finally, in the wee hours of the morning of October 12, 1876, Cynthia Wells gave birth to a healthy son with a thick shock of black hair and all his fingers and toes. There was great commotion around her then. She could hear the baby crying, feel herself being washed. Someone was pushing on her stomach to get the afterbirth, and then someone was laying the freshly washed baby beside her.

"Here is your son, Cynthia," her mother told her.

Cynthia met the woman's eyes, and she knew that no matter how this child had been conceived, her mother

304

understood the universal love of motherhood.

"And my grandson," the woman added.

Cynthia's eyes teared. "Thank you for loving him, Mother."

The woman took her hand. "We'll get through this, Cynthia. We'll help protect him and help raise him to be a fine boy. If you want to tell him about the ways of his people, and the love under which he was conceived, then he should know."

The baby pinched at her breast with tiny red fingers and started crying again. Cynthia looked down at him and wept. A son! Red Wolf's son! If only he could know! But he was far, far away, perhaps not even alive anymore. It was all changed now. There was no going back.

She opened her gown and the baby began sucking at her milk. Cynthia studied his skin, unsure just how dark it would turn out to be. For now it was very red and somewhat wrinkled. His hair was very fine, but thick and very black. His face seemed perfect. He was beautiful, just like Red Wolf. Cynthia wiped at her eyes. "I want to call him Freedom," she told her mother. "Freedom is something Red Wolf and his people wanted so badly." She looked up at the woman. "Freedom Wells. Surely God loves him the same as any child born of a Christian marriage."

The woman smiled, touching the tiny, soft cheek. "Surely he does. If you want to call him Freedom, then that is how he will be christened. Freedom Wells." The woman smoothed back her hair. "We must go on from here, Cynthia. We must look to the future and forget the past."

Cynthia did not reply. Yes, she would look to the future, for Freedom's sake. But she would never forget the past, nor the man who gave life to the tiny boy who lay feeding at her breast.

Part Three

Cynthia walked the brick walkway laid out neatly through well-manicured green grass. She missed the soft quiet of South Carolina, and wondered what Red Wolf would think of the bustling campus of Princeton, and the hordes of whites in the state of New Jersey. The busy atmosphere was enjoyable for Cynthia. Since coming here three years ago with her family to live, she had begun to feel stronger, more at peace with herself.

Albert Wells had accepted a position with Princeton Theological Seminary as a teacher, after spending four years teaching high school back in South Carolina. To help ward off her own loneliness and continued longing for Red Wolf, Cynthia had taken some classes of higher learning herself, even though most people still considered such things unnecessary for women.

But Cynthia did not consider herself an average woman. For when she walked around the campus of Princeton, she held the hand of a little seven-year-old boy whose skin was a soft brown; whose deep brown eyes were big and beautiful and full of mischief; whose hair was straight and black. She sometimes wondered how she would have kept going these past seven years without little Freedom, whose spirit was unmistakably Indian. In him Cynthia could see Red Wolf's smile, his teasing nature, his high cheekbones and handsome features.

Freedom was a strong, healthy boy, extremely bright, already reading and writing.

"I told you his father was intelligent," Cynthia would tell her parents. "You can see by how bright Freedom is."

"He is a wonder, I'll say," her father would answer.

There was much love among all of them. Since Albert Wells was no longer preaching, it was not so important what other people thought. He was a good teacher, and that was all the seminary cared about. And Freedom was a child of such charm and with such a joyful nature that people warmed to him no matter what they thought of how the boy might have been conceived. He won people's hearts with his affectionate smile, and with charming questions and his bubbling personality.

Here at Princeton Cynthia had come to be known as the rather mysterious young woman who was once a captive of Sioux Indians. People began asking questions, wanting to know more about Indians from someone who knew about them firsthand. People on campus seemed to be more open-minded about all of it, and Cynthia was no longer hesitant to tell the truth—that she had loved little Freedom's father, but that cultural differences and the dangers Freedom would have faced whether he lived with the whites or the Sioux had compelled Cynthia to come back East to have her baby.

"There was a lot of misunderstanding then," she was telling a girlfriend now. "I was young and afraid and confused."

The two girls sat down on a bench, Freedom plunking down between them. Martha Cunningham had recently begun attending church on campus. Her own father also taught at the seminary. She was twenty, just four years younger than Cynthia, and she was engaged to be married. She was a plump girl, with plain features and brown hair and eyes. She was attractive in a simple sort of way, perhaps because of her innocence. Cynthia had only known the young woman two weeks, but Martha was easy to like, and she had a sympathetic ear for Cynthia's past experiences.

"I try to imagine what it would be like, being captured by wild Indians," the girl told Cynthia then. "You must have been so terrified at first."

"I was. But I soon realized Many Bears didn't really intend to hurt me bad. He was putting on a show for the men with him, protecting me in a sense. Then Red Wolf came for me." She said it longingly, putting an arm around Freedom's shoulders.

"That's my father," the boy spoke up proudly. "He's Indian."

"I know, Freedom," Martha told him. She watched Cynthia, detecting the near-worship in the young woman's voice at the mention of Red Wolf.

"Do you ever think of going back there, Cynthia— finding him again?"

"I think about it all the time." She toyed with Freedom's hair between her fingers. "But it's been seven years. I don't even know if Red Wolf is alive. And if he is, I don't know how things have changed. He could be married to an Indian woman by now. He probably thinks like I do that it never really could have worked. And if he's still alive, he's most likely living on a reservation. I don't doubt the Indians are not getting treated fairly and that their life on the reservation is miserable. I don't want that for Freedom. At the same time, we can't go out there and live among the whites. They would be cruel to Freedom. He would never be happy living with all that hatred. I guess it's easier here because people here haven't experienced any suffering at the hands of the Indians. Out there nearly everyone has had some kind of bad experience or has suffered a loss because of the Indian wars. The trouble is, none of them think about the terrible losses for the Indians too. They don't think of them as human, so they think nothing bothers them." She looked at Martha. "But I know different. It wasn't an

311

act of cruelty that got me pregnant. It was an act of love."

Martha reddened slightly. "What is it like, Cynthia? I mean, I'll be marrying Randolph soon, and I don't know anything about men."

Cynthia felt the stabbing pain in her heart again. Was Red Wolf remarried? She had tried to get interested in other young men, but none held any attraction for her. It had been such a long, long time since she was held in a man's arms, since she felt a man kissing her, felt a man moving inside of her.

"It's wonderful," she answered honestly. "It's the most beautiful experience in the whole world, if the man is gentle and truly loves you, and you love him. Each time is a little better than the last."

Martha smiled shyly, looking away. "You must think I'm terrible asking such a thing. We shouldn't be talking about it."

"Why not? God created us to marry and mate. There's nothing bad about it, Martha."

"I suppose not. But it just isn't very good etiquette—and I've only known you for two weeks."

"It doesn't matter how long we've known each other. It's how we feel about each other. I've needed a friend closer to my own age for a long time, Martha. For the first few years I hardly ever left the house or the grounds. I was afraid of embarrassing my parents, and afraid to expose Freedom to possible insults and dangers. Every day was the same, until I thought I would go insane with the loneliness of it. There were so many times when I was tempted to at least write to Red Wolf, try to get a letter to him telling him I was all right and that he had a son. But that would have been cruel. He's better off not knowing at all."

Freedom jumped up and ran to climb a tree, and Martha turned to Cynthia. "What if you saw him again, Cynthia? Would you be able to just turn away and let him go his way and you yours?"

Cynthia looked past her at brick buildings and

meandering students. "Never. I could never tell him good-bye again. But that is never going to happen."

Martha sighed deeply. "Oh, it's such a sad, beautiful story. What an exciting life you've had." She touched Cynthia's arm. "Don't you ever think about getting married, Cynthia? Little Freedom needs a father."

"He has his grandfather."

"But that's different. Grandfathers don't have the necessary energy to do things with a little boy that a father would. And you said yourself that your father is always wrapped up in his work, bringing papers home at night to correct. He doesn't have time right now to be raising a little boy. And you're so young yourself. You should get married, Cynthia. It's the only way to truly get over Red Wolf and start living for the future. Freedom would have a father, and you'd have even more children."

Cynthia smiled sadly. "I'm not sure I could ever love that way again. But even if I could, how many men would marry a woman who has been with an Indian and has even had a son by an Indian? It isn't easy, Martha."

"But you're so beautiful. I've never seen anyone as pretty as you."

Cynthia blushed and smiled. "Thank you. But that isn't the final say in marriage. I've had a few experiences with young men who were interested in me and would come calling. As soon as I introduced my son they found an excuse to leave."

Both young women laughed.

"Well, I don't care," Martha said. "Some man is going to come along who will faint dead away at your beauty, and Indian son or no, he'll want to marry you, because he'll see what a beautiful person you are, how brave and strong and intelligent you are."

Cynthia laughed again. She looked up into the tree that Freedom had climbed. "Look at him. He's his father's son, all right, daring and adventurous. He's my whole world now. He's all I need."

313

"I don't believe that. And I won't be happy until you're married, Cynthia Wells."

Cynthia smiled. "Then you might be unhappy for a very long time, I'm afraid."

"Oh, I hope not."

They laughed together again and got up from the bench. "Come down out of that tree, Freedom," Cynthia told her son.

The boy swung down and hung by his arms, then dropped, landing on his feet and rolling backward. He was immediately back up and running ahead of them as they headed toward a park square. It was summer, 1883. Flowers bloomed everywhere, and birds sang. As the two young women approached the square, they noticed more people were gathering. Some stared at Cynthia when the little Indian boy ran back to her to grab her hand, calling her Mother. There were a few whispers, but Cynthia had grown used to the looks and the gossip. Those who knew her story understood. At least most of them seemed to. They were at least accepting and kind, and all were tolerant of Freedom.

"Oh, look, they've built a platform," Martha said. "There's going to be some kind of speaker here."

"Don't you know?" a young man said then, looking from Freedom to Cynthia. "Seems to me that might be why you came here."

Cynthia met his curious eyes. "My friend and I are just walking to enjoy the weather. Who is going to be speaking here today?"

"Why it's a young seminary graduate who is also an attorney—Richard Holmes. He's thinking of running for Congress and we're here to see what he has to say. It's, uh . . ." The young man looked down at Freedom again. "It's said that he favors Indian rights—some kind of advocate for protecting the American Indian, they say—wants to be sure they don't get cheated. Siding with the Indians seems to be a rather popular opinion these days—wins votes, you know."

"Does it? I didn't know," Cynthia answered rather sarcastically. She didn't like the young man's insinuation that a man would side with the Indians only to win votes rather than because he believed in what he was doing and truly did sympathize with the Indians.

The young man smiled nervously then. "Well, at any rate, I just thought that with the little boy there . . . Is he adopted, Miss, uh . . ."

"No, sir, he is not adopted. He is mine."

The young man reddened deeply and literally lost his voice. He turned and mixed in with the crowd, and Cynthia turned to Martha. "See what I mean?"

Martha just laughed. "Let's stay and see what the speaker has to say," she said then. "You should be interested in anyone who wants to fight for Indian rights, Cynthia. Surely you're interested in listening to him."

Cynthia looked up at the platform. "Yes. I *am* interested. Do you mind staying and listening?"

"Oh, no. I just wish Randolph were here too. I really should get back soon. Randolph is picking me and Mother up to go shopping for my trousseau for the honeymoon." The girl reddened again, and Cynthia felt a deep longing to belong that way again, to be a wife and have a home of her own. But she could not shed the memory of Red Wolf, nor bring herself to have any interest in any of the young men who had called on her, even those who hadn't run the moment they met Freedom.

The crowd grew bigger, and finally a carriage rolled up near the platform. Cynthia and Martha stood close and could easily see the young man who stepped out of the carriage. And for the first time since being forced to leave Red Wolf, Cynthia felt the familiar little tug at her insides, felt a slight flutter of the heart.

If the young man stepping up to the speaker's podium was nothing else, he was indeed handsome, with a grand physique and compelling blue eyes. He flashed a winning smile, and his features were uniquely masculine, with finely etched lips and a square jawline. What hair she

315

could see from under his hat looked neatly cut around his ears. His clothes were immaculate and of the latest fashion. His pants and jacket were dark gray cheviot, the pants fitting tightly at the ankles, the jacket cut to the waist in front but with tails at the back. The lapels of the jacket were silk, and his high-necked white shirt was graced at the neck with a small black bow tie, and he wore a silk top hat and shining black boots.

"Would you look at him?" Martha declared. "Now there's a fine, handsome, fancy man for you, Cynthia."

Cynthia smiled and reddened, turning chiding eyes to Martha. "Don't talk that way, Martha Cunningham."

"Don't tell me you don't see he's absolutely beautiful—and surely a man on his way to the top. I wonder if he's single."

"Martha, stop it!"

Cynthia looked up at the young man again, who she guessed to be in his late twenties or early thirties. He removed his top hat, revealing thick, wavy, light brown hair. People were clapping then, and he bowed slightly. As he rose again his eyes fell on Cynthia, showing in them an appreciation for her beauty, as well as an immediate curiosity, for he could not help noticing she held a little boy's hand, a little boy who looked very Indian. He looked at Martha then and nodded as he straightened, moving his eyes back to Cynthia for a moment before scanning the entire crowd.

"Ladies and gentlemen, my name is Richard Holmes. Thank you for gathering here this morning to give me a moment to speak to you." His eyes kept scanning the crowd, but always came back to Cynthia and Freedom. "I graduated from this very institution eight years ago, and I am now a practicing attorney in the state of Maryland, where in another two years I plan to run for the office of United States Congressman."

There was more applause, and Cynthia watched, struggling to ignore the pleasant stirrings the handsome Richard Holmes created in her. She told herself that after

316

seven years it was foolish to feel guilty for having such feelings, and yet she could not help them. It almost saddened her, as though to suddenly be attracted to a man after all these years was some kind of final good-bye to Red Wolf. How could she ever truly face the fact that he was never going to be in her life again? How could she give up the dream, the still-burning torch in her soul? And yet how could she expect to finish out her life alone, with no man to hold her and provide for her, no father for Freedom?

"I know you're wondering why I am here in New Jersey speaking to people rather than in Maryland," Holmes was saying. "Well, I am originally from New Jersey, and I am here to fulfill a promise I made to my now-deceased parents, who were very concerned about the rights of the American Indian. I promised them that when I was established in my career, I would carry on their efforts at doing what they could to ensure that the noble savages of this land, those red men of the mountains and the rivers and the great West, receive fair treatment, now that they have been confined to reservations throughout the country. I won't go into the details of why my parents felt a need to support the Indian. Suffice it to say, it is something that must be done. We citizens of good conscience must do what we can to take care of those we have displaced, those who gave up their lands for the great dream of Manifest Destiny. And so, I made up my mind that every year I would take time to travel to surrounding states and talk to people like yourselves—to ask you to now have mercy on our red brothers; to write letters to Congress urging fair treatment of the Indians; to stir your Christian consciences into action and do what you can to prevent some of the horrendous cheating that is taking place on some Indian reservations; to insist that Congress provide proper medical care for the Indian, provide enough food and supplies, adequate housing."

Cynthia could not remove her eyes from him. She tried

317

to determine if he was truly sincere, or if he was just spouting off words to appear the concerned Christian. Supporting the American Indian was a rather popular position in the East. Did this man even know any Indians? Had he been to a reservation? His eyes kept meeting hers again, and they were kind. She didn't see there any cockiness or lies, and she wondered what possible link this man who apparently had always lived in the East could have with the American Indian.

Holmes went on about the selling of whiskey on the reservations, filthy living conditions, inadequate housing and medical care, underhanded agents who sold the good government supplies to outsiders for a profit, then gave rotten meat and poorer-quality goods to the Indians. Cynthia pulled Freedom closer, pressing him against her legs and resting her hands on his shoulders. Was it all true, what Mr. Holmes was saying? She ran her fingers through Freedom's straight, black hair. Her parents had been right then. Freedom was better off where he was. She would never want to raise him amid the kind of conditions Holmes was describing. But what about poor Red Wolf? Her heart ached at the thought of it. How was he living, if he was even alive at all? How sad the reservation life must be for him. If it were not for Freedom, she would go to him and suffer whatever she had to suffer. But here Freedom had good schooling and a pleasant home, with grandparents who loved him, and with plenty of the proper food to eat. He was accepted, an absolute pet of some of their closest friends. In the West she did not doubt Indians were still hated. The only alternative would have been for Red Wolf to come East, but surely it would be like taking away the very air he breathed. He would never survive in this world.

"—write your Congressmen," Holmes was saying. "Tell them you will not tolerate the current Indian abuse that is taking place—that we must respect the red man as the one who was here first, who gave up everything, including hundreds of thousands of lives, so that we whites could settle in their lands."

"I have to leave, Cynthia," Martha was saying. "Tell me later what happens."

"Happens?" She faced Martha, seeing a sparkle in the girl's eyes. "What do you mean?"

"You know what I mean. Do you see how he keeps looking at you? And I don't see a wedding band on his hand."

"Oh, Martha, just go, will you? You're being silly."

The girl giggled and patted Cynthia's arm, then hurried away.

"Mama." Freedom tugged at her skirt and Cynthia knelt down beside him.

"What is it, Freedom?"

"Is he talking about my father?"

Cynthia kissed his brown cheek. "Yes, I suppose in some ways he is."

"Is my father going to die?"

Cynthia's eyes teared. "Darling, I don't even know if he is alive anymore."

"Why don't we find out?"

She hugged him close. "It's hard to explain, Freedom. You and I wouldn't be able to survive where your father is, and he would never survive here. So it's best just to leave things as they are. If we were to see him and find out he's still alive, it would just hurt more, because we wouldn't be able to be together. He probably has an Indian wife by now. He lives in a land far, far away from here."

"Maybe I would like it there."

She studied the beautiful brown face, the dark eyes, the uniquely Indian features that made her heart ache for Red Wolf. She would never know that kind of magic again, that kind of wild freedom. She could see the yearning in her son's eyes, and it struck her that even though Freedom had been brought up in the East, he still had an Indian's spirit. She wondered how long she could keep him close to her.

"When you grow up, Freedom, if you want to go West and try to find your father, I would never stop you. By then you will be well educated, and better able to understand all of this. And I know you'll be the kind of man your father would be so very proud of."

People were clapping again and Cynthia rose to see Richard Holmes coming down the platform steps right toward her. Her heart pounded and she felt as flushed and nervous as a much younger girl.

"Excuse me, ma'am," Holmes said as he approached and stood over her, his physique even more commanding up close. "I couldn't help noticing the handsome young boy with you. Might I inqure if he is Indian, and where he comes from? One doesn't usually see little Indian boys wandering about college campuses." His smile was infectious.

Cynthia swallowed, keeping a tight grip on Freedom's hand. "His name is Freedom. He's half Sioux Indian," Cynthia answered, overcoming the flustered state caused by the inquiry about Freedom. Always she was instantly ready to defend her son, and herself, against the looks people gave them when they found out the truth about Freedom. "Freedom is my son, Mr. Holmes."

The man's smile faded slightly, and his eyes moved over her curiously. "Your . . . adopted son?"

"No." Cynthia held his eyes squarely. "My son by birth."

Holmes reddened slightly, his blue eyes moving over Cynthia again, then to Freedom. "Well, well," he commented. He broke into another brilliant smile. "How fascinating! I must hear about this, Miss, uh, Mrs. . . . Oh, do forgive me. I never even asked your name."

Their eyes held for a moment, and Cynthia again felt the lovely stirring she had not felt for years. "My name is Cynthia Wells. My father is Albert Wells, a preacher. Right now he's teaching here at Princeton. We live on campus and I take Freedom for walks every morning."

The man put out his hand. "And I am Richard Holmes."

Cynthia took his hand hesitantly. It was warm and reassuring as he wrapped it around her small hand. "You should know it's *Miss* Wells, Mr. Holmes, although at the time Freedom was conceived I considered myself married to his father. A union in the eyes of God is just as valid as any union declared legal by a piece of paper."

The man's eyebrows arched and he bowed slightly again. "I don't mean to pry, Miss Wells. I suppose my question seemed rather bold, since I have just met you. But as you just heard, I have a keen interest in the American Indian, and I was so surprised to see this young man standing beside you this morning. My curiosity just wouldn't let me leave without inquiring."

He released her hand and Cynthia moved an arm about Freedom's shoulders. "Well, thank you for not jumping back in shock and running away, Mr. Holmes. That's what most strangers do when I tell them Freedom is my son."

Holmes laughed lightly. "Well, I am not so easily shocked. And you are much too beautiful to run from. Could we perhaps walk together for a while? I would be glad to walk you back home."

Their eyes held again, and Cynthia felt a lovely warmth under his gaze. "All right," she answered, wondering why she had said it. Was it wrong to have feelings again for a man? "Come, Freedom, we're going back home."

Holmes turned to the man who had driven him there in a rented carriage and told him to wait for his return. Freedom ran ahead of them then, climbing up into trees along the way, then dropping down to run ahead of them again.

"Freedom. What a fascinating name," Holmes told her, putting on his top hat. He put out his arm and Cynthia took it as they walked together.

"I named him Freedom because freedom was all his

321

father ever wanted. His spirit is as free as the eagle, just like his father's was."

"And who was his father?"

Cynthia didn't answer right away, the pain stabbing at her again. "He was called Red Wolf." She sighed deeply, watching Freedom. "When I was sixteen my family moved to Deadwood, South Dakota. My father wanted to take the word of God to the sorry lot of miners and harlots who lived there. One day the miners rode in with a captured Sioux man. They dragged him down the street and beat him. They were going to hang him the next morning." She stopped walking and turned to face Holmes. "I felt sorry for him and I snuck out of the house that night and went to where they had him tied. The man watching him had fallen asleep, and I cut the Sioux man down and let him escape."

"Red Wolf?"

Cynthia nodded. "A couple of months later I wandered too far from the house and was captured by Sioux Indians. I thought I would be"—she turned and watched after Freedom again—"violated . . . tortured and killed. But I wasn't. And when we got to their village, Red Wolf was there. He found out who had been brought in and he rescued me from the tipi where . . . where captive women are taken." She folded her arms, unable to look at him then. "It was much too dangerous for Red Wolf to take me back just then—dangerous for him. So I stayed with him, and by the time it was safe to try to take me back, I didn't want to go. I had fallen in love with Red Wolf, and he loved me."

She finally turned and looked up at Holmes, her cheeks crimson. "Does that shock you, Mr. Holmes? I didn't want to go back to my people. I wanted to stay with the Sioux."

He smiled softly. "It doesn't shock me. It only stirs an intense curiosity—how a well-bred, innocent young woman could have such a change of heart—how she could be willing to adapt to an entirely different way of living. I have heard of this happening before. But I have never had the privilege and opportunity of talking to someone who had this happen to them firsthand. I truly admire your courage and stamina, Miss Wells, and your willingness to say right out that Freedom is your son."

She studied the blue eyes, so sincere. He had called knowing her a privilege! "Thank you, Mr. Holmes." She smiled nervously. "This is so strange. I have never told so much at once to a total stranger. You have a way of getting things out of people, don't you?"

He winked. "A future politician has to have such a talent, don't you think?"

Cynthia laughed lightly. She had not felt this good and this comfortable around a man in years. "Yes, I suppose so. Tell me, Mr. Holmes, why did your parents have such an interest in Indians?"

They started walking again. "Well, I must say there is a little guilt involved. My parents, you see, became quite wealthy from Indian lands they settled on in Georgia— land purchased through a lottery after the Cherokee were sent to Indian Territory. Gold was discovered on their plot. Oh, it wasn't a huge fortune, mind you. The mine played out quickly enough. But it certainly netted them enough to live comfortably the rest of their lives, and to afford me a good education. They sold the property and moved to New Jersey because my father hated the hot summers in Georgia, and to be in a more populated area for my father's law practice. He was also an attorney. Then they had me, very late in their marriage. My mother died when I was only ten, my father just five years ago. At any rate, they often heard of some of the things that are going on with the Indians on the reservations, and they both always felt a little funny about moving onto land that once belonged to a very prominent, educated Cherokee, and getting rich off that land; while the Cherokee man probably lived in poverty in Indian Territory. They felt it their duty as Christians to do something for the very people who had lost everything

323

they had, while my parents took it all over and got rich. Does that sound silly or pretentious to you? They were truly sincere in their feelings about the Indians."

"It doesn't sound silly to me at all. I think it's commendable of them." She looked up at him. "Have you ever been to the reservations yourself?"

He frowned and reddened slightly. "I must confess I haven't. But I have people with whom I keep in touch, who tell me what is going on out there, and there have been many proven cases already of terrible cheating going on. The only help the Indians will get is from the East and the North, where there are people who have gotten over their prejudice and hatred and who recognize the injustices inflicted upon the first Americans."

Cynthia stopped walking again and faced him. "I would really like to think you are sincere, Mr. Holmes, and not just supporting the Indians because it might be the popular thing to do right now."

He frowned, studying her blue eyes, fascinated by her beauty and thinking what a fine flower of a wife she would make on the arm of a congressman. "I assure you, Miss Wells, I am very sincere. I have sent money and supplies back with men who travel to the reservations for me. And I petition men in Congress constantly to act on the various Indian legislation that is always pending. I can show you—"

"It's all right." Cynthia smiled. "I believe you, Mr. Holmes."

"Please, call me Richard?"

Cynthia reddened slightly. "I will if I ever see you again. But that isn't too likely."

"It is if you will allow me to escort you and your son to a Wild West Show next week in New York City. I would pay all expenses, and we could ride up on the train— bring your mother as an escort if you wish."

Cynthia's eyes widened in surprise. "Mr. Holmes, I mean, Richard, you hardly know me!"

"I know enough already. You are beautiful, brave,

strong, a good mother, honest, and straightforward. You don't flutter your eyes and tell lies. I want to get to know you better, Miss Wells. I want to know all about your life with the Sioux, your opinion of the Indians, your understanding of their outlook on life and of the white man. I want to know why you think it's so hard for them to live like us—why this reservation life is killing them. I want to get to know your son better." He removed his hat. "What difference does it make that we just met? Some things are meant to be, are they not? I think we were supposed to meet today. I am utterly fascinated by your beauty and your background. Please allow me to come calling this evening and meet your parents formally and ask their permission to take you to Buffalo Bill's Wild West show. Have you heard of it?"

"I've read about it." Her eyes lit up. "Oh, I would love to see it. So would Freedom. He could get a taste of the West, and his Indian heritage."

The warm, winning smile spread across his face again. "Good! Good! I've seen the show once. Do you know that Buffalo Bill Cody uses real Indians in his show? They stage an attack on a stagecoach, riding nearly naked on painted ponies—just like the real thing. Oh, it's quite a thing to see!"

Cynthia felt the old agony again. She had seen such a thing—only for real—naked warriors, painted and whooping, brandishing their weapons as they rode their ponies as though they were a part of the horse. Red Wolf! Was it a good idea to go see the Wild West show? It sounded so exciting. She had lived almost like a hermit since Freedom's birth, with hardly any socializing outside her own family. In spite of the ache of having thoughts of Red Wolf stirred again, and of wondering if it was wrong to be attracted to another man, she could not deny that she wanted to live again—truly live. She wanted to laugh and visit and see something different. Most of all she wanted to feel the strength of a man again, to be looked upon by a man as something beautiful and treasured, the way Red Wolf used to look at her. It felt good to have a man look at her with respect and admiration, rather than with shock and scorn.

"Yes, do come to the house tonight. Come by six o'clock and dine with us, Richard." It was so easy to call him that. "And call me Cynthia."

Their eyes held and he bowed slightly. "Cynthia it is, then. It's a pretty name." His eyes moved over her. "For a pretty woman."

Cynthia blushed and looked away. Richard Holmes took her arm and they continued their walk to the Wells house at the south edge of the campus. His touch sent a tingle through Cynthia's blood, and she felt the woman in her coming alive again. She had left passion long buried, had told herself she would never let it come to life again. Surely she could never again experience the passion she had known with Red Wolf. But she was hardly more than a child then, and that was another time, another world, another Cynthia. Perhaps it was finally time to let go of the dreams, the memories, the heartache. Perhaps it was time to look to the future. And perhaps Richard Holmes was right in saying they were surely meant to meet this morning.

Chapter Twenty

Cynthia stared out the window at passing trees and home. How far away and unreal the Dakotas and Red Wolf seemed to her now. Here were huge oaks and maples and elms; rolling green hills and now and again a glimpse of the ocean. Was there really a land where no trees could be seen for miles around? Was there really a land where the snow blew wild and furious, moving and drifting over hundreds of miles of nothingness, burying here and there small villages of tipis, inside which dark-skinned people huddled under buffalo robes and sat around campfires? Had there really been a time when those people rode free on barren plains, following herds of buffalo?

Only yesterday she had read an article about how the buffalo were fast becoming extinct. Suddenly their skins had become valuable to the white man over the last several years, and buffalo hunters had killed them off by the millions. Men even scavenged for the bones left behind, for which the white man had also found use, and the article told of how buffalo bones were piled as high as mountains around train stations, ready to be hauled back East.

How sad it must all be for Red Wolf and the Sioux. But she must not think about Red Wolf. She must think about a future for herself and Freedom, who sat across from her now beside his grandmother. Sixteen-year-old Alex sat beside Cynthia, eager himself to see the Wild West show. Albert Wells had insisted the whole family go to the event and make a holiday out of it. Cynthia knew how secretly happy her father was over her interest in Richard Holmes. Richard had called on her regularly for a full week. He got along famously with Cynthia's parents, who were thrilled that such a handsome, successful man was interested in their Cynthia, for they were afraid their daughter would never find a man who would want her for a wife because of Freedom. But Richard Holmes seemed to be heading in that direction. He was thirty years old and had dedicated those first thirty years to becoming successful. Now he was ready to settle, he had told them. Ready to settle.

Cynthia could still hear the words. Did he mean with her? She was afraid to believe it, for he seemed too handsome and accomplished for her to hope he would want to marry her. She supposed she could believe his intentions were in that direction more easily if he had kissed her before he left on the train for Maryland. But he had only lightly embraced her. She was ready now, ready to start life anew, ready to fall in love and be loved by a man again, ready to be a wife and have a father for Freedom. Richard was kind and fun. He was good to Freedom, and Freedom liked the man. Richard was easy to talk to. In no time at all Cynthia had come to feel she had known him all her life. He was full of stories about his experiences as an attorney, and she already knew all his political dreams. She wanted to be a part of those dreams, to be beside him when he won a seat in Congress, to go with him to balls and dinner parties.

Now he waited for them at the ferry docks in New York. He had come up from Maryland, and together they would go to the Wild West show. Cynthia had not seen him for a week, and to her surprise and delight, a week seemed much too long. She was happy to discover she could love again, and she knew now after being away

328

from Richard that she loved him. It was a different kind of love from what she had held for Red Wolf. It was calmer, more mature. It wasn't quite as passionate, but then she was no longer the foolish, fiery, brazen young girl she had been then. She had mellowed. She was a mother. Perhaps this was the way it was supposed to be when a woman got older. She had had her moment of youthful, wild passion. Now it was time to be sensible, practical, mature. Still, when she pictured seeing Richard again, she imagined running to him and being swept up in his arms, telling him she had missed him terribly. She imagined he would give her his first real kiss, a long, sweet, tender kiss. It had been such a long, long time since a man kissed her that way.

"What are you thinking, Cynthia?" her mother said, interrupting her thoughts.

Cynthia blushed and smiled. "Why do you ask?"

"Oh, I was just watching the longing look on your face while you looked out the window. You aren't letting yourself go back to a past that can never be again, are you?"

Cynthia looked back out the window. "No. I was thinking of Richard."

"Good. You just *keep* thinking about Richard. He's a wonderful young man and I'm sure he is very much taken with you. I can't tell you how happy your father and I are about it."

Cynthia met the woman's eyes again. "Thank you for being so understanding all these years, Mother. I know how hard my problems have been on you both."

"Hey, sis, you just brought lots of excitement to the family, that's all," Alex told her, patting her arm.

Cynthia turned to him and smiled. Alex was six feet tall now, with sandy hair and blue eyes and handsome features. He was an intelligent young man who would enter Princeton this fall.

"Remember that night you cut Red Wolf loose and you made me promise not to tell? Keeping that secret was the biggest thing that had ever happened to me—my brave big sister, going into Deadwood to free a wild Indian."

Cynthia smiled.

"Now, none of that, Alex," his mother chided. "I just got done telling Cynthia not to think about the past."

"I know. But that's pretty hard to do with Freedom sitting right there beside you."

Freedom grinned. "Was it fun, Mama?"

Cynthia felt the old pain wanting to return. "I didn't think of it as fun at the time, Freedom. I only saw a young man who was being treated unfairly, who was hurt and afraid. I set him free."

"And then later the Indians stole you and you saw my father again," the boy put in.

"Yes." Cynthia had never told her son that Red Wolf had killed a white man that night. Nor did the boy quite comprehend just how wild and vicious the Sioux could be at that time. He had as much trouble envisioning the Indians as any white person who had never been West, even though his own skin was as dark as his father's. He did not comprehend what a man and woman did to get a baby, or fully understand how others looked at an Indian-white relationship as wrong. Such explanations would have to wait until he was old enough to grasp what had really happened between his mother and father.

Cynthia knew Freedom must be told everything about his father in such a way that he would love and respect the man, for that was what Red Wolf deserved. Freedom must understand his Indian heritage, understand why Red Wolf would surely have been among those at the Little Bighorn, understand the cultural differences between whites and his father's people. He would have to understand the prejudice and hatred, things that his innocent nature could not now comprehend.

In time she would tell him everything, but to wait another few years would make it all even harder, for some of the memories were fading, so that it all seemed so unreal. Only the memory of Red Wolf himself, his face, his embrace, his voice, his kiss—that memory was still very much alive; and as her mother took a pair of scissors from a sewing bag on her lap, Cynthia suddenly thought about the knife, her mother's favorite knife, lying on an Indian burial scaffold next to Red Wolf's old grandmother. The memory brought tears to her eyes, and she looked out the window again.

Richard. She must think about Richard.

Cynthia stared at high, brick buildings as the ferry that had carried her from Jersey City across the Hudson neared Manhattan. She had never been in such a big city. A large crowd waited at the docks, women in their lovely dresses and high-button shoes, men wearing waistcoats and top hats. Carriages stood waiting here and there, and at first Cynthia half expected Richard not to show up. Perhaps he had changed his mind about her once he got away from her. Surely a man on his way to the top wouldn't want to marry a single woman with an Indian son, a child considered illegitimate by most "civilized" people.

But then she saw him standing in the waiting crowd. Her heart beat faster. "There he is, Mother." A blondhaired man stood next to Richard, both men smiling and watching as the ferry docked. Cynthia waited impatiently as the passengers slowly disembarked. Finally she was off the ferry. She called out to Richard, and he came toward her, reaching up for her.

"Cynthia, you made it!" he exclaimed, taking her into his arms, just as she had imagined. He hugged her tightly, and it felt good to be held in strong arms. She waited for the magical kiss, but he only kissed her cheek, and she noticed the blond-haired man watched them strangely, a look on his face Cynthia could not read because it almost looked like jealousy, but it surely couldn't be, because only a woman friend might get such a look on her face.

"Darling Cynthia," Richard was saying. "You look so beautiful!" He set her on her feet and stepped back, looking her over with the blue eyes that brought back old desires. He turned to Freedom and hugged the boy, then greeted Alex and Cynthia's mother. "I am so glad you all could come," he told them. "We've already seen the show once. Oh, you'll just love it! Freedom, you'll want to run out and ride one of those painted ponies yourself. Wait until you see some of those real Indians. It will be exciting for you."

He turned to the blond-haired man, who had stepped closer. "Oh, and I want all of you to meet a longtime friend of mine, Stewart Reynolds. We graduated Princeton together and have shared an apartment in Maryland for quite some time."

"Yes, well, I have a feeling I will be living there alone in the not-too-distant future," Stewart said with a smile, looking Cynthia over. "She truly is as beautiful as you told me she was, Rich." Stewart took Cynthia's hand and bowed slightly, kissing the back of her hand. She thought his lips seemed a little cold, and there was something about his smile that didn't seem right, as though it was painfully forced. He greeted Alex and Freedom and Mabel Wells, and quickly all baggage was picked up by Stewart and Richard. The two men led Cynthia's family to a waiting carriage, and from then on Cynthia was too swept up in the sights of New York City to care about Stewart Reynolds's fake smile.

Richard had come. That was all that mattered. They toured the streets of Manhattan, settled back in a seat together, Richard's arm around her. He seemed to know everything about everything as he explained what they were seeing. Stewart drove the carriage through bustling streets filled with thousands of people and carriages and young boys running around scooping up horse dung. Horses pulled streetcars back and forth, the poor beasts looking tired. Drivers of the streetcars clanged bells as they approached each crossway, and again Cynthia felt the tiny hint of guilt as she sat in Richard's arms wondering what Red Wolf would think of a place like New York. If he came here he would understand why the supply of white people coming West from the East seemed endless. If the Indians could have seen early on how many whites there were here, perhaps they never would have bothered to try to fight them.

"Here is our hotel," Stewart announced. He pulled the carriage to a halt, and everything became wonderful and exciting and magical. Cynthia and her mother settled into one room, Alex and Freedom in another, and Stewart and Richard would share a room. The evening was spent dining in an expensive restaurant. As they dined Richard kept watching Cynthia, and she felt the lovely flutter of desire again. The meal was delicious and more than Cynthia could eat. Richard paid for everything, then took Cynthia out dancing after settling the rest of her family back in their rooms. Stewart went along, taking turns dancing with her.

"You love Richard, don't you?"

She blushed at the question. "Surely he knows it, doesn't he?"

"Oh, yes, I believe he does. Richard is easy to love, he's so generous and kindhearted."

"Yes. I'm surprised he doesn't have a dozen girlfriends or isn't already married by now. And you too, for that matter."

Stewart smiled. "You flatter me. At any rate, we've both been busy building our careers. I suppose now I am going to have to go out and find myself a woman. I have a feeling I am losing my best friend to a wife."

"Oh, but that shouldn't change anything for you and Richard. You would always be welcome in our home."

The strange, almost jealous look came into his eyes again. "Oh, I should think I'd be in the way. I'd see plenty of Richard at the law offices and in our business gatherings—perhaps you would allow him one night a week to share a few drinks with an old friend?"

Cynthia smiled. "I hardly think I even have to think about that yet. Richard hasn't even said that he loves me or wants to marry me. I've only known him a little over two weeks."

"Ah, but he does love you. He's just afraid to say it—the bashful sort, you know."

"Richard? But he's so outgoing and successful."

"Yes, well, in the way of winning votes and influencing people and conducting his business, yes. But when it comes to his personal life, his innermost feelings, he's quite bashful."

"You must be very good friends to know him so well."

Stewart's smile faded. "Yes," he answered. "We are very good friends. We've bunked together for a long time, you know. I have no family, and neither did Richard these last five years."

He held her eyes, as though trying to tell her something. "You will take good care of him, won't you?"

Cynthia thought the statement rather strange, like a father telling a potential son-in-law to take care of his daughter. She smiled nervously. "Well, if it comes to that, of course I will."

"You are quite beautiful, Cynthia. You and Richard make quite a handsome couple. Someday you'll turn all eyes when you walk into an important political dinner or stand on a platform together while Richard gives one of his illustrious speeches. Everyone will look and say what a beautiful wife Congressman Holmes has."

Cynthia laughed lightly. "You are getting way ahead of things, Stewart."

"Oh, I don't think so." He whirled her around to a waltz, his eyes occasionally catching Richard's, who looked back at him with a strange sadness in his eyes.

It was an adventure never to be forgotten. Women gasped and children screamed and laughed, and some cried out of fright, as in the arena below a stagecoach circled, painted Indians whooping and chasing it, doing tricks on their horses as they pursued the coach while men fired at them from the stagecoach with blanks.

"Mama! Mama! Look!" Freedom was beside himself with excitement. "Is my father there?"

Cynthia watched with a heavy feeling in her chest, for she had not expected such reality. The Wild West show brought it all back to her, even a little of the fear she had felt the day she had been abducted. Richard took her hand and squeezed it.

"Are you all right?"

She looked at him and smiled. "Yes."

Stewart had not come with them that day, and for some reason Cynthia was glad. It seemed when he was along she had to share Richard with the man, and they couldn't talk as intimately as they did when they were alone.

"This must bring back some memories for you," Richard was telling her.

"I'm afraid so. But it was a long time ago, Richard."

She heard the bugle call then. Soldiers were coming. She stiffened at the sound, remembering . . . remembering . . . Soldiers were coming to take her away from Red Wolf. Her throat tightened then as uniformed cavalry rode into the arena to chase the Indians, who mimicked falling dead under gunfire. Cynthia remembered the real death she had seen, remembered Flowing Waters.

"Maybe I shouldn't have brought you," Richard told her, putting an arm around her.

She looked at him. "It's all right—really. It's fun for Alex and Freedom." Their eyes held, and suddenly he leaned forward and kissed her lightly. For Cynthia the crowd noise and the shooting and yipping going on below dimmed in her ears. There was only Richard, handsome Richard. His kiss had been light and tentative, as though he actually thought she might not like it. She tried to discern the look on his face, as though he had experienced something for the first time. She attributed it to the fact that it was the first time he had kissed her in

335

particular, for surely a man his age and with his handsome looks had dated many women and kissed not a few. He smiled then.

"I know this is a ridiculous place to ask," he told her, keeping his lips close to her ear so that she could hear him. "But will you marry me, Cynthia? I mean, not right away. I know we need more time, but I just feel as though this was all meant to be, and I want you to be thinking seriously about it."

Her eyes widened in surprise. She felt suddenly caught in a strange realm of unreality, for below her rode real Indians, people of Red Wolf's blood, people from a world she at one time never wanted to leave. Before her sat a man who represented a world as different from Red Wolf's as it could possibly be, and he was asking her to marry him. That meant taking that last step in putting Red Wolf behind her forever. She told herself it must be done.

"I will think about it, Richard. Am I being silly to want to say yes right now?" she answered.

Richard's face lit up with joy, and he kissed her again, harder this time, but still with an almost experimental feel to it. "Of course not! But we'll see more of each other first. I'll come back to New Jersey in another week. I just need some time to set my business matters in order so that I can get away for a while." His hand was strong as it pressed her own. "I'd be good to you Cynthia. I'll give you everything you could ever want."

"All I want is your love, Richard, and your acceptance of Freedom."

"You already know that is no problem. I'll have the most beautiful wife in Washington, D.C.! That's where we'll end up someday, you know." He looked at her lovingly. "I couldn't wait to ask you, to at least know you would consider marrying me. I'm sorry I did it here in the middle of a Wild West show."

Cynthia laughed lightly. "It's all right, Richard, really. But we do need a little more time, mainly so that it looks

336

better in the eyes of others. My parents would probably think we are crazy to decide this soon, but I feel like you do, as though it's meant to be. You're the first man who has come along who has not let Freedom interfere with his feelings for me, who has looked at me as just a woman, capable of loving and needing a man."

He squeezed her hand again, and her heart swelled with love for the terribly handsome Richard Holmes. She turned back to watch the show, clinging to his strong hand. Her eyes teared as she watched the Indians below ride out of the arena, as though Red Wolf were symbolically riding out of her life forever now. She felt an urge to run after them, to ask if any of them knew Red Wolf. How old would he be now? Twenty-eight. It was hard to imagine. How proud he would be of Freedom if he could see him.

But her life must belong to Richard now. She was twenty-four years old. She needed a husband, and Freedom needed a father. Richard could give her a future, a fine home, security. He loved her and wanted to marry her. She could be a normal woman, a wife, a mother. She would have a man who loved her and her son. It was unrealistic to think she could have a life now with Red Wolf. This was surely the only right thing to do, and at the moment she had no doubts in her heart. There was only the lingering memory of Red Wolf, and a special place in her heart for her first man. But she would have to bury those feelings, and never reveal them to Richard.

She did not feel the same passion for Richard as she had for Red Wolf, but then maybe it wasn't supposed to be there. And surely when she lay naked next to Richard, much of that passion would come alive—all the wonderful, beautiful feelings Red Wolf had stirred in her soul would be awakened again.

She tore her eyes from the disappearing Indians and looked at Richard. "I love you," she said softly.

He kissed her nose. "And I love you, Cynthia. One month. We'll wait one month before we make an announcement. During that time we'll get to know each other even better. Perhaps we can be married at Princeton. Your own father could marry us."

"Oh, yes, he would love that."

"It's settled then. In August you will be Mrs. Richard Holmes. I'll get us a town house in Baltimore and you can decorate it however you like when we move there."

Cynthia breathed deeply with excitement. "Oh, I would love that! A home of my own. I've never had one. I'll miss my parents, but it will be wonderful having my own home."

"I already know of the perfect place. It's not far from where Stewart and I live now. You won't mind if he visits?"

"Oh, of course not. But we should try to find a wife for Stewart too. Wouldn't that be nice? I hate to think of him being alone once we're married. He won't hate me for taking away his best friend, will he?"

A hint of guilt and sorrow passed through Richard's eyes, but Cynthia was too much in love to see it. "Of course not. Stewart wants me to be happy, that's all."

"And we will be, Richard. We'll be so happy." She felt the lovely ripple of desire move through her insides at the thought of Richard making love to her. Yes, this was surely the right thing to do. She must get on with life.

Chapter Twenty-One

The next month was one of the happiest Cynthia could remember in years. Only after deciding to love and stay with Red Wolf had she been this happy; only then her happiness was plagued by the knowledge that her parents would not approve and were surely terribly worried and despondent. She could never share Red Wolf with her family, but she could share Richard. There were times when she knew down deep inside that although this courtship and impending marriage were approved and would be sanctified through a real ceremony, her relationship with Red Wolf had somehow been richer, deeper, more passionate. She had been even happier than she was now.

But she refused to let those thoughts dominate her mind and heart now. That was another life, another man; and she decided it just seemed more special because Red Wolf had been her first man. She simply had to remember that Richard loved her just as much, and that he was simply a man very different from Red Wolf, but just as handsome and strong and wonderful.

For the whole month she was showered with gifts of flowers and jewelry and clothing, all from Richard. After another week's separation when Cynthia returned to New Jersey, Richard came to Princeton, just as he had promised. They were together almost constantly, taking long walks or carriage rides, picnicking in the country, dining with Cynthia's family.

There were times when Cynthia thought herself too bold, for she wanted Richard to kiss her, touch her. She wanted a hint of the beautiful wedding night to come. Surely if Richard wanted to marry her, he had urges that were difficult to control until the wedding. But there was only an occasional embrace and a few light kisses. She was amazed at how much he seemed to respect her, and she told herself she must stop comparing him to Red Wolf, who had always made it perfectly clear what he wanted from her, and who showed his love in a most physical way.

Deep in the night she would think of Richard, and then would come thoughts of Red Wolf. She missed the warmth that was in Red Wolf's embrace, the delicious desires he drew from her when he touched her breasts and kissed her so tenderly, so softly. She had yet to know how she would feel if Richard touched her breast, for he had never tried. Nor had his kisses lingered to a deeper, passionate state. She kept telling herself he was simply waiting until she was his wife, and she loved him all the more for affording her such respect. It was a nice change from the way other young men had looked at her and treated her.

Richard and Freedom got along famously, and Richard never objected to Cynthia wanting to keep Freedom aware of his heritage. She would explain to both her son and to Richard what she knew about the Indian way of life, their religion and beliefs. Richard was just as fascinated as Freedom. He wanted to know all he could, and he vowed to continue his work in supporting the American Indian, telling Cynthia he would do even more if he could get elected to Congress someday.

"I know that you will, Richard," she assured him. "Anyone can tell what a fine Congressman you would make."

"And with a beautiful wife like you at my side, I'll get

even more votes," he added.

It was just five days before the wedding was to take place, and they sat on the porch of the Wells house. Freedom had gone to bed, and Richard and Cynthia talked alone. Cynthia sat with her head on Richard's shoulder, his arm around her.

"Tell me, Cynthia, did you love Red Wolf more than you love me?"

The question surprised her. She turned her head and met his eyes, his lovely, blue eyes. "That isn't a fair question, Richard."

He had a sad, far-away look in his eyes. "Yes. I suppose it is unfair, yet I can imagine Red Wolf was quite the man, with all that raw power and wild daring. He rode the warpath, hunted, killed men. I've never done those things."

Cynthia nestled into his shoulder. "Of course you haven't. Your life is simply completely different. You're a man in other ways—you do your fighting in court. And you have your own free spirit, one that compels you to be the best at what you do, just like Red Wolf tried to be the best at what he knew. And you have the courage to stand up for something that is not so popular with some people." She looked up at him. "And you have the courage to marry a woman who was once a captive of Indians, who bore a half-breed child. You're man enough to look beyond those things and love me for who I am. You are not so different from Red Wolf, Richard."

She tried to discern the look in his eyes, as though he again was trying desperately to tell her something. But he only came closer then and kissed her. This time the kiss lingered, and he moved his hand to lightly caress her breast. The touch brought fire to Cynthia's blood, and she kissed him harder, circling her arms around his neck, overjoyed that he had finally touched her and that she felt the wonderful warmth and desire she had wanted to feel. But then Richard moved his hand away, and he left her lips, embracing her lightly.

341

"I shouldn't have done that."

"It's all right. I wanted to know what it would be like. It just makes me more anxious for our wedding night," she said in a near-whisper.

Richard did not reply. Cynthia suddenly felt awkward and embarrassed, and she decided to change the subject. "Will Stewart be coming to our wedding? I suppose you'll want him to be best man, won't you?"

Richard sighed deeply. "He won't be coming. We're just too busy at the office. He took over my cases until I return."

"Oh, that's too bad. He should be here, Richard."

"No, no, it's all right. Alex or Freedom can be best man."

"Are you sure?"

"Yes," he answered almost sadly. "Quite sure. Besides, Stewart doesn't know anyone up here, and you and I have been together almost constantly." He hugged her close again. "I truly do love you, Cynthia. You believe that, don't you?"

She frowned, wondering at the anxiety in his voice. "Of course I do. I'm marrying you, aren't I?"

He smiled nervously, then suddenly rose. "I had better be getting to my hotel. It's getting late."

Cynthia wanted him to stay, to kiss her again, touch her again. But surely she was being too forward. "Yes, I suppose. Good night, Richard."

He kissed her on the forehead. "Good night, Cynthia. I'll see you tomorrow."

She watched him walk off into the darkness, and she felt an odd emptiness in her heart, suddenly longing for Red Wolf. She swallowed back a sudden urge to cry, telling herself that she was just having last-minute jitters and old feelings of guilt over Red Wolf. To think of him now was foolish and stupid. She was marrying the most wonderful man a woman could ask for, and there could never again be a Red Wolf in her life. She told herself that the vague doubts she sometimes felt about Richard were just a form of nervous apprehension over getting married, and the result of her struggle to put Red Wolf behind her forever, which was the only right thing to do. Everything would be wonderful once they were married. She would finally be one with Richard, and then she would know where she belonged. She would have her own home, and be one with a man again. She would stop being a burden to her parents and look to a husband for support, rather than her poor mother and father, who had put up with so much.

She turned and went inside to her room, where she undressed and pulled on her flannel gown. She stood there a moment, and Red Wolf's memory suddenly came to her in vivid detail. She moved a hand to her breast, breathing deeply and massaging it, thinking of how Red Wolf used to touch her. Tears came to her eyes then, and she felt consumed with guilt for having thought of such a thing just five days before she was to be married to someone else. Richard was everything a woman could want. Why did she have this empty feeling? She should be so happy.

She climbed into bed and curled up. She could not stop what was going to happen. People would think she was out of her mind. Her parents would be terribly disappointed. She would not disappoint them again. They were so happy for her, and Freedom liked Richard so much. No woman could ask for a better man. These odd doubts she had been having lately were ridiculous, and nothing more than last-minute wedding jitters. She finally managed to fall asleep, but it was to the memory of the first time Red Wolf made love to her.

Everything became a whirl of showers and rehearsals and gifts. It felt good to Cynthia to be getting married the right way, and she knew it made her parents very happy. Friends and acquaintances would stop by and ogle Cynthia's wedding dress, which she and her mother were hastily making themselves. Women would comment on Richard's handsomeness and his money and success, telling Cynthia they envied her such a wonderful husband. Arrangements were made at a nearby Methodist church. Albert Wells would perform his daughter's ceremony. Alex would walk her down the aisle and Freedom would be the best man. Martha Cunningham would be her maid of honor. Everything was coming together perfectly. Mabel Wells and her lady friends worked on a huge cake. The reception would be in the Wells home, after which Cynthia and Richard would go to the fanciest hotel in the city of Princeton. After their initial wedding night they would leave by train to travel to Maryland, stopping at fancy hotels along the way, taking their time, dining at the best restaurants, and finally arriving at their new home in Maryland, a town house that Richard had described as roomy and elaborate—"a fine place to entertain important people," he had said.

"I think I had better take a course on etiquette, Richard," she had replied. "I'm not accustomed to being around Congressmen and the like."

Richard had laughed. "I will help you. And if you want to study up on it, there are classes you can take. You'll do fine. All they have to do is see how beautiful you are, and they won't care if you use the right kind of dinner forks."

At last the wedding day arrived. Cynthia was so nervous and excited there was no more time to think about any of her doubts. She was sure it had all been ridiculous. After today she would be Mrs. Richard Holmes, a respectable wife. Freedom would have everything he could ever want, including the best in education. Perhaps one day he would be a lawyer too, and could somehow help his people.

Mabel Wells helped her daughter into her wedding dress, and the whole family ooohed and aaahed over how she looked. Her blond hair, which had taken on a soft wave as she got older, hung long and thick down her back, the sides drawn up, with a lily of the valley pinned into it. Her dress was a beautiful shade of blue, matching her eyes, and she carried a bouquet of lilies of the valley, white daisies, and blue irises. The satin dress was fitted through the waist, showing her slender waist and full breasts. The high neckline was graced with white lace, and lace covered the full skirt. A satin sash made her waist seem even smaller, and it tied into a large satin bow at the back.

Mabel Wells took one look at her daughter and started crying. "Oh, Cynthia, you're so beautiful! We're so happy for you!" The two of them embraced.

"Thank you, Mother, for all your patience and understanding," Cynthia told her. "I know the last few years have been hard on you, and that you must have grown tired of having to explain Freedom to people."

The woman drew back and wiped at her eyes. "Oh, Cynthia, I never minded. You know how much we love Freedom. We're just glad you finally got over your feelings for Red Wolf and got your life straightened out. Richard will make a fine husband. It's so nice to know you'll be well provided for. You'll have such a wonderful life now."

Cynthia wanted to tell the woman that she had never "got over" her feelings for Red Wolf. But then no one had ever really understood how much she had truly loved the man. Her parents still believed she had somehow been drugged or hypnotized or beaten into submission and that for a while she had somehow "lost God." But they had been good to her, and she had long ago given up trying to make them understand. It was enough that they had supported her and loved Freedom. Now it was time to stop being a burden to them. If she did not love Richard quite the same way she had loved Red Wolf, what did it matter? Tonight she would be Richard's wife in body, and she knew she would gradually learn to love him just as much, for she would be giving herself to him completely now.

345

The carriage arrived, and Cynthia was whisked outside and into the carriage to the church. It seemed only moments then before she found herself walking down the aisle, Alex holding her arm. At the front of the church stood her kind, patient, forgiving father, the man who had been so understanding when he found out she had freed Red Wolf. The look of pride on his face was all Cynthia needed to know she was doing the right thing. She moved her eyes to Richard, who stood watching her lovingly. No man could be more handsome than Richard Holmes was this moment, standing there with his brown hair lying in perfect waves, his blue eyes glittering with love. Cynthia was too happy and excited herself at this moment to detect the hint of terror behind Richard's blue eyes.

She came closer, and now it was Richard who was beside her, tall, strong, tanned. He took her arm, and in the next moment they were saying their wedding vows before her father and before God.

"Good-bye, my sweet Red Wolf," Cynthia was saying secretly as she repeated each vow. Her eyes teared, and everyone thought it was because she was so happy and so much in love. No one knew the tears were for Red Wolf.

The ceremony was quickly over.

"I now pronounce you man and wife," her father was saying.

Richard leaned forward and kissed her lightly, but strangely, Cynthia did not feel a hint of things to come. She did not detect the urgency and desire that a man would surely feel at this moment. They turned then, and Albert Wells announced Mr. and Mrs. Richard Holmes.

Cynthia moved through the rest of the ceremony automatically, going to the back of the church and greeting the guests. She and Richard climbed into the carriage, decorated with streamers and flowers, and the driver drove them through Princeton and around the campus, ringing a bell and attracting the attention of strangers, who smiled and waved at the happy couple.

Then they returned to the house, where people waited to greet them. Gifts were opened, cake was served, and all the general visiting that went with such an occasion took place.

In no time at all it was dusk. Cynthia went to her room to change into a lovely pink dress with a matching veiled hat and a ruffled parasol. Her bags were packed for the wedding night. They would return in the morning for the several bags she would be taking to Maryland. Freedom would stay with his grandparents until Cynthia and Richard were settled in their new town house. That would give the newlyweds some time alone their first few days together. Then Albert Wells would bring his grandson to Maryland by train.

People whisked both Cynthia and Richard to the carriage, throwing rice at them and shouting teasing words about the wedding night. The carriage was off. They were headed for the hotel. Richard grasped Cynthia's hand, and she felt the excited anticipation. Soon! Soon she would lie naked next to her new husband and they would be one. Richard would see her naked, would touch and taste her breasts, would invade her and make her his own, would erase all her lingering doubts. She interpreted the way he grasped her hand as the anxiousness on his part to mate with her. She did not perceive it as a different kind of anxiety—the nervousness of a man who had never made love to a woman.

Richard checked into the hotel, and Cynthia noticed he looked pale. She put a hand on his arm as he turned away from the desk. "Richard? Are you all right?"

He grinned, taking out a handkerchief and pressing it to his forehead. "Well, if you must know the truth, I'm not feeling my best all of a sudden. Isn't that a good one? I believe it's the woman who is supposed to get a headache or something, isn't it?"

Cynthia reddened and dropped her eyes. "Don't tease,

Richard. I truly am concerned if you don't feel well. Let's get up to our room."

"Yes. Maybe a little wine will help. I've ordered some brought up." He put an arm around her and gave her a squeeze, then led her up the stairs, followed by a young boy who carried their bags. Richard led Cynthia into a large, elegant room, with a mahogany, four-poster bed and an array of fine, matching furnishings. A red and gold brocade rug covered the floor, and matching curtains hung at the windows. An open door showed a private bath, with a porcelain tub, a sink, and a flush toilet, its tank situated high above it for gravity. Another tank of water hung over the tub and sink, and a small gas stove in the main room with a steam kettle provided served for heating water.

"Oh, this is lovely, Richard," Cynthia exclaimed. "I never stayed in such nice places until I met you."

"Well, I'm glad you like it." Richard paid the boy who had brought up their bags, then closed the door.

Cynthia felt a flutter at the sound of the door closing. They were alone at last as husband and wife. She looked around the room, studying the elegant wallpaper, the fine finish of the furniture, the beautiful velvet bedspread. She thought for a moment about the tipi she had shared with Red Wolf, so primitive compared to this. Yet she had been so very happy in it. She had not needed a fancy bed and furnishings, nor running water, nor beautiful clothes. She had needed only Red Wolf. She felt suddenly guilty for having thought of Red Wolf again when here she was, preparing to go to bed with her new husband. She turned to face him, and Richard was watching her with an almost frightened look in his eyes.

"Richard, what is it?"

He smiled nervously again. "Oh, nothing. I just . . . I don't want to move too quickly." His eyes moved over her. "I mean, I don't want to offend you on our wedding night. It's . . . it's been a long time for you."

She felt a flush on her cheeks and she walked closer,

348

putting her arms around his waist and resting her head on his chest. "Yes, it has. But I love you, Richard. I want to be your wife in every way. I promise not to pretend any headaches." She laughed lightly, then looked up at him.

Richard put a hand to her face, his heart aching at the hope and joy and willingness and love written all over her face. He had been so sure he could go through with it. He must go through with it, for he truly did love her as a dear friend and a beautiful woman. And if he was ever to get anywhere with his career, he had to have a wife and lead a normal life. How could he tell her about Stewart? He had hoped marrying a woman who had already been with a man would help make it all easier; and someone like Cynthia would be more willing to wait for things to get better. She needed a husband.

"You are so beautiful," he told her. He leaned down and kissed her mouth, struggling to bring forth the passion he knew she wanted him to show. He held her close then. "Why don't you go into the bathing room and slip out of this dress?"

She blushed more, turning and picking up her bag and going into the bathing room. The wine arrived and Richard poured himself a glass, drinking it down in nearly one gulp. He needed the courage. He had to go through with this, to be a normal man for his wife. She was too sweet and beautiful to lose. He needed her badly. He had to make this work. He drank down another glass of wine, then removed his shoes and jacket and shirt.

Cynthia came out of the bathing room, wearing a silky white gown and robe. She felt warm desire sweep through her at the sight of Richard without a shirt. He had a magnificent build. The dark hairs of his chest moved in a Y shape down his flat, muscled belly to his belt buckle. Surely that part of him below the belt was as magnificent as the rest of him, and a man so experienced in everything else would be wonderful in bed. She needed a man again more than she realized. Every nerve end came alive as she walked closer to him, their eyes holding. She touched his bare chest, then kissed it softly, and Richard forced himself to stop thinking about Stewart.

"Have a little wine," he told her, handing the glass to her.

She took it and sipped some of it, then handed it back to him. "I'm not used to wine."

He grinned. "I know. I thought if I got you drunk we'd have an even better time," he joked.

She smiled, holding his eyes. "Are you feeling better?"

"I'll be all right. Are you sure you don't want a little more wine?"

"I'm sure. I don't need wine to make me drunk for you, Richard." She untied her robe and let it fall. "I'll let you do the rest," she told him.

He stared at her, still looking pale, then guzzled the rest of the wine. He set the glass aside and began untying the satin laces of her gown. He pulled it open, and Cynthia closed her eyes as he pulled it off her shoulders and let it slip to the floor, revealing her nakedness. She felt him toy with her breasts, little knowing he looked at them more out of curiosity than desire. How long ago was it he had done this, only to find women did not excite him? Never had he hated himself more than he did at this moment. He could not have asked for a more perfect wife. He must make love to her. He must.

He pulled her close, pressing her breasts against his bare chest. Cynthia whimpered in desire as he kissed her hungrily. She flung her arms around his neck, and he moved a hand down over her bare bottom. But to his horror nothing was happening. How could he explain this? Perhaps if he got into bed with her.

He carried her to the bed and lay her on it. Cynthia pulled back the covers and got under them while Richard blew out the oil lamps. Cynthia felt a rush of disappointment, thinking he would want some light so he could see his new wife; and she in turn wanted to look upon her new husband. But maybe the first time it was best this way, a little less awkward. She thought for a moment how there had never been an awkward moment with Red Wolf. There had been nothing but passion and need. Everything had taken place so naturally.

She felt Richard getting into bed, and then his naked body pressed against her own. She didn't feel the hardness at her belly that she expected to feel. He began kissing her hard but almost clumsily, his passion seeming forced. His hands moved over her breasts and she whispered his name. He moved his mouth down to her breasts, and her breath came in quick gasps. How long it had been since a man tasted her breasts! It felt wonderful. She could not imagine anything more beautiful now than to have Richard surging inside of her, to share bodies and at last be one.

Suddenly he drew away. "I'm sorry," he said quietly.

Cynthia lay in shock for a moment, trying to grasp what he was saying. She was ready for him. To have him suddenly pull away left a horrible emptiness in her soul. She turned to him, reaching out to feel his back. He was sitting up.

"Richard? What's wrong?"

He sighed deeply. "I guess I feel worse than I let on. Must be the flu or something. I'm damned sorry, Cynthia."

Her eyes teared from embarrassment and frustration. "Are you really ill, or is it me?"

"No. It isn't you."

"It is, isn't it? You're thinking of me being with an Indian man! It bothers you more than you thought it would."

"No, I swear!" He turned and pulled her into his arms. "It has nothing to do with you, Cynthia, I swear to God. Let's just lie here, all right? We'll just lie here and be together . . . sleep together. I'll be all right." He held her tighter, almost like a frightened little boy. "Don't leave me, Cynthia. Please don't leave me."

She frowned to herself, totally confused by his

351

actions. "Why would I leave you, Richard? Is that what you think of me, that I'd leave you just because you don't feel well on our wedding night?"

He laughed nervously. "No. I just . . . it must be a terrible disappointment to you, our wedding night and all."

"It's all right, Richard. We have the rest of our lives together."

"Of course we do." He sighed deeply. "It's been a long day. We're both tired. Let's just get some sleep tonight."

She lay in his arms, and he petted her hair. Cynthia struggled not to cry. Something was very wrong, but she could not imagine what it was. Was there some reason he didn't want her to see him in the light? She imagined perhaps he wasn't made like a normal man at all. Or perhaps he had suddenly decided he had done the wrong thing by marrying her and was afraid to tell her so. A million thoughts passed through her mind, and she wanted to scream and run away. But he was her husband now, and perhaps there was really nothing wrong at all.

It was as Richard said. It had been a long day. They were both tired. Yet she could not imagine any normal man not being able to make love to his new wife on their wedding night, especially when she was willing and ready. It made her feel inadequate, foolish, embarrassed, frustrated. A hundred emotions swept through her, but the biggest one was disappointment.

She lay there for seemingly hours. Finally Richard pulled away and turned over, breathing deeply in sleep. Quiet tears slipped down Cynthia's face, and she turned over herself and cried into her pillow. Again she thought of Red Wolf, and she curled up in intense frustration. This was not how she had pictured her wedding night at all, and she wondered what kind of man she had married. She could not help the horrible feeling that it was more than his not feeling well. Something was very wrong, but she was too innocent of such things to understand. She had never considered or even heard of a man not being attracted to a woman, but she realized now with cold reality that all along the passion and desire had been missing on Richard's part. She had let herself believe it was mere respect for her, that he was saving everything for their wedding night. But it was more than that. She simply could not imagine what it could be.

She wept quietly. She had taken her vows and she must keep them. Not one person in the outside world would understand if she had her marriage annulled. Why would any woman not want to be married to a man like Richard Holmes? Her parents would be devastated with disappointment. She had no choice but to stick this out and hope she was just letting her imagination run wild. Richard Holmes was just as normal as the next man. He just didn't feel well, that's all. By tomorrow night things would be normal. She was Mrs. Richard Holmes, and she should be happy and proud. She would suffer this alone. She would not disappoint her family, nor would she be a burden to them any longer. If Richard had some kind of problem, she would help him work it out; but it was probably nothing.

Chapter Twenty-Two

Cynthia dreamed of the wide open plains. She rode free on a fast horse, her long hair blowing in the wind. A dark man rode beside her, both of them laughing, his hair nearly as long as hers. They raced over rolling hills, and the sun shone down on them, warming their backs. They passed a great herd of buffalo and called out to them.

"Hello, buffalo! Come and run with us!"

The buffalo followed, and it seemed in the dream that the horse she rode moved across the land without touching the ground. She floated slowly over the plains, as though she were flying, and suddenly she *was* flying, on the back of a great eagle. Now the dark man was sitting behind her, his strong arms around her, and together they flew above the clouds, then arched and circled down again. The eagle landed and let them climb off and she turned to the handsome dark man, who pulled her into his arms and kissed her. It was Red Wolf. She was with him again, and she knew the only true happiness she had ever known. This was where she was meant to be, free and wild on the Dakota plains, in the reassuring arms of Red Wolf.

Suddenly she stirred awake, realizing she was not in Red Wolf's arms at all. It was Richard Holmes who held her. The room was dimly lit from a rising sun. It was morning, and in her sleepy state she realized she was being rudely awakened with fumbling kisses and groping hands. Richard was moving on top of her, feeling around between her legs with one hand.

"Cynthia! Cynthia!" he gasped. "I'll make you my wife, I will!" The words came out as though he considered it a determined duty, rather than a desire.

Cynthia sucked in her breath when suddenly he shoved himself inside of her. She was barely completely awake, and there had been no foreplay. It was simply a quick, hard thrust that at least told her he was indeed built like any other man. But there was no time to enjoy it. His release came quickly, and he made a strange grunting sound, then rolled off her.

Cynthia lay shocked and frustrated. She was hardly aware of what had happened to her. Would it always be like this? The whole thing had taken place as though he was in a hurry to get it over with. Richard sighed deeply, then raised up on one elbow, a look in his eyes as though he had just accomplished something wonderful.

"Are you all right?" he asked, petting her hair. "Was it satisfying, darling?"

She frowned, wanting to scream at him that it was horrible, that it was not satisfying at all. But he looked so eager. He reminded her of how Freedom looked the first time he climbed a tree and yelled for his mother to come and look. What was wrong with her husband?

"Yes," she lied. "But I wouldn't mind being more awake first, Richard. I hardly knew what was happening."

He laughed lightly. "I just woke up and felt better," he answered. How could he tell her he had to turn away and think of Stewart before he could perform for her; and even then he had to do it quickly or the fact that he was with a woman would spoil it for him again. He leaned down and kissed her cheek, her breasts, wishing he could be a better lover to this treasure of a woman. Perhaps in time . . .

"Let's do it again, Richard," she was saying. "We have

all day, and I want us to enjoy each other. Let's do it more slowly this time."

He nearly froze at the words. Wasn't what he had just done enough? Didn't most women consider this a burden, simply something to please their husbands but something they would rather not do? She had been so willing the night before, but he had hoped it was simply to show him what a good wife she could be. He wondered how long he could fool her, for he had apparently married a woman who actually enjoyed making love.

"Ah! Ah!" he said jokingly. "I think I have a married a woman of lust!" He frowned, kissing her lips. "Bad girl. We have a train to catch, remember?"

"Not until this afternoon."

"Ah, but I have a wonderful breakfast planned. Come on now. Up with you."

He got out of bed, and Cynthia stared after him as he walked into the bathing room. His build was magnificent, and everything necessary was there. But somehow she suddenly had trouble thinking of him as a whole man. Someone not so handsome and not so well built and not so wealthy would have satisfied her much more, if he truly loved her as a whole woman and knew how to *make* love to her. Richard had had all the other wonderful qualities, and she almost wished he had tried to make love to her before their marriage. Then she would have known he had strange ways in bed. But then it hit her full force that he had *never* tried to make love to her, and he had always seemed nervous when they got intimate.

He came out of the bathing room looking handsome and dapper. "Your turn, darling," he told her. He came over to the bed, handing her her robe as though he wanted her to put it on. She would have thought a new husband would want to see his wife naked just once more before she dressed, but he turned away when she got up and pulled on the robe.

"I have something for you, Cynthia," he told her. He went to his suitcase and took out a small box, coming

357

back and handing it to her. "To celebrate our union."

She took the box, amazed he could call what had just happened a union. But she told herself to stay calm. Things would get better as they got used to each other. Maybe he really hadn't felt good the night before. And maybe he really had just suddenly awakened and wanted his woman. Maybe the next time would be slower, but why was he so anxious to jump right up and get dressed?

She opened the small box, and a devastatingly beautiful emerald and sapphire ring sparkled inside.

"My special wedding present to you," he told her.

Cynthia felt a deep dread as she took out the ring. Was this how she would be loved the rest of her life—with "things"? This man could be so good and understanding. They were great friends and could talk for hours. But that didn't fill the great emptiness that had been left when she was torn from Red Wolf's arms.

"It's beautiful," she told him. She burst into tears then, but he didn't understand why.

"Darling, I didn't think you would be this touched!" He held her and petted her hair. "Come on now. Put the ring on and we'll go down and have some breakfast."

Cynthia cried hard against his chest. "You do love me, don't you, Richard? Tell me you love me."

"Of course I love you. Why do you ask such a thing?"

"Make love to me again. I need you to make love to me, Richard."

He felt the terror building in his chest again. "Now, Cynthia, we have the rest of our lives to make love. I just got dressed." He petted her hair. "I must have moved too quickly this morning. Maybe I hurt you. This has all been a difficult change for both of us. We'll adjust, though, you'll see." He pulled away, grasping her arms. "Come now, don't cry, Cynthia. Wait until you see your new home. You'll be beside yourself. Aren't you anxious to get there and decorate? I'll let you do anything you want with it."

She wiped at her eyes and slipped on the ring. "Yes,"

she told him despondently. "I'd like to see my new home." She turned away and walked to the bathing room to wash herself of what little life he had managed to spill into her. She closed the door, then heard him go out of the room. Cynthia let loose of the tears then, crying until she felt sick. She began washing then, looking at her nakedness in a mirror and wondering if something was wrong with her instead of with Richard. But she saw nothing different from the woman Red Wolf had loved. Was she attractive only to an Indian? She hardly thought so. Other young men had always been attracted to her beauty. It was only the fact that she had been an Indian captive and had a half-breed son that chased them away.

She washed the tears from her face, suddenly seeing things that she had refused to see before. Why had Richard been so eager to marry her? Why had he so easily ignored her half-breed son, as though it didn't bother him at all. It was big of him, but it seemed he would have had some apprehension, at least at first. And why had he asked her not to leave him last night, as though he carried some terrible dark secret that might make her run away? She told herself she must stop inventing things in her mind. She must give this marriage some time. Perhaps she was being wrong to compare Richard to Red Wolf. Richard was Richard, and Red Wolf was out of her life.

She brushed out her hair and walked into the main room to dress. She pinched her cheeks for color, but her eyes were red and swollen. Richard finally returned, asking if she was ready for breakfast. She wore a yellow skirt and jacket, and a yellow ribbon in her hair.

"You look wonderful," he told her, coming up and kissing her cheek.

"Richard, maybe we should have breakfast brought up to our room. I look terrible from crying."

"Nonsense. People will just think it's the trauma of a woman's wedding night. Come! I'm starved."

She followed him out reluctantly, getting the impression that he actually wanted people to think she had been the frightened but conquered bride. It made him look more manly. She felt the stares and whispers as they found their way to a table in the hotel's dining room. They sat down across from each other, and Richard took her hands, holding them out to study the huge diamonds of her wedding and engagement rings, and the elegant sparkle of the new ring he had given her that morning.

"Do you see now the kind of wonderful life you will have, Mrs. Holmes? You will want for nothing. I promise you."

Want for nothing? She had a horrible feeling that this man would never give her what she needed most. She looked at the rings, suddenly feeling as though he had bought her like a piece of merchandise. Again she thought of Red Wolf, and the simple tipi. The glory of being in Red Wolf's arms was worth all the diamonds and town houses in the world. But she had made her decision now. For the sake of everyone else involved, she must live with it. "Thank you, Richard. The ring is beautiful. Let's eat so we can go home and look at all our gifts. We have a lot of things to pack."

He squeezed her hands. "Thank you, Cynthia. You are a good friend. I will make you as happy as I possibly can. I promise you. And little Freedom will have the best of everything. I give you free rein with the house and with your son."

"Perhaps there will be more children, Richard. I would like to give you children."

The odd fear moved through his blue eyes again, and this time Cynthia detected it. "Yes." He put on the fake smile. "Yes, I would like to have children. That would be nice." He squeezed her hands and let go of them, turning to the menu.

Cynthia picked up her own, but she did not see the words inside, for new tears stung at her eyes. She breathed deeply and blinked them away, telling herself she had to be mature about this and be patient. Her marriage was barely one day old. In time things would get better, and all her fears would be alleviated.

Cynthia caught the concerned look on her mother's face when Richard hastily explained they had come early to pick up their things because they were anxious to get to Maryland and their new home.

"Cynthia is dying to start decorating her very own place," he told them, lighting a thin cigar and looking over some of the gifts. "I just hope we can get all this stuff packed and on the train."

"Well, you can leave some of it and I'll bring it when I bring Freedom down," Albert Wells told his new son-in-law.

Cynthia followed her mother to the kitchen to help finish some clean-up work from the day before. "I hope all of this wasn't too much for you, Mother."

"Nonsense. We're so happy for you." The woman eyed her daughter closely. "Is something wrong, Cynthia? You don't seem as happy as you should be this morning. I must say I thought the two of you would still be in bed, if I may be so forward. A man as virile as Richard—"

"Mother, please!" Cynthia reddened, quickly turning to put some cups away. "I'm very happy. I'm just tired. And Richard is right. I'm anxious to get into my new home, but I'll miss you and Father and Alex terribly."

"We'll miss you too, Cynthia, very much."

Cynthia turned and saw tears in her mother's eyes. She went to the woman and they embraced.

"Oh, Cynthia, I hope you aren't still pining after that Indian. I hope you haven't let that interfere with your relationship with Richard."

How could she explain? If Richard were the husband he should have been last night, her thoughts wouldn't stray so readily to Red Wolf. But what was the use trying to make her mother understand? She certainly couldn't announce that she wanted to annul her marriage, and technically it had been consummated, if that was what one could call what Richard had done to her this morning. Surely she was just being stupid and spoiled. Maybe when they were more settled in their town house, things would be better.

"Nothing is wrong, Mother. I love Richard very much. We just got anxious to get going, that's all." She pulled away. "But just because I have a husband now doesn't mean I can just forget all about Red Wolf. I loved him, Mother. He's Freedom's father. Why haven't you ever been able to accept that I loved him?"

The woman dabbed at tears with her apron. "Oh, I guess I have. It's just that it was all so wrong for you. Now you have everything. Your life is as it should be. We're so happy for you. We just want you to enjoy life now, enjoy your new husband and your new home."

Cynthia buried the terrible hurt of last night and this morning. Surely she had no other choice now. "You and Father will come for Christmas, won't you?"

"Oh, we would love to."

The conversation quickly turned to the gifts and the good time everyone had had. Richard and Cynthia's father finished packing everything, and Cynthia took a walk with Freedom.

"Grandpa will be bringing you to me very soon, Freedom," she told the boy. "You'll like it in Maryland. You'll be going to a fine school and make lots of new friends."

"Will we see the Indian show again?"

"Oh, I don't think so. They have traveled on to Europe."

"Was my real father with them, Mama?"

Cynthia struggled against the old pain. "I don't think so, Freedom. I would have recognized him."

"Would you really?"

Her throat tightened and tears came to her eyes. "Yes. I really would. I would never forget your father, Freedom, how he looked, how he spoke." "*How he made*

362

love to me," she finished secretly.

"Will you still let me go out West some day and find him?"

"Of course I will."

"I want to ride a horse and be all painted up like those Indians I saw. Did my father do that?"

"Oh, yes. He was a very good rider." She knelt in front of him. "But for a while you shouldn't talk too much about your real father in front of Richard, Freedom. Richard will be your father now, and he wants all that is best for you. You do like Richard, don't you?"

The boy nodded his head. "He's fun. Richard is nice. Are you happy, Mama?"

She hugged him tightly. "Yes," she lied. "Mama is very happy. And now you will have the best. Oh, I love you, Freedom. I love you more than anyone in the whole world."

"More than Richard?"

"Yes, more than Richard."

"More than my father?"

She struggled against the tears. "Yes, even more than your father. Mothers love their children above all things, Freedom. That's just the way it is for a mother."

"I love you more than anybody in the whole world too."

"Oh, thank you, Freedom." She kissed his cheek. Such a beautiful, dark, precious creature he was. As long as she had her Freedom, she could bear anything life presented to her. She was not quite sure what kind of trials marriage to Richard would bring her, but at least she had Freedom. At least she had this wonderful piece of life that was a part of Red Wolf.

They returned to the house, and everything was ready. Cynthia hugged her parents, and Alex.

"I'll miss you, Cindy," her brother told her. "You happy now?"

"Yes," she answered with a smile.

Alex frowned, studying this sister he had known

363

closely all his life. Cynthia didn't seem happy at all. He still missed the Cynthia he had known before the night she went to cut down Red Wolf. Everything had changed since that night. And even after having to be separated from Red Wolf, Cynthia's sadness had not been the kind he saw in her eyes now. Before she had had some spunk left. She had been sad to leave Red Wolf, but she had also kept her pride and admirable strength. Now it seemed the pride was somehow missing. It was as though someone had destroyed all her hope. He gave her a strong hug.

"Did Richard treat you okay?" he asked quietly as the others visited, all talking at once.

Cynthia reddened and pulled away. "Richard is very kind. I'm just . . . having to get used to this sudden change, that's all."

"Well, you know you can talk to me about anything, Cindy," he told her. "Just send me a note, and I'll come and visit."

Their eyes held, and she knew her brother sensed more easily than her parents that something was wrong.

"Thank you, Alex. I'll remember that." She put on a smile and looked him over, stepping back and looking up at him. "I can't believe you're my 'little' brother. I wonder if you'll grow even more before I see you again."

Their eyes held again and he squeezed her hands. "Good luck, Cindy. God be with you."

"And with you, Alex."

He leaned down and kissed her cheek, and she realized she felt more strength and support from her own brother's embrace than she had gotten from Richard. She turned away from him, hugging Freedom once more. She didn't want to leave. She wanted to scream at all of them that Richard wasn't at all what they thought he was. But they would never believe her. She boarded the buggy amid more hugs and kisses and good-byes, and the carriage was off. Cynthia Wells Holmes was headed for her new home in Maryland, with her handsome, successful new husband. Her whirlwind romance and

364

beautiful wedding and the wonderful life she would lead as a proper lady of Baltimore were the very stuff of which dreams were made. The prince and princess were headed for their new home.

Life was not a fairy tale. It became a nightmare for Cynthia, who put on a grand show of the happy new wife. Richard was gracious and generous, a good father, an excellent provider, giving in to everything Cynthia wanted to do to the town house. In so many ways he was everything a woman could want, and they shared many conversations about politics as they sat beside the hearth on cold winter nights. Richard had every respect for Cynthia's viewpoints, and he listened with all sincerity to her talk about the Indians. Through a barrage of beautifully written letters, he actually had managed to turn one Congressman's thoughts about Indians from being against a bill that would keep certain reservation lands out of the hands of white speculators, to being for the bill.

There were a lot of things about Richard Holmes to love. But Cynthia was starved for the kind of love she needed most—that intimate, sweet, physical lovemaking that to her was all a part of loving a man. To her deep humiliation he had made love to her only once on their trip south, and that time just as clumsily as he had that first morning together.

Once they were settled in, lovemaking dwindled to hardly more than once a month. Cynthia felt starved and lonely and humiliated. She began to think there must be something very wrong with her, but Richard was so kind in every other way, and she was being the best wife she could be. To discover that her handsome, seemingly virile husband had no interest in sex was devastating. She had turned to him because she was ready for a man again, because she needed that part of her life fulfilled. Now she was just as starved and lonely as she had been before meeting Richard; more so because now she had found a man she thought she loved and who she thought loved her. It was much harder to be around a man and never receive affection, than to be without a man of any kind.

She gradually found herself learning to hate Stewart Reynolds. He visited daily, often staying for supper and hanging around for long chats in Richard's study, going over court cases and matters that Cynthia thought should be left at the office. Many nights she went to bed alone, but soon it didn't matter, for even with Richard in her bed, it was as though he wasn't there at all. She said nothing to him about Stewart, for the two men were close, and she knew the worst thing she could do was come between them. And she did not complain about the lovemaking, or rather the lack of it. She had taken her vows. She felt she was surely lucky to have a husband like Richard, and she suffered her loneliness quietly and secretly. No one else knew or suspected, except Alex. Alex had a way of looking at her when he visited that let her know he knew she was very unhappy. But she told him nothing.

How could she share such a thing with her brother, or with anyone for that matter? No matter how she explained it, it made her sound like some kind of wanton woman. And the way some of the women in the sewing club and the group of lawyer's wives she had joined talked, a woman was better off if her husband left her alone. They talked as though sex was some kind of burden to be suffered in order to get children. But Cynthia had known another kind of physical love, with a man who had opened a world of beauty and ecstasy to her. Sex had never been a burden with Red Wolf. And she couldn't imagine that all these women thought that way, for some had teasingly joked that it might not be so bad with a man like Richard.

If only they knew. Her hopes of getting pregnant were gone. No woman could get pregnant when her husband mated with her hardly more than once a month. And even then, it was always quick, with no foreplay, no long, lingering kisses, no deep, pushing thrusts that would ensure that his seed was planted good and deep.

Days turned into weeks; weeks into months; months into years. Cynthia suffered alone. Richard Holmes's law practice grew, and more men were hired. Cynthia busied herself with sewing circles and card parties with prominent women, who quickly warmed to the beautiful Mrs. Holmes, all of them acutely curious about Freedom and his father. Cynthia spared the details. She knew that these women would never understand her love for Red Wolf, and that love was actually growing deep in her heart rather than fading. Richard's physical starvation only enhanced her memories of Red Wolf. There had been many lonely, hurt-filled moments when certain women shunned her for having been "soiled" by a wild Indian. But for the most part, Cynthia's charming personality and her beauty, along with the obvious fact that the successful Richard Holmes truly loved his wife, seemed to win over even the most skeptical.

For six years Cynthia lived in her lonely world, putting on a grand show for outsiders. She was a marvelous hostess, and at all public occasions Richard showed her the fullest attention, even to saying he owed his continued succcess to the wonderful woman he had married. He ran for Congress and lost, but he and his colleagues were confident that he had a good chance the next time around. He simply had to stay in the public eye and keep campaigning. He and Cynthia traveled around the district together, and Cynthia would sit nearby, giving the picture of the wonderful, supportive wife, while Richard gave eloquent speeches.

Freedom was happy. Richard taught him everything he knew about practicing law, and by thirteen the boy already had a head start on things even college students didn't know. He was doing well in school, already planning on finishing high school by sixteen and then attending Princeton to be an attorney like his stepfather.

Freedom was very smart, and in so many ways he reminded Cynthia of Red Wolf. She remembered how intelligent Red Wolf had been, too intelligent to waste himself away on a reservation. She wondered if he had ever used that intelligence to better himself. She remembered how she had told him he should get more schooling and use his intelligence to help his people. But back then all he was interested in was fighting the white man physically.

Having Freedom and thinking of Red Wolf often were all that helped Cynthia keep her sanity. She plunged deeper and deeper into outside activities to stay as busy as possible so that at night she would fall to sleep exhausted and not long for Richard to hold her and make love to her. Richard went on about life as though it was perfectly normal, seeming to think that their sex life was just as it should be. He seemed perfectly happy, and many ways their marriage was normal and happy—in every way but at bedtime. In her kind and innocent heart, Cynthia simply did not see what was really wrong with her husband. She was sure he simply had a strange outlook on sex; that perhaps something was wrong with him mentally or even physically in that respect. She had thought of suggesting they see a doctor, but she feared such a suggestion would hurt him so badly he would alienate her in other ways, and she couldn't bear to be shut out of his life in any other way. Their marriage became more the life of two good friends living together.

It was not until a night in January 1891 that the years of strain took their toll on Cynthia. It started with the news of a terrible massacre of Sioux and Cheyenne Indians at Wounded Knee, South Dakota. The stories poured in through Eastern newspapers. Soldiers had killed a great number of Indians in a skirmish for which no one had an explanation. The number of Indians killed varied from a few to several hundred. Some newspapers called it a battle which the soldiers won. Others called it a slaughter of innocent Indians. No one seemed to know the reason, except that because of some new religion the Indians had been celebrating, whites had feared a new uprising. Fear and confusion had led to the final skirmish, and there were stories of a mass burial of Indians.

Fourteen-year-old Freedom was upset, fearing his real father might have been involved. Cynthia tried to console him, reminding him how capable Red Wolf was. But the news brought back all the old memories for her— that awful day the soldiers picked her up, Flowing Waters lying there raped and murdered, the babies dead, women mutilated.

Had it happened all over again at Wounded Knee? How had things come to this after so many years of relative peace with the Sioux? Surely things were just as bad on the reservation as Richard had been told, for the Indians were apparently still very unhappy. Her heart ached for Red Wolf. If he was still alive, he surely had been a part of this latest skirmish. Maybe he had even been among those killed. All the memories came back to haunt her, and it upset her to see Freedom so worried.

She went to bed early that night, for Richard and Stewart had a lot of work to do in the study. Richard intended to begin a new campaign of letters to Congressmen demanding an investigation into the conditions on reservations and the matters that had led up to the massacre. Reformation of various laws governing the Indians was going to be one of his goals if he could ever get into Congress.

Cynthia slept restlessly, jumping awake every few minutes, thinking of Red Wolf. A chapter in her life had been left open, and she felt helpless to ever close it. She was married to Richard now, but she wanted so much to see Red Wolf just once more, wrong as it might be. After fourteen years, he should have been out of her life. And he would be, if only Richard had loved her fully as a

369

woman and had given her the physical attention she needed. But Red Wolf was there in her heart.

She sat up deep in the night, wide awake. The room was dimly lit, and she looked over to see that Richard had never come to bed. She got up and pulled on her robe. She had taken all she could. She could not go on this way. She would talk to Richard about how badly she needed him physically, gently suggest he see a doctor. Tonight, more than ever, she needed him to hold her. She hurried quietly down the circular stairway and down the oak-lined hallway to Richard's study. She saw a light under the door, but heard no voices. There were only soft groaning sounds.

Cynthia frowned. Was Richard ill? She hurried inside, then stood frozen in place, horror coming into her eyes when she saw that both Stewart and Richard were naked, and in an obviously lustful embrace.

"Cynthia!" Richard exclaimed. He pulled away from Stewart and began pulling on his pants, but Cynthia had already fled the room, her mind racing wildly, her stomach lurching from the shocking, sickening sight. How could she not have seen it all these years? She realized now it had been there all the time, but she had been just afraid to face it. No! Not Richard! Not her handsome, virile, successful, kind Richard! He was every woman's dream! He was her husband! She managed to make it to the bathing room adjoining their bedroom, where she vomited into the water closet.

She straightened then, her breathing coming in great gasps as deep sobs of indescribable sorrow welled up from her soul.

"Cynthia, please let me explain."

She turned to see Richard standing in the doorway, wearing only his pants. His face was red, his eyes teared.

"Please, Cynthia," he was begging. "You've got to let me explain."

She made a sound like an animal, coming at him with gritted teeth, kicking at him and flailing at him with her

370

fists. Little squeals and grunts came from deep in her soul as she hit at him over and over until a blessed blackness came over her. She felt herself collapsing, felt Richard lift her in his arms and carry her to the bed.

"My God, Cynthia, I never wanted to hurt you," she heard him sobbing. She could not reply. Nothing would move, not even her mouth.

Chapter Twenty-Three

For two weeks Cynthia lay in a state of nervous exhaustion and emotional shock, unable to do anything but cry. Freedom was in Princeton visiting his grandparents. Neither he nor Cynthia's parents knew about her collapse. And so she lay suffering alone. But she knew that even if her parents knew about her condition, she would never be able to explain what had brought it on.

Richard! Richard! She could not get the picture out of her mind, and suddenly she was consumed with an agonizing exhaustion that prevented her from even getting out of bed. She spoke to no one, and Richard stayed away on doctor's orders. Every time he entered the room Cynthia would groan and become nearly hysterical.

"I don't understand it, Mr. Holmes," the doctor would tell Richard. "I would think she would want her husband beside her."

"I don't understand it either, Doctor," Richard would answer. "She will get better, won't she?"

"In time. I can't really find anything physically wrong with her, but I know how hard your wife has been working on various community projects and such. I think she has simply worn herself down. This happens sometimes—all the pressures of being married to someone as prominent as you are. She'll need a good rest, especially if you intend to run for Congress next year. You just have her personal servant keep her sedated a few days. I'll come by every couple of days to check on her."

Cynthia could hear conversations. She wanted so badly to speak, but nothing would come. It was as though she was too tired to do barely more than breathe. In the deep recesses of her mind she remembered that Freedom was visiting his grandparents, and she was glad of it. But she was so desperately lonely. If only she could explain to her parents. But they would never believe her. Again she must suffer alone, and again she turned to memories of Red Wolf for comfort. It seemed that was all she had left now—a past to which she could never return, and a bleak and lonely future.

After two weeks she was finally sitting up in bed and eating on her own. But her body felt like dead weight. She wondered if perhaps it was just her heart that weighed so much. Perhaps she was doomed to a life of unhappiness for her sin of cutting loose an Indian man sixteen years ago. Or for loving a man supposedly forbidden to her. Maybe it was because she had helped Red Wolf kill the men who had attacked her. The only real happiness she had known since being taken from Red Wolf was the son he had given her. Thank God, at least, for Freedom. Without him she would have nothing.

There came a light tap on the door. "Who is it?" she asked in a weak voice.

"It's me—Richard. Can I come in, Cynthia? I must talk to you."

She felt the sick feeling come into her stomach again and her head ached. "Come in," she answered, setting aside a food tray.

The door opened slowly and he came inside, looking as handsome and virile as ever. Cynthia was astounded at his manly bearing, now that she knew the truth about him. Bitterness and hatred shone in her eyes as he closed the door and walked hesitantly closer. His own eyes actually teared, and he reddened some, pulling over a chair to sit down beside the bed. He swallowed and cleared his throat.

"I, uh, I want to thank you—first—for not screaming all over Baltimore about . . . about what you saw."

She looked away from him. "Why, Richard? Why did you marry me? Just for looks? Did you think a pretty wife on your arm would help win votes? That's it, isn't it?" She turned to look at him accusingly. "You married me to show the public what a wonderful family man you are! It was all just a great pretense! A cover for what you *really* are!" She made a little choking sound. "It sickens me to think I've let you touch me! Don't you ever, ever come to my bed again, or even think about kissing me!"

She broke into quiet sobbing and Richard rested his elbows on his knees, putting his head in his hands. "I don't suppose you would believe me if I told you I am genuinely sorry," he said, his voice broken. He began crying himself then, pitiful sobs that tore at her heart in spite of how she felt about what he was.

She closed her eyes and listened to him cry, wondering how such a beautiful man could have such a problem. This was her first encounter with such a thing. It was a subject she had hardly ever heard of and one she had never believed really existed. Now she wondered how she could have been so ignorant of the obvious all these years. It was partly her fault, for marrying him when she had doubts—for not annulling the marriage after that first disastrous wedding night.

She wiped at her eyes with a handkerchief. "Did you ever love me, Richard? Did you ever really care about Freedom?"

He took several deep breaths, wiping at his own eyes. "I did love you, Cynthia. I still do. I have the utmost . . . respect for you. I love you for the friend you have been—for the strength and patience you have had with me all these years—for putting up with the loneliness. Did you think I didn't know how lonely you were—how much you needed what I couldn't give you?"

"You couldn't have loved me and put me through that."

He blew his nose. "It wasn't that I didn't love you. I do. I never meant to make you suffer, Cynthia. I swear to God that I really tried. I really wanted it to work. You were so beautiful and so patient and sweet. I thought in time . . . I could change. I *wanted* to change, Cynthia. As God is my witness! Please tell me you believe that."

She closed her eyes again. "I don't know what to believe anymore. I feel so . . . empty. You've taken my best years, Richard. I'm thirty-two years old. If I leave you I will not only be a white woman who once lived and slept with an Indian, I will also be a divorced woman. No man will touch me. My family would never understand and I don't have the slightest idea how I would support myself. And yet I suppose I am going to have to live with all of that because I can't stay with you—not now."

"Don't talk that way, Cynthia. I can give you everything, just as I always have. Please stay with me, please! At least until after the election next year."

She met his eyes, the lump in her throat swelling painfully. "Do you know how it feels—to know you married me just for convenience? Do you know how that makes me feel about myself? You deceived me, Richard, in the cruelest way a woman can be deceived!"

"Not completely, Cynthia." He leaned closer. "Cynthia, listen to me. Please try to understand. I swear to God that I love you and I always did. I married you with the full intent of changing my life." His eyes teared anew. "Do you think it was easy for me? Do you have any idea the hell I live with? It's as though . . . as though a demon has always had control of me. Look at me, for God's sake! I know how others perceive me. I look in the mirror, Cynthia, and I see the man I should be—the man I *want* to be! But . . . the demon keeps after me. I try to think and act the way a man should. And all my political ambition, my desire to help the Indian, all my work as an

376

attorney—all of that is real, Cynthia. All of that is sincere. And so are my feelings for you. All these years I have adored you. Haven't I given you everything you ever wanted?"

He looked down at his clasped hands. "Everything but the physical love you need. I know that." He met her eyes again. "But I would do anything for you, Cynthia, and no matter how much you hate me, if you will just stay with me a while longer, I'll continue to provide for you as I always have. I know I've hurt you terribly, but I beg of you to just hang on a while longer, for the sake of the friendship we at least shared—and for Freedom's sake. I'm begging you, Cynthia, stay with me until a year or so after the election, and please . . . please don't ever tell anyone the truth about me. If you still want to go away, I promise, as God is my witness, that I will continue to support you with whatever you need until the time should come that you marry again."

She smiled bitterly. "Marry? Who would marry me now?"

"You're a beautiful woman, Cynthia."

"I already told you why no man would have me."

He quickly wiped at more tears that slipped down his cheeks. "I wish I could make you believe . . . how sorry I am . . . how much I really wanted it to work. If you would just believe that much . . . if you would understand just a little bit . . . what life has been like for me. That's why I've dedicated myself to work . . . to helping those who need it . . . to getting into politics, where I can have the power to change the things that are wrong with this country. If I can't change my personal life, then maybe I can at least change things outside that life. I can't tell you sincerely enough what your friendship means to me, Cynthia. If you must leave me, then at least let us part friends."

She watched him, trying to grasp the certain hell he must have been suffering for years.

"I guess we've both been suffering our own kind of

377

unspoken loneliness, haven't we?" she said then, her voice filled with sorrow.

He just nodded, crying again. He quickly wiped at his eyes and took deep breaths, trying to gain control of himself.

"You have me trapped, Richard," she said wearily. "I'm probably the biggest fool ever born, but I don't have the heart to give away your secret and destroy you. How about that for being a fool? I would like to blame you for ruining my life, but I suppose I've done that myself. I thought about having the marriage annulled after that first night, but I was too proud; and I thought maybe there was something wrong with me. All these years I've blamed myself, wondering what I was doing wrong; but deep inside I knew it wasn't me at all. I just didn't want to face it. You were so good to me in every other way, and you've been a good father to Freedom." She sighed deeply. "If for no other reason, I'll never tell anyone about you for Freedom's sake. I wouldn't want him to know that. I wouldn't know how to begin explaining such a thing."

She faced him again. "I want your promise that no matter what, Freedom will have the best education he can get."

Richard wiped at his eyes again. "You know I would do that for him."

"I want separate bedrooms. Lots of couples have separate bedrooms. That shouldn't be difficult to explain and it's no one's business anyway."

He nodded.

"And I never want to see Stewart Reynolds in this house again. If you must be with him, then do it someplace else, not under my roof."

He swallowed. "Stewart . . . is leaving the law firm," he answered, sorrow evident in his voice. "He's going to Boston to start his own practice."

Cynthia's eyebrows arched in surprise. "The damage has already been done."

378

"I know. Believe it or not, we care very much about each other. It isn't the ugly, perverted thing you think it is. It's always been . . . just Stewart. And because he cares about me, he decided it was best to go away for a while. He thought . . . perhaps there was some way you and I could survive together if he was out of the picture . . . and he doesn't want any more risk of this being found out by the public. He's doing it for me. Believe it or not, he is a great friend, Cynthia. He understood when I married you that I was going to try to live like a normal man. And no matter what you think of it, it will be a great loss to me when he goes." He smiled sadly, new tears coming. "I suppose . . . it's a bit like you and Red Wolf. He meant very much to you and now he's gone. So I guess we will both be very lonely, won't we? We'll have that much in common. Maybe that will help us to be closer."

She looked away from him, wishing she could hate him more, but suddenly the hatred was leaving her. "We will never be really close, Richard. I can never be a wife to you in the truest sense. But I will make you a promise, if you do the things I asked." She looked at him again. "I won't tell anyone the truth. I'll stay by your side through the election and play the happy wife. I'll put on a pretense for Freedom's sake, and I'll support your causes. I can't predict how long I can live this way, but I'll stick it out for a couple more years at least. You have given me all the comforts and luxuries a woman could want, and you've been good to Freedom. But if I reach the point where I simply can't live this lie any longer, I'll have to leave you."

He nodded. "I understand." He met her eyes, another tear slipping down his cheek. "Thank you, Cynthia. My deepest regret . . . is that I have never been able to take advantage . . . of the wonderful woman I married . . . the sweet love she had to offer me." He sniffed and wiped at his cheeks, forcing a smile. "I truly am glad to see you are better. If there is anything—anything you need, tell

379

me right away."

She shook her head, her own tears coming again. "You can't give me what I need," she sobbed.

He sighed deeply, running a hand through his hair. He got up from the chair, leaning over her and hesitantly touching her hair. "If you could . . . see your way to forgive me, Cynthia . . . I could never ask for more in this life."

He quickly left the room then, and Cynthia rolled over and hugged her pillow close, remembering the time another man had held her, a man in every sense of the word, his arms so strong, his kiss so sweet, his love so pure and devoted. Oh, for the feel of those arms, the sound of his voice! But now it was even too late for that. Even Red Wolf wouldn't want her anymore, after all these years.

There followed a year of mad campaigning, and a considerable amount of entertaining was done at the Holmeses' lovely and "happy" home. After a few weeks' rest Cynthia had again busied herself with parties and benefits, against the doctor's wishes. She added politicking to her schedule, traveling separately from Richard to make speeches for him, representing her would-be congressman husband in a most fitting manner that would make any man proud. She knew of no other way to mask the hurt and loneliness than to stay as busy as possible, and she thanked God that at least her husband stood for causes she too believed in. She could at least support him in that respect.

People commented about how difficult it must be for the beautiful couple to have to be apart so much, and when they were together publicly, Cynthia smiled and seemed to enjoy being beside her husband. Occasionally Richard would kiss her lightly on the cheek. But at night in their hotel rooms Richard slept on the floor or in a chair, and at home Cynthia slept completely alone.

Cynthia's parents were ecstatic over the popularity of their son-in-law. Occasionally Cynthia would visit them for a few days—"to rest from the wild campaign schedule," she would tell them. Martha would visit her old friend and carry on about what a glamorous, wonderful life Cynthia led. "What is it like being married to a man like Richard Holmes?" she would ask. "Oh, Cynthia, you have everything! I'm so happy for you."

Only Alex noticed something was wrong. For years he had suspected his sister was not happy. Alex was twenty-six now, a teacher himself but still living at home. He had met a young woman at Princeton whom he intended to marry, and he understood now what love was all about, what it felt like. He knew how a woman in love should look—how Cynthia had looked when she used to talk about Red Wolf—the light in her eyes. That light was not there when she talked about Richard. It had never been there. And it seemed that all the spunk and daring she had shown as a young girl had long ago left her.

On her last visit before the November 1892 election, Cynthia and Alex both sat up late talking in front of the hearth—talking about Alex's impending marriage, the campaign, Richard's goals, Freedom's future.

"What about you?" Alex asked her then. "You never talk about you, Cynthia. Are you happy?"

She met his eyes, surprised by his insight. "Of course I'm happy. Why shouldn't I be? I have everything."

"Do you?" He searched her eyes. "I know you better than anybody. You haven't been happy for a long time. Is Richard treating you all right?"

She looked at her lap. "Richard is very good to me. Isn't that pretty obvious?"

He shook his head. "Something's the matter, Cynthia. I wish you'd tell me about it."

Her throat tightened. "I can't, Alex. You just have to trust me that Richard is very good to me. It . . . it has nothing to do with Richard."

"Red Wolf? You never really got over him, did you?

You've never really loved Richard like you loved Red Wolf."

She met his eyes again, her own tearing. "You mean you understand that I truly loved him? You believe me when I tell you I was never forced or drugged or tricked into being with him?"

"I always believed you." He smiled. "I figured if anybody is crazy enough to love an Indian, my sister would be." He studied her lovingly. "You never, never got over him, did you?"

She broke into quiet tears. "You don't know . . . how good it feels . . . to know somebody understands that. I've never . . . loved another man that way, Alex . . . God forgive me."

He leaned forward and grasped her hands. "Forgive you? For loving somebody?" He squeezed her hands. "You do know it never could have lasted, don't you? You do understand Mother and Father did what they thought was best for you—and that this life has been much better for Freedom than what he would have had on a reservation."

She nodded. "I know. But . . . I'm so unhappy, Alex! It . . . feels so good just to . . . tell somebody." She cried harder and he reached out and petted her hair.

"Poor Cynthia. You've never really loved Richard that way. You've got to let go, Cynthia—let go of the memories and give all of yourself to Richard. He's a good man. You've got the best. Let him love you. You can't go on like this the rest of your life."

She shook her head. How could she tell him? She had promised never to tell anyone. She only wept. "Don't tell anyone, Alex, especially not Mother and Father. They would be so disappointed. They think the world of Richard."

"I know. I won't say anything. But I told you once you could come to me if you've got problems, Cynthia. All I can tell you about this one is that you've got to wake up and realize what you have. It's been sixteen years since we left the Dakotas."

"To me it's like yesterday," she said wearily.

"My God, Cynthia."

She raised tear-stained eyes to meet her brother's. "Every time I look at Freedom I see him. Every time I close my eyes he's there. Richard could buy me the world, but my heart will always belong to Red Wolf. My whole marriage is a lie, but I keep up the pretense because it's all I have, and I don't want to disappoint Mother and Father."

"Cynthia, you can't go on like this. I can't imagine that a man like Richard hasn't helped you forget—hasn't won your heart."

She put her head down. "You don't understand," she whispered.

"What don't I understand?"

She shook her head. "It's all right. At least you understand how much I loved Red Wolf." She met his eyes again. "You're a good brother, Alex. We've always been close. I'll always remember how you tried to cover for me when I snuck out of the house that night."

His eyes teared. "When I see how you've suffered, I wish I'd waked up sooner and stopped you from going at all. Everything might have been different then."

"Yes," she whispered. "I suppose it might have."

He leaned forward and kissed her cheek. "I'll always support you, Cynthia, whatever you do. I want you to be happy. You've got to let go and let Richard make you happy."

If only she could tell him. But she couldn't bring herself to betray her promise to Richard. She was still his wife. "I'll try," she answered, feeling the final loneliness of not being able to share her worst disappointment with her brother. "I'll try."

Red Wolf watched the changing scenery as the train rumbled across the Nebraska-Iowa border. In spite of his

383

education, and in spite of having already made this trip several times before, he still had lingering feelings of panic when he knew he was leaving his homeland, especially when he was headed into the "land of the white man."

It was no wonder that those Indians who had been put onto reservations hundreds, sometimes thousands of miles from their homeland, died in alarming numbers, sometimes from little more than broken hearts. Red Wolf knew he would not want to go on living himself if someone told him he could never return to the Black Hills.

But Red Wolf and his people were among the "lucky" ones, if it could be called lucky to be completely defeated by and under the thumb of the white man's government. They were lucky only in the fact that the Rosebud Reservation lay nearly in the heart of Sioux country; and the Standing Rock Reservation north of it was also in Sioux country. They were still "home," so to speak; but living conditions on the reservations were pitiful, and the government seemed to be able to use the land however they chose. Red Wolf felt more like they were simply being allowed to live on someone else's property.

"So, again I go into the land of the rising sun," he thought. *"The land into which my Cynthia disappeared so long ago."* He had tried so hard to forget her, the beautiful white woman he had once called his wife. In his heart she was still his wife. He had never taken another.

How he had hated the white man after they took Cynthia away! How good it had felt to shoot at Hard Backsides and his men, for it was bluecoats who took Cynthia away all those years ago. But the days of freedom and warfare were over. He recognized now the ugly truth—that the white man was here to stay; and he had never forgotten Cynthia's words: *"You're different, Red Wolf. You could help your people."*

He had done just that—and only for Cynthia. He had risen above his hatred, conquered his fear of leaving his homeland. He had let white men teach him to read and write; he had traveled all the way to Pennsylvania and attended the Carlisle Indian School. He would never forget how shocked he was to discover the white man's cities in the East, and to see the unending supply of white men who lived in the land beyond the Mississippi. Once he had traveled East, he'd realized life would never again be the same for the Indian.

To see so many changes for his people saddened his heart. More whites were moving onto land that was supposed to belong to the Sioux. A man considered himself lucky now if he spotted a buffalo. Screaming, belching locomotive engines had invaded Indian lands; and a few of his people lived in little houses now. But others, especially the old ones, insisted on remaining in tipis, for they found houses too hard and cold, too removed from Mother Earth, too confining of the inner spirit.

Red Wolf lived in a small house now himself. He wondered what Cynthia would think of it—what kind of life she was living herself. And most of all he wondered if she had had the child she was carrying when she was taken from him. How he longed to know, to see the product of his seed, his only child. He wondered if his son or daughter had even been told about its father. But knowing Cynthia, her strength, her determination, her love for him—surely she would not raise the child without telling him or her all about Red Wolf, and the way life once was for the Sioux.

He looked out the window again, watching a white man plow a field with a team of horses. How he still hated seeing Mother Earth torn up like that! But he could no longer stop such things. Lieutenant Wilson had been right. The only way to continue fighting for what little Indian lands and Indian rights were left was to get a white man's education and use the white man's own system of justice to ensure treaties were obeyed. Red Wolf had studied diligently, always keeping Cynthia in mind, her encouragement to use his intelligence for his people.

He was a teacher now on the Rosebud Reservation. It was not an easy task, although he was more successful than most of the white teachers because his people trusted him more. Even at that, many still refused to send their children to school. It was Red Wolf who had fought for schools on reservation lands, rather than taking children from their families and sending them far away to school. To send them away was to kill their spirits; and it only made the older ones even more distrustful. And young ones who were sent away were often forbidden to speak their own language or to do or say anything related to their heritage.

It was with bitterness Red Wolf remembered his own experience at Carlisle. He'd been a grown man at the time, but had been allowed to attend because of his potential, on the recommendation of the lieutenant. But again the whites had tried to cut his hair. It was only Red Wolf's threat to kill anyone who touched his hair that had kept them at bay; but he had not been able to stop those in charge from cutting the hair of the children who came there, and it still pained Red Wolf's heart to remember their little faces, sober Indian boys and girls, their hair cut short, all of them wearing the clothes of white children, their happy spirits destroyed. He'd vowed then to get the best education he could, and to fight to keep Indian children home with their families and on their own sacred lands. The white man wanted to destroy the Indian culture. Red Wolf would not let that happen.

That was part of the reason he was again heading East. He would speak before Congress on behalf of a bill being considered that would ensure more money for schools on reservation lands. With these whites who understood little about Indian culture and the Indian spirit, keeping the Indian ways alive was a never-ending battle in Washington. But there were some who were sympathetic, and Red Wolf had been told about one man in particular, a man running for Congress in Maryland, who had done a considerable amount of lobbying on behalf of the Indians. His name was Richard Holmes, and since he was running for a seat in Congress, he could be important to Red Wolf's cause. Red Wolf had already decided that since this was an election year, after he spoke before Congress he would go to Maryland and find this Richard Holmes. Men like that were important allies, and voting on the new bill might not take place until after the new Congress was in session.

He watched out the window again, imagining he was riding beside the train on a swift pony, wearing only a loincloth instead of the binding white man's clothes he wore now, his pony keeping pace with the iron horse that had replaced the four-footed kind. And beside him, on an equally swift pony, there rode a woman, her skin tanned but still much more fair than Red Wolf's, her long, blond hair blowing straight out from the fast ride.

"*Cynthia*," he whispered. Apparently the aching emptiness left in his heart would never go away.

Chapter Twenty-Four

The park was crowded with people who had come to meet the candidates for Congress. A marching band paraded through the middle of the crowd, and various candidates stood on platforms scattered here and there throughout the park in Baltimore, each man touting his attributes, spouting off promises, kissing babies. The election was only a week away.

Red Wolf wandered with the rest of the crowd, always astounded at the antics of the white man, their love of parades and the way they believed the campaign promises of the white men who spoke with forked tongues. There were not many politicians he trusted, and he wondered now just how many of those in Congress who had smiled at him and shook his hand after his speech would really end up voting for his cause when the time came.

Games. That was what life was for the white man. Just games and strategy. It sickened Red Wolf that he sometimes had to play by the same rules. Here he was, mingling with this crowd of people, most of whom were simply putting on a show. He was going to find Richard Holmes, and he would talk to the man, smile for him, praise his work, pretend he was the greatest person who ever walked. He would do all that, play it the white man's way, if it meant better education back home. But he hated every minute of it. He had already spent a week in

Washington. He wanted to go home. But Richard Holmes could be an important contact. He had fought his desire to jump on the next train West and had come to Maryland instead. Richard Holmes was to speak here in this park today. Red Wolf would listen. He walked tall and handsome and proud through the crowd. People stared at the "real Indian"; women took second glances when their husbands weren't looking, moved by his physique, his proud carriage, the mystique he carried with him by just being Indian. Red Wolf searched for the grandstand where Holmes would be speaking, pushing his way through the crowd, wondering how whites could stand to live in such congested areas. This park was their attempt at keeping a piece of "country" within the city, but this was not like the quiet Black Hills at all, and he almost felt sorry for the struggling trees and grass in the park.

He approached a grandstand surrounded by a growing crowd and decorated in the white man's United States colors of red, white, and blue. A man and woman stood talking together on the platform, both of them very well-dressed. "Mr. Holmes!" he heard someone shout.

"So, this must be the man I'm looking for," Red Wolf thought. He watched Holmes for a moment, intending to go up and introduce himself, but then Holmes turned and put up his hands to silence the crowd, ready to begin his speech. The woman with whom he had been talking also faced the crowd then as she sat down.

When Red Wolf caught sight of her face, his heart nearly stopped beating. If any woman fit the picture of how he imagined Cynthia might look now, this woman did. Seeing her instantly stirred old memories. This woman was beautiful! She was apparently the wife of Richard Holmes. How ironic that this man who fought for Indian rights was married to someone who looked so much like Cynthia. Red Wolf stared, trying to ignore the shivers that ran through his blood at the thought that perhaps it really *was* Cynthia. He told himself he was letting his imagination and old memories get the better of him.

A group of young men approached the platform then, one of them talking to the blond woman for a moment. To Red Wolf's surprise, the one talking to her looked very Indian. Again his suspicions were aroused, and he wondered if being in this white man's world too long had taken away his ability to think clearly and sensibly.

The group of young men left the platform then and headed in Red Wolf's direction. Red Wolf watched the Indian boy approach as the crowd pushed against the grandstand and Richard Holmes began delivering his speech. Red Wolf dropped back. The Indian boy glanced at him and smiled and nodded as the young men walked by. Red Wolf could not help following, feeling drawn by some supernatural force.

"Excuse me!" he called out, suddenly rushing up to the young Indian man and touching his arm. It seemed everything in his body tingled strangely at the touch. The boy, who appeared to be about sixteen, turned to face him.

"Yes, sir?"

Red Wolf struggled to find his voice. "I . . . I'm just wondering if the man on the platform is Richard Holmes. I've come to talk to him."

The boy smiled. "About Indian rights?"

Red Wolf nodded.

The boy glanced up at the speaker, then back to Red Wolf. "Yes, sir, he's Richard Holmes. He's my step-father. I guess you can tell he's for Indian rights, since he is such a good father to me."

Red Wolf smiled. "Yes, I suppose."

"Are you a real Indian?"

Red Wolf laughed. "You mean you have never met one?"

"No."

"But *you* are Indian."

"I know. But I've always lived here in the East. My

391

mother and I were taken from the Sioux Indians before I was born. What kind of Indian are you?"

Red Wolf struggled to keep his smile. No! It couldn't be! Was this why his inner spirit had urged him to come to Maryland?

"I am Sioux," he answered, deciding to avoid giving his name yet.

"You are?" The boy's eyes widened. His white friends urged him to come with them, but he waved them off. "I'll catch up," he told them, his eyes on Red Wolf. "Maybe you know my father!" he told Red Wolf. "My mother says someday I can go out to the Dakotas and try to find him if I want. But first I have to finish college. I already started this year—Princeton. I only came back to Maryland for the elections. My stepfather is running for Congress, but I guess you probably know that."

Red Wolf just stared as the boy rambled on with the eagerness of his youth. Yes, it could be! A young Red Wolf stood before him. He said he had been stolen away before he was born—and if Richard Holmes was his stepfather, that meant the blond woman on the platform with Holmes would be this boy's mother!

"My real father's name was Red Wolf," the boy was saying. "Do you know a Red Wolf? How big is the reservation? Would I be able to find him?"

Red Wolf turned away for a moment, pretending to clear his throat. He forced himself to be calm, told himself he had no right telling this young man straight out that he was Red Wolf. There was still a remote possibility this was all just some crazy mix-up. If this young man standing before him was his own son, he had to be sure before saying anything or the boy might be terribly disappointed. Somehow he had to talk to the blond woman on the platform.

"I . . . I'm afraid I don't know a Red Wolf," he answered, smiling. But inside he was weeping. He wanted to hold this boy, to grab him and shout that he was Red Wolf, that he might be his father! He wanted to fall to the ground and thank the Great Spirit for bringing him here; and yet he told himself this might not be what it appeared to be. "What . . . what is your mother's name?" he asked. "Perhaps back on the reservation someone would recognize it."

"Cynthia. Cynthia Holmes. Her maiden name was Wells."

Red Wolf's eyes began to tear against his will. "And what are you called, young man?"

"Freedom. My mother named me that because she says my father always wanted to be free."

A sharp pain moved through Red Wolf's heart. Yes, that would be like Cynthia—to remember how important freedom was to him! What a beautiful name she had given their child!

The young boys who had been with Freedom returned then and began tugging at him. "Hey, the prettiest girls you ever saw just walked over toward the fountain. Come on, Freedom."

Freedom laughed and waved at the Indian man as the boys dragged him off. "Hey, maybe I'll see you again later!" he called out. "Come to the Fountain Hotel tonight! My parents are holding a cocktail party there. You can look for Red Wolf and write me. . . ." His words trailed off as he ran off with the other boys.

Red Wolf stared after him, his heart pounding wildly, his throat tight. Could the handsome young man he had just met really be his son? He felt dizzy from the shock of it. He wanted to call out to him, to run after him. But he had to be careful. What did the boy know? He blinked back tears and turned toward the platform. He walked cautiously closer, his legs feeling suddenly weak. Richard Holmes's eloquent words went unheard. Suddenly Red Wolf didn't care what the man was saying or what he was doing about the Indians. All he wanted was to get another look at the blond woman sitting behind him on the platform.

He stayed deep in the crowd. If the woman with

Richard Holmes was his Cynthia, he didn't want to shock her or cause a commotion—not here in public. He realized now he was almost afraid to look again, but he had to know. He moved his dark eyes to where she sat, and he knew in that moment it was all true. Mrs. Richard Holmes was his Cynthia! She was older, but still utterly beautiful! There was the blond hair, the blue eyes, the creamy skin. She was still slender and appealing. How could he have even doubted when he first saw her?

"Cynthia!" he whispered.

Cynthia's eyes scanned the crowd, suddenly catching sight of a handsome Indian man. Their eyes held for several long seconds, and for both of them the crowd noise was gone. There was only an Indian, and a white woman.

The Indian man suddenly turned and mixed into the crowd. Cynthia stared after him, her heart pounding wildly. She wondered if she was finally losing her mind completely. The man she had just glimpsed could easily have been Red Wolf. But maybe after all these years any Indian man would look like Red Wolf to her. She searched the crowd frantically, wishing she could get up and run after the man as she caught sight of him in the distance then, leaving the park. But she was compelled to sit still while her husband continued his speech.

She put a hand to her chest. Where had the Indian man come from? What was he doing here? Had he come to see Richard? She felt suddenly warm all over in spite of the cool November air. The eyes! The dark eyes! The handsome face! It couldn't be! But the way he had looked at her, the intense emotion she had felt the moment their eyes locked. He had looked at her as though he knew her. Still, it couldn't be. What would Red Wolf be doing in a place like Baltimore? She told herself her years of pining away for him were taking their toll on her mind.

She tried to concentrate on Richard's speech then, but

her heart raced wildly. Seeing the Indian man had awakened all the old feelings. She watched the place where she had seen him disappear, scanned the crowd in hopes he had come back. But there was no sign of him.

Red Wolf entered the hotel dressed in a fine, black twilled worsted suit. The dinner jacket was waist-length in the front, with pointed lapels finished in black silk; and the back hung full to the back of his knees. His white, high-necked shirt only accented his dark skin, and a fancy bow tie decorated the collar. He wore a silk top hat only because here in the East it was the thing to do, but he had never gotten used to hats. His high, black boots were polished, and he was as well dressed as any man at the gala cocktail party.

He removed his top hat as soon as he was inside the lobby, and his tall, commanding appearance, and the fact that he still wore his black hair long and tied at the base of his neck, drew stares.

He could hear whispers about "the Indian," but he ignored them. His only goal in coming to Maryland had been to see Richard Holmes. Now that goal had changed. Now he was here to see *Mrs.* Richard Holmes, to catch one more glance of her, perhaps get a chance to talk to her. He had considered leaving right away and not causing any trouble. He still did not want to make trouble, but he could not leave without seeing Cynthia again, without hearing her voice, finding out if she was happy.

And now he knew he had a son! He had seen the boy with his own eyes. There could be no doubt who his father was. Cynthia had had a son, and she had apparently raised him into a fine young man. Right or wrong, Red Wolf was not about to go back to the reservation without seeing the boy again.

He moved toward the entrance to the banquet room where Richard Holmes was treating his supporters to a buffet meal and drinks. Red Wolf stopped occasionally to speak to people who pulled him aside, shaking his hand, asking who he was.

"Joseph Red Wolf, eh?" one man asked, his nose red from too much whiskey. "Why, I've never met a real Indian. You here to ask our future congressman for some kind of support for your people, Mr. Red Wolf?"

"Education. I am a teacher on the reservation. We need more teachers, better buildings, more supplies."

"Well, Holmes is the man to see. He's been a big supporter of Indians—even married a woman who had a son by an Indian. Can you imagine that? She was once a captive of the Sioux. Does all kinds of things to a man's imagination, if you know what I mean." The man laughed, patting Red Wolf's arm, and Red Wolf felt a keen desire to hit him. "But she's a beauty, I'll say, and every bit the refined lady. That boy of hers is right intelligent—going to Princeton next year to study law and theology. His grandpa is a preacher and teaches college too."

Red Wolf scanned the crowd, hardly listening to the man babble on. "Thank you," he finally spoke up. "Nice meeting you."

He had caught sight of Cynthia. She was walking toward the back of the room, stopping here and there to talk to people. He stayed behind her, able to keep track of her easily, as he was taller than most of the men in the room. He kept sight of her blond hair, mounds of it piled high at the crown of her head in an array of curls, while the rest of it hung down the center of her back. She wore an exquisite, deep brown satin dress, the bodice cut deep and exposing the milky white skin of her chest, with a tiny bit of the full white mounds of her breasts exposed. He had never forgotten the feel of those breasts in his hands, the taste of their sweet, pink fruits. The shoulders of the dress sported big satin bows, and a wide satin sash and bow accented her still-tiny waist. The skirt was fitted through the hips, then flared at the bottom into a small train.

Red Wolf held back, following her until she went through a door at the back of the room. He quickly followed, opening the door and peering into a hallway to see the train of the skirt disappearing through another door into the women's rest room. Red Wolf went through the door and stood in the hallway, where everything seemed suddenly quiet. He moved a few feet back, watching the door to the rest room. Two women came out, but neither of them was Cynthia. He prayed she would come out alone. He fingered his hat nervously, suddenly feeling like a young boy instead of a grown man, remembering how he'd felt when he wanted Cynthia all those years ago and had to patiently wait for her to want him.

It seemed incredible that the beautiful, refined woman he had seen today and this night was the same Cynthia he had known and loved all those years ago. It was difficult to picture the beautifully coiffed and fashionably dressed woman at this banquet riding free on a painted pony, wearing only an Indian tunic, her hair long and straight. Surely now she lived in some fancy home, probably with servants. But once she had lived in a tipi and was perfectly happy.

Again he considered just turning and leaving. There was obviously no hope of ever expecting her to live on an Indian reservation, even if she was free. But she was not free. She was Mrs. Richard Holmes, married to a man soon likely to be a congressman. Her son seemed perfectly happy. He had the best of everything and would get a good education. Yes, Red Wolf should leave all this alone and get the hell out of Maryland and never come back.

He turned to leave, but then the door to the rest room opened, and there she was, his beautiful Cynthia, the woman who had been stolen from him all those years ago, the woman who had once loved him with such devotion

397

and passion, the woman who had borne his son. Cynthia! She was moving across the hall toward the door to the banquet room. He could not stop himself.

"Cynthia?"

She stopped, a shiver moving through her at the familiarity of the voice. She turned, then gasped, putting a hand to her breast. She blinked and stood frozen in place.

"It is I—Red Wolf," he told her, stepping hesitantly closer. "Do I look so different?"

Cynthia stepped closer, her legs feeling like rubber. "Red Wolf?" she whispered in disbelief.

He smiled the familiar, beautiful smile. "You probably do not know me in these white man's clothes. I wear them only to fit in. I am sorry to shock you this way, but I—"

"You're the man I saw earlier today!"

He nodded. "I came here to meet with Richard Holmes. I did not know you were his wife until I saw you sitting beside him." Now he stepped closer, close enough to touch her. "I met an Indian boy in the crowd at the park. We talked, and he told me about his mother and said that his father was called Red Wolf. He said his name was Freedom." His dark eyes moved over her lovingly. "I am afraid I could not leave without knowing for certain—if he is my son. When he pointed out his mother—"

"Red Wolf!" she squeaked. "My God!"

She looked ready to faint. He reached out and took hold of her hands, then moved to put an arm around her waist and led her down the hall and around the corner to a love seat meant for public use. No one was about. He made her sit down in the love seat, then sat down beside her.

"I am sorry. I have shocked you. I do not mean to come and disrupt your life, Cynthia. I had no idea I would find you here."

She met his eyes, reaching out and grasping both his hands. Her eyes were teared. "How can this be?" she asked, her blue eyes studying him with all the love he had seen there years before. "It's like . . . like a miracle! Is God really letting me see you again? How on earth did you come to be here?"

He squeezed her hands. She looked so thin and tired. "I am a teacher now, Cynthia. I got an education, like you always said I should do. I teach on the reservation. Every year the government sponsors trips for some of the tribal leaders to come East and plead their cases before Congress. I have been to Washington to speak in behalf of education on the reservations. I came to Maryland to talk to your husband, since he does so much work on behalf of the Indians. But I . . . I never dreamed I would find *you* here!" His eyes drank in her beautiful face, the tempting fullness of her bosom displayed at the satin bodice of her dress, her milky shoulders, her full lips.

"Red Wolf!" she whispered, a tear trickling down her cheek. "You . . . look more handsome than ever! You look wonderful!"

He smiled, his own eyes tearing. "And you are the most beautiful woman in all this land." He squeezed her hands, little knowing how wonderful his warm, firm grip on her hands felt to her—the hands of a man who was all man, strong and skilled and sure. "I suppose we should not be sitting here like this. I should not be telling you how beautiful you still are."

She shook her head. "It doesn't matter. I never wanted to leave you, Red Wolf. You know that, don't you? The soldiers took me, and then my parents convinced me it was best for my baby if I didn't go back. They took me away, and things got worse with the Indian wars—and then I didn't even know if you were alive or dead, and—"

"It is all right, Cynthia. They were probably right about our son. I can see already what a fine future he has ahead of him. And things are still bad at the reservation—very bad. There is much work still to be done. You must know about the terrible slaughter at Wounded Knee."

Her eyes teared more. "We heard . . . many versions. But I knew what probably really happened."

He nodded. "Many Bears and Basket Woman were killed there. But their children are grown now and they will be all right."

She felt suddenly overwhelmed with memories and sorrow. Many Bears, the man she had hated at first, then learned to love. She thought about Flowing Waters and the dead babies, about Red Wolf's old grandmother. To see him sitting here now, to remember the days of wild love and exquisite freedom and happiness, combined with all the trauma of her years of loneliness and unhappiness, brought on a sudden torrent of tears as she hung her head and wept bitterly.

Red Wolf was beside himself with concern, worried that he had surely done the wrong thing by making his presence known. He took a handkerchief from his pocket and handed it to her, wondering what kind of trouble he might get into in this white man's world if he was seen holding hands with the wife of such a prominent man and she was crying so pitifully.

"Take me . . . out of here, Red Wolf," she sobbed. "We have to talk more."

"But your husband will miss you soon. It is not right that we walk out of here alone. I did not mean to upset you so, Cynthia."

"It's all right," she sobbed, wiping at her eyes. "Richard . . . won't miss me for a while . . . with so many people around. And I can't just . . . see you for a moment and then let you walk away from me. Please, let's find a back way out of here."

He frowned with concern, but if she was willing, he was more than happy to go off alone with her. There was so much to talk about. It seemed so strange that being with her this way seemed to erase all the years. Something about her had not changed at all. He had half expected her to be aloof and cool, to be friendly and gracious but far removed from the young girl he had loved all those years ago. He had not expected these tears, nor the strangely possessive and desperate way she clung to his hands. In that one moment she became his Cynthia again, and he felt the old manly emotions of possessiveness and protectiveness. He was suddenly in command of the situation. She was looking to him for help and support, and from deep within came the old, powerful love and protective instincts.

"Come," he said softly, rising. He kept an arm around her waist and led her down the hallway, opening a door and peering into an alley. No one was about. He removed his jacket and put it around her shoulders. "It is warm for a November night, but still too cool for your bare shoulders."

He led her outside, and Cynthia continued to cling to his strong hand, relishing in the warmth of it, finding strength in it. In that one touch she felt more manly protectiveness and love than she had felt in years with Richard. She felt absolutely no apprehension in going with him, had no concern as to whether it was right or wrong. In her mind this man was still her husband, her only true love, the father of her child. She would talk with him alone and she didn't care what anyone else thought of it. He led her through the alley and across the street to the park where earlier the speeches had been made. He remembered a vine-covered gazebo he had seen earlier in the day, and he led her to it and sat her down on a bench inside.

The park was empty now, and inside the gazebo no one would know they were there. A full moon shone down through the top of the vines, and Cynthia raised her eyes to meet his dark ones in the moonlight, still clinging to his hands.

"I can't believe you're here, Red Wolf. For so many years I had to wonder if you were even alive! And you look so wonderful!" she told him. "To see you so handsome and strong and well—and to see you've got yourself an education . . . a teacher? My Red Wolf

401

is a teacher?"

He frowned at her use of the word "my," as though her husband didn't even exist. "It is true." He searched her eyes. "Tell me about our son, Cynthia."

"Oh, he's such a good boy, and smart like his father. He has already graduated high school and is going to Princeton this year. He's been such a good son, Red Wolf, and all his life he has asked about you. It has been his dream to someday meet his real father. I never hid you from him, Red Wolf, or lied about you to him. He has always known the truth—that he was conceived in love . . . that he . . ." She stopped, a sudden, fiery passion sweeping through her at the realization of what she had just said. She looked down for a moment, unable to keep looking into the dark eyes that had always had a hypnotic effect on her. "You must meet him again, Red Wolf. He must know who you are. You can't go back without him knowing."

His jacket was warm around her shoulders, and she caught the familiar scent of him, the wild, clean scent that was not shrouded by colognes and hair creams.

"What about your husband?" he asked then. "Perhaps he would not be very happy about this at all."

She met his eyes again. "Richard would understand. He loves Freedom very much. He's been a good father to him. Freedom was seven years old when I married Richard."

"And are you happy, Cynthia?" His heart was torn by the terrible sadness in her eyes.

"I . . . have everything a woman could want."

His eyes held hers for several long, quiet seconds. "No. That is not what I asked you. A woman who is happy with her husband does not cling to another man the way your hands grip mine now, not even an old friend and lover."

She made a little whimpering sound and hung her head. "Life is so cruel," she almost whispered. "I should be the happiest woman in the world, but I'm not."

"But your husband—he is a very successful man, and

I see with my own eyes he is strong and good-looking. And surely with all the causes he works for, he is a kind man."

She nodded her head, unable to speak. "I . . . shouldn't have told you," she finally sobbed. "It's something . . . I can't explain, Red Wolf. I'm so sorry. I never should have said it." She breathed deeply for self-control. "What about you? Are you married? Do you have a family?"

She met his eyes, and again they sparkled with love and concern. "No. I never married. I wanted no one else."

The words tore at her soul. "Neither did I," she whispered. She wanted nothing more than she wanted his lips covering her own, to feel the arms of a real man around her again. She turned away and stood up, walking away from him, pulling the jacket close around her. "I can't believe I said that. After all these years . . . and a second husband . . . I see you after all this time and in five minutes I'm telling you I never stopped loving you. It's . . . it's like it was only yesterday that we were parted. I always thought . . . if I did see you again . . . you would be like a stranger."

"We were too much in love to ever feel like strangers. It is the same for me. I have no right sitting here telling another man's wife I never stopped loving her. But to me you are still my wife. We never divorced, Cynthia—not in our hearts."

She choked in another sob and stepped farther away. "I felt I had been a burden to my parents long enough. They thought I needed a husband, and I did, for support; and Freedom needed a father. Richard came along, and he was the first man who wasn't scared off by the fact that I had been an Indian captive, or at least that's the way everyone here looks at it. He accepted Freedom right away, and Freedom liked him. Richard represented security. And he's a wealthy, handsome man. He would have been so easy to love, and at first I truly thought I did love him. But it was never the way I loved you. You have

403

always been first in my heart."

"What do you mean, he *would* have been easy to love?"

She wiped at her eyes, her back still to him. "It's a long story, Red Wolf. Richard has . . . problems. I have stayed with him in spite of it. I promised him I would stay by his side through the election, but I'm not sure how much longer after that I can hang on. I'm doing it only because he's a good man and has done so much for me and Freedom. He needs the appearance of a happy family in order to win votes. I discovered after the marriage that that was part of his reason for marrying me in the first place, just to have a wife."

"Is he cruel to you?"

"No. He's very kind."

"I am afraid I don't understand. Is he untrue to you? Does he run with other women?"

Cynthia laughed bitterly. "I would be happier if he did."

"Happier?"

She put her head in her hands. "Please let it be, Red Wolf. I can't believe I'm telling you any of this." She wiped at her eyes again. "I must go back." She turned to face him. "We have to meet again, Red Wolf. We must talk more before you see Freedom again. Where are you staying?"

"At the Congress Hotel—up the street."

"What room?"

"Two Twenty-One."

"Elections are the day after tomorrow. I'll tell Richard that I have some shopping to do before that—that I want to get away from all the pressures and have a day alone. He won't object. We live in a town house at the north end of Baltimore. I'll take a carriage into the city and tell him I want to walk for a while. I'll take a back entrance into the Congress and come up to your room. Would ten o'clock be all right?"

Their eyes held. "Cynthia, if someone saw you—"

404

"I don't care. I couldn't bear it if this was all I got to see of you after all these years. Let people think what they want. I'll try to make sure no one sees me. But if they do I don't care. Richard and I haven't been a husband and wife in the real sense in years—actually we have never been."

He frowned, studying her beauty. "This I cannot understand. You have had no children?"

She looked down. "No."

"I am very confused, Cynthia. You are such a handsome couple. I cannot imagine living with you without loving you fully. The two of you should be very happy."

She met his eyes again. "I have never been more unhappy in my whole life. I have never known a truly happy moment since the soldiers took me away from you, Red Wolf."

He stepped closer. "I should never have made myself known to you. I am sorry, Cynthia, if this is causing you great grief and trouble. I did not come here to make things bad between you and your husband. I did not even know—"

"Things were bad between me and Richard long before you came here, Red Wolf." She touched his arm. "God surely led you back to me just as surely as He led me to free you that night in Deadwood. I am not going to let you go away from here without seeing you again, without letting Freedom meet his father. It's so good to know you're alive and well. All these years I've wanted to be able to tell you that I never forgot you, that I never wanted to go away that day. The soldiers had to tie me at first. After a while we were so far away that I wasn't sure how to get to you even if I did manage to run away. Then I was afraid for the baby. I thought, if I was never going to see you again, I wanted that baby more than anything in the whole world. And when he was born, I wanted so badly for you to know. But my parents kept telling me it was best for me and Freedom both if we stayed in the East and just left you out of our lives." She studied his dark eyes. "Now that I see you standing here before me, see the kind of man you have become, I'm thinking they were very wrong, and I was very wrong to believe them. I was happy with you, Red Wolf, in spite of the hardships of life. With Richard it's been just the opposite. I've had everything a woman could want, but I've never been happy—not the kind of happiness you and I had."

She turned away. "I'm sorry. I must be embarrassing you and making a fool of myself. I shouldn't be telling you all these things. Here we've been apart all these years, and my husband is running for a seat in Congress— and I'm out here spilling intimate secrets to a man I haven't seen for seventeen years."

"I am not embarrassed. And there is nothing wrong with telling me these things, Cynthia. We were once the best of friends. We shared many secrets, as well as sharing our bodies. We loved each other. Time and circumstance cannot change such love. Freedom is proof of that love, a lingering reminder of what we once shared. I did not expect such a reaction from you. It only tells me what a lonely and unhappy woman you must be, and it makes me very sad. I do not like knowing you are so unhappy."

She shivered with the realization of how forward she had been with him, as though she expected him to help her, perhaps take her away from all of this, as though she thought he would be ready to just pick up where they'd left off and sweep her away. She didn't even know if he still felt the same! Even if he did, she was married to someone else. Did she think that in five minutes this man would grab up another man's wife and ride off with her into the sunset?

"My God, what have I done?" she murmured. She removed the jacket and handed it to him. "If you don't want me to come tomorrow, I won't. I'm afraid I've made a royal fool of myself, haven't I?"

His eyes studied her lovingly. "No. And I do want you

406

to come tomorrow, Cynthia."

Their eyes held, and fire ripped through her at the memories. Red Wolf! He stood before her in all the same magnificent splendor. She could picture him without the fancy suit of clothes, standing there in only his leggings, his magnificent chest bare, his hair undone and falling about his shoulders. She had a terrible urge to run to him and beg him to hold her. Instead, she turned and ran back across the street and into the alley. She heard him call after her, but she did not stop. It would be too dangerous to stop, and she knew it would be dangerous to go and see him tomorrow. Perhaps she shouldn't go at all. How strange that when she was near him it was as though they had never been apart.

Chapter Twenty-Five

Cynthia dashed inside the hotel and into the rest room, where she sat for a few minutes to regain her self control. She smoothed out tear marks and waited for her eyes to lose their redness. Every part of her body felt warm and clammy, and her heart ached from beating so furiously.

Red Wolf! A grown man now—handsome, accomplished, and right here in Baltimore! Her mind whirled with the danger and excitement of it. He was just as forbidden now as he had been years ago, yet he was always the only man she had ever truly loved. Why had God brought him here? To torment her? To simply let her glimpse a man she could never have again? He said he had never wanted another woman, but that didn't mean he still loved her now as he had once loved her. Surely she had told him too much. She had bared her unhappiness to him as though she expected him to do something about it, when each had only just discovered that the other still existed.

She walked out of the rest room, half expecting to see him standing in the hall again, but he was not there. Had she only dreamed all of it? Was she indeed mad? She looked down then and realized his handkerchief was still in her hand. No! She was not mad at all. He truly had been there. And now she had to decide whether to go and see him in the morning. How wrong would it be? And how dangerous? Just being near him again had brought alive all the buried passions and emotions and needs. She didn't know how he felt about her. She must not make a grand fool of herself. And she was still legally Richard Holmes's wife.

She entered the banquet room, and immediately several women descended on her. "Cynthia! Where on earth have you been?" They had this to show her and that to show her, this person and that person for her to meet. She went through her duties as a candidate's wife mechanically, hardly hearing what people said, looking past them into the crowd to see if Red Wolf was there. But he was not. She was soon ushered over to where her husband stood talking with others. Richard introduced her, and there was a round of compliments about the beautiful Mrs. Holmes.

Richard put his arm around her, but she felt no warmth in the embrace, drew no strength from it. All she could think of was how it would feel to have Red Wolf's arms around her. In his embrace she would feel warm and loved; she would feel like the woman she had longed to be for years. She could think of nothing now but seeing Red Wolf again. She smiled and shook hands and spoke graciously with voters, who never dreamed that the beautiful Mrs. Holmes was standing there thinking about an Indian man she had loved seventeen years ago.

An orchestra began playing, and people urged the happy couple to dance for them. Richard laughingly obliged, sweeping Cynthia out into the middle of the floor and whirling her around with ease. But Cynthia could not help noticing how cool his hand was as it held her own. There was no strength there, no support. She realized that all these years it was Richard who drew strength and support from her, rather than the other way around. There was something about him that made her pity him in spite of how she had suffered being married to him. Richard Holmes was a very confused, unhappy man. She was his wife. Perhaps it was her duty to stay with him

410

forever; perhaps in time her unfaithfulness and support would bring him around to being the man he should be.

She was wearing his jewels, and beautiful clothing he had paid for. Freedom was going to a good college on Richard's money. She had married him in the eyes of God. Surely it was wrong of her to go and see Red Wolf, to be thinking of Red Wolf, envisioning what it would be like to be in his arms together. Richard had deceived her, had brought her nothing but unhappiness. Still, she was his legal wife. She had led this lie for years now, and she wondered what Richard would do without her. She was a Christian. She must be the faithful wife and not go and see Red Wolf in the morning, for she could not trust her emotions.

"Stewart came down for the elections," Richard told her then. "I hope you don't mind."

The smile she had put on for show began to fade. "I thought you were done with Stewart. You said you would try eventually to pull yourself away from that."

"I know." He looked around at the crowd and smiled, whirling Cynthia around to the music.

"Richard, you have a good chance of being elected to Congress. I've done everything for you, given up any chance I might have had for a normal marriage. I've been faithful to you, in spite of being starved for the affection you can't give me."

"I know all that." He sighed deeply, meeting her eyes. "Just one day, Cynthia. Stewart wants to take me to dinner tomorrow. We'd like . . . we'd like to spend the day together."

She looked away from him, the old, sick feeling coming to her stomach again.

"I'm sorry, Cynthia. Please bear with me. I know I'm going to get better. Stewart and I never had a last good-bye." He pulled her closer. "God, I'm sorry, Cynthia. I can't tell you how grateful I am for the way you've stayed with me. If I win this election it will all be because of you."

411

She struggled against tears. "Go ahead," she told him. "I was going to spend the day shopping anyway."

He kissed her forehead. "You're a dear. You have a good day. Buy anything you want."

She wanted to scream at what a farce her marriage was. If he had given one hint that he was better—that he wanted her the way a real man should want a woman— she could have changed her mind about going to see Red Wolf. But nothing had changed, and dangerous as it might be, she would go and see Red Wolf tomorrow; and she would ask him to hold her. Just hold her. There was nothing she wanted more at this very moment than to feel a man's arms around her. She was tired of being the strong one. She wanted someone else to be strong.

Cynthia knocked hesitantly at the door, half expecting that Red Wolf would not be there. Perhaps he had thought it best just to leave. But the door opened, and there he stood, tall and magnificent, his hair hanging long this time. Surely he had dressed just for her, a headband around his forehead, wearing cotton pants and a calico shirt and moccasins. He smiled the warm, beautiful smile.

"When I am in my room I like to be comfortable. You know how I hate the white man's clothes. I would even rather be in buckskins than these." He stepped back, and her blue taffeta dress rustled as she entered. "I hope you don't mind how I am dressed."

She looked him over lovingly. "I dont' mind at all. You simply look more like the Red Wolf I used to know."

He closed the door and reached out his hand. "I will take your coat for you."

She unbuttoned a velvet coat, her cheeks reddening slightly at being alone in the room with him. She removed the coat. Her high-necked dress was perfectly fitted through the bodice, revealing her full, lovely figure. Red Wolf wanted nothing more than to hold her again, taste her lips again. But it had been a lot of years, and she belonged to someone else now. He was not sure just how she felt anymore, except that both of them had never forgotten the love they once shared. He hung her coat on a hook and turned to face her. She stood with her hands clasped nervously.

"This is a little awkward, isn't it?" he asked.

She blushed and dropped her eyes. "I guess it is."

He sighed deeply and came closer. "We left so much unsaid, Cynthia. I wanted to come after you, but it was too dangerous, and I could not get anyone to come with me and help me. We all rode north and west to gather our forces. We soon became very strong in numbers, and then some of our scouts caught Custer in the midst of us. You know what happened then."

She met his eyes again. "You were there, weren't you?"

He nodded. "I was there."

She shivered, folding her arms and picturing him riding naked and painted into battle with Custer's men. How strange to be standing alone in this room with a Sioux Indian who had actually ridden with the wildest of them; and yet who had been so gentle and good to her, had fathered her child.

"I wanted to die when they took me away," she told him, staring at the floor. "I saw Flowing Waters lying there mutilated—her babies. They shot the baby I was trying to protect. I knew you were out there somewhere but I had no way of knowing you were all right, except that I insisted the soldiers let me search the camp. Your body wasn't there, and I was so glad."

She met his eyes, her own eyes tearing then. "I know it sounds forward. I'm married to someone else now, and I have no idea how you feel anymore, Red Wolf. But if I don't say it, I'll lose my mind." She swallowed. "I thought about it all night, and I realized this might be the last I see of you. I just want you to know I never stopped loving you—not for one minute. You were my first love,

413

and the only man I have held dear to my heart. There was no other. I . . . I tried with Richard, but only because of my parents and because of Freedom. But I never loved him . . . the way I loved you . . . and I still love you that way."

Tears ran down her cheeks and he came closer, touching them with his fingers. "It is the same for me," he told her. "Just like you I took the advice of others and told myself it was best not to try to find you. But all these years my heart has been sad." He placed his hands at either side of her face, wiping at her tears with his thumbs. "Many times I would ride out onto the open plains and I would think of you. I would look toward the land of the rising sun and wonder where you were, how you were, if you had a healthy baby and what my child was. When they took you away, it was as though a part of my breath left me."

Her tears came harder, and then his arms came around her, the blessed, strong, warm, reassuring arms. Her sobs came then in great, heaving agony over all the lost years. How wonderful it felt to be held again. She wrapped her arms around his waist and clung to him, releasing all the pent-up emotions in a torrent of tears, wondering all the while how she had found any more tears to cry. He just held her, stroking her hair, whispering her name, telling her everything would be all right. Nearly ten minutes went by before she gained control of herself enough to speak.

"Help me, Red Wolf," she sobbed. "I need your help so badly."

"What is it, Cynthia?"

"I'm so unhappy. And I still love you so. My marriage isn't a marriage at all. From the very beginning I've been so terribly lonely."

"You must tell me what is wrong, Cynthia."

She finally pulled away slightly, blowing her nose and wiping at her eyes. "We've been married . . . nine years . . ." She turned away. "In all that time Richard has made love to me only once a month at most . . . if you could call it making love. The last year or so he hasn't touched me at all."

"My God," she heard him whisper. "He is impotent?"

How could she tell him the whole truth? And she had promised Richard she would not damage his career. "Yes," she answered. It was enough that he knew her husband could not make love to her. "He's . . . tried . . . but he just can't. The worst part is . . . he knew before he married me. Once I was his wife, I kept waiting for things to get better. But they never did . . . and I've just grown lonelier and lonelier. He as much admitted he married me for show. He truly does love me in his own strange way, and he's been good to me and Freedom. But he . . . can't give me the one thing I need the most from a man. And my life has been so empty. I promised him I would stay with him until after the elections, but he knows I can't go on much longer. I also promised I would never reveal his problem. You must never tell anyone what I have told you."

"Cynthia," he said softly, putting his hands on her shoulders. "Such a terrible secret you have had to live with."

She wiped at her eyes again with shaking hands. "You're the only person I have ever told. It's so strange . . . after all these years of being apart that I can tell you . . . when I've never been able to tell anyone else close to me. I can't imagine what you must think of me."

"I think of you as my Cynthia, the wife who was stolen from me. In our hearts we are still husband and wife, Cynthia. When I first took you from Many Bears and told you how I felt about you, you fought it, for always you were worried about doing what was right, instead of what made your heart happy. Finally I taught you how to be free, how to be happy, how to follow your heart. Your heart probably told you years later to try to find me, but again you worried about what was right and wrong. I made the same mistake. I did not follow my own advice. I did not search for you, as my heart told me to do. I am so very sorry. Because I did what I thought was best, you have suffered all these years."

She shook her head. "Don't blame yourself, Red Wolf. There is no one right answer. And right now the only thing I am sure of in this life is that I love our son dearly, and I have never once stopped loving you."

He gently turned her and she rested her head against his chest. "For years I have dreamed of being with you again," she told him. "May God forgive me."

He pressed her close. "Forgive you for what? For longing for the only man who has truly loved you? The only man to whom you gave your heart? The man who was first inside of you? What is there to forgive, Cynthia?" He kissed her hair. "Many years ago I told you a piece of paper did not make a marriage. Now you know what I meant." He grasped her hair, gently forcing her to look up at him. "We will work it out, Cynthia. No more tears. Do not ever be afraid anymore. I will not let you be unhappy any longer."

Their eyes held, and all the years seemed instantly erased. They were not in a tipi, yet it seemed she could hear drumming and dancing and rattles shaking. She could smell the smoke of a campfire and see paint on his face. It was there in the eyes. He had not changed. His education had not changed the Indian in him; nor had the years changed their love at all.

"Make love to me," she whispered, surprised at her own boldness. "I need you to make love to me, Red Wolf. I think I knew from the moment I agreed to come here that was what we would do."

He smiled softly. "You have the same look in your eye—of the innocent young girl who pushed me away for so long and then decided she wanted me." He traced a finger over her lips. "My Cynthia."

He came closer, and in the next moment he kissed her lightly, his tongue feathering her lips. Fire ripped through her, and she reached around his neck. Such a long, long time it had been since a man did this to her! He pressed her close, and she felt his hardness through her dress. Her passion knew no bounds then. Red Wolf! He was right here, holding her, kissing her again, his familiar arms around her. He was all man and he needed her as much as she needed him.

From that moment on ecstasy became too mild a word to describe what she was feeling. His own groans and heated kisses told her it was as necessary for him as it was for her. He finally released his hold on her, moving his hands to the collar of her dress, beginning to unbutton the long row of buttons at the front.

"So many clothes you white women wear," he said, smiling almost boyishly. She clung to his arms, her cheeks reddening as he worked his way down the front of the dress, the backs of his hands softly touching the fullness of her breast, on down to where the buttons ended just below her waist. "It has been a long time for you," he said as he carefully pulled the dress over her shoulders. "I will make it nice for you."

She felt nearly faint from the glory of his touch. Every movement was so gentle, yet so distinctly manly in his knowledge of how to treat her. There had never been these wonderful preliminaries with Richard, never an indication that he thought it might be important that she enjoy it. The dress fell to the floor, and then he was unhooking her undergarment. It fell away, and her nipples came pink and alive as she closed her eyes and knew he was looking at her breasts.

"Still so beautiful," he almost groaned, moving his hands to cup her breasts and massage them gently. She trembled under his caress. He worked his hands up over her breasts, massaging her shoulders, her neck, back down over her breasts to her waist. He knelt down and pulled off her slips and bloomers, pulled down her stockings and unbuttoned her shoes so she could step out of them. He massaged her legs as he came back up, kissing at her thighs, lightly kissing that secret place that had

417

really never belonged to any other man, kissing her belly, eagerly tasting her breasts.

She grasped at his hair as he moved a hand under her hips then and picked her up, carrying her to the bed. He laid her on it, then stood up to remove his clothes. Cynthia watched every move, every beautiful muscle, from the powerful shoulders to the bared chest, the flat belly, and on down as he disrobed, boldly drinking in his masculine splendor. Never had she seen Richard this way. Never had he reminded her of a splendid stallion.

She moved under the covers, her eyes glazed with desire. It had been too long. And in her heart she had never belonged to Richard. If he had been a normal husband, she knew she could never do this. But she was too starved for this affection, too lonely, too broken. Red Wolf was right. The piece of paper had meant nothing. He moved into bed beside her, and it was as though there had never been a gap in their relationship. It was as though they had done this just the night before, except never had Cynthia's needs been this keen. Never had she felt so alive.

Their eyes held and their lips met, and she was his to do with as he pleased. She lay like a limp rag doll as he moved over her, pulling each breast into his warm mouth and drawing forth gasps of ecstasy. He moved his mouth over her flat belly, lightly licking, searching secret crevices. His fingers searched her hot moistness as he moved back toward her breasts, and after just a moment of his gentle touches the wonderful explosion she had not felt in years rippled through her insides, her muscles contracting wildly as he buried his fingers deep inside of her. She arched toward him, gasping his name, and he moved between her legs.

In only an instant he was inside of her, stifling her cries of ecstasy with heated kisses while he surged deep into her belly, meeting her urgent, rhythmic movements. They had not lost the perfect rhythm they had once shared. His tongue searched her mouth while his hands

418

moved under her hips, pushing her up to him, wondering how he was able to go so deep into such a small woman. He fought to hold back his release, realizing how badly she needed this. He raised up slightly, drinking in her naked splendor as he held her hips and continued the teasing rhythm that made her wild with desire. She grasped his powerful forearms, noticing through blurred vision how dark his skin was next to her hands.

This was more wonderful than it had ever been, for now they were man and woman instead of hardly more than boy and girl. Never had this been more fulfilling for Cynthia than now. He grasped her bottom then, pushing hard and moaning something in the Sioux tongue, coming down close to her then as his life spilled into her. She took it gladly, wondering if she could still have a baby. Of course she could! She was still young enough. She could not imagine anything more wonderful than having another child by Red Wolf. She had hoped when she first married Richard that she would have more children. She wanted more badly. But Richard had put an end to such dreams. Red Wolf's seed was surely potent, and he knew how to plant it deep. If she could be with Red Wolf . . .

He lay down beside her and pulled her into his arms. "We will do it again before you go," he told her. "We have many years to make up for."

She kissed his nipples. "I haven't been this happy since before the soldiers took me from you. You're the only happiness I ever really knew, Red Wolf. I don't know what you think of me now, and I don't care. I have never known anything so beautiful."

He toyed with her damp hair. "I will tell you what I think of you." He pulled the covers up over them. "I love you, as I have always loved you. The Great Spirit has brought me a wonderful gift, leading me here to where you were, letting me be one with you again. We belong together, Cynthia. It can be no other way. The Great Spirit did not lead us back together in order for us to part

419

again. I will not let you go this time."

She kissed the palm of his hand, relishing the strength that lay there, closing her eyes and pressing his hand against the side of her face.

"It was so wonderful, Red Wolf. And it's the same for me. I want to be with you forever."

"Then it is decided. You will leave your husband and we will be together again, only this time nothing will ever make us be apart." He settled into the pillows and stroked her hair. "But you must know it is a hard life on the reservation. You have known such a wonderful life here. I cannot give you that kind of life."

"It doesn't matter. It has never mattered. I could live anywhere with you."

"What about Freedom?"

"Freedom's biggest dream has been to meet his father. I know if I ask him, Richard will pay for Freedom's education at Princeton. He owes me that much for staying with him all these years. Once Freedom's education is finished, he can decide where he wants to live. He might want to use his education to help the Sioux, like you have done."

"I must see my son again."

She sighed deeply. "I know how it pains you to know he exists and not be able to see him. But we have to be careful, Red Wolf. I don't want to hurt him or cause too much confusion in his soul by leaving Richard. I have to think about how to go about all of this. He doesn't know how unhappy my marriage has been. He doesn't know anything about Richard's condition."

"I understand." He kissed her hair. "Do you want me with you when you confront Richard?"

She sighed deeply, remembering Richard's tears and pleading eyes. "No. I promised him I would stay until after the election. I'll wait a few days before I tell him. This will hurt a lot of people who don't understand, but I can't help that. I'm tired of being alone, Red Wolf, tired of being the strong one. I can't keep going this way. I've already had one breakdown." She kissed his hand again. "As long as I know I have you to fall back on, I can get through it. I only have to know I can come out to you, to the land I learned to love with all my heart, to the Black Hills. It's as though my heart has always been out there with you." She searched his warm, dark eyes. "Maybe you shouldn't see Freedom again before you leave."

Red Wolf frowned. "What do you mean?"

She traced a finger over his dark eyebrow. "I don't want anything to mar how Freedom feels about you, Red Wolf. Right now he has this dream of coming out to you, of finding his real father. But he has grown to care very much about Richard. Maybe we should just wait until I am free of Richard, and then I can tell Freedom I am coming out to you. He doesn't have to know we've seen each other here, at least not yet. He might think you came between me and Richard. But you never did. There was never anything there for me and Richard in the first place. Freedom will go back to Princeton soon. I'll just have to explain before he leaves that I am leaving Richard. I'll have to find some way to make him understand. As soon as he leaves, I will have Richard start divorce proceedings."

"What if there is a problem? What if he won't let you go?"

She shivered and huddled against him, kissing at his chest. "Then I will live in sin. I'll come out to you anyway, divorce or no divorce. Nothing matters to me any more but being with you. I don't care what Freedom or my parents or anyone thinks. I can only pray Freedom will understand."

He kissed her cheek. "Still my strong, independent, brave Cynthia, aren't you?"

"I don't know if I'm brave or just reckless."

"I don't like leaving you here alone to handle it all."

"Please let me do it this way." Her eyes teared. "I don't like the thought of going several more months without you again. And I know it isn't fair to tell you you can't see

Freedom. But I think it's best for now." She took his hand and kissed it. "I don't want Freedom thinking anything bad about you. Once I'm free of Richard, Freedom will understand my wanting to come out to you. He'll want to come too. He'll want to meet his father." She met his eyes again. "Only then will I tell him he's already met you. I don't know how else to do it, Red Wolf. I hate to ask you to wait to see your own son."

He sighed deeply. "I waited seventeen years never even knowing he existed. Now I have seen him—so tall and strong and handsome and intelligent. It is enough to know what a fine son I have. I only wish I could have watched him grow." He pulled her closer, kissing her hair.

"Maybe when this is all over and we can be together, we'll have more children of our own. I can still have children, Red Wolf. I was just never with Richard enough to get pregnant."

His grip on her tightened. "It sickens me to think of how he treated you. How can any man live with such a beautiful woman and not want her that way?"

"He can't help it," she said sadly. How could she tell him her husband was with another man today? Richard lived in his own special hell. She would not break her promise of not telling anyone what she knew about him. She would not even tell Red Wolf.

"It is sad for him then," Red Wolf told her. "But he should not have done that to you, such a beautiful, trusting woman." He tangled his hand in her hair. "Come out to me, Cynthia. Promise you will go through with it, and that if you need me you will send for me."

"I promise. You know now that I've been with you again I could never go without you. It just gives me that much more courage to go through with leaving my husband. I would have done it anyway, eventually." She kissed at his chest again. "Give me an address and I will write you and let you know when I am coming."

"I will tell you where to write."

422

"Be there, Red Wolf," she whispered. "You've got to be there. You're all I'll have left."

"You know I will be there. I have always been there, waiting . . . waiting for my Cynthia. My house is plain and small. I do not even own a buggy. I do not have a lot to offer."

"Oh, you're wrong, Red Wolf. You have everything to offer. I'll have your love, your sweet, beautiful, true love. That's all I've ever wanted or needed."

Their lips met again in a long, sweet, passionate kiss, and already he wanted her again. She had forgotten it could be this way, that a man could take a woman and take her again soon after. What a contrast to Richard. Her heart pained at how hard she had tired to love Richard, how innocently she had married him. The hurt of their wedding night would never leave her. Now here was Red Wolf, his kisses so full and warm and sweet, his dark skin damp from heated lovemaking, his manliness probing at her again.

She groaned with the wonder of it, opening herself to him and letting him quickly enter her again. There was no foreplay this time. It was not necessary. She had not really come down from the first sensuous peak. Now all he did was take her temperature from hot to steaming again, moving over her as only her wild Indian man could move. Red Wolf. Her wild, reckless, daring Red Wolf was in her arms again, sharing her body again—such a beautiful man now—so changed in many ways, yet not changed at all in the ways she had loved the most.

Nothing else mattered now—not her good name, not all the material possessions, the jewels, the fancy clothes, the lovely town house. None of it mattered. There was only this—Red Wolf and Cynthia. This was all it ever should have been. Let others think it wrong. She would never let them talk her out of this again, never throw away such happiness because of what others thought was right. If they didn't understand, it didn't matter. She would find a way to be with Red Wolf forever.

He moved inside her again with his own perfect rhythm, and she did not see the room at all. All she could see was a tipi, its lovely paintings of horses and buffalo and men making war floating all around her. Again she heard the distant drumming, women singing and chanting, bells jingling, the whinny of a horse. A dark man moved over her, claiming his woman, his long, black hair shrouding her face. She was his. She had always been this warrior's woman.

Chapter Twenty-Six

They met once more, a lonely white woman who had everything but the love she wanted most in life, and the Indian who had brought her more happiness than all the furs and jewels and comfortable living had ever given her. As she lay in Red Wolf's arms, Cynthia wondered why she had ever listened to those who told her what was best for her. This was what was best for her, even if it meant returning to a hard, more primitive life. In these two days she had known more joy and ecstasy then she had known since the last time she lay in Red Wolf's arms. She felt more vibrant, healthier, her mind and body more relaxed, with a peace she had not known since that awful wedding night. To tell Red Wolf good-bye again was agonizing. But this time it would not be forever. Whatever she had to suffer to be with him again, she would suffer, including the scorn and gossip that would surely accompany a divorce.

Red Wolf left on a train the day of the election, his own heart heavy for Cynthia. He did not like leaving her behind to face what was coming. But he respected her wishes. He could not help the awful dread that perhaps she would never go through with it. Perhaps she would never come out to him. The train rumbled out of the station, and the past two days seemed suddenly unreal to him, a strange, beautiful dream. Surely it had not really happened. Surely he had not come to this white-man's land and just walked right back into Cynthia's life. And to find he had a son! Such a fine boy his Freedom was. He could only pray Cynthia's plans would work out and they would both come to him. If not, he knew he would have to come back. He would have to see his son again. But what if Freedom ended up hating him because of the divorce? He realized now that to know his son existed and that he might never get to see the boy again hurt more than if he had never known about him at all. He could only trust his beautiful, courageous Cynthia would find a way to bring Freedom through all this without hard feelings. He would go home now, home to the Black Hills—home—to wait for Cynthia and Freedom.

Cynthia entertained a few close friends at their town house the day of the election. As she walked into the kitchen she heard a distant train whistle. Pain stabbed at her heart, and she set down her wineglass, walking through a back door and listening for it again. There it came. Her eyes teared. Somewhere in Baltimore a train was pulling out. Red Wolf would be on it, headed back to his beloved homeland, the rugged, sacred Black Hills that Cynthia longed to see again.

"Red Wolf," she whispered, her body on fire, her heart spilling over with love.

"Cynthia, come in," Richard said then from the back door. "We are getting word on some of the early returns."

She turned and stared at him. How sad. Such a beautiful man he was.

"Cynthia, are you all right? You have the strangest look on your face."

"I'm fine," she answered quietly.

"If you're upset over Stewart being here for our party—"

"No. Let him stay. I don't care anymore."

426

She came back inside, walking past him quickly. He grasped her arm and she looked up at her husband.

"Thank you for sticking it out, Cynthia," he told her. "I'm . . . I'm getting better, you know. And once I win the seat in Congress, you'll have a fine life in Washington, Cynthia."

She shook her head. "No. You aren't getting better, Richard. If you were, Stewart wouldn't be here. And you wouldn't have spent the last two days with him. And if you go to Washington, I won't be with you, Richard."

She left him then, feeling an urge to scream and run when she heard the distant train whistle again.

Richard Holmes lost his seat in Congress by a very narrow margin. Even though the race was close, Richard's disappointment ran deep. Cynthia knew her husband well enough to know how difficult the loss was for him, and she did not have the heart to demand an immediate divorce, in spite of her longing to be with Red Wolf.

They continued to entertain and socialize as husband and wife. Freedom returned to Princeton, and Cynthia was even lonelier with her son gone. But she knew that waiting was all for the best. Red Wolf was removed from this life, and she did not intend to involve him in any of the scandal that was sure to come. A man like Red Wolf did not belong in the headlines of Eastern newspapers. He was a Sioux Indian, a man who belonged to another world, a world apart from gossip and frivolities and accusations. Red Wolf was a part of the earth, in many ways something pure and innocent, free of white man's greed and lust and need for material things.

Stewart moved back to Baltimore and began visiting often again. To Richard's curiosity, Cynthia did not complain. Cynthia had never been able to hate her husband, in spite of what he was. She had grown only to feel sorry for him. Perhaps he was only happy with

Stewart the way she was only happy with Red Wolf. It was something she would never understand, and something she realized now Richard could not fight. His problem was far bigger than anything she was capable of handling, and so they continued to live as strangers under one roof for six months after the election.

Cynthia wrote Red Wolf often, spilling out her love for him on tear-stained paper, promising that it would not be much longer until she would come to him, begging him not to write back. She didn't want anyone seeing mail come to her from a Sioux Indian. Someone might suspect. She lay hugging her pillow at night, dreaming of Red Wolf's embrace, longing for the ecstasy of sharing bodies with him. And often she remembered the awful certainty of never seeing him again so many years ago. But God, the blessed, merciful God who she thought had long ago deserted her, had brought Red Wolf back into her life. Surely it was the final sign that she belonged with Red Wolf.

Spring arrived early, and with the budding of flowering trees and shrubs and the appearance of daffodils and lilacs, Cynthia's love for Red Wolf and her need to be with him burst forth from her heart, giving her the courage she needed to bear the final burden. She walked into the study, where Richard and Stewart sat pondering over a legal case they were handling. She met Stewart's eyes boldly. "I would like to speak to my husband alone, Stewart."

The man picked up a folder of papers and rose from a leather chair. "It's getting late anyway. I'll get back to my own apartment." He nodded to Cynthia, an odd smile on his face, as though he were some kind of victor.

"I am so sorry for both of you," Cynthia told him quietly but firmly.

His smile faded and he reddened slightly, then left the room. Cynthia faced Richard, who sat behind his desk. She stepped closer.

"I want the divorce, Richard. Handle it however you

428

must to save your own reputation. I just want out."

He paled slightly, rising slowly from his chair. "Cynthia, I thought—I thought perhaps you had accepted all this. You didn't say a thing—"

"I just gave up, that's all. Believe it or not, Richard, I want you to be happy. You have done all you could for me to make up for the one thing you could not give me. I don't blame you for anything, and I don't hate you. But I just can't live this way any longer."

His eyes teared. "Where will you go? What will you do?"

Her throat felt tighter. "Richard, think of how you feel when you're with Stewart and you're really happy. That's how I feel when I think about the West, the Dakotas. I never wanted to leave, Richard. And now I intend to go back."

His eyebrows arched. "Back to that uncivilized place? Cynthia, there are still no nice cities out there—no luxuries—no—"

"I don't care," she interrupted. "I don't need those things, Richard. Grateful as I am for all you have given me, I don't need any of it. I only need the feeling of freedom and total happiness I knew when I lived among the Sioux. I need to see the Black Hills again, to breathe the air, to see an eagle, to smell the pines. I need to get away from this artificial life and all the etiquette and worry over the latest fashions. Years ago I learned about a whole different kind of life, a life of nature's beauty, of peace within. And the only real love I've ever known was in the arms of Freedom's father."

"But . . . you don't even know if he exists any longer. And if he does, how do you know he would even want you anymore."

"It doesn't matter. I'll find that out when I get there. Just tell me what I have to do to be free of you. You promised me a long time ago that if I stayed with you through the election I could have my freedom later. I think waiting six months has been a fitting length of time.

Freedom will be out of school for the summer soon. He could go with me to the Dakotas to try to find his father."

Richard closed his eyes and nodded. "I, uh, I'm so terribly sorry to have to injure you even more, Cynthia. But if I'm to save my reputation for future elections, I can't be accused of something like adultery. And we do need some specific reason for the divorce." He met her eyes and she felt the sick feeling creep into her stomach.

"Are you saying you will accuse *me* of adultery?" she asked.

Another tear slipped down his cheek, and she wondered how such a big man who was so strong in his outside convictions could be so weak about his personal life. "I'm damned sorry, Cynthia. I'll give you a good settlement."

"I don't want anything from you, Richard—not one thing. All I want is enough money to make sure Freedom can finish his schooling at Princeton."

He nodded. "I will miss you, Cynthia."

She felt weak at the thought of being publicly accused of adultery. Yet she realized it was true, for she had spent two days with Red Wolf. But she was determined no one would ever know. People would have to guess who her "lover" was, and tongues would wag viciously in spite of her innocence.

"You'll get over me quickly enough, Richard. You'll have Stewart," she choked out. "Just do it right away, will you? You're a lawyer. Speed things up if you can. I'll move out tomorrow. For the moment I'll go back to Princeton and live with my parents. When I get there I'll talk to Freedom—try to explain all of this to him."

Richard swallowed nervously. "You won't . . . tell him about me?" he asked tentatively.

Cynthia closed her eyes and turned away. "No. How could I explain something like that to a boy his age? He'll probably never understand. He might even hate me. But I see no other way out of this hell."

"I really am sorry, Cynthia," Richard repeated. His

voice choked as he spoke the words. "I'll give you a few days after you've left—then I'll file for the divorce."

"Fine." She turned and left, wondering at how easy it was to leave a man she had called her husband for ten years. But then he had never really been her husband at all.

Cynthia waited nervously in the parlor of her parents' home. Freedom was home for spring break. Breakfast was finished, and it was time now to explain the divorce to her son. The news would break in all the papers any time. So far she had not even told her parents what would be happening. It only seemed right to tell Freedom first. Even so, she still couldn't tell the boy the whole truth— that she had already seen Red Wolf. He still must not know, not yet. Freedom might build up a hatred for Red Wolf before he even met the man.

Freedom came into the parlor then, and she studied his handsome physique. In the past six months he seemed to have grown even more, and the older he got, the more he reminded her of Red Wolf.

"What is it, Mother?" he asked.

Her heart pounded with dread. "Close the door, Freedom."

The boy frowned, closing the door behind him. He realized the somber look on his mother's face meant something was seriously wrong. "Is something wrong with Father?" he asked. "Is he sick or something?"

Cynthia motioned for him to sit down beside her. She took his hand, her throat so tight it hurt. She drew a deep breath. "Richard and I are getting a divorce, Freedom."

She felt him stiffen. "A divorce! Mother, why!"

Her eyes teared. "A lot of reasons." She met his eyes. "Freedom, I have never been happy with Richard. I pretended to be. I worked very hard at helping build his career. I did everything I could to be a good wife. But there just . . . just has never been enough love there . . .

on either side. Richard is so involved in his career there is little time left for me, and we just . . . grew apart."

Freedom's eyes teared with disappointment. "I don't understand." He pulled his hand away and rose. "You never let on you weren't happy."

"I know. Freedom, I'm sorry. Part of the reason I married Richard was because you needed a father, and because I knew you would get the best of everything. And while you were growing up I wanted everything to be nice for you—happy and secure. And I really thought I loved Richard at first. But a person can live in total unhappiness for only so long, Freedom. I've already had one breakdown. You never knew about it. But I continued to wait for this—wait until I felt you were old enough and mature enough to understand. This whole thing is going to be very hard, Freedom. I'm begging you not to hate me for it. I need you to understand. There's never . . . never been another man I loved more than your real father. I thought Richard could take his place, but it just didn't work out that way."

The boy quickly wiped away one tear and faced his mother. "I have to think about this for a while."

"I know." She closed her eyes. "Freedom, you're going to hear bad things about me." She rose and walked to a window. "Because of Richard's career . . . we decided that in order to be sure he comes out unscathed, the divorce will be blamed on me. We must have definite grounds for the separation. I'll be accused of adultery."

She waited as the room hung silent. "Is it true?" the boy asked brokenly.

The words pierced her soul. "No," she answered in a near-whisper. She turned to face him. "It's true only in the fact that it's always been your real father I have loved, Freedom. Deep in my heart, he's been the only man I ever really wanted. And much as I love you, my son, I have to think about survival—about my own sanity. Surely you know how unhappy I must be by the simple fact that I would risk losing your love to do this.

People calling me names, gossiping about me—those things can't hurt me. I can bear them. The only thing I could never bear is losing my son's love and respect. Please don't turn away from me, Freedom. When all this is over, I intend to go out to the Dakotas and find Red Wolf. I'm hoping you and I will still be close, that you'll want to come with me."

Another tear slipped down his cheek and he nodded. "If my father is the reason for all of this, then I suppose I *should* meet him, shouldn't I?" He quickly wiped at his eyes again and let out a bitter laugh. "It's crazy—him still affecting you this way. I never knew your feelings for him were still so strong. You should have told me, Mother."

She watched his dark eyes, seeing there the wonderful compassion he had apparently inherited from Red Wolf. "Yes, maybe I should have. I wasn't sure you would understand."

He shrugged, trying to smile. "I'm not so sure I do yet. But I don't think it's right for Richard to let you take the blame like that. I don't like my mother being accused of something so ugly."

"I'm sorry, Freedom. But I agreed to it. I felt I owed that much to Richard for marrying him without loving him as I should. I wanted this divorce, Freedom. I couldn't expect Richard to take the blame."

The young man studied his mother's blue eyes. It was difficult for him to imagine her with a man, loving a man so passionately as she must have loved his real father. No boy his age could imagine his mother in a man's arms. But he knew how much this divorce would hurt her character, and until now he had never realized how much the man called Red Wolf must have meant to her.

"I don't really understand it all yet. But you know nothing would make me stop loving you, Mother."

Her own tears spilled out then, and she hung her head, unable to talk. In the next moment her son was hugging her, and she thought of Red Wolf, and how welcome his

433

arms would be at this moment.

"Thank you, Freedom," she whispered. "You'll come with me, won't you? You'll come with me to find your father?"

The boy sighed, his own curiosity keen now. "I'll come with you," he answered, unsure at the moment if he should love the man or hate him.

The Baltimore papers seemed to relish the scandal, with headlines about the prominent attorney Richard Holmes filing for divorce on the grounds of adultery. The circle of high-society friends and acquaintances Richard and Cynthia had known buzzed with curiosity about who the secret lover might be, and not a few wives began questioning their husbands, for many had commented on the beauty of Mrs. Richard Holmes.

"She seemed so sweet," some would say. "It just seems so impossible."

"And she worked so hard on the committees to aid the poor and unfortunate."

"You just never know. I always wondered myself, her being an Indian captive once and all. After a woman had been through that, who knows what it does to her mind?"

"Well, look what she's leaving behind! A handsome, successful man who will now need a wife!"

Mothers began bringing daughters to social events where Richard would be in attendance, a man now alone and surely lonely. Headlines began to read that Richard Holmes was seen in the company of such-and-such and so-and-so. After all, such an eligible, good-looking single man was not a man to go long without a pretty woman on his arm. And because it was his wife's infidelity that had broken up the marriage, no one thought the less of Richard Holmes for being seen in the company of women before his divorce was final.

Back home Cynthia's mother had at first been beside herself with grief. "How could you! How could you!" the woman carried on. "Cynthia, you can't leave Richard! Look at the grand life you have been leading! Look at what he can give you! Such a beautiful, beautiful couple you made. The man could still end up in politics. You could have lived in Washington! Oh, Cynthia, we were so happy for you. How can you do this to us?"

Cynthia's only comfort was knowing Freedom was trying to understand; and that Alex seemed to understand better than anyone. That very first night when she told her parents, Alex only nodded and smiled faintly to her while her mother threw a fit. Albert Wells said nothing. He simply stood staring at his daughter like she was some kind of stranger.

"You will both hear that the divorce is because of my adultery," she told them boldly.

Her mother gasped, and Albert slipped a supportive arm around his wife's waist. "How can you come here and tell us such a thing?" he asked his daughter. "Do you really think you can commit adultery against a man like Richard Holmes, and then just come home and live with us?"

Her eyes teared. "So, you would believe it that easily, Father?"

He paled slightly. "Cynthia, I . . ."

"Never mind. Richard and I have never had a good marriage, Father. We haven't lived as a true husband and wife for years. I am not going to go into details. We needed grounds for the divorce, something more than just not loving each other. After all, everyone thought us the happiest couple in the world. We put on a grand show, didn't we?" She turned away, walking to the fireplace mantel and staring at a painting of an Indian her father had been given a few years earlier. "Richard had a good future ahead of him. In order to save his reputation and keep people from gossiping about his own conduct, we agreed to put the blame on me."

Mabel Wells broke into tears.

"That's ridiculous!" Cynthia's father exclaimed.

435

"It's all right, Father. Please don't ask me to explain all the details, why I agreed to the disgrace." She turned to face him. "I'm just glad to be out of the marriage. I'm terribly sorry it breaks your hearts. I married Richard to make you happy—not for myself. But a person can live a lie only so long, Father. Can you understand that?"

He closed his eyes and sighed, hugging his grieving wife. "I suppose we will *have* to understand." He studied his beautiful daughter, who had never seemed truly happy since they came back from the Dakotas. "You never got over that Indian, did you?"

Her eyes teared. "No. I've already explained all of this to Freedom. And he has agreed to go with me to the Dakotas after the divorce is over and try to find Red Wolf. I'm sorry if that shocks both of you and breaks your hearts. It seems I have managed to hurt you over and over again. I never once meant to do that. But in order to make up for that hurt, I have lived a horrible lie for ten years. I even had a breakdown two years ago. You never knew about it. By trying to please others, I have been destroying myself. Now it's my turn, Father. I'm going to go to the Dakotas, and I'm going to try to find Red Wolf. If he still exists, and he is free, and we discover we still love each other, I will stay with him. I won't come back. And I know now that I should never have left. I know you thought it was best. I don't blame you for any of my unhappiness. I only blame myself, for ignoring what was in my heart, for living a lie all these years."

She left the room, going outside to get away from the sound of her mother's crying. A moment later she heard the door open, and she turned to see Alex behind her. She turned away again, wiping at tears.

"You already know he exists, don't you? You've seen Red Wolf. He's already waiting for you out there."

She covered her mouth and her shoulders shook as she wept quietly. Alex put his hands on her shoulders. "You did it again, didn't you, Cindy? It's like the time you snuck out of the house and went to cut him down that night. It was all your wonderful secret."

She turned and wept against his chest. Alex held her while she cried, then led her off the porch and through the backyard to a bench, where Cynthia spilled out her story to the only person besides Red Wolf she knew would understand—including the fact that Richard had never been able to make love to her, though she made Alex promise never to tell anyone.

"This is just like the time you told me about freeing Red Wolf," he told her jokingly, trying to cheer her up. "Hell, Cindy, nobody would blame you for still loving Red Wolf. I always did know how you felt, and I knew from the beginning you weren't very happy with Richard. I told you once you should stay with him, but I didn't know it was that bad." He kept an arm around her. "Don't you worry about Mother and Father. They'll get over it. They always recover, and they love you, Cindy."

"That's just it. They've put up with so much because of me."

"And you have to stop worrying about how other people feel about something. Worry about yourself for once. If you still love Red Wolf and want to go to him, then you should do it."

She wiped at her eyes, looking at her brother lovingly. "You were always my buffer, Alex, and my biggest supporter." She smiled through her tears, then kissed his cheek. "Thank you. Don't ever tell Mother and Father everything I've told you."

"Heck, we've always kept secrets from them."

They both laughed lightly. "I hope you and Betsy are happy, Alex."

He grinned. "Betsy is a good wife. When I think about how happy we are and think about what you've been living through all these years, it makes me sick." He grasped her hands. "You go out to Red Wolf, Cindy. You go out there and you marry him if you want. Just be happy. For once in your life quit trying to please

437

everybody else and think about yourself. If the Dakotas are where you belong, and if the only man who makes you happy is Red Wolf, then go, and don't you take one backward glance."

Her heart swelled with love and a new excitement. Yes! She would be shed of the heavy weight of trying to please others, of living a lie and keeping the terrible secret about her husband. She would leave this false life behind and go back to where she belonged, to the place where she had known love and peace and freedom, and to the man with whom she wanted to share those things. She would return to Paha Sapa, the sacred Black Hills, and to the man who was as much a part of that place as the pine trees and boulders. And she would not look back. She would never, never look back!

Chapter Twenty-Seven

The train whistle blew, and Cynthia sat staring out the window at the changing terrain. How many years had it been since she had first come to Deadwood as a sixteen-year-old girl? Nineteen years! The ugly divorce had taken longer than expected. It was now the spring of 1894, and it had been nearly eighteen months since those two splendid days she had spent in Red Wolf's arms. But she had kept that secret, even from Freedom. She had written Red Wolf, but had insisted he never write back. Now all Freedom knew was that they were going to the Dakotas to try to find his father. Cynthia could only hope that Red Wolf had received every letter and would be waiting for them at Fort Robinson. She turned her eyes to study her eighteen-year-old son, the image of a young Red Wolf. Freedom had been so understanding about the divorce. He did not believe for one minute that his mother had been untrue to her husband. But now it was time to tell him he had already met his father and didn't know it. Again she felt the fear of rejection. But now that everything was over, and they were really going to see Red Wolf, Freedom had to know.

He smiled at her. Yes, surely this beautiful son of hers would understand. He had so much compassion, and he understood emotional pain. He had suffered some rejection and abuse because of his race, but he had risen above all of that and already had tucked away two years at the university. He had a certain spirit that had kept him from being spoiled by the good life he had enjoyed when they lived with Richard. His wealth and intelligence and education had never gone to his head, and Cynthia attributed it to the Indian spirit that lived inside her son.

Yes, he was Red Wolf's boy, and even though he had never lived like an Indian, he seemed strangely untouched by living the white man's way all his life. In so many ways he was totally Indian, his spirit free and happy and innocent, his heart good and pure. He wanted nothing more than to meet his real father, and already he talked about using his future law degree to help the Sioux if there was anything he could do for them.

Soon they would arrive at the reservation. Cynthia had told Red Wolf she should arrive at Fort Robinson the second week of May. It seemed so ironic, for it was also in May, nineteen years ago, that she'd first come to Deadwood.

She looked out the window again, taking a deep breath for courage as she watched the open prairies of Kansas, dotted here and there with settlements and farms. Here was a land that was once barren of the white man, a land where the Indians once rode free, chasing the great herds of buffalo. The buffalo were gone now, and the old days of freedom for the Indian were gone. How sad it must all be for Red Wolf. And how sad that he had had to suffer the changes alone. She could not help admiring his courage and determination in getting an education. But then Red Wolf had always been courageous—strong and sure and reckless and determined. In a few days she would be with him again, would lie in his arms and be safe and loved forever.

She looked back at Freedom. "It will only be a couple more days, Freedom. Are you excited?"

He shrugged. "Kind of scared, I guess. Maybe he won't like me for some reason—or won't want us there."

"Oh, he'll want us, Freedom. And he not only likes

you, he loves you. You've already met him, Freedom."

The boy frowned. "What do you mean?"

She twisted her gloves in her hands. "Do you remember about a year and a half ago—in the park in Maryland where Richard was giving a talk before the election? You ran into an Indian man from the Rosebud Reservation."

The boy thought for a moment. His eyes widened then. "That man? That Indian man was my father?"

She nodded, watching the confusion in his eyes.

"But . . . I remember I told him my father's name. He never said anything!"

"He wasn't sure then. It was a strange accident, the two of you meeting like that. Then again, perhaps it was meant to be. Red Wolf thinks the Great Spirit brought him to Maryland that day. It was only after talking to you he realized who I was. He didn't say anything because he wasn't positive at the time, and because he didn't feel he had the right."

Freedom ran a hand through his thick, dark hair. He glanced out the window, trying to sort out his thoughts. He looked back at his mother. "You saw him! He must have spoke to you! Is *that* why you divorced Richard? Did Red Wolf come between you and Richard?"

Cynthia sighed and leaned forward, taking his hands. "Yes, I saw him. But that wasn't the reason for the divorce, Freedom. Richard and I had many problems long before God brought Red Wolf back into my life. And I know it was God's doing. It was His way of giving me the courage to do what I knew I must do eventually, in spite of Red Wolf—divorce Richard. I just might have put if off a little longer is all." She squeezed his hands. "Red Wolf is a good, good man, Freedom. He would never have deliberately broken up a marriage. But it was the same for him as with me—he never stopped loving me, Freedom. He never married again. You are his only son, and there is nothing he wants more now than to win your affection, to see you again, be able to embrace you and get to know

441

you. I know he's so proud of your accomplishments. And your father has accomplished a lot himself. He got himself an education. He's a teacher now on the reservation. He's traveled East many times and has spoken before Congress on behalf of his people. He's an intelligent, educated man who I know you will quickly learn to love. Please give him a chance, Freedom."

The boy kept a frown, turning to look out the window at country he had never seen before—barren, open land.

"Was he really at the Custer massacre?" he asked.

Cynthia let go of his hands and sat back. "Yes."

Freedom shook his head, still watching the terrain. "He actually rode like a wild Indian—painted and everything?"

Cynthia smiled. "Yes, he did. He was considered a skilled warrior. He belonged to the Strong Heart Society."

He turned to meet her eyes. "What is that?"

She watched his dark eyes. "You have so much to learn about your own people," she told him. "I've already told you a lot about them, Freedom, but I'll tell you more before we get to Fort Robinson, if you really want to understand."

He nodded. "I do. I can't help them if I don't understand them. But it seems so strange to know my father was as wild as any of them and now is a teacher."

"That should tell you the quality of man he is, how wise he is. He understood that to survive, and to help his people, he had to get a white man's education. It isn't easy for a full-blood Indian to learn white man's ways, Freedom. But Red Wolf has forced himself to do just that. You could be so much help to him, Freedom. Together the two of you could do so much."

He shook his head, shivering. "It kind of gives me the chills to know I met my father and didn't even know it. That must be why I got such a funny feeling that day. I thought about him for the longest time. I just never said anything to you."

442

"I'm sorry I didn't tell you sooner, Freedom. But I didn't want Red Wolf's name dragged into the divorce. He's too good a man for that, and he's too innocent of white man's gossip and cruel ways. And to bring his name into it might have hurt his own struggle to get better education for the Indians. Not even your grandparents know I saw Red Wolf. Only Alex knows."

"Uncle Alex?"

"My brother has always understood my feelings for Red Wolf."

Freedom leaned back, watching out the window again. "Tell me everything you know, Mother. I especially want to know about my father—all the things you left out."

"Everything?"

He nodded. "Everything." He faced her. "I don't want to hate him. I'm grown up now, Mother. I understand things. I know what usually happened to white women captives. He didn't do that to you at first, did he?"

Cynthia reddened, realizing with almost a shock just how much of a man her son had become. "No. It was never that way with Red Wolf." She looked out the window herself again. "I had wandered too far from the house when I was first captured by a Sioux warrior called Many Bears," she began. *"Poor Many Bears,"* she thought. *"He's dead now."*

They rode the Kansas Pacific over the prairies and plains to Denver, Colorado. Cynthia was astonished to see a booming city in a land that had been void of white men not so many years ago. They rode the Denver Pacific north then to Cheyenne, Wyoming, another booming white man's town. At Cheyenne she and Freedom caught a stagecoach. Cynthia breathed deeply of the dry air, not even minding the dust. This was the West she had once loved so much, the West she had missed all these years.

In the distance lay the dark outline of the Rocky

Mountains, and as she left Cheyenne she could see the rising peaks of the Bighorn Mountains to the north. She pointed them out to Freedom, telling him about another time, when she traveled with a tribe of Sioux and Cheyenne, wearing an Indian tunic, riding beside her Indian husband. They had covered hundreds of miles of this land, through Powder River country and the Bighorns, into beautiful Yellowstone, where she and Red Wolf had bathed in warm waters. She told Freedom about the Grand Tetons and riding through the Rockies on their way back toward the Black Hills. That had been the most wonderful year of her whole life. She knew it could never be quite that way again, but she would be with Red Wolf again, and that was all that mattered.

Freedom watched her eyes light up as she talked about Red Wolf and her days with him so long ago. Never had he seen his mother look this happy, this animated. He realized now that he had been so busy growing up and getting his education that he had been oblivious to the sadness in his mother's eyes over all those years. What a sad and lonely life she must have led.

The stagecoach clattered and bounced over hard-packed earth to Fort Laramie, then on toward Fort Robinson. They had slept on trains, in stage stations on benches, in rooming houses of tiny, unknown towns, and at Fort Laramie. The journey was a difficult one, yet Freedom realized his mother did not seem wearied by the journey. She had lived such a pampered life for several years, yet she'd actually laughed once at the dust on her dress. Another woman in the stagecoach with them looked at her as though she were crazy. Cynthia had laughed harder, and Freedom grinned at the thought. His mother was as excited as a much younger girl. The closer they got to Sioux country, the happier she seemed. She had given up so much to come out to this seemingly godforsaken country—to live with an Indian no less.

Cynthia watched the dust roll past the window of the coach. She was lost in her own thoughts now. She had entered that strange, different world that belonged to men like Red Wolf. The prairie stretched naked before her, and in the distance she could see Fort Robinson. Her heart pounded wildly. What if for some reason Red Wolf was not there? Would he change his mind? Was he still all right? What would poor Freedom think if the man didn't show up? It seemed to take an eternity for the stage to arrive at the fort. She had forgotten how deceiving distances could be in this land. Something could look so close, but be miles away.

Finally the coach rattled into the fort, the other young woman on board fussing about what a mess she must be. "If my husband wasn't stationed out here I would never be here. I just hope he gets sent back East soon," she grumbled. "I don't know how long I can stand to stay here."

Cynthia's eyes were lit up with happiness. "I hope I can stay forever," she answered, grasping her hat and leaning down to climb out of the coach as the driver came around to open the door for her. The young woman with her stared after her, shaking her head at how strange the pretty blond woman riding with her was. She looked at Freedom.

"I think that woman is a little touched. Now you—you look like you *belong* out here."

Freedom was beginning to understand the hatred Red Wolf once felt for such people. "My mother belongs here more than I do."

The woman's eyes widened. "Your mother!" She sat back and fanned herself, and Freedom exited the coach. He watched his mother, who had walked a few feet from the coach and was looking around anxiously. The driver unloaded their baggage.

"Is he here?" Freedom asked Cynthia.

"I don't see him." She forced herself not to seem worried. The old fear gripped her again, that the two days she had had with Red Wolf were all she would ever have of him. Her eyes teared in a sudden panic as the stage

445

driver asked what he should do with her bags. She looked around desperately. "I . . . I don't know yet. Just leave them right here," she answered.

The man shrugged and walked away. Cynthia dusted off her blue cotton dress, and soldiers and civilians alike stared at the beautiful, sophisticated-looking Eastern woman standing in the street with a young Indian man beside her. Finally Cynthia called out to a soldier who walked by close to her.

"Yes, ma'am?" he asked, looking her over appreciatively.

"Do you know an Indian named Red Wolf?"

"Joseph Red Wolf? The teacher?"

"Yes!" Her eyes lit up with hope. "Do you know how I can find him?"

He grinned. "I don't think you'll have to. Just wait a few minutes and he'll show up. The stage got here early. Joe's been here every day with his wagon, waiting for somebody to get off the stage." He frowned then. "Are *you* the one he's waiting for?"

She smiled with relief, quickly wiping at tears. "Yes."

The soldier looked her over again in astonishment. "Joe said a woman was coming who was his wife once . . . said he has a son eighteen years old."

"Yes," Cynthia answered eagerly, turning to Freedom. "This is our son—Freedom."

The soldier blinked, looking from Cynthia to Freedom and back to Cynthia. "*Our* son?"

"Yes. Mine and Joseph Red Wolf's."

The man's smile faded slightly. "You're the mother?"

"Yes." Cynthia smiled. The man removed his hat and ran a hand through his hair. "I thought it would be an Indian woman."

Cynthia met his eyes boldly. "It's a long story. But I've never been happier than I am right now."

The soldier looked at her as though there must be something wrong with her. He stepped away from her and pointed through the gates of the fort. "I reckon that's

Red Wolf coming now, ma'am."

Cynthia looked to see someone coming far off. "Oh, would you please stay here and watch my bags? Please?"

The man was astonished at the love and joy that shone in her eyes. "Sure. Everybody around here likes Joe Red Wolf."

"Oh, thank you!" She started running toward the gate, and men stared curiously as she hurried through it and ran toward the approaching wagon. Two horses pulled the clattering buckboard, and as Cynthia got closer its driver slowed the horses, then finally drew to a halt and put on the brakes.

Cynthia stopped, staring at an Indian man in buckskins. He had dressed the old way just for her. She smiled, an aching lump in her throat.

"I was afraid you wouldn't be here," she squeaked.

"And I was afraid you would not really come."

He climbed down and stood there tall and handsome, every bit the warrior she had left so many years ago, but even more than he had been then. Here he was all Indian. There were no white man's clothes like in Maryland. There was no fancy hotel room.

"I have made a camp in a special place," he told her, searching her eyes. "It is very pretty there . . . and private." His eyes moved over her lovingly, hungrily. "I . . . I hope you do not mind sleeping in a tipi tonight. I thought perhaps you would like to."

She ran to him then, and in the next moment he swept her into his strong arms. She was home, home where she belonged, where she had left her heart so many years ago. She would no longer wear fancy dresses and live in a town house. She was not meant to be a congressman's woman. She was meant to be a warrior's woman, and she would have it no other way.

Freedom understood that now, too, as he slowly approached them. Red Wolf met his eyes, and already felt he had known him all his life. "Father," he said softly.

"What treaty that the whites have kept has the red man broken? Not one. What treaty that the white man ever made with us have they kept? Not one. When I was a boy the Sioux owned the world; the sun rose and set on their land; they sent ten thousand men to battle. Where are the warriors today? Who slew them? Where are our lands? Who owns them? What white man can say I ever stole his land or a penny of his money? Yet, they say I am a thief. What white woman, however lonely, was ever captive or insulted by me? Yet they say I am a bad Indian. What white man has ever seen me drunk? Who has ever come to me hungry and unfed? Who has ever seen me beat my wives or abuse my children? What law have I broken? Is it wrong for me to love my own? Is it wicked for me because my skin is red? Because I am a Sioux; because I was born where my father lived; because I would die for my people and my country?"

The words of Sitting Bull, from *Touch the Earth*, compiled by T. C. McLuhan, Promontory Press.

I hope you have enjoyed my story. If you would like more information about other books I have written, as well as names and publication dates of future books, please send a self-addressed, stamped envelope to my attention through Zebra Books, 475 Park Avenue South, New York, N.Y. 10016. Feel free to include a letter. Thank you so much for your support.

—F. Rosanne Bittner